NEW LANARK

SPINNING NEW LIVES

C A Hope

First published in Great Britain as a paperback original in 2013 by

Marluc

www.completely-novel.com

ISBN 978-1-84914-2922

Printed and bound by Lightning Source International
Front cover produced by ronindreamer
All rights reserved.
Front cover Artwork by Lane Brown
Titles and Texts by Lerom Lee
Back cover photograph of New Lanark by C A Hope

For my beloved sons with all my love.

And to David Dale, for whom I hold the
greatest admiration and respect: a truly good man.

Contents

Foreword

The River Clyde springs from a hillside in the heart of lowland Scotland. Growing larger with every mile it weaves through Lanarkshire's wooded glens and barren moorland.
Until suddenly, just shy of the market town of Lanark, the landscape changes and the riverbed drops sharply away into a deep gorge.

The water pours relentlessly over great shelves of rock to cascade hundreds of feet in a thundering, crashing spectacle of waterfalls: the Falls of Clyde.

It is this incredible natural wonder which attracted the attention of wealthy Glasgow businessman, David Dale. He had plans for a new cotton mill and needed water-power to drive the pioneering machinery.

One afternoon in 1784, with the engineer Richard Arkwright, he took a stroll to see the already famous beauty spot for himself. The location was perfect so, there and then, they pledged to build a Mill Village at the foot of the Falls.

It would be called New Lanark.

This is the story of the first formative and eventful years of the village, told through the lives of the people who lived there. All the true events have been meticulously researched as have the lives of the actual characters of David Dale, his successor Robert Owen, their families and contemporaries.

Chapter One

"For a long period it was by the working people themselves
considered to be disgraceful to any father who allowed his child to
enter the factory..."
'Alfred' (S Kydd)

October 9th 1788

On Thursday, October 9th 1788, another arduous day of production
was underway at the New Lanark Cotton Mills. There was nothing to
suggest that this day would be any different from all the rest. Even
the weather was unremarkable, overcast and dull with a slight breeze
shivering across the surface of the slow water in the mill lade.

One massive, seven storey stone mill, the first of the proposed four
mills, stood proudly on the banks of the River Clyde. Around it,
rising from terraces hewn out of the steep hillside, was the next phase
of the newly emerging village. A nearly completed row of tenements
to house the workers clung to the rocky hillside and, below it, by the
river, the foundations were already in place for the second great
building. Hundreds of men laboured on the project and the air was
alive with their voices amid the hammering, sawing and clatter of
horses and wagons.

Mill One had been spinning cotton for over nineteen months now
and every room was active. The water wheels were running to full
capacity, sucking in the smooth lade water to power the machines
before spewing it out into the river again in bubbling torrents. The
upper floors hummed with the incessant rumble of the spinning
jennies turning out yarn from over five thousand spindles. Lower
floors housed the looms with men bent over their frames, children

scurrying to their beck and call and in the basement were the carding rooms and storerooms, kitchens and offices.

It was an enormous factory, drawing its energy as much from its hundreds of employees as from the river. There was little chance to rest; Overlookers kept a vigilant eye and insisted on unremitting labour. High demand meant that every day wagons rolled down the hill bringing more bales of the raw material. Those same wagons were filled with the processed yarn and hauled away again. Ironically, a good deal of the cotton was returning to clothe the very slaves who were picking it from the plantations.

Deep in the bowels of the great mill, amongst a crowd of other children, Fiona, an orphan from the Highlands, knew nothing of this, nor did she care. Her interest lay outside the walls. She had been at New Lanark for less than a week and because she only understood Gaelic, she had at first believed she was in a Work House. Now, she understood it was a cotton mill and was full of anxiety, not knowing how long she was supposed to remain there.

Could she just leave? She had asked Mhairi, a fellow Gaelic speaker. When would they be paid? They were never paid, she was told. How could that be? Mhairi could not answer; her child's mind had no reason to question what would happen in the future. Today they would work, eat their meal and attend classes. What else was there?

Mhairi was young, only eight or nine years old, and was accustomed to poverty on Glasgow's streets or in bleak workhouses before being brought to David Dale's new village. Fiona was older. For much of her fourteen years she had known freedom, happiness and a loving family, so she felt the difference keenly.

An ache of longing for her old life gnawed away inside her. Working alongside dozens of other children in the carding room, she pushed the raw cotton between the spikes on the hand card and let her mind run free.

There was so much that she missed. Her family, of course, but it was quite unbearable to think of them and her mind shied away from those memories. There were simple pleasures, naively taken for granted at the time, like paddling among the rock pools on the beach, gathering crabs and mussels to take home to eat, and looking for beautiful shells. She could almost feel the burning sand between her toes on a hot day, smell the salty seaweed. When would she next see terns soaring high over the waves, then plummeting straight down, wings folded tightly back, to plunge like arrows into the water?

Half way through the day the carding room door opened and several gentlemen entered. Immediately the supervisors jumped to attention, calling 'Wheesht!' to the children as they straightened their own aprons and tucked stray hairs beneath their caps.

It was the works' manager. He stopped in the doorway to talk with the other men, bewigged and elegant in dark coats and colourful brocade waistcoats. They took a cursory look around over the sea of children's heads and discussed the imminent arrival of the new carding machines which would replace the laborious hand card system. The dim, lamp lit air was thick with white floating fibres, causing one of the men to draw out a handkerchief and hold it over his nose and mouth. After a few minutes the men retreated, flicking at the film of fine threads on their jackets.

Fiona glanced over at a fair-haired girl, Sarah, who looked up from her work and caught her eye. They exchanged a rueful smile and carried on carding.

Sarah was also struggling with the thought of being trapped in this claustrophobic life.

Like Fiona, she was older than most of the other children and she was also a newcomer to the mill. However, unlike Fiona, Sarah had a family and returned to them each evening. Forced by their dire circumstances, she and her younger brother and sister were now obliged to be there for four full years. Papers had been signed, a meagre wage would be paid: they were bound apprentices. She also knew, because her older brother had told her when she was bemoaning the length of her indenture, that she was more fortunate than Fiona. Orphans were contracted to the mill for seven years.

She looked at the wane faces and scrawny limbs of those children who had no homes or families. This was all they had, this was their whole life. She felt like throwing down the hand-cards and sobbing.

A noise from the corridor brought her attention abruptly back to the present.

The door burst open and a man charged inside.

'Get out!' he shouted. 'Get out!' He started grabbing at the children nearest to him and pushing them roughly towards the door. 'Fire! Fire! The mill's on fire!'

There was a scramble of flying cotton, writhing limbs and swishing hair as everyone jumped to their feet and fled for the door.

3

The doorway was only three feet wide, with a narrow passage beyond it leading to a spiralling staircase. At first there was silence, a hush born of shock and confusion, but when they found they could not easily escape, a nervous babble rose into hysteria. The more the mass of small bodies pushed and shoved the more tightly the ones at the front were jammed together, some being grazed and squeezed against the walls; the little ones slipping, in danger of falling over. Fiona and Sarah were thrown together as they all crowded along the corridor.

'At least it's only the one stairs!' Sarah shouted over the panic-stricken cries.

Fiona was not sure what the commotion was about but from the fearful cries and the man's urgent shouts, she knew it must be something terrible. Once up the steps, they joined a mass of fellow workers flooding through the hallway and out the front door.

It was only as they dashed out into the daylight and ran from the walls that it became clear what was happening.

Smoke billowed from the upper windows, first in the central part and then spreading to either side. With a terrific crash a window blew out and a scream went up as people threw their hands over their heads and ran for cover from the showering glass. Another crack and then another, more windows exploded and huge snaking tongues of flame shot out, sending sparks spraying into the air. Tinkling shards of glass rained down, spattering across the ground.

Figures were streaming out of the door, eyes wild, their faces contorted with sheer terror. All the builders working on Mill Two were rushing to help, frantically snatching up buckets and organising themselves into a chain to pass along water as soon as it was scooped from the lade.

Even as they started, they knew it was a hopeless cause.

Pushing urgently past those fleeing from inside, the men tried to make their way upstairs to the seat of the flames but were met by workers scrambling down, shouting at them to get out. By the time they reached the third floor the smoke and heat were unbearable and they were forced to retrace their steps, choking and coughing, shielding their scorched faces with smoke blackened hands.

The fire was totally out of control.

Among the throng outside, wagon drivers drove their terrified, squealing horses away from the building. Yelling orders above the mayhem, they stood up to haul on the reins, wrestling to hold them

4

back from bolting as the acrid smell of smoke triggered the great animals to leap into flight.

Within minutes, brilliant flashes of scarlet and yellow licked through the roof. First wisps, then a spreading shroud of smoke rose up in a plume. Suddenly, with deafening cracks, the roof timbers erupted into flame.

Sarah was screaming for her family, pushing recklessly among the crowd, tears coursing down her cheeks. She yelled their names and peered frenziedly into the faces of strangers. All around her, others were doing the same. It was a deafening scene of complete chaos and panic.

'Sarah!' Rosie threw herself into her sister's embrace.

'Where's Cal? Hae ye seen him?' Sarah demanded, so frightened that the words came out in an angry torrent. The little girl shook her head before burying it against her sister's skirts, crying uncontrollably.

The mill was now a roaring furnace. Flames flared from every window and the heat was so intense that the crowd were forced to shrink away from it, moving further and further back beside the lade. Some of the stronger men and women persisted, withstanding the blaze as long as they could bear to hurl water on to the partly built lower floors of Mill Two.

There was a terrible desperation to their actions. This was their livelihood. Without the mills they would have no jobs and without jobs they and their families would starve. Young and old, they swung the heavy splashing buckets to one another. Sweat glistened on their tense faces, their mouths open as they grunted and puffed from the exertion.

Fiona crept to the back of the crowd and dropped to her knees, heedless of her long cotton tunic pressing into the mud. Her whole body was shaking. She bowed over and covered her head with trembling hands. The sight of the flames overwhelmed her with a feeling of dread, causing images from her past to flood over her, drowning her in memories. A group of crofts, their thatched roofs blazing, screams... her mother's anguished face as she pleaded in vain for mercy... their home destroyed.

After that, she thought life couldn't get any worse, but it did. And now? Now what was to become of her?

Just yards away, Sarah was lost in her own agony. Clinging to Rosie, she searched in vain for her brothers through the jostling,

5

gabbling mob. Little Cal would have been working on the upper floors of the mill when the fire broke out and from what she saw when she ran from the burning building, that was where the fire had started. Please God, she prayed fervently, let him be all right. And Joe? Where was her older brother? Surely he was safe, he should not have been in the building but what if... what if...?

It had been Joe's idea to come to New Lanark: he saw it as their salvation. Yet now, staring at the raging fire consuming the mill, she saw their security, their hopes and survival for the years ahead, crumble and burn.

She pulled Rosie closer. Just four days ago she had not set foot in New Lanark yet now it held all that was precious to her and her family.

'I can bear anything,' she thought, 'the workhouse, the coal pits... *anything,* just, please God, let my brothers be safe.'

Six days earlier.... Friday 3rd October

The mill bell broke the silence of the sleeping valley as the first streaks of dawn brightened the eastern horizon. A new day was approaching New Lanark.

Joe's eyes opened. It was pitch black in the room, only the small window showed as a grey rectangle. He shut his eyes again, sighed heavily and then forced them open once more. Waves of sleep were threatening to pull him back into unconsciousness but he couldn't succumb. He listened to the slow rhythmic rings, counting them silently, as he did every morning. Then, on the tenth stroke, he pushed the blanket away and swung himself off the bed.

The three other men in the room did not start work for another hour or more and had easily dismissed the bell and returned to their slumber. Yawning and rubbing his eyes, Joe envied their snores and longed to crawl back onto the warmth of the mattress and draw the cover up over his head. Instead, bracing himself against the cold, he groped around in the darkness for his cold, crumpled smock and started to dress.

Minutes later, he was criss-crossing through Lanark's narrow vennels, his footsteps echoing among the deserted streets of the old market town as he headed down towards the valley.

The bell now sounded loud and insistent. With its chimes, movement began appearing on the hills, barely discernible at first against the grey landscape. A cawing cloud of rooks rose from their roost, farm dogs barked and the first morning calls of cockerels echoed in the still autumn air. As the sky grew lighter the progress of Joe and hundreds of other hurrying figures became clear.

Steadily, the steep hillsides came alive. From all directions they streamed towards the bell, their arms flailing jerkily to gain balance as the paths dropped them deeper and deeper into the gorge.

Those approaching from the west clustered in little groups on the riverbank to ready themselves for crossing the water. An unusually long dry spell made it possible to ford the Clyde opposite the newly built mill village, saving hours of walking to the nearest bridge. Those with boots to remove paused on the rocky shore, lagging behind the rest who, already barefoot, stepped straight into the rushing water. The women hoisted up their skirts and clutched each other for support before wading across, gasping and shrieking at the biting cold, the younger among them fighting back tears.

They were a ragged, lean-faced crowd but, as they joined fellow workers, bursts of laughter mingled with trampling footsteps and shared gossip. There were men, some carrying small children on their shoulders, and a lot of women, grasping their shawls tightly around them, the hems of their thick skirts stained dark and heavy with dew, and there were children, scores of children.

United in one aim, they flocked towards the mill to earn their living.

Like a great funnel, the almost sheer slopes of the valley drew them together and poured them into the village. The last toll of the bell echoed away against the cliffs, leaving just the rush of the river to accompany the stragglers running to the mill door before it closed.

Joe and the other construction workers, the only remaining figures moving inside the village, set about the first duty of the day; lighting braziers for warmth and light. They were working on the foundations and lower ground floors of the second mill. It would be another hour before there was enough daylight to see what they were doing for any serious work but heaps of rubble could be moved and buckets of sand and lime needed to be filled and made ready for mixing.

'Joe!' a high pitched child's voice came from the darkness beyond the flames. 'Joe Scott?'

'Aye!' Joe pushed his cap back and walked towards the voice.

'Mr McCulloch wants yer!'

A little boy stood precariously on a boulder, his bare feet gripping the relatively smooth surface. He was jigging about, peering at the ground around him which was littered with sharp stones and discarded nails.

'He wants yer!' He repeated, his anxious face lit by the fire.

'Whit fer?' Joe didn't expect an answer. He waved through the gloom to attract his friend's attention. 'Tam! Oi! McCulloch wants me, don't s'pose Ah'll be lang.'

'Till efter sunrise if he's gaun' tae lecture ye on the deils o' drink! He must hae seen ye in the tavern!'

It was a joke but as he followed the hopping child through the building site, Joe realised there was an element of truth in Tam's words. McCulloch was an abstainer and had called men in for less, saying it was his duty to save them from the sins of alcohol.

Joe had taken a lot of ale the night before but no more than anyone else. It had been a good evening, with a warming fire, a few songs

8

when Tam's brother arrived with his fiddle and the bar maid was giving out generous measures. He remembered a blue-eyed girl with a cheeky smile but, to be honest, he couldn't remember going back to his lodgings. Still, as he woke up in his own bed, surely nothing too terrible had happened?

Doubts were creeping into his mind and he was nervous as he stamped the worst of the dirt from his boots, pulled off his cap, smoothed his hair and stepped through the office door. Mr McCulloch might be a slight figure but it was he who hired and fired and therefore he was to be respected and feared in equal measures.

McCulloch had his back to him, holding an oil lamp high and rifling through a pile of papers. Shadowy shelves of books and ledgers crowded round the walls of the small room, a newly lit coal fire flickered feebly in the grate, more smoke than flame.

'Sir?'

McCulloch immediately turned round and, setting the lamp down on the desk between them, surveyed Joe from head to foot.

He was surprised by what he saw. Was this the Joe Scott he engaged two winters before? He had expected a thinner, shorter youth with brown hair. In front of him was a tall, well muscled young man with a shock of blonde hair and dark complexion. Of course, he was a labourer and the summer had been especially hot, bleaching his hair and colouring his skin. Also, McCulloch, himself in his forties, realised the lad was probably not yet even twenty years old and had bolted up like a colt.

'I have here a letter, carried over from Douglas this morning.'

Joe's heart missed a beat. His family were in Douglas. The very mention of the name enveloped him in the fumes of coal dust, damp wool, rank dung-heaps and an uneasy feeling of guilt.

McCulloch picked up a piece of paper and held it out to him.

'Ah cannae read, sir.'

'Very well,' the older man had hoped he would be spared giving the news directly. 'Well, it is to inform you that your father has been killed in an accident.' He hurried on in case there was any display of grief. 'The letter itself was written by the foreman of the mine and he states that the accident was not in the pit itself. It seems a horse shied when being backed between the shafts and overturned a cart. Regrettably, your father was crushed and died shortly afterwards.'

A silence followed. Joe was caught in so many swirling emotions that no words could be found. He looked down at his hands,

9

unconsciously clasping and unclasping them against the dirty cotton smock. Samuel, his elder brother, would know what to do. Sam would know what to feel and say at this moment, but Sam was away, far away. Oh God, how he missed Sam.

Now their father was dead, so the whole reason for Sam running away was gone.

After some moments, McCulloch became uncomfortable and busied himself with flicking his coat tails away and taking a seat behind the desk.

'Do you wish to see your family? I take it you have family?' He glanced up for a response.

Joe raised his head slowly, as if he was pressing back against a great weight.

His piercing blue eyes looked directly at McCulloch, 'Aye.'

'You will be grateful to know that Mr Dale is sympathetic towards occurrences such as close familial bereavements, not all employers are so generous. In consequence of his benevolence you may be excused from your labour for the remainder of the day. '

He dipped his pen in the ink well and made an entry in the register.

Joe nodded, 'Thank ye, sir.' Still no coherent thoughts came into his head.

'Off you go then,' McCulloch gestured to the door, 'Oh and ... my condolences.'

Joe nodded again and left the room. It was only as he felt the cool outside air on his face that he realised he was being marked as absent which meant he would receive no wages for the day.

'Whit wis a' tha' aboot?' Tam asked cheerily as soon as Joe joined the group again.

'Ma faither's deid. Ah've bin gie'n the day tae gae hame an' see tae... things.'

The laughter and chatter stopped abruptly. There were murmurs of sympathy and some of the men turned away, awkward and at a loss as what to say.

Tam gave Joe a push on the shoulder, 'Aw that's rough. He wis a miner, eh? Did he die doon the pit?'

Joe told them what McCulloch had said and then looked around him in preparation to leave. A pale gold glow was now spreading into the remnants of the night, fading the stars and gilding wispy clouds in an otherwise clear sky.

'At least it's anither dry day. Ah'd best be aff.'

Now that morning production was underway in the mill, water was being diverted through the water wheel so there was even less water in the riverbed than an hour before. Tam accompanied him down to the river bed and they picked a spot just below the waterfall, where the Clyde divides around a long, narrow island.

Joe sat on a rock and untied his laces to pull off his boots. 'Sure the wheel's turning?'

They peered towards the outlet from the water wheel where white sprays of splashing water sparkled in the dawn light.

'Aye, yer safe enough tae cross, the lade's fu' an' yon wheel's workin'.'

The dangerous time was when they stopped sending water through the mill lade and a sudden wave would raise the river level so fast it could knock a man to his knees. If the river was already high it would carry him off downstream to almost certain death.

'Here,' Tam fumbled in the drawstring bag slung round his waist. 'Ye'll miss yer porridge, tak this.'

It was a cooked potato wrapped in cloth.

Joe was touched by the thoughtful gift. He was already hungry and had a long walk ahead of him.

'Tha' wid be grand, ta!' He stuffed the potato into the toe of a boot, jamming it securely with his thick, rolled up stockings. 'Ye'd better get back up tae the site, Old Mack will be dae'in his roonds ony minute. Tell him whit's happened, will ye? Nae doubt he already kens frae McCulloch, but Ah dinnae wan' grief frae him when Ah get back.'

He watched his friend scramble up the bank towards the busy figures moving in and out of pools of smoky fire light. Behind them, beyond the piles of materials for the second mill, rose the great stone walls of Mill One, soaring seven storeys high into the sky. He was gripped by immense pride that he, Joe Scott, had played a part in building that colossal structure. There it stood, bold and gleaming, its highest windows flashing with the first rays of the morning sun.

He wanted to stand and gaze at it all day, knowing that as soon as he turned away and waded into the river he would have to confront the task ahead. He would have to come to terms with the fact that his father was dead and face up to all the changes it would mean for him, his mother and younger brother and sisters.

Eventually, he tied his boot laces together, slung them around his neck and set off across the river.

11

***

Forty miles downstream from where Joe forded the river, the Clyde had grown into a vast body of foul, brown water. It snaked its way through Glasgow gathering waste from thousands of households and factories, a putrid open sewer. Urchins and beggars picked over the flotsam washed up on its soiled shores, fighting over their meagre finds: fire-wood, rope, a blanket. Little boats rowed from side to side, larger crafts docked with goods for the markets and, in the deeper water approaching the mouth of the Atlantic, huge cargo ships discharged their bounty.

It was these ships that brought wealth into the city. Walking the same streets as the starving beggars were merchants, strutting between their private clubs and coffee shops. Flourishing gold topped canes, they took to flaunting their riches by tucking sheafs of pound notes into their hat bands.

Fiona Macdonald was one of the poor. Her short life started among the vast open spaces of Argyllshire, where she could roam freely along windblown beaches or lie among the heather and watch skylarks soaring overhead. Now, she was trapped inside a glowering red sandstone institution; Glasgow's Town Hospital.

There was pitifully little left of the light-hearted child who used to sing as she mended nets with her mother and laugh with her friends when they harvested the crops. Her once waist length auburn hair was shorn to her head, uneven and spiky, her slight body swamped by a grey, ankle length smock; her own brightly coloured skirt and shawl having been ripped off her and burnt on arrival. Scrubbed and scoured for lice, her skin was still broken in places and she had taken to picking at the scabs, increasing the wounds and discomfort. Somehow the physical pain eased the misery she felt inside, giving momentary distraction from her dreadful predicament.

She was lying on her bed with her eyes tight shut, trying to blot everything out, when a voice boomed at her side.

'Come wi' me!'

A stout woman with a face that did not brook disobedience, caught hold of her shoulder and pulled her off the bed and down the ward.

Fiona was thrown back into the chaos of the workhouse. All around them was the drab world of row upon row of wooden framed beds, high echoing ceilings and dozens of little girls, orphans. When not at work, as now, some would just curl up on a mattress, others sat sucking their grimy thumbs, rocking to and fro. The more energetic among them squabbled and shrieked at one another, playing made-up games and fighting.

There was a lot of fighting.

Out into the long wood-panelled corridor and other sounds joined the cacophony; boys voices from the dormitories at the far end and, eerily muffled from the floor above, the unearthly wailing from ill and mentally deranged patients.

Fiona was alarmed by this sudden turn of events. For weeks now, the day to day routine had never faltered. When they left the dormitory it was always as a group, marching in pairs. She had not been singled out before and, unable to ask what was going on, she half ran, half walked ahead of the woman, trembling inside and sick to her stomach with nerves.

The Town Hospital was where you ended up when there was nowhere else to go. It was one step up from complete hopelessness. Here the inmates were fed, given shelter and, if able, put to work. Surely they were not going to throw her out? Terrible though it was among these walls, her time on the streets had been so traumatic that it was a constant battle to banish it from her mind.

Fiona was propelled down stairs and then, with a push, ordered to stand by the wall.

The woman knocked on a door and disappeared inside.

'She's here. Ye want her brought in, Sir?'

The Superintendent of the Hospital was accompanied by John Laverty, a heavily built, be-wigged gentleman who turned in his chair as Fiona was pulled into the room. He raised his eyebrows in objection to the rough handling.

'She only speaks the Gaelic,' the woman responded. 'She does nae understan' a word we say.'

'I see, but perhaps a little less force is required?' Laverty's expression remained stern.

The orphan was clearly frightened, her large brown eyes reminding him of a fawn. Sometimes he felt a terrible revulsion towards the burly assistants who paraded the children before him with less respect than an auctioneer at a cattle market.

13

James Anderson, the superintendent of the establishment, bristled with annoyance at his staff's display of ill-treatment. He cast her a disapproving look. He knew all too well that this was her usual manner with the children, whether they could understand verbal commands or not. In an attempt to retrieve the situation in front of his visitor he gave her a harsh rebuke, following it up with the threat of dismissal if she acted that way again.

John Laverty was not just any client, he was the agent of Mr David Dale and, quite apart from the fact that Mr Dale was a Magistrate and mill owner, he was also a Director on the Board of the Town's Hospital. It would never do to have it reported that he, Anderson, had condoned bullying and rough behaviour, it could cause him all sorts of problems.

Cheeks flaming, the nurse left the room and Fiona shrank back against the nearest wall.

She had stepped into another world. A world of richly coloured fabrics, glass fronted mahogany bookcases, oil paintings in gilded frames and, beneath the marble mantle shelf, the delicious warmth of a fire's leaping flames. On the floor in the centre of the room was a thick pile rug with such intricate patterns of red, green, yellow and blue that she couldn't believe its beauty. Why would anyone put such a lovely piece of material on the floor and then stand on it? She longed to touch it, feel the shiny threads between her toes.

It was true, she did not understand the streams of words they directed at her and since arriving in the building, she survived by keeping her head down and doing what she was bid. The saving grace, the one thing that kept her from losing all hope, was the work she was set. For many hours every day she and upwards of twenty other girls attended a room where they made lace. A kind lady, who they called 'ma'am', taught them the art. To Fiona, she was like an angel. Her voice was low and coaxing and, when she leaned close to show a particular way with the thread, there was a fragrance of lavender.

'Well,' said the Superintendent, 'as you can see the child is in good health.' He stroked his luxurious moustache. There was no point in adding that the nurses felt she might be a little backward.

'How old is she?' Laverty smiled benignly at Fiona who was staring at the floor, wriggling her bare toes on the floorboards.

'We believe she is around thirteen or fourteen years old, give or take a year or so. I don't think she knows herself. She was brought in to us just over a month ago. She was begging on the street beside what was first believed to be a pile of rags. It turned out to be her mother, her recently *deceased* mother.' He wrinkled his nose in uncontained disgust. 'When she first arrived she wouldn't say a word. Indeed, it was believed she was a mute until she was caught fighting with one of the other paupers. Then it was clear she had a voice, so we asked Mrs Orr, who speaks a little Gaelic, to see what she could find out.'

Laverty was appalled by the story.

'And? What did she find out?'

'Very little, except her name is Fiona Macdonald and she came from near Mallaig, up on the west coast. She seems handy with a needle so perhaps she has some previous experience. I have good reports from her teacher on her lace making skills. She also confirmed that it was her mother's body which she was found beside.' Anderson leaned back in his chair. 'It's the usual tale. These Highlanders think the city's going to give them work but what can they offer Glasgow? Do we need kelp pickers in George Square?'

Laverty shook his head gravely, 'You say she is skilled at lace making?'

'As you know we are very proud of our production of lace here and Mrs Sinclair is an excellent teacher. Yes, the girl is good with her hands. Neat, quick. I thought of Mr Dale immediately. I am sure she would be a useful apprentice in his mills.'

'I agree. At least under Mr Dale's care she will receive an education. I fear a girl such as this would attract the wrong sort of attention under the wrong sort of employment.'

The two men exchanged a worldly look. Fiona might be young but her heart shaped face and blossoming body, evident even beneath the orphans' regulation shift, would lead her into ruin if left unguided.

Anderson pulled a bell cord on the wall behind him and within moments the brusque assistant returned and whisked Fiona away.

'So,' Laverty stood up and adjusted his blue silk waist coat. 'I am going to Charlotte Street now to report our arrangements to Mr Dale. That will be nine new apprentices and the two older women. We will take them all into the New Lanark Mills. Blantyre is not at full capacity yet but we will soon be looking for more labour over there.'

'And how is Mr Dale's other new mill progressing? The Ayrshire venture?'

'Catrine? Excellently, excellently! His plans may be adventurous but we all know when David Dale does something, he does it properly.'

Upstairs, curled up on her bed again, Fiona replayed the scene and wondered what had just happened.

It seemed something was decided about her, but what that might be, she had no idea. However, for now, she was just very relieved to be back in the dormitory because it would have been a disaster to have been sent away immediately. Hidden under the corner of her mattress was a small parcel containing her most precious possessions: her only possessions.

Somehow, she decided, she must carry them with her at all times.

***

John Laverty strode up to the entrance gates of the exclusive, private street where David Dale and many of the other richest merchants in Glasgow had built their homes. On being recognised by the gate keeper, he barely faltered in his step before they swung open.

'Afternoon, sir!'

Laverty inclined his head in acknowledgment and approached the impressive frontage of his employer's city residence.

Over the years, he had always enjoyed his meetings with Mr Dale but the last five years, since this splendid new house was constructed, it was an added pleasure to be received in such style. Charlotte Street was very peaceful after the dirty, clattering city streets. There was no through traffic here, no hawkers or beggars, dung heaps or lines of grey, tattered washing to offend the senses.

Apart from a coachman readying a private carriage in front of one of the other substantial stone houses further down the road, the crisp sunshine bathed only scattered autumn leaves and chirping sparrows taking a dust bath.

He was greeted by Renwick, the butler, who, after taking his hat and gloves, showed him into the library while he informed Mr Dale of his arrival.

Laverty wandered idly about the room, casting his eye over the book lined walls and the bronze figurines on the mantel shelf. He knew this room well but there was always something interesting to note on each visit. Perhaps a new book lying open on the desk, a collection of ivory miniatures arranged in a group on the wall, or on one occasion, a fine brass standard oil lamp.

There was a sweet perfume mingling with the other faint aromas of coal smoke and leather. He leaned down close to a bureau, its intricately inlaid wood warmed by a shaft of light from the window. Polish; beeswax polish. That was the pleasing scent. After a tour of the room he took up a stance with his back to the fire. If he ever had the good fortune to be able to afford such a fine home, he could wish for no better example.

Renwick returned and he was escorted up the sweeping flight of stairs to Dale's study.

As soon as word of Laverty's visit reached the housekeeper's ears, she hurried upstairs to consult her mistress. With a brief tap on the door she entered one of the children's rooms.

The eldest daughter was standing perfectly still in the centre of the bedroom with her arms held out from her body. Her curly dark brown hair was swept up in a silk scarf and secured high on her head to leave her neck and shoulders free. Around her worked a young woman, pins gripped between her lips, draping and securing scarlet material.

Anne Caroline Dale was ten years old and this was the first fitting for her new winter outfit. She was taking it very seriously and did not even dare to move her eyes lest it distracted the seamstress.

'It will be charming, quite charming!' her mother encouraged from her seat by the hearthside. Mrs Dale, also named Anne Caroline, but referred to affectionately by her husband as Carolina, enjoyed these quiet times in the comfort and warmth of her own home. It was such a pleasure to relax in a loose day dress with no need for hairstyling, high fashion or toe pinching shoes. A blessed relief.

She turned her attention to the housekeeper, Mrs Breen.

'Did I hear a visitor?' she asked; if someone was calling on her, then their journey had been wasted. She was definitely not receiving today.

'Ma'am, Mr Laverty has arrived and is with Mr Dale at present. Would you wish tea to be served for them?'

'Yes ... and cake. Mr Dale particularly enjoyed the fruit cake yesterday. If there is any left, please have it taken up.'

'Yes, Ma'am.' Breen glanced quickly round the room, noting the waning glow of the coals. 'Smith will bring more coal and attend to the fire. Is there anything else?'

Before her mother could reply Anne Caroline piped up.

'Don't you think this is going to be beautiful, Breen?' She chanced a beaming smile in the housekeeper's direction. 'Oh, I hope it snows this winter because even it is very cold I will still be warm inside this wonderful wool.'

'It will be very fine, Miss Anne Caroline.'

The child suppressed a rising giggle. 'It's such a bright red I will look hot even if I am not!'

Her little brother, William, wriggled himself backwards up onto the high bed. His legs stuck straight out in front of him and he started to bounce them up and down, enjoying the way his petticoats rose and fell with the movement.

'William! Please be still.' Mrs Dale softened the rebuke with a smile. 'You must learn to be patient. Learn from your sister, see, she doesn't footer and jump about.'

'She would, if she had to wait. I wish I was the oldest. Then I wouldn't always have to be second.'

'You should just be grateful to have *any* clothes, my dear.' His mother chided. It worried her that maybe she was spoiling her children but it was only right that a magistrate's family should be well dressed.

'I think we should all have cake,' she announced brightly. 'Please also bring some tea, Breen. When the fitting is over the children will be going for a walk, so a little tea now will see them through to their meal.'

Cheered by the thought of the food, William slid off the bed, gathered up one of the boxes of trimmings which lay open on the floor and took a seat by his mother.

'Will you be coming out with us today, Mama?' he asked, picking out swatches of silk braid and arranging them neatly on his lap, narrowest to widest.

'No, I think I will have a little nap.' Mrs Dale stifled a yawn. The last week had been a terrible strain. Two dinners at friends' houses, a formal reception at the Bank and an interminable concert. She had eventually found the concert unbearable and persuaded her husband to leave early. Dear man, she remembered, his expression was so anxious when she told him she would like to go home before the programme was complete.

'Do you feel unwell, Mama?' Anne Caroline asked now.

Since the birth of baby Margaret, just two months earlier, Carolina was still feeling weaker than usual.

'Don't fret. I am quite well enough for a walk, if I wished it. Just a little tired. And, goodness me, we are entertaining ten for dinner tomorrow night. I shall rest while I have the chance.'

Their tea arrived, the fire was replenished and the seamstress was invited to join them in sampling the cake; plain sponge with raspberry jam, the last of the fruit cake having been taken to the master of the house.

So, it was a cosy domestic scene that greeted David Dale when he entered the room.

'My, that's a sight to gladden the heart!' he exclaimed in his deep, Ayrshire tones. 'No... no.. stay as ye are!' he added, as his children started to rise to greet him. The seamstress, already on her feet, bobbed a respectful curtsey.

This was the great David Dale.

On all her previous visits he had been either ensconced in his study or away from the house. His fame extended across the city and she was quite in awe of him from his fine reputation. He walked past her to reach for a slice of cake, holding a hand under his chin as crumbs dropped onto his chest.

Dale was a short man in height, but his stout body and broad shoulders made a much larger impression. He was dressed to go out, immaculate from his neatly curled and powdered white wig to glossy leather shoes. As cake crumbs gathered among the folds of his dark wool coat, his wife levered herself up from her seat and flicked them carefully away with a napkin.

He finished his last mouthful, raising his chin good naturedly to allow her to fuss over him.

'And what do ye think of the 'turkey red' cloth?' he asked, waving a hand towards his daughter's new coat.

The coloured wool was from her husband's own Dyeworks at Barrowfield.

'It is certainly an eye catching red! 'Dale's Red' I hear they are calling it now.' she told him. 'I can understand its popularity.'

'I shall not be long, Carolina,' he said, patting her arm. 'There is business up at the Church to attend to, after which I will return.' His

19

square face lit up with a contented smile as he looked down at their two eldest children. 'May we be thankful to the Lord for these pleasant times.'

He ruffled William's golden locks and made for the door, the silver buckles on his shoes and breeches gleaming white amidst the rest of his black attire.

Anne Caroline looked lovingly after her father. She savoured every moment with him and wished their times together were not so fleeting

***

It was after midday before Joe reached the brow of the last hill and looked down on the cottage which he had once called home.

The family lived in the end part of a row of miners' houses strung along the roadside. Houses were too grand a description for the shabby collection of stone walls and ragged thatched roofs. Smoke hung above them and here and there activity could be seen, mainly small children and old folk going about their daily tasks.

He was hot now. Even in the autumn air, his exertions from the cross country trek had worked up a sweat. He wiped his sleeve across his mouth. He was thirsty. The last stream he passed was several miles behind him and his throat was dry, his tongue parched. Or maybe, the imminent meeting with his mother was the cause of his discomfort.

As he stood on the skyline a girl appeared near the cottages, the sun catching on her long hair, the colour of sun-dried hay. She was hanging washing out on the line and glanced up to the horizon. Joe recognised her at the same moment as she dropped the peg basket and started running up through the long grass towards him.

'Sarah!' he called, arms outstretched to catch her up and whirl her round.

'Oh Joe!' she cried, flinging herself against him. 'Oh Joe, thank the Lord ye've come!'

Brother and sister hugged warmly, then he held her away from him and looked afresh at the girl he had not seen for over a year.

'Yer sae tall! An' yer hair? Sae lang! Whit e'er hae ye done wi' ma wee sister?'

20

She laughed and caught up her tousled locks, throwing them back to fall in a wave behind her shoulders. 'An' see ye? A grown man noo!'

'Ah heard tell ye were fruit pickin' doon the valley.'

'Aye, that's where Ah've bin since the spring.'

'An' how wis it? Yer lookin' awfy well. Broon as a conker!'

'Och, it were fine. The ither lassies were guid company an' we ate well enough. The work wis hard, mind, an' at the start Ah thocht Ah'd break ma back wi' a' the stooping.' She shrugged. 'Naw, it wis fine. Ah just felt... sort o' bad aboot leavin' Ma an' the weans.'

Joe drew her to him again. 'Ah felt the same goin' tae New Lanark.' Guilt cut into him with its icy knife. 'How long ha'e ye been back here?'

'The news aboot faither came last nicht an' Ah managed tae cadg' a ride o'er tae Lesmahagow on a cart an' arrived while they were sleepin'. Only Meg wis awake.'

Meg, his baby sister. The knife sliced deeper.

'How is she?'

'The same, but bigger.' Sarah's pale eyes flooded with sudden tears and she blinked them hurriedly away and smiled. 'Ah think she wis pleased tae see me though?'

'She would be, and tha's a fact.'

They looked solemnly at one another. There was so much to say, too much to ever be said.

Then Sarah burst out, 'Oh Joe... Joe... he's deid. Faither's really deid.'

There were no tears now. There would be no grieving for Duncan Scott. This was a moment they had both privately craved for most of their lives.

There would be no more beatings, no more rows and drunken brawls leaving their mother sobbing and broken on the floor. Their father had ruled them with angry words and violent abuse. An illiterate, frustrated man, he was bitterly resentful of his lot in life. He deemed that the daily grind at the coal mine earned him the right to treat his family in any way he chose, so it was on them that he vented his pent up rage. They were utterly dependent on him so they were obliged to obey him and do his bidding without question. The children grew up fearful of his cruel ways and as soon as they were old enough they learned how to keep out of his way.

'How's Ma?' Joe asked as they set off downhill, arms around each other's waists.

21

'Aw... she's greetin' 'cause she does nae ken whit will happen tae her. And, weel... she's bin on the grog since she got word o' the accident.'

It was rare if Marie Scott was not drinking. It was her way of dealing with her life: drunk, numb and blissfully disconnected from day to day matters.

'Weel, she'll ha'e tae sober up when the jug runs dry. There will be nae mony fae mair booze.'

Joe paused by the doorway, the foul stench from the midden nipping his nostrils. It would be no better inside the hovel, just a different odour of coal, unwashed bodies and whatever his mother was burning in the cooking pot that day.

He gave thanks to God for his freedom from this dreadful place then, bracing himself, pulled off his cap, ducked beneath the low lintel and entered the gloom.

'If its no' ma wee boy! Joe! Joe!' Marie was lolling back on a bed among the folds of her dishevelled shawl and skirts, her calloused bare feet dangling over the side. 'Come away in...' she waved a beckoning hand.

He bent over her and, holding his breath, laid a cheek against hers. He was appalled by her condition and that of the room. There had always been some order to the place when he lived there but now the floorboards were covered in discarded rags, mud and withered vegetable leaves, left over from meals in days gone by. This was more than a day's worth of mourning for her husband, this was weeks or months of slovenliness. He shuddered to think what life must have been like for his younger brother and sisters.

His eyes were adjusting to the dimness and he cleared a space on the bed beside her, sending bed bugs scuttling into new, dark hiding places.

Sitting down, he took his mother's hand. What to say? She stared at him from beneath her grubby muslin cap, straggling grey hair escaping into her eyes; bloodshot, red rimmed eyes. Her creased, swarthy complexion showed little of the woman he remembered from his early childhood. Loose bags had formed beneath her eyes, and her nose, broken many times, was an unhealthy purple colour. She had long since lost most of her teeth and now only one remained, a brown stump in the front of her bottom jaw.

A movement from the other side of the room caught his attention.

Meg was raising an arm in greeting to him.

He rushed to her side and scooped her up in his arms. Like a fragile doll she hung limply against him, her one good arm wrapped tightly round his neck, her little head resting on his shoulder.

He rocked her gently and hid his tears amongst her hair. Unlike his mother, Meg was in clean linen, the blanket on her bed neatly tucked in at the base. A part of his mind registered all this in a second, instantly connecting Sarah pegging out the washing. What terrible state had their poor little sister been lying amidst before Sarah arrived?

As a small child, still unsteady on her legs, Meg tumbled down the steps by the well and hit her head on the wall at the bottom. He remembered her screams and the following hours when she staggered around, bumping into everything, restless, agitated, in pain. The crying went on all day and when their father returned he couldn't stand the noise. In a fury he snatched her up and shook her with such force that when he threw her down on the cot she just lay there; no more crying, no more sounds at all.

From that day, Meg never uttered another sound. Her limbs, all except her right arm, were lifeless and useless. How much she could hear or see they did not know, but when they looked into her eyes there was still a spark of personality and understanding.

Their father blamed her condition on the fall at the well steps, but his family knew better. Duncan Scott caused the catastrophic injuries that paralysed his daughter. Terrified of him, their mother withdrew into the bottle. The younger children suffered their knowledge silently but his eldest son, Samuel, dared to speak out and stand up to him.

Joe pulled himself out of the memories. Sam left them the same week of Meg's accident.

Sarah came through the door with fresh water and filled the kettle, prompting Joe to lay Meg down again. He tucked the blanket over her and tenderly smoothed tendrils of hair from her brow. Now that she was nearly four years old she no longer had the baby sweetness in her face. He was saddened to see how gaunt and pale she looked, with dark shadows around her eye sockets, her mouth narrow and drawn down on one side.

'Dear God,' he thought, moving away from her to help Sarah prepare some food. 'Is it any wonder I feel guilty? how can I drink and laugh with my friends when I know what's happening here?'

23

They found a sack of oatmeal, cobwebby from moths but, after careful inspection for any grubs, Sarah prepared some porridge and they supped bowls of weak, sugared tea. All the while, Joe was thinking of what was going to happen to the family in the coming week.

The cottage was tied to the mine and he knew they would be evicted within the next few days. The mining company was covering the expense of the burial, which was a small consolation, but after that as far as they were concerned, the Scott family were no longer their problem. Every time he turned the conversation to the subject of where his mother would live, she threw herself into a fit of wailing tears.

Duncan's sudden death may be causing them to lose their home but in a very real way it was giving his family a new lease on life. Marie, through all her sobbing and moaning, was mainly concerned about the spectre of being thrown out into the street. She never gave more than a moment's thought to the cold, disfigured body lying on a trestle in a back room up at the pit office.

As the afternoon wore on, she lay back among her louse infested blankets, lost in an alcoholic haze, and was soon asleep, mouth open, snoring loudly.

Sarah and Joe brought Meg over to the fireside and took turns to hold her on their knees as they talked. Despite their dreadful straits, there was a tangible relief and buoyancy to the atmosphere.

Sarah, at fifteen years old, was three years younger than Joe, but the two of them had always been very close. So it was not long before they were joking and laughing, recounting anecdotes from their time apart and reminding each other of past shared incidents. Joe was full of stories of his exploits with Tam and the daring fishing trips they took, dodging through a private estate, to the mighty Corra Linn waterfall.

For her part, Sarah confided the delights of her first weeks of gorging on strawberries, so much so, that now she could hardly bear their scent without retching. She also had much to say about a delivery boy who would seek her out and recite poetry to her whenever he visited the orchard.

By the time their younger brother and sister came in from work, blackened with coal dust, the sun was setting in a fiery crimson ball. Great stabs of red light pierced the dim interior when the door swung open, illuminating Joe and Sarah sitting with Meg, their mother sprawled unconscious in the corner. The children were very pleased to see Joe again and although physically exhausted, soon gained a second wind. They too were affected by an inner excitement caused by the dramatic change to their circumstances.

'Ah had best get back tae Lanark,' Joe said, when they had been together for a while. It was good to see Calum and Rose and he realised how badly he had missed them all.

In his urgency to leave home and spurn everything to do with his father, he lost touch with the rest of his family. He blamed his father for that as well, but now, back with them again, he knew it was as much his own fault. He should have been mature enough to do what was right, not cowered away from his father, out of sight, out of mind.

With Samuel away, he, Joe, was now head of the family, so he should rise to the responsibility and look after them. Properly, as his father should have done.

While he was taking his leave of them, Sarah went to the line of hooks on the wall just inside the doorway.

'Ye will hae use o' this noo,' she said firmly, holding up a trench coat.

Joe took the heavy garment from her. He could see his father before him again, storming through the door, the coat swirling round him, heavy brows pulled down: a menacing figure.

''Tis a coat, Joe.' Sarah said softly. 'Jist a coat. Feel how thick it is... winter's comin' on us. Let it do some guid fer a change, eh?'

'Walk wi' me?' he asked.

'If ye tak the coat.'

'Fair enough.' He made no move to put it on.

She gathered up her shawl and they went out into the dusk. A light frost was already shimmering on the grass, stars starting to show amid the black sky above them.

'Ma and the weans...' he wasn't sure how to broach the subject because he needed Sarah's support.

She waited for him to continue, linking her arm in his beneath the folded trench coat.

'Sarah, Ah have an idea... Ah think it might work but Ah'll need ye tae agree 'cause it will nae be easy. It will affect us all.'

She nodded and pressed encouragingly against him, 'Oot wi' it!'

'Ah ken where we all could live and get jobs... at New Lanark...'

25

'In the mills! Och Joe, are ye mad? Mills? Ah couldnae bare it! Closed up a' day, an' the noise an' machines! It's gie dangerous an all! Naw Joe, Ah couldnae! Rosie couldnae!'

'It's no' as bad as tha' at New Lanark. It's cotton they're spinnin' an' the bairns look fine and healthy when they come oot a' the end o' the day. Mr Dale's a guid church-going man. He treats them weel, an' feeds them.' He stopped and turned to her imploringly. 'Yer work in the valley, how lang d'ye still hae tae be there?'

'It's over.' She looked downcast. 'They paid me aff when Ah left to come up here last nicht. In ony case, the fruit's a' pulled, the season's o'er. I wid ha'e bin sent aff in the next few days whether this had happened or no'.'

'Then ye need a job. If ye came wi' me tae New Lanark we could rent somewhere. With ye, Cal and Rose workin' we could manage the rent, Ah'm sure.'

'Whit aboot Ma?'

'She has tae see tae Meg. We could do it, Sarah. Wi' ma wages ... we could do it.'

'An' Ah have a wee bit o' money put by,' she bit her lip, it was to have been for some shoes for winter, maybe new cloth for a dress... she saw these hopeful luxuries melt away.

He noticed the uneasiness on her face and, misreading it, sought to comfort her. 'The mill work's no' that bad. No worse than the coal mine, at any rate! But we would ha'e a place to sleep. A safe place fer Meg.'

'Ah dunno, you hear such stories about the mills. Terrible accidents an' the weary toil o' every day the same.'

'An' pickin' apples and damsons wisnae like that?' He straightened up, feeling the cold of the evening air seeping into him. With a dramatic flourish, he shook out the coat and plunged his arms into the sleeves, hoisting it into place around his shoulders. Then, with a belligerent grin he pulled the belt tight. 'If Ah can wear tha' auld bastard's coat, ye can help me look efter Ma an' the weans.'

'Joe Scott! Ye can jist tak tha' coat aff again if ye think it compares at a'!' Her serious expression gave way to a small, apprehensive smile. 'D'ye really think we can get work a' the mills and find lodgings?'

'At least let me ask?' Joe could see she was relenting.

'When will ye ken? The man frae the mine will be alang tae move us oot efter the burial.'

'Ah'll ask t'morra. If it's all richt, ah'll come back t'morra nicht an' get ye al'.'

'An' if its no' all richt?'

Joe kissed her on the forehead and set off quickly across the dark hillside, calling behind him, 'We will jist ha'e tae pray that it will be!'

Saturday 4th October....

Fiona had a plan.

The first meal of the day was drawing to a close with the Town Hospital's manager expressing gratitude to God in a rousing prayer to his one hundred and twenty two inmates as they sat at long tables, their empty bowls in front of them. Every man, woman and child sat silently, heads bowed, hands folded in their laps. Even the youngest child knew the procedure, their eyes tightly shut and obediently sitting still.

Fiona didn't know what he was saying but she knew the moment was approaching when they would be released and sent off to the work rooms.

'May the Lord have Grace upon us all. Amen.'

The whole company rose as a wave, with a great roar of noise.

Bowls and spoons were clattered together and piled up to be taken to the kitchen, benches grated against the flagstones. Bodies rustled as they jostled to leave the room with hurried chatter, their voices rising in volume to compete with the din. The explosion of sound echoed up into the lofty ceiling. Within seconds the hall was emptying, each knowing where they were heading, what part they were taking in the day's routine.

Fiona was heading to the sewing room. For hours, she had pondered as to how to keep the small parcel of her personal things safe and about her person. Eventually a plan formed. At first, she was thrilled and very pleased with herself. It would work, it would be simple. However, the more her mind focused upon it, the more she worried and picked holes, finding flaws in every aspect. It entailed stealing a good length of ribbon or binding, enough to secure the cloth around her parcel and then tying it around her waist beneath the shift.

What if she couldn't get the opportunity to be near the big ribbon bobbins at the end of the room? What if she couldn't take the scissors with her? What would she say if she was caught cutting the material? Where could she hide it before returning to the dormitory?

It was such a fraught exercise that her head began to ache with the problem, but she knew she must carry it out. The rich gentleman might return at any moment and she would be taken from the building. And that was another concern: what did he want her for? Where was she to be taken?

Frowning, lost in her worries, Fiona fell into line with the other girls and trooped up the back stairs towards Mrs Sinclair's room.

'Fiona Macdonald!'

Fiona swung round. The one thing she did recognise in English was her name.

The oldest of the nurses, a haggard woman with hairs sprouting from her chin, was pointing directly at her.

'Yes, you! Come here! There will be no sewing for you, you are leaving us today.'

Fiona approached her warily, confused.

'Come on, hurry up!' Then the woman remembered that this was one of the ones who didn't understand what she was being told. She grasped her by the arm and marched her back down the stairs and towards the front hall.

To Fiona's horror she saw several other girls being taken out of the open front door. A long covered wagon stood on the street outside, its heavy horses standing alertly in the shafts. As she neared the door, one of the other inmates took a shawl from a pile beside her and held it out towards Fiona.

'Take a shawl and follow the others!' instructed the nurse, letting go of Fiona's arm and turning away to fetch the remaining paupers destined for New Lanark.

It was happening: she was leaving. No, not yet, not without her parcel.

She whirled round and scampered past the others in the hallway, dodging the old nurse's outstretched arm and then racing up the flight of stairs. She could hear the shouts and footsteps behind her but pressed on, her bare feet hardly making a sound as she flew down the corridor and, grabbing hold of the door jamb, swung herself into the dormitory.

Her bed was at the furthest end, by the window, but she managed to reach it and snatch her things from under the mattress.

'Come here, girl!' came a wheezy shout from the nurse, out of breath and holding her side from the hurried chase up the stairs.

Fiona sat down on her bed and enjoyed making the woman walk the entire length of the room to reach her. She hated the nurses with their tight black bonnets tied down over frilled caps and their high-buttoned, dark grey outfits, keys jangling on a chain at their hip. They reminded her of hooded crows.

Let them think what they like about her, she didn't care. None of them had shown any kindness towards her, so why should she make their job easier? Make the horrid old woman work for her pay. From beneath her lashes she watched the approaching figure, her dark eyes fixed on the distorted, ugly shapes of the nurse's mouth as she let forth a tirade of meaningless but obviously furious words.

For a moment Fiona toyed with the idea of jumping up and moving around between the beds, always keeping just out of her reach. Like cat and mouse. It brought back visions of the cats at the croft, mercilessly playing with their prey. It was cruel. It had made her cry sometimes and there was many a time she took the mouse's side and chased the cat away, rescuing the poor little creatures.

Who was the cat and who was the mouse, in this strange situation?

It was these memories, mere flashes of the past, which brought her to her senses. She stood up just as the woman's hand made contact with her head in a well practised slap.

'Get down those stairs! Now!'

Her little package tucked safely under her armpit, Fiona did as she was told.

The journey quickly took them out of the city and into country side. Hours of being rattled and thrown about, mile upon mile, made the occupants weary and sore. They were all female, Fiona noted, and most of them were younger than herself. Where ever were they being taken? Maybe a farm? But it was autumn and the crops had already been gathered. She could see plots of cultivated land among the passing heather, bogs and stony hills with little squares of run-rigs and areas of new bright green grass coming away where oats, barley or maybe wheat had been recently scythed. As the wagon rolled on, she strained to see work horses and haystacks, looking longingly at the wide open views and distant hills.

She hoped she was going to a farm.

After several stops and a change of horses, she was soon too tired to do anything but lean her head on the shoulder of the older woman next to her and drift in and out of a jolting, disturbed sleep.

She must have dozed off because the next thing she knew, she was waking up with a start. The coach had stopped and there was a loud exchange going on outside between the coachman and a couple of young men on the road.

Disorientated and nauseous, she looked about her.

It was late afternoon and the sun was low in the sky, sending long shadows out from the trees. On one side, a hillside ran up to houses, where other roofs and a spire could be glimpsed. On the other she couldn't see anything, except, far in the distance, a heavily wooded and very steep hill. From her seat inside the coach, they appeared to have stopped on the edge of a precipice.

At least they were in the countryside.

They disembarked from the comparatively warm interior of the wagon to stand in a huddled group. It was cold and the road's compacted stones were hard and rough on their bare feet.

With a lot of laughing and calling to one another, the coachman waved to the two men and sent the horses forward in a wide, creaking circle to head back up towards the town. The women looked at each other in astonishment. They seemed to have been deposited in the middle of nowhere.

Fiona eyed the men warily. They were dressed alike in knee length brown coats with red collars, matching brown breeches and long black boots. It struck her that they had a military look to them, yet their unkempt hair and the evident wear and tear to their clothes gave them a scruffy appearance. Perhaps they were servants from a grand estate?

An estate! A mansion with fine ladies in beautiful dresses, handsome footmen, a well stocked kitchen! Her lips parted in a smile, that would not be so awful. Maybe the rich man at the Town's Hospital had acquired a country house and sought to staff it with needy, homeless people. It gave her a warm feeling of hope.

'Richt then! Follow me!' One of the men raised his hand and walked briskly towards a gap in a hawthorn thicket and disappeared from view almost instantly

'In the name o' goodness!' shrieked one of the women. 'He's vanished in tae thin air!'

As a group, they pulled back from the bushes, some of the smaller children running behind the older women's skirts.

'It's a path, a stairway, ye dafties!' called the other man, laughing and guiding them towards the edge again. 'It's nothin' tae be scared aboot!'

Fiona had no fear of heights. She had scaled cliffs in search of birds' eggs and clambered among rocky ravines many times, so she moved to the head of the group and took the lead down the steps.

It was not until she was half way down the hill that she raised her head and looked into the valley. Nothing could have prepared her for what she saw: it took her breath away.

A silver ribbon of water tumbled down a waterfall and wound past a small wooded island, but closer to Fiona, running beside the river, was a canal and at the furthest right of her view, was the largest building she had ever seen in all her life.

Its vast sandstone bulk dwarfed tiny moving figures hurrying around in the open space at its base. Row upon row of windows looked up and down the gorge and its roof was crowned with a bell tower. Here, surrounded by green hills, trees and the shining beauty of the river was a massive man-made structure worthy of the centre of Glasgow.

Beside it, in its shadow, she could see the roof of one long row of stone tenements, their ground floors embedded into the cliff side. There were signs of habitation, puffs of blue smoke floating up from dozens of chimneys, washing hanging out from the upper windows.

People lived here.

The buildings looked utterly out of place. Like chunks of a city randomly dropped into the lush valley. Yet there was a fascination to it. The sheer size of the houses was extraordinary. Constructed on terraces to make the most of such a narrow strip of land, it was almost cut off from the rest of the world by the precipitous valley sides and the flowing water.

The women behind Fiona were urging her to move on and she tore her eyes away from the sight and carried on down the steps.

As they descended, the buildings grew larger, until, when the steps gave way to level ground, the stone walls towered over their heads.

Fiona stared up at them and was filled with a dreadful panic. This was no castle or dwelling house, this was something else... a factory? Another work-house?

Her first instinct was to run away, just run, as fast and as far away as she could get from this strange, terrifying place. Despite the open sky above her head, she felt trapped, just as she had felt in the Town Hospital. At least in Glasgow she knew where she was, having walked there from her home, but it was different here.

Shaking with fear, she was shepherded towards the huge building and through its yawning doorway to be swallowed up into the dark, cavernous lower floors.

***

Before he started work that morning, Joe had been to see Mr McCulloch. The meeting went well, he thought, all things considered. He started by stating his family's plight and describing his younger siblings as 'willing and strong workers'. Should McCulloch see fit to take them on at the mills he would personally ensure, from his own wages, that prompt payment was made for their lodgings. He added that he would live with them and take full responsibility for them.

This was greeted with an agreeable nod of the head.

Joe then broached the subject of his 'poor, bereaved mother and crippled sister.'

This was of little interest to McCulloch, but he wanted to know if all the family were in good health, no disease was to be brought into the community.

Eventually, satisfied that he would be hiring three able-bodied new workers and, with Joe's contribution, that the payment for their rent would be sustainable, McCulloch agreed to take them into New Lanark. He made one condition. He only had Joe's word for the health and ability of his family so when they arrived at New Lanark they would be inspected, as all employees were, and if found to be unsuitable they would not be hired.

All day Joe laboured on the site and when the bell pealed to signal the end of work, he threw his tools down, pulled the coat around his shoulders and set off to tell Sarah the news. Although the next day was Sunday, he was expected to work from midday but had asked for, and been granted, the time off. It would mean that he would now be a further half day down on his wages that week so they would have to rely on Sarah providing enough money to pay their first week's rent.

It was a concern, but he had another more serious problem that churned around in his head. He had no qualms about McCulloch accepting Sarah or Rosie, and Calum, although moody and despondent by nature, was used to long hours and tiring work. It was his mother that worried him. One look at her ravaged face and bedraggled posture and a man like McCulloch would easily be able to tell that she drank to excess.

This was still preying on his mind several hours later when he let himself quietly into the cottage. It was the dead of night and the room

33

was in complete darkness. After pausing by the door to allow his eyes to adjust, a faint glow from the dying embers in the grate showed him a direction to follow. He started to mend the fire with some sticks which were stacked neatly by the hearthside and as the fire flickered into life he could see the floor was swept and two clean pans sat at the hearthside.

'Joe?' Sarah whispered from behind him, where she lay with Rosie and Calum.

'Aye,'

She came to join him and they sat on the floor together, hugging their knees and watching the burning sticks send flashing sparks licking up the chimney.

'It's gaun tae be fine,' Joe said, keeping his voice low and hushed. 'We ha'e a place tae gae.'

She cuddled up against him, kissing him on the cheek. 'Ah have nae bin idle either.'

'Ah saw. Ye've tidied up.'

'Oh aye, the bugs wer' nipping tha' bad Ah couldnae stan' it, an' Ah think Ma wis feedin' a' the rats o' the village. Ye should ha'e seen the nest at the back o' her bed! Bigger than that yin you an' Sam used tae torment up at the auld farm? But tha's no' whit Ah meant. Ah've bin askin' aroon' tae see if onyone's goin' Lanark way. Ma's no' able tae walk that far, an' whit wi' Meg an' a'.' She sighed. 'Faither's tae be buried t'morra mornin', an' Bel MacNab said her man could tak us o'er tae Lanark in his cart when tha's o'er.'

'Tha's good o' him.' Joe's words were slurring. 'Ah'm no' workin' the morra, so Ah can gi'e ye a haun.'

'Ah ken it's fae the best, an' ye ha'e found us a place tae live... but, aw Joe, the thocht o' the lang days o' workin' at machines...Ah'm fair scared o' the whole idea o' workin' in a Mill.'

She waited for a response and when none came she turned her head to look at him.

His eyes were closed, lips slightly parted, fast asleep.

Very gently, she shifted her position to let him lie down, cradling his head on her lap.

She gazed into the fire, idly stroking his long thick hair, her mind filled with jumbled thoughts and memories. Tears smarted in her eyes. There was no going back to the old, terrible days of her father's time, and they had no alternative but to leave this place. There had been such misery between these squalid, rough stone walls, such suffering, but it was familiar and its very familiarity held a certain comfort.

Now they were leaving, everything was changing. The tears overflowed and ran down her cheeks as she swallowed back sobs. She wondered if she would be able to bear the future her brother was providing for them. He needed her help and she would give it, willingly, but in those dark, pre-dawn hours she was overwhelmed by the enormity of it all.

Through brimming eyes she looked down at Joe. He looked so young, vulnerable, in his sleep. He was doing the best for them, the very best he could do, and her heart went out to him. He had secured a new home, kept them together as a family, what more could she ask? How selfish and silly she was to complain about the mill work.

Winter would soon be here. The frosts had started, fieldfares and redwings were now flocking in the trees, skeins of geese cackled across the skies heading south. There was no work in the winter for the likes of herself and the weans. Ma was unable to provide for them so it would only be a matter of time before they would be forced to knock on the Poor House door.

She shivered, drying her wet cheeks on her shawl and reaching carefully across Joe to throw more wood on the fire.

They separated families at the Poor House, one of the women at the orchard had told her all about the horrors of those ominous institutions. Men with men, women with women and what would happen to Meg?

Crying had helped release some of the raw anxiety bottled up inside. She felt calmer. There really was no other choice open to them so the road ahead was plain. Instead of snivelling, she would put on a brave face, encourage Cal and Rosie to look positively on their new life and, whatever it was like, no matter how bad, she would try and act as an example to them.

Her fate accepted, Sarah's practical mind moved to the pressing problem of what they should take with them, and how to make Meg comfortable for the cart ride.

Sunday 5th October....

During the night, a blanket of low cloud rolled over the skies above Clydesdale, bringing with it the threat of rain. For weeks on end there had been a drought, shrivelling crops and causing the clay soil to dry as hard as stone. Few could remember such a long, hot summer and while it was welcomed in June, it was cursed by harvest time.

The lack of rain was also a concern for the mill-rights at New Lanark.

A weir had been constructed upstream of the mill and, in a project worthy of the brilliant engineer John Smeaton, a thousand foot tunnel was excavated through solid rock to allow water from the river to be channelled into the mill lade. It was a mighty feat of engineering.

Months of low rainfall saw the Clyde's water levels drop considerably. There was still enough water collecting above the weir to do the job, but the sight of heavy grey clouds looming over the valley was greeted with hopeful eyes.

The dark, wet day was not met with the same pleasure by Fiona.

She woke to the sound of a clanging bell. It came from somewhere above her head and she was momentarily bewildered, expecting to find herself among the stark walls of the Town Hospital. Instead she was in another dormitory, a longer room which stretched the whole width of the building, tucked under the low roof rafters. It smelt very clean and the heather mattress on her bed was surprisingly comfortable.

She was sharing the bed with a young red-haired, freckled girl. On meeting, Fiona gave her a smile but she just glared back from her pale blue eyes and stuck out her tongue. Fortunately, the child was so much smaller than herself that she was able to stretch out and even enjoy the luxury of lying on her back. In Glasgow, the beds were narrower so the occupants were jammed together in an awkward, squashed manner that left little room for comfort and led to outbreaks of angry kicking and pushing in the middle of the night.

While the rest of the girls enjoyed a few more precious moments in the warmth, two of them rose and busied themselves with lighting the whale oil lamps positioned down the room. It took a few minutes before their flames diluted the blackness into a spreading glow, gradually drawing bed frames, rafters and sleepy faces out of the gloom. When it was light enough to allow them to rise, wash and make up their beds, a ripple of activity stirred through the room.

Fiona followed the routine by watching what everyone else was doing.

The evening before, she was measured and handed new linen undergarments, two white cotton tunics, two pairs of thick woollen stockings and, to her amazement, two pairs of stays. She had never worn stays before and looked down at her breasts, pushed up with the support, and was surprised to note how much they had grown over the summer.

No-one questioned the package she carried and no-one pushed her about or scolded her when she did not immediately understand what they were saying. She was unused to being treated kindly and it left her a little wary.

The door burst open and a woman came in carrying a lantern.

'Come now, everyone get ready! Hurry up!' she shouted, but the words were said brightly, cheerfully.

She walked down the centre aisle pointing out where a stocking had fallen or a cover was not tucked into the mattress. The wide skirts of her dress swished along the floor, brass buttons flashing in the lamp light. Mrs Docherty liked everything to be in order. She was a methodical woman and ruled the orphans in her charge in a systematic manner. Slovenly behaviour was not tolerated, but she did not punish an offender, neither verbally nor physically, because there was no need. In a quiet, civil tone she told them clearly 'it should not happen again.'

Respect, she told her employer, was what she commanded. The girls respected her and would comply with her wishes because they knew she was right to demand it of them.

Her methods worked wonders on almost all of the girls, although, even she had to admit that there were a few among them who 'God in His divine wisdom had seen fit to make lazy and untidy.'

Mrs Docherty was pleased to note that the new intake of girls from Glasgow appeared to be obedient.

On her way back to the door, she paused beside Fiona.

'You are from the north?' she asked briskly. 'A Gaelic speaker?'

Fiona's brown eyes showed her dilemma as she tried to express that she did not understand the question, '*Chan eil mi 'tuigsinn,*'

Mrs Docherty's lips curved into a smile and she turned to face down the room. 'Isla? Mhairi? Come here.'

Two little girls ran towards her, one still trying to button up her tunic.

'Please explain to Fiona how we do things here.' Her eyes darted across the rows of beds. 'You three all speak Gaelic so I shall place you together. Tell her to move into the bed beside you.' She assessed Fiona's height and age: she was larger than most of the others. 'Indeed, she can take the whole bed for the time being, and Jinty and Cathren, being so small, can take her place and share with Susan'.

There was a sharp gasp from Susan. She was not at all happy about the change in arrangements and narrowed her eyes at Fiona.

Throughout this conversation Fiona was standing by her bed, anxiously looking from one to the other as they spoke. She could see the girls were being asked to do something and whatever it was, it seemed to involve her in some way. They all kept looking at her, then looking down the room.

Then the matron turned on her heel and carried on supervising the bed making.

The taller of the two girls, dark-haired and skinny, smiled at Fiona and touched her on the arm.

'*Is mise Mhairi,*' she said in Gaelic, '*bring your things, you are going to be sleeping down at the far end with us.*'

'*A bheil Gàidhlig agat? Do you speak Gaelic*?' Fiona cried, covering her mouth as she tried to contain a great outpouring of relief. '*Oh! Oh! You speak Gaelic*!'

The younger child grinned at her, showing a wide gap where her new front teeth were just appearing.

'*O'course we do!*' she laughed. '*It's Scots we find hard, but we have been here for so long we can understand quite a lot.*'

Tearful with this wonderful turn of events, Fiona gathered up her bundle of new clothes and her special personal items and followed the girls to her new bed.

Suddenly, a warm feeling surged up through her body. She had been distraught when her mother died because she loved her mother, but in the weeks following her death there was another reason why she felt chilled to the core and so desperately sad. Loneliness. Unable to speak to anyone in Gaelic or even understand the most basic words, had shut her away from proper contact with other human beings. Now, with Mhairi and Islay, she could return to the world.

The delight of being able to talk to someone, ask questions and join in with conversations marked a momentous day for Fiona. Even when she was separated from the girls, she carried with her a lightness of heart she wouldn't have thought possible only minutes before.

Fiona's first morning was spent cleaning the dormitories, scrubbing corridors and emptying the smelly buckets from the girls' closets. Then, it being Sunday, she joined all the paupers to endure several hours of catechising and preaching from two fervent, evangelical ministers.

After these services, the new girls from Glasgow were drawn away from the others and told to wait in the dormitories until they were allocated a work area. On Mrs Docherty's word, they made their way downstairs, passing different levels where Fiona could hear the ominous whirring, clattering noise of machinery. Even through the thick walls the sound was frightening, like a caged bear, growling and dangerous. She found herself wishing she was back in Mrs Sinclair's sewing room.

So, when they were finally led into the carding room, in the basement, Fiona let out a sigh of relief to find it was quite quiet, not a cranking, roaring machine in sight.

It was a large room, like everything at New Lanark. The walls were stacked with bales of cotton surrounding a space in the centre where a crowd of children were gathering to start work for the day. A young woman, not much older than Fiona, took charge of the new batch of Boarders, boys and girls. Without delay she dispensed hand-cards to each of them and set them to learn the task of carding cotton.

Fiona fingered the wooden blocks with distaste, gingerly holding the handles and turning them this way and that. The flat surface was covered in leather, embedded with rows of short angled spikes. A pile of cotton, just a mass of white bobbly tangled fibres flecked with debris, was then thrown down beside them.

A brief lesson followed on how to pick over the cotton and work it between the spikes and then, turning the cards around, scrape it off in rolls. These rolls of material, cardings, should end up about an inch wide and a foot long, and were then laid aside to be taken upstairs and spun into continuous thread. It was not as easy as it first looked and they were left to practise and struggle-on to perfect the knack; their first uneven efforts being thrown back onto the pile to start all over again.

After several hours of dozens of children pulling and teasing the fine white threads, there was a mist of wafting fibres hanging in the air. Fiona was absorbed in her work but the others chatted and even sang.

39

So long as they were constantly busy with the task at hand, the two Overlookers took a relaxed attitude. Occasionally the door would open as messages were brought or cardings removed, and the draught sent clouds of loose cotton drifting across the floorboards.

When the bell started ringing again there was an immediate scramble to the door. Fiona was as eager as any of them to leave the dusty room, but her haste was driven by the thought of being able to seek out Mhairi or Islay, her new found friends.

It was a good feeling.

***

The rain was falling in a steady, drenching curtain when the Scott family finally arrived in New Lanark.

McNab's cart was piled high with pots and pans, baskets of blankets, clothes and any other useful paraphernalia they could salvage from their home. Huddled between the household goods sat Ma, holding Meg in her arms, a heavy blanket draped over her head to try and give shelter from the worst of the rain. Rosie rode up beside Bill McNab. She had shared this position with Sarah, swapping at every stop.

Like her mother, Rosie was hunched under a blanket, gripping it tightly under her chin like a hood, her face spattered with mud. Raindrops spiked her lashes and left shiny clean streaks through the grime on her cheeks. Her expression was solemn. They were a tired, sodden party.

Joe and Cal had walked the whole way beside the cart and were weary and footsore. The journey took much longer than they had planned, partly due to the age of the horse which required frequent stops, but also due to the circuitous route chosen by McNab. When Joe walked home, he went directly across country, which was about eight miles. He was young and fit so he could stride out without stopping and cover the distance in just a couple of hours. However, keeping to the roads as they twisted and turned uphill and down through valleys, had added several more miles to the trip.

Being the Sabbath, the hillside beside the great mill was empty of the usual wagons, horses and workmen. Its grassy slopes were wet and littered with puddles, heavy raindrops bubbling the surface of the muddy water.

Joe left his mother and Meg on the cart, pulled in close to the mill walls to catch a little shelter, and took his brother and sisters with him to the office.

McCulloch would only be at his duties between two o'clock and four o'clock that day and Joe was worried they might be too late. However, as they entered the building a young clerk was on his way out of a meeting with the manager and drew away from the soaking figures he met in the hallway.

For a moment the two young men looked eye to eye. Joe, soaked, dirty, his hair straggling round his shoulders with water dripping from the rats' tails onto his worn trench coat. The clerk was clean and fresh, his dark hair neatly tied back in a black ribbon. His clothes were fashionable, the high collared white shirt, smart cut away black jacket and cream breeches proclaimed his success in the world. For all that they were the same age, the contrast in their lives was starkly evident.

Joe's confidence and the pride he felt in looking after his family, was shattered. Here he was, a mere labourer, coming cap in hand to the mill manager to ask to be taken into the village. His solution to their dire situation was to condemn his brother and younger sisters to years of toil. He was about to display them for inspection, like goods to be scrutinized to see if they were good enough. It made him cringe inside to see the other man step aside, holding himself away from Sarah as if he might catch something.

McCulloch was quick in his appraisal of the children. He was used to seeing paupers, their rancid clothing, greasy, louse ridden hair and unwashed faces had long since ceased to have any effect on him. All he needed to confirm, on behalf of his employer, Mr Dale, was that they were sound of body and could do the job. He wrote their names and ages beside the date and told them to sign with a cross where he indicated.

Sarah, Rosie and Cal were now bound to the New Lanark Mills for a four year period.

They were assigned a room in the tenements and after more paperwork, instructed to report to the front door of the mill at six o'clock the next morning.

Within minutes of walking through the office door, the Scotts walked out again.

McNab was relieved to see them emerge from the mill so quickly. He took the tired old horse by the head-collar and they set off to retrace their steps to a higher terrace. Although the workers' housing was right beside the mill, it was on a higher level, perched above a sheer cliff face where the hillside had been hacked and blasted away to create flat ground for construction.

If Sarah was as disappointed as Joe at the first sight of their new home, she hid it very well.

'Look, a cast iron grate wi' a swee!' she exclaimed, seizing the swivelling iron arm where their kettle could hang above the range. 'Ah will lay a fire richt awa' an' we can start to get dry.'

Joe tried to throw off his own low spirits and match her light tone.

'See how cosy we will be in here, an' we ha'e a windae on each side, it'll be much lighter than in yon auld place.'

Cal went to the window overlooking the mill and beyond it to the river curving away down the valley. The valley was so deep that the wooded hill on the opposite bank blocked out any view of the sky.

At that moment the bell in the tower rang out.

'Whitever's tha'?' he called over his shoulder to Joe.

'Och, ye'll be hearing that every day. They ring it tae start the day, then tae call ye tae the meals and again at the end, so ye ken when tae gae hame!' Joe made a good attempt at laughing it off. 'Thank the Lord ye dinnae ha'e the bell ringer's job. He's the first up an' the last tae leave.'

From this high window Cal could see the bell moving, swinging to and fro, the peals matching the movement. He hated it already. He hated the whole wretched place from the sinister, overbearing walls of the mill itself to this dingy, damp, lime-smelling room.

He ran a finger down the window pane, feeling its smooth surface. It was real, yet he felt shaken and at odds with all around him. It was new and stark. Where were the sparrows chirping in the thatch, the butterflies, closed winged and tucked into the gaps in the stone walls to sleep for the winter? He wanted to hear the sounds of sheep bleating and the collie dogs barking from the high farm, smell the damp grass outside the door. This was a stone box, perched high on other stone boxes. He couldn't stay here, he would runaway.

'Cal!' Joe was calling, 'Rosie's awa' tae bring Ma up the stairs wi' Meg an' we need tae clear yon cart.'

Cal turned to follow him down the steep wooden stairs, a dour frown on his face. He was fair haired, like all the children, but his eyes were dark and deep set. In his ten years of life he had known little of comfort or fun. His father had knocked the child out of him a long time ago and he looked at life suspiciously, expecting the worst.

As soon as the cart was emptied, McNab was eager to be on his way. His thoughts, as he left them, were a mixture of resignation that at least the Scotts had a roof over their heads, and compassion. He would never put any of his family into a mill and he couldn't think of any of his neighbours who would allow it either.

Yet, he could understand that after Duncan was killed, they had few options open to them. Working with machines though, it wasn't right. He shook his head and muttered to the horse all the way up the hill to Lanark and then on into the stable yard at the back of the inn.

Meg refused their offers of a drink or food and fell asleep even before they laid her on one of the set-in beds. Apart from lying out on the grass beside the washing green in the summer, the paralysed child spent her entire life indoors. The experience of the cart ride from Douglas was taking its toll, she was floppier than ever.

Beneath the two wide beds set into the wall were two hurlies; low box shaped beds with wheels on them so they could be rolled out of the way during the day. Sarah pulled one out.

'If Ma an' Meg had one o' the big beds, an' Cal and Rosie had the ither...' she looked up cheekily at Joe. 'Ye an' Ah could tak a whole bed each!'

Their mother, slumped in a chair with her dress billowing round her, groaned and held her head. 'Ah cannae sleep wi' Meg. Ah'd crush her if Ah rolled o'er.' She moaned again. 'Ma heid's fit tae burst! Let me lie doon, darlin'. Just fer a wee minute, then Ah'll be wi' ye... help ye wi' the dinner...' She lurched across the room and fell onto the bed where she instantly passed out.

Sarah rushed to pull off her mother's wet clogs before they soaked the new mattress.

'She's drunk!' She cried, 'She cannae lie in a' these drookit things...' she started to unfasten the drenched skirt. Rosie joined her and between them they rolled their mother this way and that, tugging the wet clothes away.

'Whaur did she get the grog?' Joe asked.

He and Cal started to pick apart the baskets littered around the room.

'Aw naw...' Cal found a stoneware bottle jammed beside some boots.

Sarah pulled out the cork and with one sniff she knew. 'Bye, she's a crafty yin. She sed it wis watter! How did she get this? She's bin swiggin' at this a' the way here. It's tha' auld man Jock's brew, Ah'm sure o' it, it smells like neeps! But she said there was none left in the hoose?'

'Some folk were bringing her things when we pu' Da' in the grun'.' Cal said quietly. 'Tha' bread we ate? That wis frae Sal, an' there wis a sack o' tatties, Ah pu' them on the cart.'

'Frae this minute, there's tae be nae drink in the hoose,' Joe said firmly. 'If we are a' oot workin' we cannae ha'e her here drinkin' hersel' stupit.' He was enraged by his mother's crass behaviour. 'Every penny we earn will be needed, an' if we dinnae watch her she'll pour it doon her throat.'

'How'll we stop her?' asked Rosie, laying the cooking pots by the hearth.

Sarah was looking for the basket of kindlers and coal. There was no point leaving good coal, she had thought, and gathered as much as she could before they left Douglas. Now, she was even more grateful of having made the effort. A fire would cheer them up and she could boil some potatoes with the kale she'd picked.

'If we're workin' every day,' Rosie continued, 'it will be Ma who'll be buying the food. She'll ha'e the mony... so, how do we stop her frae spendin' it on drink?'

'Ah dunno' Joe said wearily, even his bones were tired. 'But we'll starve if she does, so we'd better think o' summat.'

There was a commotion on the stairs and then a loud rap on the door.

Sarah opened it to find a wiry little woman smiling up at her from under a lacy cap.

'They cry me Bessie Jackson, Ah live o'er the landing wi' ma sons. If ye need onythin' jist chap the door.'

As she spoke her button eyes were scanning the room, taking in the chaos of baskets, blankets, brushes... Ma's discarded clothes, all in a haphazard mess on the floor.

'That's fair kind o' ye,' Sarah smiled at her, 'we ha'e jist arrived, as ye can see.'

'D'ye have summat for yer meal? Dinnae gang hungry on yer first nicht, noo. No' wi me next door!'

44

Both Sarah and Joe thanked her for her offer but declined, they had food with them. Neither of them wanted Mrs Jackson to venture further into the room and see their mother sprawled on the bed.

'We'll need some watter, tho',' Joe said, picking up a bucket. 'Is it frae the river?'

'Aye, if ye wish, but the lade's fresher. There's talk o' stand wells but Ah widnae haud ma breath fae that!' She was looking them up and down. 'Is it jist the four o' yous?'

'An' oor Ma and wee sister...' Sarah decided she didn't want to say more about Meg, not yet anyway. 'Ma's sleeping, she's awfy tired... it's been a lang day.'

'Ah weel, as Ah say, jist chap the door if ye want me! Cheerio!'

'Well,' said Sarah, closing the door. 'That wis kind.' For the first time that day, she felt herself relax.

They had done it. They were all safely in New Lanark, with a job to go to in the morning, food to eat, coals for the fire and a friendly greeting from their neighbour.

She smiled across at Joe and he returned it with genuine warmth.

'Richt noo,' he said decisively. 'let's get yon rug on the flair, Cal ye come wi' me and we'll fetch up some watter and start gettin' this place sorted oot.'

***

As the Scotts were drying out their blankets and settling into their new home, Fiona was standing in line with her bowl, ready to receive the evening meal.

The delicious smell of beef made her mouth water and when two large ladles of broth were emptied into her bowl she raised it to her nose. She couldn't remember when she last tasted meat. She hurried to take her place, impatient for everyone to be served, Grace said, and permission granted to start the meal.

The broth was more like a thin stew, each portion having four large chunks of meat among the barley and carrots. She carefully halved each piece of meat and ate slowly, savouring every mouthful of the soft boiled beef. She wondered if it was a special occasion, or why else would they be eating such a rich meal?

45

Life was so much better. In just one day, the sorrowful girl was transformed. She still yearned for Mallaig, pined for her friends at the crofts, the salty air and her past life, but now it did not constantly fill her mind. Mhairi and Islay were going to help her understand the new language and had already told her many useful things to make her days easier.

Working on a Sunday was very unusual, they told her, for it was the one day they could have a little time of their own, between church services and Sunday school.

'*If Mr Kelly thinks he's getting behind wi' stuff,*' Mhairi said, '*he sometimes has us Boarders working on the Lord's day. I've heard Mrs Docherty being mad with him about it. You were just unlucky it was today.*'

They filled her in about which of the supervisors to avoid and which were pleasant; where to go for the two hours of lessons after dinner; quick 'rat runs' to get around the huge building and where the closets were if she needed the toilet. This had been an embarrassing problem and was probably the most valuable piece of information of all.

She now also understood that she was in a mill, a cotton mill. As well as the girls in her dormitory there were at least as many boys who slept in a separate dormitory, all of them orphans or abandoned by their parents. She and the other orphans were just a portion of the hundreds of people who worked there every day.

The lessons, taken by an austere, bearded man, were unintelligible to Fiona. She could not grasp or separate even one word from the next. The words he drew on a black board with a white piece of chalk, were just circles and lines with gaps between them. Mr Lyme, the teacher, noted Fiona as a new pupil and from time she saw him looking at her in a thoughtful way but he did not approach her and nothing was said about her inability to understand the lesson.

When the meal was finished and they were all dismissed, she met Mhairi in the corridor and together they went up to the school room.

As Boarders, as all the orphans were called, Mr Dale expected them to attend the school every day. He was eager for them to be able to read and write which was a generous and Christian gesture. However, after twelve hours of hard factory work and then eating the largest meal of the day, by the time the children sat down to be taught most of them could hardly keep their eyes open.

Mr Lyme guided Fiona to the front of the room and sat her with a group which, apart from an older boy and girl, were predominantly much younger children. Islay was among the group so Fiona squeezed onto the bench beside her.

Mr Lyme had spoken with the managers about all the new apprentices. In Fiona's case they discussed the fact that she did not know any English and he agreed with Mrs Docherty that it made sense to place the Highlanders together. From past experience she knew this made for a happier outcome on all sides. It was decided that those Gaelic speakers who had been at New Lanark longer were best placed to instruct the new arrivals and it saved time and effort on the company's behalf. Besides, from the growing stream of Highlanders heading to the Lowlands, there could well be more of these people coming to the mills.

'*I don't know why he's put me here?*' Fiona whispered to Islay, in their native tongue. '*But I'm glad we can sit together.*'

'*It's because he thinks you're stupid.*' Islay whispered back. '*This class is for all the wee ones and the dunces. See, Molly and Nat there,*' she nodded to the older children, '*They don't own a brain between them!*'

'*But you're here! An' you are not stupid?*'

'*I am with this! See those things he calls letters? I can't make head or tail of them. They jump about and make no sense at all.*'

Mr Lyme stalked across to them, 'Stop talking! Islay, you can relate to Fiona what I have asked you to do but I will not have chatter.' He gave her a serious look, raising his eyebrows and giving a curt nod to punctuate his instructions. 'So, get to work children, copy down what you see on the board.'

Islay passed on his instructions and stared at the blackboard, chalk in hand. She knew she was in for another long session of trying not to go to sleep while pretending to scratch something on the slate. After over a year of the same routine, she was used to it.

Fiona applied herself to the task with deep concentration.

The passage written on the board was from the Bible but, to Fiona, it was random symbols running in lines. Nevertheless, she painstakingly drew an accurate depiction of the design on the board.

On seeing her sit back, lay down her chalk and rub her tense neck, Mr Lyme picked up her slate to judge her efforts.

He was pleasantly surprised. It was crude and many of the letters were misshapen, but overall it could still be read without too much difficulty. He praised her and handed her a sheet of paper with the alphabet neatly laid out, each letter illustrated with a picture.

'*He wants you to copy this.*' Islay translated.

In no time at all the bell was ringing to end the school day. Fiona couldn't believe it, having been totally absorbed in making clean white lines and perfect loops the time had flown past.

She handed in her slate and waited for his remarks, quietly pleased with herself for her efforts.

He burst out laughing, shaking his head and removing his glasses to wipe his hand over his eyes. The rest of the pupils were shuffling out from behind their desks and gathering by the door, but his loud guffaws stopped them in their tracks.

All eyes turned to Fiona.

She was mortified, feeling the blood rush to her cheeks and knowing her face was crimson.

'This is a fine piece of work, Fiona,' he said at last, still smiling broadly. 'I required you to copy the letters, not the pictures as well. Although, I have to say you have made an admirable job of it! Well done!'

He held up her slate so the other children could see not only the apple and ball, but a beautiful cat, it's paw raised to bat a fly, and beside the letter D, a deer, lying in long grass with its legs curled beneath it.

Islay giggled and quickly comforted her embarrassed friend, explaining that he was praising her pictures.

Fiona was still flushed and disconcerted when they retired to their dormitory. She did not like to be the centre of attention, especially when there were boys in the room. Feeling upset and worn out, she started to undress. As she laid her tunic neatly by her bed, she reached under the pile of clothes and drew out the little parcel of her own, personal things.

Carefully, she unfolded the material and looked upon her treasures. A bracelet made of shells and horse hair, a shiny metal thimble, a wooden spoon and three pebbles. Each one held precious memories. They were irreplaceable, imbued with the magic of emotional connections to a time gone by. People loved and now lost, places now changed beyond all recognition. Her childhood was embodied in the objects on her lap.

'What are those?'

Fiona looked up sharply, instinctively wrapping up the parcel.

Susan was standing beside her, a smile pulling at her lips, an earnestly friendly expression on her face.

'Let me see?' she leaned towards her, her frizzy red curls tickling Fiona's cheek. 'My, aren't ye special?' the smile was slipping, her voice rising. 'Teacher holdin' up yer drawings, a whole bed to yersel... and ye have summat there that looks gie pretty but ye willnae share it!'

Mhairi was climbing into the next bed. 'Leave her be Susan. Away to yer end o' the room. Gie us peace!'

Susan made to turn away but in a flash, swung back and grabbed the parcel from Fiona's hand and ran off towards her own bed.

A wild chase ensued: Fiona clambering over the beds, jumping from one to the other with Susan scrambling to keep ahead of her as they tumbled and fought down the length of the dormitory.

The other girls joined in with cheers and shouts, bounding out of the way and shrieking. For a second Fiona caught her, pinned her to the ground and was trying to prise the parcel from her hand but Susan squirmed herself free and slid under a bed. Then, snatching the mattress for support, pulled it half off the bed and pushed it between herself and Fiona.

The barricade didn't last long and she whipped round and leapt onto the next bed, followed closely by Fiona. The wooden frames thumped on the floor, beating out their progress, adding to the great rumpus.

Suddenly, Susan tripped and crashed headlong onto the floorboards and Fiona was down on her like a falcon grabbing its prey. This time, she seized her things and fled back to her bed.

'Whit's all this carry on!' Mrs Docherty came rushing through the door, lantern swinging.

There was not a sound from anyone. They all froze like statues.

'What are you doing on the floor, Susan? And this mattress? Shona, put it back in its place at once!'

She walked to the end of the room, assessing the situation. No damage seemed to have been done, although there was a scattering of heather on the floor where the mattress had been thrown.

'I don't know what happened here, but it will not happen again. Am I understood?' She glared at each girl in turn as she made a slow and stately return to the doorway.

'Shona and Susan, I expect better from you.' She sniffed in disapproval. 'Janet and Flora, turn out the lamps.'

The girls who were still half undressed hastily pulled off their outer garments and slipped quietly into bed.

Mrs Docherty raised her voice to reach the furthest corners of the shadowy attic.

'I would remind you, that you are here by the grace of God and Mr Dale.' The sixty two orphans all looked at her from where they lay in their rows of beds. 'While you eat his bread and are sheltered by his mercy, you will behave in accordance to the rules of his house.'

With that, she left the room, pulling the door closed behind her to pitch them into darkness.

Fiona tucked her mementoes beneath the mattress and turned on her side. She had not expected Susan to be so horrid and knew that she would probably try again to take her stones. The next morning, she vowed to herself, I will put them into one of my spare stockings and tie it round my waist, then they will always be with me.

Within moments, she was asleep.

***

Mrs Dale was dozing among a pile of down filled pillows. The candles on her bed stand guttering in a draught from the fireplace, an occasional gust of wind rattling the windows. It was growing cold in the bedroom but she was warm beneath the blankets and the beautiful new silk cover, a present from friends recently returned from Paris.

In her sleepy state, she recalled their anecdotes of the trip to the Continent. Mr Dale was also interested to hear of their exploits but when she asked him later if they might travel to these exotic places, he was less than keen. There was much unrest in France at present, he told her, best to let it simmer down awhile.

Drowsily, she opened her eyes and gazed around the room. The long brocade curtains and fine carved panelling were splendid, even in the flickering candlelight. Adam, the architect, had thought of every convenience and highlighted the grand rooms with intricate plaster cornices, ceiling roses with dangling chandeliers and elaborate fireplaces. Why would she wish to go anywhere when she had this beautiful home and her lovely children?

In the dozen years since they became man and wife, their union had created eight children. All daughters, except William. She thanked God for those surviving, but struggled with the almost unbearable loss of the three little girls who were no longer with them.

50

After their first born, Anne Caroline, sweet little Arabella arrived, only to succumb within months. Christian, a special gift after the grief of losing Arabella, appeared to have a strong grip of life and filled the nursery with laughter and mischief, only to leave them just weeks before her fifth birthday. Then their fourth little girl, Katherine, so healthy in her first months, fell victim to the dreaded chin-cough and never reached her first birthday.

For seven anxious days and nights she nursed little Katherine, tense with horror at the ghastly whoops she made as she struggled to gasp in air after bouts of coughing. Each suffocating attack left her tiny body so weak she could barely open her eyes. In the end, the effort was too much and she died.

The memory of her lifeless child lying in her arms brought tears afresh. In those dark months following their bereavements, Carolina thought she would never be able to smile or feel pleasure in anything again. She clung to her husband, both physically and as a soul companion in her grief. He, in turn, looked to the Church for guidance. Every day, she thanked God for giving her the strength to carry on.

Amongst those awful years of tragedy, her beautiful little boy, William, had arrived and then three more perfect, healthy daughters: Jean, Mary and baby Margaret. Yet her happiness was constantly tinged with the dread that they too might be taken from her.

Her thoughts were disturbed by her husband coming into the bedroom.

He was walking quietly, candelabra held high to light his way and was surprised to find his wife awake.

'My Dear,' he cried, 'I thought you would have been asleep long ago.'

She pulled herself higher on the pillows. 'Is it very late?'

'Past eleven o'clock. I was taken up with the new plans for our cottage in New Lanark.' He went through to his small dressing room to change into night robes.

'And is it looking promising?' she called to him, smoothing the silk counterpane, tracing the outlines of elaborately painted flowers.

'Indeed it is. I also wish to build another house alongside it. I think my brother or William Kelly should live on site to manage the Mills. No suitable accommodation can be made for a manager in the tenements.'

He reappeared in a long night shirt, his curly grey hair in disarray.

Placing the candelabra at his night-stand, he plodded over to the smouldering remnants of the fire. 'I fear the weather is changing. We may be in for a cold spell now, cold and wet.'

Using long tongs, he carefully placed more coal into the middle of the embers. 'It is on nights like these that I fear for the poor wretched souls of the homeless. Too many die in the winters in this city, indeed, across the whole country, God rest their souls. It is a disgrace. For the want of a little shelter! It hurts me to think on them, but God willing I will have the means to better the lives of some of them.'

'You are a good man, David.' his wife told him fondly. 'And I am not the only one to think it of you, either.'

'I wish I could do more.'

'You do plenty,' she sat up and rearranged her pillows in preparation for sleeping.

Dale climbed onto the high bed, heaving himself the final few inches and sinking into the mattress with a groan of both effort and pleasure. He drew the covers up high over his hefty stomach.

Every year his weight increased and his favourite breeches were altered to cater for his expanding girth. He liked dining well, he enjoyed good wine and had an impressive cellar to prove it. Why should he not indulge himself now he could afford it?

'I was thinking...' he said, after relaxing for a few minutes.

'Mmm...' Carolina was nearly asleep.

'I am minded to take Anne Caroline with me to visit the new mills. What would you say to that?'

'I think that would be a very nice idea, Mr Dale. Giggs would go with her. Yes, I think she would enjoy being with you and her mind needs more to occupy it nowadays than a walk on The Green.'

'I will be staying with Claud Alexander at Ballochmyle House. He runs a splendid house so I have no reason to believe she would not be comfortable.'

'I am sure you wouldn't take your daughter anywhere unsuitable.'

There was a long companionable pause.

'Perhaps we will spend a night at Stewarton, on the way home. It is some time since I saw my father. I am sure she would like to see her grandparents again.'

'And they will be delighted to see you both.'

Dale snuffed out the candles and lay back, closing his eyes.

'She is a clever girl, our Anne Caroline,' he mused, remembering her enthusiasm and the intelligent questions she asked when he first showed her the master builder's drawings for the New Lanark mills.

'As are all our children,' his wife murmured.

He opened his eyes again to the soft glow from the fire and rubbed her shoulder affectionately, 'Of course. William is yet a little young, but I greatly look forward to him leaving the nursery and joining me on trips like these.'

The next morning, before his customary visit to his church, the Old Scotch Independents in Greyfriar's Wynd, he called in at Hopkirk's Land where he leased an office to run the city's branch of the Royal Bank of Scotland.

Some years before, he acquired the position of agent for the Royal Bank in Glasgow, going into partnership with an Edinburgh merchant, Robert Scott Moncrieff.

Dale was involved with so many ventures that the brunt of the bank's work was carried out by Scott Moncrieff, an astute financier who was also the Receiver of the Land Tax for Scotland. Dale's value to the Bank was the high regard in which he was held by Glasgow's tradesmen and merchants alike, thereby encouraging a healthy clientele.

However, on that morning he requested a withdrawal from his own account, the proceeds of which were to be sent anonymously to a reputable coal merchant.

He knew from a reliable source that Tolbooth prison was suffering from a severe shortage of funds and were unable to purchase enough coal for heating. Conscious of the cold, dark days ahead and of his own warming fireplaces, he felt it his Christian duty to provide the necessary fuel. He had learned, since finding himself sufficiently wealthy to be able to give charity, that it was best not to give money. Whether it was oatmeal for the poor of his home town, Stewarton, or sacks of provisions for starving highland villages, he bought what was needed and sent it directly to their door.

Satisfied that a wagon load of coal would be delivered to the prison gate every week throughout the winter, he donned his tricorn hat and went to church.

***

To Sarah, the most alarming part of their first morning in the mill was when Cal and Rosie were led away from her and she saw them disappearing up a stairway among a crowd of other children. She was consumed with dread and thought she would faint from the pounding of her heart and a giddiness in her head.

Since waking, she had been trying to remain calm and even pretend she was looking forward to starting work. All the time her stomach was clenched in a ball of anxiety, made worse by a forced show of brightness.

She only owned two dresses and one was so worn and marked with fruit stains that she was forced to wear the plainer of the two. Its hem was frayed and the blue and white stripe was all but washed away in places, but it would have to do. Her hair was a problem, but after trying several alternatives she settled on one long plait. Rosie copied her and for a while they were immersed in these simple tasks by the light of the only lamp in the room.

By the time the bell was ringing at six o'clock, they were ready to go.

Now, her bravado was vanishing into the gloomy, lamp lit hallway of the great mill as she waited to be told what to do. There were people hurrying this way and that, all of them purposeful, some even laughing. She swallowed hard and pulled her shawl closer. What should she do? Perhaps they had forgotten about her?

'Sarah Scott? Yer startin' in the carding room. Follow me.'

A tall woman in a smart, full-skirted, dark dress, escorted her down into the basement.

'No stains or frayed hems for you,' thought Sarah, noticing the woman's muslin bonnet and the stiff white bows under her chin. Candles and lamps gave sufficient light to make out the winding stone steps but it seemed to grow darker as they descended. Sarah held her skirts higher to see where to place her feet, apprehension making her breathless.

At the bottom of the stairs the woman turned to look her, 'Are ye unwell?'

'Naw,' Sarah steadied herself against the wall, 'In body Ah'm weel enough, but in spirit Ah'm that feart, Ah think ma heart is aboot tae stop.'

'Whit nonsense! There's nothin' tae be feart o' here. Ye'll see.'

'But the engines... the jennies, Ah've heard tell they can pull ye in an' kill ye!'

'That they can... but yer no' gaun near any spinning jennies the day.'

'Ah'm no'?'

'They're up the stairs, ye'll be doon here carding fae the next few weeks onyway. Unless they need mair help up there.'

Up the stairs? Another wave of panic: Cal and Rosie had been taken up the stairs.

The woman was irritated by the girl's prevarication. She walked on and opened the door into a long room, glowing with lamps and filled with children, most of them sitting on the floor. Sarah entered very hesitantly, peering round the walls and into the dark recesses in search of lurking horrors. There was nothing but bales of cotton.

It didn't take her long to learn the skills required and soon she was sitting cross-legged in a circle of others, picking cotton and working it off into cardings.

When the muffled chimes of the breakfast bell sounded through the building, Sarah stretched and yawned. If this was her new work, she could manage it. Although it was boring and repetitious, it was not difficult and it certainly was not dangerous.

Caught up with the crowd, she collected her bowl of porridge and found a space at one of the long trestles. Large jugs of water were laid out down the tables with a couple of smaller pottery bowls beside each one. When she saw that everyone was using the bowls to fill with water to drink, she helped herself. The luxury of milk on her oats was an unexpected pleasure as well.

Spooning in the food, she kept her eyes on the slow moving line of workers queuing for their food. She was nearly finished when she saw Rosie's fair head appear by the doorway, talking to the girls around her, her face bright and animated. Relieved, Sarah kept watch for Calum.

When there was still no sign of him by the time she had to leave her place at the table, she began to get worried. Taking up a position near the entrance, she folded her arms and looked at everyone who came through the door.

Hundreds of workers, men and women as well as children, were piling into the dining hall, eating their fill and leaving again. Sarah saw some of the older boys taking their bowls to the back of the line, shovelling the porridge into their hungry mouths as they queued and then having the bowl refilled before going to find a seat.

At last, Calum appeared in the doorway. He was behind some men, with a gossiping group of women clustered at the back of him. He saw her and shrugged his shoulders, looking down at the ground.

'Cal,' she moved to his side and put out a hand to touch his arm.

He shook her off.

'Ah'm no' a bairn, an' ye're no' ma Mither! Leave me be!'

She pulled her hand back, scalded by his words.

'Whit's the matter wi' ye?'

'Nuthin'!'

'Cal..?'

He kept his eyes lowered and took a step forward, leaving her by the doorway.

Upset, Sarah went in search of Joe. The front door of the mill was open so she stepped outside, half wondering if she was allowed to leave the building. There was a fine drizzle in the cool, fresh air and she paused to take stock of the scene before her.

The air was alive with hammering and sawing, huge brown horses were trailing heavy wagons of sand, rocks, wood and all manner of tools and iron bars. Men buzzed around them, attending to the horses and unloading and shovelling what they needed from the carts. Mill Two was rising from the lower terrace and with two floors nearing completion, its raw materials were now lying in expectant heaps on the same level as Mill One's entrance.

Pulleys had been erected over the walls of the second mill and massive beams were being lowered into place. There were so many men carrying timber and dragging laden handcarts that she knew right away that she would not be able to find her brother. A wagon, stacked with long pieces of cut timber, was being manoeuvred round the end of the mill lade, just yards in front of her.

With shouts of guidance from men on all sides, the driver sent his four heavy horses forward, inching his way, step by step. It was a tight, difficult operation, the load being much longer than most, but with the harness creaking, they took up the strain, moved a few feet, stopped again, pulled again. The muscles on the massive Clydesdales stood out from under their rain slicked coats. Their enormous iron shod hooves digging into the ground, throwing up grit and splashing water from the puddles, their shaggy legs so caked in mud that the feathers swung like bunches of rope.

Eventually, tossing their big heads, metal bits jangling, they made it round the corner and plodded off along the flat ground to discharge their load.

Sarah glanced up the hill at the long row of tenements, their symmetrical lines of windows staring out across the valley. Their room was on the second floor but she couldn't tell which of the many windows was her own. From where she stood, the long building looked precariously close to the rock face beneath it.

If you fell out of the window you would fall hundreds of feet straight to the ground. She shuddered.

What were they doing in this strange, half built place? Her stomach churned. Was it only a few days ago that she was raking windfalls from out of the long grass under apple trees, and watching dopey wasps feed from the rotten fruit? The soft, green orchards further down the valley seemed like a distant dream. All she could see here was mud, stone and water.

Her gaze alighted on a figure standing by itself.

It was a girl, her back so straight she was almost tilting back, her face turned up to the sky, arms held loosely at her sides. She was soaked in the rain, her dark hair clamped to her head like a cap.

The girl's body jerked as the bell swung into action, calling them back to work. It was only then that she noticed Sarah watching her and a slow, enigmatic smile spread across her face.

Curious, Sarah waited for her by the door. She recognised this girl from the carding room, but although they were about the same age and worked on the same batch of cotton, they had not yet spoken.

'Yer soakin'!' she cried, 'Ye'll catch yer death o' cold!'

The girl's brown eyes were sparkling, 'Rain!' she said, giving that odd smile again. 'I like rain!'

The words were said slowly and separately with an unusual accent.

Sarah pulled a face. 'Ne'er thocht aboot whither Ah like it or no'!' she said, 'but we had better get doon tae the basement or we'll be in trouble and it's only ma first day.'

They fell into step together and made their way down the stairs and into the peculiar gloomy, dust-laden world of the carding room.

It was just as well that Sarah had not ventured out to find him, because Joe was not on the building site. All the labourers were allowed half an hour for breakfast. While some went into the mill for porridge, which was included as part of their wage, those who lived in the village chose to take a little extra in pay and go home to eat.

Joe had decided to go back and see how his mother was faring but as soon as he walked through the door, he wished he hadn't bothered.

Meg was lying in soiled linen and his mother was curled up under a blanket on her bed.

After a life time of withstanding his father's rages, Joe was seldom given to outbursts of temper but this time his patience snapped. He demanded that his mother got out of bed and looked after his sister. Then he snatched up a bucket and ran out to get more water.

Cursing her all the way to the lade and back, he slammed the splashing bucket down by the hearth and hastily relit the fire.

'Dinnae let this gae oot! D'ye hear me? Keep the fire in, its too cold fer Meg. An' boil some watter fer the washing. See, Ah've brought ye plenty.' He dragged the tin bath out from the corner. 'In the name o' God, will ye get oot o' bed an' get on wi' it!'

'Ah'm no weel, son.' she whimpered. ' Ah'm sick. Can ye no' see tae yer wee sister...?'

'Aye, yer sick! Sick wi' the drink. There will be nae mair o' that, Ma. Ah've tae be back at work! Make sure ye ha'e a meal ready when Sarah an' the weans come in!'

He couldn't bring himself to look at Meg, her pale clammy skin and sunken eyes were too distressing. 'After work', he promised himself, 'after work I will spend time with Meg.'

Back down working on Mill Two, he picked up a sledge hammer to break up stones for filling the walls. It was arduous work but today he laid into it ferociously.

'Eh, Joe!' Tam shouted to him. 'Ye mad aboot summat?'

Joe straightened up, wiping sweat from his brow. 'Aye, Ah'm.' he raised the heavy tool and brought it crashing down on a slab of sand stone. It shattered into several pieces.

He was filled with resentment towards his father: a brute when he was alive and a menace to his family in death, leaving all his problems for Joe to sort out.

It was dawning on Joe that the carefree life he had taken for granted for the past two years had come to a shuddering halt. Now it would just be a round of work, dealing with Ma and Meg and trying to make their meagre wages provide for the family.

He threw the sledge hammer down and clambered down the steep embankment to the riverside.

Tam watched him out the corner of his eye but left his friend to fight his demons on his own terms. A short while later, Joe returned, a resigned, defeated slope to his shoulders.

'Ye ken...' Tam called, 'Mike Torrence caught a crackin' trout up by Corra Linn the ither nicht. A great big brownie! Peggy wis fair pleased wi' him. They dined awfy well, Ah can tell ye!'

Joe set about choosing the next rock to break.

'How aboot we go up the nicht,' Tam carried on, 'an' find a couple of big ones fer oorsels?'

'Ah cannae, Tam.'

'Aye, ye can!'

'There's things tae be done... Ah cannae leave Sarah tae dae it.'

'For one nicht? Anyway, ye wid be daein' them a' a favour puttin' food on the table.'

'There's tha' aboot it.' Joe looked over at Tam, who gave him a broad wink.

'Come on, Joe! Leave the hoose tae the wimen folk, let's gae fishin?'

'Ah ha'e tae get ma rod an' things frae Lanark ...but mibbee anither nicht? Friday?'

' Naw, ahm awa' up tae Nemphlar tae see that lass ah telt ye aboot! Thursday? nuchin happens on a Thursday.'

'All richt, Thursday. Ah'll ask Cal along, ma wee brither.'

Tam grinned at him. 'Ye dae that!'

They returned to their work and Joe saw a light flickering in his otherwise black future. An evening on the river, showing Cal the wondrous waterfalls in the gorge: that was more like it.

Wednesday 8th October...

Anne Caroline could hardly contain her excitement. From the moment her father told her about their forthcoming trip to Ayrshire, she could think of nothing else. Laura Giggs, the nursery maid, was to go with her, and as Giggs had never been out of Glasgow before, she was as delighted as the little girl.

The morning of departure dawned with a raw wind hissing through the city's streets, moaning at door jambs and window frames. Trees, their branches still heavy with foliage, were tossed and shaken in sudden gusts, scattering the roads with restless, shifting drifts of leaves.

Renwick stood in the entrance hall directing his staff as they ran in and out of the house packing Dale's carriage. The four Cleveland bays in the harness were champing their bits and pawing the ground. Fresh from the stables and disturbed by the wind, the groom had to throw his whole strength into keeping them under control. On the roof of the carriage the coachman and one of the footmen braced themselves as they organised piles of luggage and secured it in place with leather straps.

Their progress was hampered by the violent flurries, pushing them about and tugging and nipping at their clothes. The general rush and roar was punctuated by embarrassed shrieks from maids, their skirts caught up and sent billowing above their knees, earning cheeky quips from the men and causing much hilarity.

Travelling with the father and daughter was not only Giggs but also a quiet, thin young man, Charles Duncan, who was David Dale's valet. They set off as early as their master's substantial breakfast would allow and crossed the river to take the road south towards Ayr.

Every turning brought a new marvel to Anne Caroline and she hugged her happiness to her and revelled in the adventure.

The adults soon grew weary of the motion of the carriage and, after depleting their magnificent picnic, spent much of the journey sleeping. Dale, completely at ease, lounged in his seat with his head lolling, snoring happily. The two servants, however, tried valiantly to remain awake and hold themselves neatly upright, worried in case they might appear too familiar by sleeping in front of their master. The pure monotony and discomfort soon overcame them and they crumpled together in a jolting, uncomfortable heap.

Catrine, the newest of Dale's mills, was being constructed near the Ayr River amid beautiful rolling Ayrshire countryside. In the same way as he was planning with Blantyre and New Lanark, he wanted to build a whole village around his factories and change people's unfavourable perception of this style of manufacturing.

One of his previous business partners, Richard Arkwright, with whom he had first started New Lanark, had made a success of his workers' village at Cromford in England. Dale was keen to expand this exercise. It made sense for those employed in the mills to live close to their place of work and he felt strongly that provision should also be made for the education of the children. His deep religious beliefs did not sit easily with causing suffering or neglect to others and he was steadfast in his commitment to the best possible conditions for all his employees.

This came as no surprise to his colleagues and friends. Dale was a devout believer in practising what he preached and every Sunday, without fail, he would give sermons in his Church or, if he was out of Glasgow, to any gathered company.

The party were to be staying with Alexander of Ballochmyle, Dale's partner in Catrine Mills. Ballochmyle was an extensive estate and Claud Alexander himself was excellent company so Dale was looking forward to his hospitality. It was late in the afternoon before the carriage drew up in front of the portico of the country house.

Giggs, eager to impress her employer with her diligence and care, had made sure the child was awake before they stopped. She combed her hair and, making her stand up in the rolling carriage, smoothed out as many creases as she could from her jacket and skirt.

The horses had no sooner drawn to a halt, the carriage still swinging on its springs, than two footmen ran out, one to take the lead horse's head, the other to draw down the steps and open the door for the guests.

Ballochmyle House was large and sprawling, its frontage appearing more like a cluster of buildings joined together but running off at different angles and heights. During their journey, her father told Anne Caroline that the architect for this impressive house had been the father of their architect, Robert Adam. The child vaguely recalled being dangled on this gentleman's knee, but her memory was of an old man in a thickly powdered wig, so she had difficulty in imagining what *his* father would be like.

The flag-stoned hallway with its ornate panelling was magnificent but Anne Caroline was used to great houses and was much more interested in the unusual paintings and furniture than the architecture. Alexander's time in India with the East India Company was evident everywhere, especially in a wonderful portrait depicting him with his brother and an Indian servant. The servant's white robes and dark skin captivated the little girl's attention and she had to be reminded, twice, to leave the adults and go with Giggs.

Claud Alexander and his wife, Helenora, had several small children and another on the way, so the servants were used to catering for children's needs. However, as Anne Caroline and her maid discovered, the nursery wing was very basic and cold compared to the reception rooms.

They were taken up through a maze of narrow, creaking corridors to a bedroom where their bags were deposited on the floor.

It was a surprisingly spartan room but had been freshly aired, a warming pan placed under the bed covers and a fire lit in the grate, which offered a little comfort.

Supper was served to them in their room and a chaise longue placed beside the bed so that Giggs could sleep beside her charge. After the initial disappointment of being relegated to such an unwelcoming and distant part of the house, they were so tired from the journey that Anne Caroline took little persuading to retire to bed straight after the meal.

They were both still fast asleep when there was a knock on the door and a maid carried in a tray of porridge and hot milk. Giggs was startled, she wanted to be dressed and have Anne Caroline awake and washed before breakfast, now they would have to hurry to be ready for the day ahead.

Dale and Mr Alexander were already in the hall when Anne Caroline came down the stairs but they seemed in no hurry to leave for Catrine. Wilhelmina, Claud's spinster sister was with them, dressed to go riding in a dark blue velvet jacket and voluminous grey skirt. Her hair was tucked neatly into a net, crowned by a matching dark blue hat, held in place by sparkling jewelled hat pins.

She took Anne Caroline by both hands and complimented the child on her outfit.

Dale smiled proudly at the kind remarks concerning his daughter. He had spent a very agreeable night with the Alexanders, enjoying some delicious pheasant at the meal and rounding off the evening with a fine old brandy by the fireside.

'We will spend time together when you return this afternoon,' Wilhelmina said sweetly to the little girl. 'We have an excellent pianoforte, do you play?'

'A little,' Anne Caroline glanced shyly at her father. 'A teacher comes once a week, but I am not very good.'

'No matter, it will be fun! And maybe some poetry? Do you like poetry?'

'Oh, I do! Mama likes me to read to her and she especially enjoys Thomas Gray.'

'Oh yes, he is a favourite of mine too. I like his witty, light hearted pieces, just as much as his profound work. Do you read the works of Robert Burns, my dear?'

The little girl only knew a little of Burns but she saw Wilhelmina's eyes brighten and her plain, pale face suffuse with pink. The change in the woman's demeanour was also noted by Dale.

Wilhelmina joined them the evening before and during the meal conversation turned to the new found fame of the local poet, Robert Burns.

Wilhelmina, flushed and coquettish, had quietly informed Dale that she was the subject of one of the bard's poems.

As well as his indisputable talent with words, Burns was also known to be quite a ladies' man and on looking at his host's sister, Dale had wondered why she might inspire the young poet. She was an even featured, not unattractive woman and in her low cut evening gown, her hair styled high to accentuate a slender neck, she could be thought quite agreeable, but nothing more.

While Wilhelmina was flattered by this attention from someone famous, her brother did not appear so enamoured with Mr Burns. Perhaps, Dale had wondered while watching them in the candlelight, Claud thought that any connection to the handsome young rake might besmirch his sister's good character. In his club in Glasgow he had heard a few of Burns' more bawdy rhymes and thought he might also be offended if that same young man wrote about a female member of his own family.

Before his sister could elaborate on the poem at the dinner table, Alexander skilfully turned the subject to one he knew Dale would take up with gusto.

'Burns is acclaimed by society now, widely published,' he said, 'and he is much in demand yet, only a couple of years ago he was about to leave Scotland.'

'Leave Scotland?' Dale was outraged.

'Aye, however, Professor Dugald Stewart... you know him? Spends his summers in Catrine House?' He looked enquiringly at Dale.

Dale did not know the gentleman.

'Highly intelligent! I have a lot o' time for the man!' Alexander barged on, 'So there was Burns, heading off to Jamaica, ye know, and he would be there now, I dare say, if the Professor hadn't been so taken with his writings when they were printed in Kilmarnock. He introduced him to his own publisher in Edinburgh. That was a couple o' years ago now. By all accounts the poet will not be joining the ranks of those leaving our shores while enjoying being feted by all and sundry in his native land.'

The touch paper lit, Claud Alexander sat back and took up his claret glass. Wilhelmina did not stand a chance of returning to her poem, Dale was straight into his views on how to stem the rising stream of Scots emigrating to the colonies.

However, gathered here in the hall this morning, with Anne Caroline as a new audience, Wilhelmina seized her chance once more to mention her association with Burns.

Dale listened, bemused.

'My poem is called the Bonnie Lassie of Ballochmyle,' she finished, clasping her hands under her chin and smiling at the child in front of her.

'How wonderful!' Anne Caroline cried, gazing admiringly at the lady in front of her.

'And has this poem been published?' Dale asked.

'Alas, no,' Wilhelmina shook her head, the tightly curled ringlets bouncing on her forehead, 'He wrote to ask if I would allow it to be published, but ... well, I did not know what to think. So, I have not replied.' She cast a quick glance towards her brother who was checking his pocket watch against the time on an ornate grandfather clock.

'Probably for the best, my dear sister,' Claud said firmly as he turned back to the company, 'Sir, shall we proceed to the mill?'

A slightly deflated Wilhelmina waved them away.

Anne Caroline sat beside Giggs in the well-upholstered coach and tucked her feet as far to the side as possible. Alexander was a tall man and his long legs and buckled shoes extended right across the carriage and she was worried in case her feet should brush against his spotless cream stockings.

There were so many unusual views passing by the window that she couldn't keep them to herself and was constantly nudging the maid and pointing them out. It felt very grown up to be included in this outing and she determined to remember her mother's advice to 'remain polite and quiet, give the least annoyance possible. Your father is a very busy man and should not be distracted by any childish nonsense.'

So, when they alighted in the village square, she walked obediently beside Giggs and a few paces behind her father. If she behaved very well he might invite her on more visits.

Catrine's Mill was very similar in design to New Lanark's Mill. It sat boldly, five storeys high plus attics, in the middle of the village square, surrounded by symmetrical rows of thatched housing making up the sides of the square. Through the village ran the mill lade diverting water from the Ayr river, sometimes necessitating arches to keep the level even and bridges to allow access from one side of the village to the other. Having invested so heavily in the construction of the lade, Dale and Alexander wanted to make full use of this power supply and planned another cotton mill on the site and also a corn mill.

The day was fresh but thankfully dry and when the gentlemen retired to do business, Anne Caroline and Giggs spent a happy afternoon exploring the village and surrounding countryside.

Just after four o'clock, the two men emerged from the office with the mill manager. It had been a very useful meeting and they were in good cheer as they walked out into the square.

A horse came galloping towards them, the rider bent forward, urging it on. From the flared nostrils and lathered sweat on its coat, the horse had been ridden hard and for a considerable distance. It came to a sliding halt at the mill steps and the man in the saddle threw himself off and ran unsteadily towards Dale.

'Mr Dale... Mr David Dale?' He asked, fighting to catch his breath.

'Aye?' Dale was alarmed. Was something wrong with Carolina? the new baby?

'I have come from New Lanark... Sir, I have to inform you that there has been a catastrophe...a fire. The Mill has burnt down.'

The men were horrified, all talking at once but Dale took a step towards the messenger.

'The Mill? Burnt? Destroyed completely?'

'Yes, sir...'

'Has anyone been killed? Injuries?'

'There is much confusion there, sir. When I left, there were no deaths reported but several were unaccounted for....'

Dale uttered up a prayer before returning to the man standing before him who was struggling to regain his breath, mopping his brow with his cap.

'When did this happen?' Dale asked.

'Just not even four hours ago. I was sent straight here to tell you, but I had to change horses .... I know the road to Ayr better than any man and would wager no one could have reached you in less time.'

Both Dale and Alexander congratulated him on his gallant effort. Then Alexander instructed his manager to take care of the messenger and see that the horse was attended to at the stables.

Anne Caroline overheard the whole story and watched her father with round, worried eyes. While the other men were loud in their dismay, he was standing quite still, his gaze directed towards the tired horse. Clouds of steam rose from its body, its flanks heaving from the chase across the countryside.

Dale did not see the horse, his normally jovial face was grey and drawn: deep in thought. Then, clearing his throat, he asked Alexander to take them immediately back to Ballochmyle, from there they would leave for New Lanark without delay.

Throughout their short journey back to Ballochmyle House, Dale sought guidance from God. This was a terrible occurrence, but buildings and machinery could be replaced, souls could not.

In the swaying coach, he led the party in a prayer for all the inhabitants of New Lanark.

***

While Dale's carriage was rapidly prepared for his speedy departure from Ballochmyle, New Lanark was in a state of uproar.

James Dale, David's half-brother, gathered his managers together and ordered them to round everyone up and count them. On hearing

66

the first warnings of the fire, McCulloch, ever efficient, had grabbed as many important documents and files as he could manage in his panic and thrown them into boxes. With difficulty, he commandeered several terrified workers to help him carry them out of the burning building. Among these papers were the records of the workforce. He earnestly searched through the boxes which were piled haphazardly in a heap on the grass, and produced the lists. His superior was not unimpressed but there was no time for praise amid the smoke and crackling, roaring chaos.

James Dale just seized the proffered papers from the little man and strode off purposefully to direct operations. He was overwhelmed by the disaster and hoped his older brother would receive the urgent message and come swiftly to take over.

Eventually, all the Boarders were lined up and, beside them, the workers on the payroll. Sarah was still looking anxiously for her brothers and as the crowds thinned and organised themselves into groups she realised that neither of them were present.

Too frightened to cry now, she cuddled her little sister and waited to be dismissed. Perhaps Joe and Cal had gone back to Ma, up in the tenement? Yet this was unlikely because no-one was being allowed to leave until they had been counted and anyway, Joe being Joe, he would want to stay and help.

It seemed to take forever for the roll call to be read and she shuffled from foot to foot. Then Calum Scott's name was called out. She held her breath. The name was repeated, shouted loud against the violent, raging fire behind them. There was no reply.

The men at the front leaned together, concerned. They gave one more call for Calum Scott then moved to the next on the list.

In all there were eleven men and boys missing.

A sudden thunderous crash came from the mill as the bell tower and roof rafters gave way and smashed to a lower level sending balls of spark filled smoke spiralling up into the darkening sky.

'We must search all round the building!' Kelly, one of the managers, demanded and pointed to six of the strongest workmen. 'Nine of those unaccounted for worked in the storerooms... go! Go round to the back!'

The men set off at a run but were forced to slow up as soon as they tried to move between the flames and the cliff side.

Cringing away from the searing heat, they drew their jackets up to shield themselves but the glowing cinders and falling debris made it impossible, singeing and then setting fire to their clothes. They ran to the lade and, ripping off their jackets, thrashed out the worst of the flames and doused them in water.

'We'll try t'other side, through the river!' one man shouted and they tore off, scrambling and jumping down through the sodden, half built walls of Mill Two.

The river side of Mill One was on a much lower level. The storerooms and basements led out the back of the mill onto a strip of land just wide enough for wagons to pass but this road was also impassable. Only by wading downstream through the river, past the outflow from the waterwheel, and emerging to scramble more easily on the island, could the rescue party find a way to the rear of the mill. Far enough away from the inferno, they left the island and plunged back into the water, staggering against the current and clambering up the bank.

A group of figures and loaded handcarts were clustered on the bank further downstream, as far from the fire as the steep cliffside would allow. They waved to the dripping, shouting men who hurried towards them, rapidly counting their heads: eleven.

Both Joe and Calum were among the group. By pure chance, Joe had been at the back of the mill when the fire broke out and his brother was collecting supplies from the storeroom. They had spoken briefly and been about to part when the cry went up.

Immediately, the store keeper appealed for assistance to save as much as possible and it was all hands on deck. It was only when the falling glass and appalling heat became too much that they gave up, but by then they were trapped.

The rain of the previous few days had swollen the Clyde to a level where it was difficult enough for a full grown man to wade downstream, but it would have been treacherous for a child to even attempt to wade upstream. Exhausted by their efforts they had all elected to stay where they were until the ferocity of the blaze died down.

There was nothing they could do except watch the building burn down in front of them. Joe took it especially hard. It was his pride and joy, the first great structure he had been part of creating and now it was in its death throes.

One of the lads who had been sent to find them, seized two broom handles to use as wading sticks and stepped unsteadily back into the rushing water to carry the good news of their safety back to James Dale.

'They're all safe! All of them!' he shouted, waving the sticks triumphantly.

A great cheer went up.

Sarah saw the man, heard his words and then crumpled to the ground in a faint.

***

The fire was still burning when David Dale's carriage took the winding road down the last mile to New Lanark. Even from the market town of Lanark, an eerie red light could be seen emanating from the gorge. It was a dark night, with clouds obscuring the moon, but as the horses made the final turn in the road, the village suddenly appeared before them, illuminated in the brilliant scarlet glow of the fire.

It was a heart-rending scene.

Only the stout stone walls of the mill remained. Its windows were just gaping empty spaces, the roof and all the wooden floors had collapsed, taking with them the bell tower, machines and cotton, to create one massive bonfire.

Instructing his daughter to remain in the carriage, Dale went to consult with his brother and the senior managers. Although Anne Caroline had slept most of the way from Ballochmyle, she had woken when they came to a halt and looked out on the devastation.

It was not exciting, it didn't thrill her to see such a terrible sight. All she felt was an awful sense of sadness. She peered out at the mass of people and was horrified to see hundreds of children among them. Little shaggy-haired boys and girls, many barefoot, sat in groups on the open ground, huddled together, several sharing shawls wrapped around their narrow shoulders. Some were not much older than her brother, William.

In the shifting light of the flames their faces showed their anguish; hollow cheeked, dark eyed. They were all looking in the same direction.

With a jolt, Anne Caroline realised that they were all watching her father.

69

Dale had hardly uttered a word during the journey. His mind was adjusting to the dreadful implications of the disaster and sorting through the scores of things that should be done straightaway. On arrival, he heard from his brother that no lives were lost, and an immense weight lifted from his shoulders.

'They have been waiting for you to arrive,' James Dale said, looking meaningfully at the crowd.

Dale could see his half-brother's anxiety from his sickly pallor and the quick, nervous glances he kept making around the open hillside. James had long since abandoned his powdered wig and his own brown hair and dark wool jacket and breeches were speckled and smudged with a coating of fine grey ash.

.'You have done a good job,' Dale stated plainly. 'No one has been killed, well done, to both of you,' he turned to William Kelly. 'Do we know how the fire was caused?'

'Some new parts were being fitted to the jenny on level four and candles had to be used to give light beneath the frames. It's gie tricky working under the gears. They say the dust caught alight and flames ran as if unfurling a carpet across the floor, before they could even call out a warning.' He sighed, rubbing at his face, his eyes bloodshot. 'It's a miracle they all escaped.'

Dale nodded and pressed his hat further down upon his wig, straightening the buckle on his jacket belt.

'I will talk to them,' he said, taking a minute to compose himself.

Arrangements were underway for the orphans to be taken in by the church up in Lanark where they would be given shelter for the night. However, he knew that the main concern was not about where the paupers would sleep that night, it was much deeper.

His proud new village was now just an empty valley with muddy tracks leading to the lade and a stricken, burning mill. Only a single row of tenements stood as testament to his endeavours of the last four years. Perched on the cliff above the river, they stood shrouded in drifting smoke, bleak and stark in the autumn dusk.

Dale walked a little way up the hill and held up his hands, beckoning to everyone to gather around.

Anne Caroline slipped from the carriage, but Giggs caught hold of her arm and pulled her back, imploring her to stay where her father had ordered.

'I want to hear what he says!' Anne Caroline insisted, 'Come with me? Just a bit nearer?'

They moved to within earshot and listened.

The crowd went quiet. Against the background crackling and groaning of the ruined mill, Dale's strong, deep voice rang out. Years of preaching in the Church bore fruit and his words reached clearly to the back of the assembly.

First he gave thanks to God for saving all their souls, telling them to reach into their hearts and pray for the strength to overcome the events of the day. The mill would be rebuilt, he told them. The village would rise from the hillside once again.

'This will take time! I shall employ every joiner, stonemason and mill-right necessary to complete New Lanark. Your jobs are *here,*' he raised his arms to embrace them all, 'and you will receive your wages every week while this work is done.'

An astonished murmur passed among the crowd. With disbelieving looks and shrugs, some of the men called out to him.

'Ye mean ye'll pay us while we cannae work?'

'Aye, that I do!' Dale shouted back 'You are all a part of this village. This devastation may have befallen us, but the Lord God has given us the will and strength to overcome. When the buildings are repaired and the machinery replaced you will go back to your work and fulfil your duties.'

He then called them to join him in prayer.

'Praise the Lord that you are spared and can bring comfort to those around you. God's salvation shall be forever and this Righteousness shall never be abolished. Let us therefore place all our hope in this Righteousness and this salvation and we shall never be confounded or ashamed world without end...'

Anne Caroline looked through tear filled eyes at the strange, bedraggled congregation standing in the smoky night air. There was a tangible change to the atmosphere, his words and his powerful, compassionate presence gave them security, hope.

Never had she been so proud of her father.

Chapter 2

'As mortals on the brink of eternity we are called to hear and believe the Gospel of Christ. Now is the accepted time, now is the day of Salvation.'
David Dale

After the fire, a whole new mood pervaded New Lanark.

Even the most world weary and embittered members of the work force grudgingly took a different attitude towards their employer, as well as their employment. Only by nearly losing it, did they fully appreciate how much they needed the mill. Suddenly, it was no longer David Dale's business, it was their business as well.

A new found loyalty was forged out of the burning wreck of Mill One.

Dale was as good as his word and, from the very next morning, he set to work recruiting labour from all over Lanarkshire. While they could not spin cotton, he kept his employees busy, especially those living in the village. Women and children worked beside the men, clearing and scraping, salvaging and washing. The few empty rooms in the tenement building were requisitioned for the orphans and hurriedly whitewashed and fitted out with beds.

New routines overtook the old ones and everyday steady progress was made clearing out and then rebuilding the mill.

Joe and his family were swept along with this wave of energy and worked harder than ever as the days grew shorter and the air colder.

By December, the mornings brought ice on the inside of the windows and the sound of persistent coughs rattled among the stone tenements. Joe would rise early before work and re-kindle the fire, while Sarah tended to Meg. Their mother was of little use and they

72

were beginning to realise that maybe the drink was only part of her problem.

Unfortunately, within a week or so of moving to the village, she discovered the stalls that were set up by local shopkeepers to service the tradesmen visiting the village. One of the stalls sold ale.

'Ah dinnae think she's richt in the heid,' Sarah confided in Joe one evening. 'She forgets what you tell her jist minutes efter ye've spoken. Ah found her wondering ootside t'other day an' she did nae knaw where she wis. Honest Joe, Ah think she's lost her mind. It's no' jist the drink. Ah'm that worrid aboot leavin' Meg wi' her.'

His sister was only saying what he knew himself and Joe just sighed and nodded. 'Well, there's no' much we can do aboot it, but keep an eye.' He glanced across at Meg's still form in the bed. 'Meg's no' well, Sarah.'

She cast a hasty look at her sister. 'She's sleeping?'

'Naw, Ah mean... the last week or so, you must've seen? She does nae look at me onymair. Not properly. Just dopey like.'

'Aye, Ah knaw whit ye mean.'

'She's gie thin. When she takes some food she does nae seem able to swallow. Perhaps we could find a medic?'

'And how do we pay for that? Ah would dearly love to see Meg well, but Joe, even if we had Mr Dale's wealth, Ah doubt we can nae buy what God does nae give.'

It was late. Behind two heavy curtains, Ma was asleep in one of the set-in beds and Cal and Rosie were sharing the other. Joe's plans to take his brother fishing had never materialised because of the fire and the darkening evenings. Nowadays, they rose in the dark and returned from work in the dark. It was impossible to dry any washing so their clothes were rank and Meg's linen, the only things which could not be left soiled, hung limply on a makeshift pulley above their heads. Already overcrowded, this made the room seem even smaller.

The air was thick with the smell of coal and tallow candles; winter was upon them.

Despite his worry about Meg and his mother, Joe was feeling much better about life in general. It was not the care free lifestyle he enjoyed before his father's death but, all in all, things were working out better than expected. The previous evening he went up to the inn with Tam and some other lads. It felt good to have a laugh and flirt with the girls. It was a long time since he had been with a girl or had even felt the desire to climb the hill and enjoy a drink, let alone anything more. Now, it seemed, his appetite for life was returning.

He was also relieved that his sisters and Cal were more settled. They were all tired, physically worn out from such long days, but their spirits were higher. Both Sarah and Rosie would sing together and chatter by the fire while cooking or mending.

It pleased him immeasurably.

Sarah yawned. She was sitting beside him on the old rag rug they brought from Douglas. 'Ah'm aff tae bed afore Ah fall over,' she pretended to half fall sideways and laughed.

'It's awfy guid tae hear ye laugh again,' he smiled at her.

'Aye, it's guid tae *feel* like laughing.' She stood up. 'Ye knaw that lass Ah talk aboot, Fiona, the one frae Mallaig? She makes me laugh. She has a strange way tae her, an' she sings songs in that odd language o' hers, but then she'll suddenly try and say summat in Scots. She's gettin' better, but doesn't half sound comical.'

'An' Ah suppose you wouldn't, if ye tried to speak the Gaelic?'

She grinned at him. 'Ah'm away tae bed.' She turned away, miming a kiss, and climbed under the covers beside Meg on the hurlie bed.

Joe stoked the fire for the night and pulled off his heavy smock and breeches. He slept in the hurlie that tucked under Ma's bed and as he drew it out he couldn't keep the smile from his lips.

When Sarah talked about her new Highland friend, it was all he could do not to ask her a hundred questions. He knew exactly who Fiona was, she only had to appear by the lade collecting water and his pulses raced. If she was pegging out washing with the other orphans he would always take that moment to walk past the green. There was something so appealing about the way she moved, her strange dark, shaggy hair, and on the two delicious moments when their eyes met, he felt as if he had been scalded.

Perhaps that was another reason why the girls up in town held little attraction for him nowadays.

In the darkest days of the year, when the sun barely rose high enough to penetrate the gorge, Joe's fears for Meg's health were realised. They came home from work to find Ma sitting beside a cold fireplace, her youngest daughter on her knee.

She rarely touched Meg, her guilt was too great, but now she was holding her close and kissing her hair. Here was the mother they all remembered from their early childhood; affectionate, warm, humming melodies to them as she cradled them in the evenings. That loving mother had died when Meg was hurt.

Now she turned lost, tear filled eyes to Joe.

'She's at peace noo, son. Yer wee sister has left us fae a better place. God will tak care o' her noo.'

Her other children knew immediately what had happened. Meg had given up the struggle to endure her achingly lonely and pathetic life. How she survived so long in her isolated, paralysed body, no one knew, nor could they even begin to understand the thoughts and emotions the little girl must have held within her silent world.

When Joe reported his sister's death to McCulloch he was granted permission to bury her in the newly laid out graveyard for New Lanark residents.

Due to the short hours of daylight, Joe asked for leave to attend to the burial. There were no grave diggers in the village, as yet only seven people were buried there, so he needed enough time off to dig the grave as well as laying her to rest.

McCulloch consulted his papers.

'This is your sister you are burying, not your spouse, your own child or your parent.' He stated, running his finger along a line of management guidelines. 'I cannot grant you a day off from your labour.' He raised his eyes to Joe, 'However, if you wish to take an hour for your midday meal, I would be agreeable to that.'

'An hour?'

McCulloch shuffled the papers into a neat wad and laid them down with precision. 'You have already taken two days away from your work in the last three months. It is an unfortunate occurrence that so many children die, but if we granted absence to all our workers for the deaths of their siblings, well... it would never do!'

Joe opened his mouth to plead his case but McCulloch held up a hand. 'I will tell your foreman that you are to be allowed an hour. Tomorrow?'

'Not t'morrow, Ah've the coffin tae ...'

He was cut short 'The day after then? We cannot have a dead body kept in the house for any longer than necessary, not even in the winter. Therefore, the day after tomorrow, 25th December.' He filled his pen and made a note. 'Very well, you may go now.'

At the end of that day's work, Tam and two of the other lads on his team offered to help with preparing the ground. Joe collected the lantern from his room and met them at the bottom of the steep steps up to Lanark. They were carrying spades surreptitiously 'borrowed' from the site and were eager to have the job done and the spades returned under the cover of darkness.

The graveyard was laid out in an open space on the grassy slope above the village with young beech trees planted at the boundary. These were no more than sparse bunches of bare twigs on that winter evening but, after walking round the area, they chose a spot and balanced the lantern on the neighbouring headstone. In this pool of yellow light they neatly cut out the turfs and laid them to the side, before taking it in turns, two at a time, to dig out the rocky soil. These were men who were used to heavy manual work and the grave soon became too deep for two men to step inside.

'It's gie small!' Tam called up to Joe. 'Ah'll have tae make it bigger or we'll no' manage tae get the depth.'

'She was only a bairn.' The grief could be heard in Joe's voice. 'An' that's another thing... where will Ah get a coffin?'

His choked words reminded them of the serious task in hand and with sombre expressions they carried on digging.

Then Rab said slowly, 'Ma Da's new wife's brother's lodger's sister is married tae a joiner.'

The other three stopped what they were doing and looked questioningly from one to the other and then back to Rab.

Rab shrugged, 'Whit?'

'An' how does that help?'

'They live next door to me, so Ah'll ask if you want?'

'That'll be your neighbour, then?' Tam said, pursing his lips to stop the smile. 'Why no' jist say 'ma neighbour's a joiner?''

'Did nae think o' it that way...' Rab shrugged again but even in the lamp light he could see the mirth in Tam's eyes.

In spite of the grim circumstances, or maybe because of the need for a relief from them, they started to chuckle. Rab was maybe not the cleverest man but he was a sound and reliable friend.

Joe watched him throwing his back into dislodging a large stone from the middle of the pit , the other two leaning in to take it from him. Their long hair was tucked behind their ears, their smock sleeves rolled up showing muddy arms; he was lucky to have such good friends. It was inappropriate, but Joe found their laughter comforting and realised that he was smiling with them.

Rab brought the coffin to the Scotts' door early on the morning Meg was to be buried. The family wrapped her little body in a clean white sheet and laid her gently inside. She was so small that Sarah rolled up an old shawl and pushed it round the edges so she was cushioned from the rough planks of wood.

'There,' she whispered, 'that's better. More comfy...' She had said those words to her little sister so often after bathing her that they came out spontaneously. The finality of arranging her in a coffin caught her breath and Joe saw her face contort with grief.

Better to get this over with, he thought, near to tears himself.

'Come, you all get aff tae work!' he seized the coffin lid and, as soon as they left the room, he screwed it down into place.

His mother, standing at his side, seemed to crumple. She reached for the back of the chair to steady herself and then dropped down into the seat.

'Yer a guid lad,' she said, not looking at him. 'Thank the Lord yer faither's blood has nae tainted ye.'

He pulled on the heavy, sacking cape he used on the coldest days; he felt chilled to the bone.

'Ah'll be back at midday, mind an' keep the fire in now.'

'Aye,' she leaned forward and rested her head in her hands. His heart went out to her. She was a helpless creature, unable to care for herself let alone her children, but she was his mother. Her greying hair drooped from under her mob cap which, like the old shawl and petticoats she wore, was dirty and torn.

He stopped at the door, hand on the latch. 'Dinnae jist sit here an' greet, will ye, Ma? Get smartened up, boil some watter and have a wash. It's cold oot,' he didn't know when she had last ventured down the stairs, 'ye'll need tae put a lot o' clae's on tae gae up the hill.'

She rubbed her hands over her face. 'Gie us some pennies, will ye?'

'Whit fer?'

Only then did she turn to look at him. 'Ah need a drink, son. Jist tae see me through the day?'

She looked so wretched that he pulled out his money bag, counted out four farthings and laid them on the table beside the coffin.

As he drew the door close behind him he heard her say, 'Yer a guid lad, Sam. A guid lad.'

Sam.

Now, she didn't even know her own children. Dear Lord, what was to become of her?

***

It was a mild winter and the rebuilding of New Lanark was able to make good progress. By March, not only was the interior of Mill One ahead of schedule, but Mill Two would soon be ready to be fitted out with machinery.

Later that spring, on a warm, still evening, Joe and Cal met Tam on the cliff path above Dundaff Linn.

Dundaff was the smallest waterfall in the valley and suffered by comparison to the mighty Bonnington and Corra Linn falls further upstream and Stonebyres Linn some miles downstream. Yet, being visible from the village, it held its own beauty, splashing down over rocky shelves just before the mills and sending white water to swirl around the island. After its tumultuous journey between the cliffs, the river emerged to become much wider and shallower, a favoured place for wildlife.

In summer, kingfishers flashed on the overhanging branches, wings a blur of brilliant blue as they hovered above their prey before slicing into the water to snatch silver minnows and jaggy sticklebacks. Dippers bobbed and sang from their rocky perches, throwing themselves under the water in search of insects and larvae before bobbing back to the surface. Lazy winged herons, legs trailing beneath them, flew slowly up the river bed to take up solitary, statue-like positions beside pools, or to land clumsily high in the trees to oversee their domain.

This evening, clouds of newly hatched flies danced and drifted above the surface of the river, a delight for grey wagtails swooping and pirouetting in the air, filling their beaks with this easy feast. Ducklings, fluffy floating brown balls, were already appearing, scooting behind their mothers and scrambling unsteadily about the rocky shore line. A group of noisy carrion crows hopped and fluttered close by, hoping to intimidate unwary ducklings to take fright and leave their mother's protection. The crows had their own hungry chicks to feed and a duckling was worth pursuing.

'It's a grand night!' Tam greeted them. He was sprawled in dappled sunshine on the grassy slope, his cap laid on his chest. 'ye knaw, it may be nearing sun down but it's still warm on ma face.'

They set off through the woodland, pushing through knee high woodrush and Cal was pleased he was wearing his boots. They were

78

too tight for comfort now but he had managed the winter with them and was glad the warmer days were coming and he could throw them away. The way he was growing, they would never fit next winter.

They followed the course of the river, first above cliffs then down to a flat broad stretch above the weir, where little sandy beaches showed tracks of roe deer, badgers and foxes who lived in the woodland. Sweet scents hung in the air, fresh from the slender budding bird cherry and aspens overhanging the water.

After crossing a burn by jumping from boulder to boulder, the ground started to rise steeply. It was no longer possible to stay by the water's edge, the river was running deep and narrow below rocks, so they moved up through old oak and chestnut trees, their trunks wide enough to hide two men. Clusters of new ferns, some bowing their heads, partially unfurled, stood tall above peppery scented bluebells. This was Bonnington Estate land and Joe cautioned Cal to be quiet and keep watch for the game keeper.

Cal held his breath and picked his steps carefully, tip toeing between dry sticks in case he snapped them. He was eager to keep up with the older boys and, although his heels were nipping with torn blisters, he was enjoying the expedition.

They were now high above the gorge, the roar of the water reverberating from a long way below. The far bank had also risen up in densely wooded hills, but opposite them, the chimneys of the mansion of Corehouse were clearly visible.

Checking first to make sure no one was around, Tam signalled to the others to follow him. In silence, keeping low among the alders and shrubby undergrowth, they all moved forward to a clearing where a stone folly stood with two ornately carved benches placed before it.

Immediately in front of the benches the slope fell away hundreds of feet to the chasm below.

'There!' Joe breathed, leaning close to his brother. 'That's Corra Linn!'

Corra Linn streamed towards them, cascading down over ever widening tiers of rock, projecting torrents of silver foaming water far out into the huge pool at the bottom. The surrounding cliffs, over a hundred feet high, formed a great semi-circle, gathering the Clyde and turning it in a deep, swirling arc to flow towards New Lanark.

They sat down on the nearest seat and stared at the spectacle, each lost in the wonder of it.

At the top of the waterfall, the remains of Corra Castle could be seen jutting out from the rocks and beneath it, on a ledge, dim lights and movement showed where a mill stood. It was growing darker by the minute and eventually, midges sucking at their skin, they pulled themselves away and retraced their steps to the sandy banks near the weir.

Fishing was almost an anti climax. Cal's teeth were chattering with cold and excitement but he wished the evening would never end. Only one fish was hooked, by Tam, but it was fun. It was thrilling. He wanted to do this every night.

In early summer Mill Two took receipt of four spinning frames and Mill One was nearly ready to start production again. With the building now sound and ready for occupation, Fiona and the other orphans returned to their attic dormitories.

She was sorry to leave the tenements. Twelve of them shared the room, three to a bed, but without the constant supervision of Mrs Docherty and her assistants, they could chatter and sing or play games much more easily. Maybe they were cramped and it was a lot of work to keep clean and the fire stoked, but it was far preferable to the stark, airy space under the rafters.

Joe was not at all happy when the orphans moved out. He had grown used to seeing them going about their chores and gathering on the green to hear sermons or take their lessons. Only in the most inclement weather were they allowed to miss these occasions and then tasks were set indoors.

Now that they were to be living inside the mill again, he would hardly ever see Fiona. The thought made him irritable and restless, like a hunger pang that couldn't be assuaged. His mind constantly turned to her; her laugh, her dark brown hair that gleamed red in the sun, the way her skirt swung from her hips as she walked... little anecdotes Sarah recalled about her....

He knew several girls in Lanark, all of them bonnie and all of them eager to take up with him. They would smile and tease, dress their hair with ribbons and try to catch his eye, giggling and smoothing their hands over their slender waists. Yet, Fiona did none of that and he found he wanted her more than any of the others.

On Sarah's birthday he waited outside the Mill door for her at the end of the day. He was leaning against the wall, wondering if he had missed her because most of the other workers had already left, then she came running out.

80

'Joe!'

'Ah thocht we could tak a look at that drapers' stall, we'll catch it afore they pack up if we hurry. Rosie said ye were hankering fae summat frae there and ... we would all like to gi'e it tae ye fer yer birthday.'

A huge smile spread across her face and she slipped her arm in his, 'Aw! Yer the very best brother!'

'Sarah!'

They both swung round to see Fiona standing by the doorway. She was holding a piece of paper and took a few steps forward to thrust it into Sarah's hand. As she did so she looked up at Joe.

This was the man she had watched climbing on the ladders, hauling chains and pulleys and walking boldly along the high gantries of Mill Two. He was just as handsome close up as she had dreamed he might be, more so. Her heart was beating violently and she could feel herself blushing and cursed this stupid affliction. She wanted to appear calm and pretty, but instead she was hot and flustered.

Then, all in an instant she saw Sarah's hand on his arm, how close they stood together, remembered their lively smiles when they turned towards her and she felt a rush of pure jealousy.

This man, the man she admired for so long from afar, was Sarah's man.

The fantasies and longings she had enjoyed through the last few months were dashed to the ground. Of course Sarah should be with him, she was pretty and sweet natured and she lived in the village, as he did.

How could she ever have thought he might have been interested in her, Fiona? An orphan, a pauper and not even able to speak his language... Yet, there had been those brief moments when she was sure he was seeking her out, those glances that lingered just a few seconds longer than needed, both of them unwilling to release contact. She had felt the magic, it was not imagined. Nor, as she looked up at him now, could she deny that she saw her own desire reflected and returned in his eyes.

They were sparkling, laughing eyes of a brilliant blue. Perhaps she had misunderstood, perhaps she amused him and he thought her a ridiculous figure in her apprentice cotton tunic, barefoot and with her hair dusty with cotton.

Sarah was thanking her, but, dismayed and quite unable to hold back the tears, Fiona whirled round and disappeared inside.

81

'It's a drawin' o' a flo'er, honeysuckle! Aw it's bonnie!' Sarah held it up for Joe to see.

He was staring at the doorway with a perplexed expression. 'Why did she run aff like tha'?'

'Och, she acts funny sometimes.' Sarah dismissed the incident. 'Ah will thank her t'morra, but it wis fair kind o' her.'

Joe could not leave it so easily. The girl had a profound effect on him and he felt out of sorts for days afterwards.

***

While New Lanark baked in the hot July sunshine, the rumbling years of troubles in France came to a violent climax. It was in every newspaper and the talk of every gentleman's club.

David Dale folded his copy of The Glasgow Advertiser and took a sip of coffee. It tasted more agreeable these days since they took to using water from one of the new hand carts supplying fresh, clean water drawn from springs. The city's public water supply corrupted the flavour of even the strongest brew.

He was seated in the corner of the coffee rooms in the Tontine Hotel waiting to meet George MacIntosh to discuss business. He was not in the least surprised that the French peasants had finally risen up against their oppressors. The violence, however, was by all accounts terrifying. On many occasions he preached on the subject of treating one's fellow man with respect and kindness and it was a subject he felt could not be stressed enough.

Dale and his wife often discussed these concepts and religious beliefs at length. At least Scotland was a peaceful, God-fearing country to raise their children, unlike France.

He urged her to embrace his church but respected her choice in following her own path to Salvation with the Baptists.

During their heart-breaking bereavements his own grief could be alleviated by praying and the distractions of trade and outside affairs. For Carolina, her daily life was wholly concerned with the household and her children. At present, all was well. Their youngest daughter, Margaret, was thriving and they were to be blessed with another baby in the autumn.

George MacIntosh arrived, resplendent in an embroidered scarlet waistcoat and velvet trimmed cream jacket. It was very warm in the club and he drew out a silk handkerchief to dab at the beads of sweat running from his brow. The day was too humid for wigs and waistcoats but he was a fastidious man, always immaculately dressed. It would never do to walk the streets in anything less than the best.

He hailed a boy to bring them more coffee and took a seat beside Dale. The Rooms were full of extravagantly dressed merchants debating the rising prices of raw materials and postulating what would happen in France. They all remembered the dreadful riot at Calton less than two years before and each had a tale to tell of their own, personal experience of mob violence.

A tide of unrest had seen a group of weavers rise up in a rage against their employers because their demand for the right to have an advance on their wages was refused. Tempers flared and cloth was set alight in the Drygate. A terrible scene ensued, Glasgow's streets were filled with rioters and the situation escalated when magistrates ordered the infantry to disperse them with gunfire. Three people were killed and thousands turned out to their funerals.

It was a salutary warning that it was not impossible for a revolution to happen in Scotland.

'I fear for the Highlanders,' MacIntosh said seriously, 'turned off the land and with not a penny between them. These are desperate people Dale, all they want is a means to earn a living. You and I know how difficult it is for them to grow anything in the north, they can barely scratch enough to eat from the earth. It's all stone and peat, nothing will grow and, apart from sheep, it is hard to even survive the winters up there. If we are not careful it will be a similar tale as we are reading of in France. Either that, or the country will be emptied of Scotsmen because they have been forced to seek a life in the colonies.'

Dale nodded, a frown creasing his brow. It was a problem they had both chewed away at for years. After the dreadful harvest of '83, MacIntosh had prevailed on him to help a starving community north of Inverness. He sent a ship from Leith, its hull full of white beans, but this, while feeding the community for a few months, did not address the fundamental problem.

'We need to give these barren areas some way of providing for themselves,' Dale said at last. 'It is of no lasting use to dole out charity to these people, they don't want charity, they want to provide for their families themselves. We must all put our minds to the matter and, God willing, we will come up with a plan.'

They turned to discussions regarding their joint venture; a dyeing factory in Dalmarnock. It was a profitable company, turning out cloth of a brilliant red, called Turkey red. The name came from the madder plant, imported from Turkey, which was used to produce the colour, although in Glasgow it was now referred to as Dale's Red.

The two men had been running this business together for over ten years and they enjoyed each other's company.

Their business concluded, Dale enquired after Macintosh's son, Charles.

'Is it true that Charles is to marry next year? It seems no time since he was a boy with ringlettes like my little William!'

The proud father puffed out his chest. 'Indeed it is, a fine lass, Mary Fisher. Mrs Macintosh and I are both very taken with her, it is a good match. Although Charles is now wishing to leave his position as a clerk and pursue his interest in chemistry. I have advised caution, perhaps a change of profession just before marriage and the possibility of children is not the best step.'

'He is a level headed young man, I wish him well.'

'Please give my regards to Mrs Dale,' MacIntosh said as they rose to leave.

'Perhaps you will both join Mrs MacIntosh and myself for a dinner next week? Wednesday? In these long summer evenings it makes for a pleasant change to dine at other houses. What do ye say?'

'That would be very kind. I shall consult with my wife and let you know tomorrow.'

When he returned to Charlotte Street he was informed that Mrs Dale and the children were in the garden. He went up to his dressing room and with a sigh of relief, removed his wig and restricting formal waistcoat and gave his head a good scratch. Then, with just a loose, open necked shirt and light breeches, he left the cool of the house and walked down the long path to a seating area under a group of elm trees.

Bees hummed among the leaf canopy and the rose arbour, where his wife sat, was scented and shadowy.

She looked up from her book and, immediately on seeing him, laid it face down on her lap.

They talked of his day and when he broached the subject of Macintosh's invitation she greeted it hesitantly.

'Think on it, Mrs Dale.' he told her. 'T'will only be the four of us present and they are well known to us.'

'You wish to go?' she asked, rearranging the folds of her skirt, absently fingering the lace trim on the outer flounces. This pregnancy was not as smoothly borne as the others. She would be thirty seven on her next birthday and her body was exhausted producing her ninth baby in eleven years. It was difficult enough to rise each day and face the household, carry out the daily routine, but to dress up and commit to spending hours away from her home?

'Yes, I would like to accept. However,' he looked at her affectionately, 'if you do not feel up to it, my dear, I will make our apologies.'

Inside, she said no, but outwardly, she nodded, 'I am not sure how I feel, but, yes, we shall go to the Macintosh's.'

He relaxed back into the seat and changed the subject, pointing out how well the lavender was growing this year and how pleased he was that they had purchased this extra piece of garden. Beyond the arbour was an open space where they could glimpse the children playing.

Giggs sat beside them on the grass, darning stockings and watching Anne Caroline and William skipping and throwing a ball to one another. The little ones, Jean, Mary and Margaret were tottering and crawling about on the uneven ground. Their squeals, softened by the warm afternoon air, mingled with the distant rustle of Glasgow's streets in the background.

'We have so much to be thankful for,' Dale murmured. 'We must not take for granted the joys we have been given by the Lord.'

***

A few months later, one bright autumn day, David Dale sat at his desk in the comfortable octagonal study of his house in Charlotte Street and set about writing to his colleague Richard Arkwright.

Arkwright was now a Knight of the Realm which amused Dale when he thought of the unrest the man had caused only a few years before. Not only did the workers hate him for replacing their jobs with mechanical equipment but he had also turned his fellow cotton mill owners against him by claiming he was the sole inventor of certain machines.

These were not only spinning machines but also intricate designs which carried out carding, drawing and twisting. There was great concern that they would either have to pay him large sums of money for using his inventions or be charged with breaking the law. When Arkwright won his first court cases, they were determined to stop him having a monopoly and united to launch an appeal. The last judgement went against him.

Arkwright had been in the middle of all that bother when they went into business together. It was one of several reasons why Dale thought it wise to end their partnership before it affected New Lanark adversely. However, it was to Arkwright's Cromford Mills that he had sent a group of his first New Lanark workers to be trained.

The memory of the young men, assembled infront him before they left for England, so proud in their specially made brown, red trimmed outfits, came to mind. It had been an interesting time, the start of a new venture. Dale held genuine admiration for the way Arkwright ran his mills and still used him as a supplier for parts and machinery. He had even heard from contacts near Manchester that he gave his workers a feast and treated them to a ball once or twice a year.

Whatever the chatter in the coffee houses said about the man, this certainly showed a humane and charitable side to his character.

In front of Dale was a neat list of equipment, plates, wheels and rollers, required for the jennies at Catrine and he paused to calculate if he should add a few dozen spindles to the order.

There was a knock at the door and the butler entered.

'Sir, Mrs Dale has requested that I inform you that she has sent for the physician.'

'Reginald Black? The baby is on its way?'

'I believe so, sir.'

Dale left his desk straight away and hurried along to the bedroom. He paused for a moment outside the door and then knocked.

'My dear, may I come in?' he did not wish to burst in and cause her embarrassment but he felt he must see her before the doctor arrived.

Carolina, her hair loose and wearing only a nightdress, was laid on her side on the bed, gripping the mattress fiercely. The normal bedclothes and silk coverlet were nowhere to be seen, instead the whole bed was draped with old sheets, the brocade side curtains tied tightly out of the way. She offered him a smile but her expression turned to a grimace as she was seized by another contraction.

'I shall not be a moment... ' he said quietly, 'my thoughts and prayers are with you my dear wife.' With that, he left the room and returned to his study.

All thoughts of business evaporated.

He was disturbed, unsettled. Any kind of suffering was anathema to him and although this was a natural process, it grieved him deeply to see his beloved wife in pain. There was nothing he could do for her and, as with the births of all his children, he knew the next few hours would be interminable until he heard she was well and delivered of a healthy infant.

He sat down by the fire and reached for his Bible, firmly placing his trust in God to keep her safe.

After enduring childbirth so many times before, Carolina knew all too well what ordeal lay ahead. Her maid, Maggie MacIntosh, or Toshie as she was called, stayed with her, calmly arranging for more sheets, soap and hot water to be brought to the room. When Mr Black arrived, she became his nurse; they had both attended Mrs Dale together before.

In the end it was less than two hours before a series of bleating cries announced the arrival of her ninth child.

It was a girl: Julia.

The whole household rejoiced at the news and Dale dispatched letters to his father in Stewarton and her parents in Edinburgh.

Anne Caroline and William clapped their hands and danced around their bedroom. A new little sister!

After visiting his wife and marvelling at the sight of his tiny new daughter, Dale walked briskly up to his church, the Old Scotch Independents, raising his cane in greeting to passersby, touching his tricorn hat to the ladies. His heart was brimming over and he wanted to spend some quiet time alone, in prayer.

***

After seeing Sarah with Joe and believing them to be romantically involved, Fiona was consumed with jealousy.

Her immediate reaction had been to rush up to the dormitory, throw herself on the bed and weep. Although she barely knew this tall, fine looking labourer, her young heart had never experienced such intense attraction for anyone before and she was seized by painful, confusing emotions.

Following the initial realisation that he was lost to her, came a gradual dawning that she would probably never be able to have a sweetheart. When could she meet anyone else? She hardly ever left the building and, if she did go out, it was always as part of a closely chaperoned group. Anyway, who would want to be with an orphan who was tied to the mill for many years to come?

The bleakness of her situation weighed heavily on her mind. For weeks she tried to avoid any direct contact with Sarah, struggling to be even civil to her, so strong was the envy that raged inside. This also made her sad because, by nature, Fiona was a friendly girl and had enjoyed Sarah's company.

The recollections of pleasant times spent together were now tinged with bittersweet pangs of resentment. All through those days when she lived in the tenements, when she was looking out for any glimpse of *Aluinn,* handsome, as she called him, it was Sarah that he was interested in, not her. When she saw his frequent glances towards them as they washed clothes by the river, she thought he was observing her. No, it must have been Sarah that he was watching.

On those tediously long summer evenings when she was shut inside the classroom with the other orphans, Sarah had probably been out strolling with him, hand in hand in the sunset... It was just too painful.

She felt foolish and stupidly naive.

In the autumn, new complicated carding machines were installed which replaced the many small hands pushing and teasing the fibres with hand cards and Fiona was taught how to work with the spinning jennies up on the higher floors. It was a more difficult job, requiring constant vigilance, but she was relieved to be away from Sarah.

As the months wore on, she threw herself into her lessons and decided to dedicate all her energy into learning how to read and write and, most urgently, master speaking Scots more fluently.

Mr Lyme was impressed with her attentiveness and she began to make steady progress up through the classes. Her life became a cycle of whirling spindles, attending lessons and falling straight asleep every night from exhaustion. There was no time to ponder on the past or contemplate the futility of her future. She still carried her mementoes with her everywhere she went, but, while she could not bring herself to discard them, neither could she look at them.

Gradually, over weeks and months of self discipline, Fiona succeeded in locking away her hopes and dreams in the same tomb which held her childhood memories.

New Lanark continued to grow.

After the completion of Mills One and Two, a third and then a fourth mill rose up in a line beside the river. More and more rows of tenements scaled the hillside to accommodate the ever increasing workforce. There were also two new smart houses under construction, one of which was to be used by David Dale and his family, the other for William Kelly.

While James Dale chose to continue to live out-with the village, Kelly was keen to be on site. He was not only a very good manager, he was also a brilliant engineer. With Dale's support and encouragement he worked on the machines in Mill Three and adapted them in an innovative way so that each employee could handle twice as many spindles.

The rapid growth and success of his mill village helped to sustain Dale through the following, devastating months.

A virulent strain of smallpox began to wreak havoc across Scotland. New Lanark kept a strict control on all newcomers to the village and managed to escape the worst of the epidemic.

Glasgow was especially badly hit and the cruel, painful disease ripped through the city with no regard for money, privilege or religion. Hundreds were dying every month causing panic and chaos in the more heavily populated areas.

More and more houses were marked as infected and quarantined. Wagons patrolled the streets collecting bodies, their very presence terrified passers by, sending them scurrying to doorways, handkerchiefs over the faces.

Tragically, young William Dale showed the early signs on a warm May day. At first it was hoped he was suffering from influenza, but then the dreaded spots appeared in his mouth.

Several of the Charlotte Street servants were taken ill and the house was divided both upstairs and down in a desperate bid to stem the infection. Despite treating the pox with every means known to them, William's symptoms worsened. The pus filled blisters gave way to a rash, bleeding and oozing, as the pox consumed his flesh until his immaciated body could fight no more. He died.

Carolina was devastated. Their beautiful, funny, energetic little boy, their only son, was taken from his family. Aware of her duties and responsibilities for her husband and five daughters, she tried desperately to carry on.

However, when another wave of smallpox hit Glasgow early in the new year, just six months after William's death, Carolina herself contracted the disease.

Dale could only watch in horrified disbelief as the virus took hold of his wife. Scorched with fever and growing ever weaker with sickness, instead of the hoped for peak and recovery, the physicians soon realised that Carolina was in grave danger.

In the later stages of the illness, when her mother was no longer infectious, Anne Caroline was allowed to read to her. Dale purchased a newly published book on impulse, eager to procure any and all comforts and pleasant distractions for his wife while she was unwell.

It was The Marriage of Heaven and Hell by William Blake and Anne Caroline held the beautiful bound edition with reverence. Its hand-coloured illustrations were a wonder to behold, even if the text was proving to be laboriously complicated.

Her mother was finding it difficult to muster the breath to even speak. Lying back on piles of eider-duck down filled pillows, her hair swept up into a loosely tied turban, she was calm and half asleep.

Mr Black was attending her frequently. As well as the awful blistered spots and rashes, her pulse was erratic. He pronounced her heart struggling to follow a natural rhythm, but, given bed rest and good nursing, she could recover.

Anne Caroline looked fondly on her mother's sleeping face. She could not bear to see her so ill. Memories of her little brother lying cold beneath the covers, and now her beloved Mama ravaged by the same disease, robbed her of all appetite or ability to sleep.

Despite Black's hopeful prognosis, the household went about their duties with bated breath and hushed voices. Their mistress was dear to them all, being, like her husband, a much loved and considerate employer.

The great Charlotte Street house without Mrs Dale? Who would choose the menus, flowers, guest lists and entertainment, or make arrangements for the little girls? While Breen and Renwick could run the house, they required the instructions and guidance of their mistress at the helm.

Dale was deeply concerned.

A feeling of dread saturated him, dulling his senses.

If it was God's will to take his beloved wife away from him, he must trust that it would be painless and that she would find everlasting salvation in the Kingdom of Heaven.

He took to spending every free moment at Carolina's bedside and on returning from an important appointment on a freezing January afternoon, found Anne Caroline already there.

They sat together in silence not wishing to disturb the patient's peaceful sleep. As they watched, her breathing became more laboured and she opened her eyes, raising a hand as if beckoning for assistance.

'Hush, me dear,' Dale leaned across and took her hand in his. His heavy black jacket and large hands at odds with the delicate lace of his wife's night robe. 'Ah'll stay by your side, you rest and recover...'

'David?' she sighed, 'It is very dark in here...'

Anne Caroline jumped up and spread the curtains wide, allowing more of the white winter daylight to flood into the room. As she turned back, she saw her father lean towards her mother and kiss her gently on the forehead, clasping her hand against him.

In those few seconds, Carolina released her last breath and slipped away.

Neither father nor daughter realised her passing for several seconds.

They stared at her, aghast.

Something terrible had happened; something different and inexplicable. Anne Caroline turned questioning eyes to her father. It was not just that her mother was still, her eyes closed, lips relaxed and parted, there was an indefinable change in the room.

It was tangible, unbearable: she had left them.

The next few days were filled with people coming and going as arrangements were made for her funeral.

Breen, Toshie and Giggs, shocked and grieving themselves, comforted the children and strove to maintain a normalcy to the routine of the house.

It was hard.

A pall of sadness loomed over the mansion, its shutters closed on the front windows, its servants subdued. Renwick turned an uncharacteristically blind eye to the many female staff crying openly as they went about their chores.

Dale's brother Hugh and close friends rallied round but they could do little to dispel his grief. In the same way as he coped with the death of his children, he sought the scriptures. Reading late into the night helped to put off the desolate moment when he had to retire to his empty bed.

Claud and Helenora Alexander, and Wilhelmina, sent their condolences straight away by letter. Then made arrangements to journey to Glasgow and stay with friends in the city so they might attend the burial and support their friend. To have his son, and now his wife, die within months of each other was intolerably cruel and the many letters of condolence arriving at Charlotte Street were written with genuine, heartfelt sympathy.

When the funeral was over, Dale appeared to outsiders to be coping well, but within the walls of his own home, he was suffering the bereavement severely.

In New Lanark, James Dale and William Kelly were sincerely sorry to hear of Mrs Dale's death and also travelled up to Glasgow to pay their respects and attend the funeral. A few of the older village residents paused to reflect on their memories of her and some remembered her in their prayers, but generally the news of her passing was met with indifference.

Had it been David Dale who had died, then they would have paid more attention. So long as their employer was still walking the earth and paying their wages, his wife's death was of little personal interest.

***

By that summer, in 1791, New Lanark was a thriving community, the largest cotton producing mills in Britain.

The Scotts were active in its success and none more so than Joe. He greeted each day with zeal, the rough beauty of the walls he helped build inspired him to greater things. His reliability leading him to be chosen as part of the team to construct Dale's house, a privilege he accepted gladly.

This was a more refined design and he held the owner in such respect that he worked on it with pride and meticulous care.

'Yer certainly handy at that!' Bill, the foreman, called up to him one morning, as Joe tapped a stone into place.

'Ah've had enough practice!' Joe shouted back. He was perched high up on the roof timbers.

'Ah ken a stonemason who's lookin' tae tak on anither apprentice. Ye could dae worse than mak a trade o' it. Ah'll put a word in fer ye, if ye want?'

'Wid ye?' Joe rested back on his heels, surprised at the sudden offer, 'Aye, Ah wid be gratefu'. D'ye ken if it's awfy dear? Ah heard t'were near five pounds tae the Master an' a year afore ye get ony pay.'

'Mibbee, yit it pays weel in the end... if ye stiy the carse!' the man added.

'Aw, Ah'd stiy the carse, a'richt.'

'Jist remember,' Bill chortled, 'ye cannae start wi' him until yon hoose is feenished!'

Joe admired the art of the stonemasons and watched them dressing the sandstone lintels and creating sweeping arches. Whenever he was working beside them on gantries and ladders, he would note their precise, expert handling of the rocks. They turned them and looked at them, as if reading their hidden lines or gauging weaknesses, and then shaped and presented them to their best advantage. Often he had wanted to seize the chisel from their hand and be allowed to try it for himself.

He carried on with his job, whistling and thinking how satisfying it would be to learn a trade. He was twenty now and he didn't want to spend the rest of his life breaking stones and shovelling sand. He had a little money put away in the Savings Bank, administered by Dale's clerk in the mill office, and he decided that if he had enough it would be best spent on a valuable apprenticeship.

His vantage point on the roof gave an open view to the comings and goings between the mills. There were nearly a thousand people employed in the village now, many of them having moved into the new housing. Among them was a lovely girl, Flora, who would return his smiles and exchange a few words whenever they passed.

He fancied getting to know her better but knew from village gossip that her father, a weaver, was devoutly religious and very protective of his only daughter. Her brothers were allowed to lark about in the streets in the light evenings with Cal and the other village children, but not Flora. She was older, perhaps older than Sarah, and she remained indoors or took walks up to Lanark with her parents.

On Sundays, dressed in their best clothes, they would join the hundreds of folk trailing up the hill to Church. Joe even toyed with the idea of going with them but he was not in the habit of attending church and, even with the promise of an opportunity to be with this pretty lass, the notion held little appeal.

He was engrossed in his work when the bell rang for the mill workers' meal break and the bustle of doors banging and hundreds of feet tramping past the lade drew him to glance down the hill.

Fiona was hurrying along with the stream of apprentices, heading to Mill Four. He had seen her many times since that strange encounter on Sarah's birthday yet never had the chance to speak to her. That was nearly two years ago and he was shocked to feel an instant rush of desire.

She looked more striking than ever and the easy swinging way she walked held his attention until she disappeared through the mill door.

All the orphans were now housed and fed in Mill Four and he found himself rapidly assessing when she would be leaving again. Maybe it was the high blue skies or the unexpected chance of training as a stonemason, but whatever it was, he was filled with confidence and galvanised to act.

When Fiona re-appeared he was waiting for her and fell into step beside her.

'Fiona, I dinnae knaw if ye understan' whit Ah'm saying but Ah would like tae ask ye tae tak a walk wi me... on Sunday?'

Her eyes never faltered from the path ahead. She quickened her pace but he matched it.

'Och, mibbee ye dinnae understaun'' he said, grasping for inspiration. 'Ah wantae see ye... get tae ken ye...?'

'An' Sarah?'

He smiled with relief, at least she could understand. 'Aye, well, Sarah can come wi' us if ye wish...'

To his amazement she turned furious, flashing eyes to him. 'Gae fer a walk wi' you an' Sarah? Och... jist... leave me alane!'

He was astounded and stopped dead in his tracks. Of all the reactions to his invitation he had not expected that one.

He gazed after her stiff back with her hair rippling round her shoulders, that wonderful mass of hair he yearned to touch. What was wrong with the lass? What had he done to upset her so badly?

He thought of the incident when she gave Sarah the drawing. That was it. Sarah must have done something to make Fiona so upset, although for the life of him he could not think how his kind-hearted sister could cause anyone to hold such a deep-seated grudge.

Fiona ran up the stairs, battling for control, feeling her face glowing with frustration and anger. How dare he? After all this time! Why would he talk to her? And about Sarah too! Maybe Sarah still wanted to be friends with her and asked him to approach her, on her behalf, thinking his bonny face and glorious smile could win her round.

'Whit wis Joe sayin' tae ye?' One of the girls asked her as they entered the work room, kicking off their clogs at the door.

Joe, his name was Joe, despite her temper she felt a warmth at knowing his name.

'Nuthin.' With deft fingers, Fiona smoothed her hair safely back into a thick plait.

'By, yer a cool yin!' the girl laughed. 'Every lass in New Lanark has her eye on Joe Scott an' when he speaks tae ye, ye ha'e a face like a skelpit erse!'

' He's wi' Sarah, why wid he talk wi' me?'

'Away! Sarah's his sister!'

'Sister?'

Fiona didn't know whether to laugh or cry! This was the happiest day of her life.

She had not misread his interest in her, he *did* seek her out. Indeed, he was asking her to walk with him. Again she chided herself on her stupidity and was mortified at remembering her curt manner and haughty rebuttal. What would he think of her? Had she ruined any chance to be with him?

Somehow, she must talk to him; explain the misunderstanding.

Automatically, she took her position by the frames ready for the gears to be set into action. Wheels turned and the deafening rattling, whirring jennies jumped to life. It was all she could do to stay in her place and work through the rest of the day. Every part of her craved to relive their conversation and she played it over and over in head. It was a dream come true and she prickled with discomfort at her harsh response.

It must be put right, straight away, or at least as soon as she could find a way to reach him.

It was still warm and dry when Joe handed in his tools and walked home to the tenements. When they first arrived in the village, only part of their row was completed. Since then two other much longer lines of housing had been constructed. These were given the unambiguous names of Long Row and Double Row. Above them, running downhill adjacent to the road, was Braxfield Row. Most of this housing was now inhabited and at the end of each day the workers swarmed up to their homes, hungry and tired. In the winter, the streets would be empty again within minutes but in the summer, as it was now, it was preferable to gather outside. Choosing places away from the stench of the dung heaps, they would chat over the day with friends. Children played with balls, rolled hoops and chased each other around.

He knew there was a commotion near his door as soon as he entered the stairwell, the raised voices carried out onto the street. Ma was going at it hammer and tongs with their neighbour Bessie Jackson.

For months these two women would call a truce and then something would set them off again, usually from Ma's side. Since Meg died, their mother alternated from bouts of quiet depression to aggressive, wayward behaviour when she would quite lose the place.

Today was one of those days.

Several times a year, supplies of dry, cut heather or straw for bedding were sent to the village under Dale's instructions. This was included in their rent and was looked upon by many as a bonus. Early that morning the wagon, loaded with heather to refill the mattresses, had delivered two loads to Long Row. In their neighbour's household, all members of the family went out to work so Mrs Jackson had taken the precaution of choosing the cream of the crop before leaving that morning and, wrapping it in a blanket, told her sons to pull it upstairs to their landing. Throughout the day most of the wives in the row had been out and collected what they needed, dumping their discarded filling near the middens.

On arriving back this evening Bessie Jackson discovered her blanket was not only half empty, but her carefully picked fresh contents had been exchanged for withered old brown bedding. She ran to see what was left outside only to find most of the good, springy, foliage had already been taken, leaving a pile of sparse, woody stems.

A tell tale trail of twigs led to Ma's door, so battle commenced.

It took some time to mollify Bessie and then only because Joe offered to collect more bedding and bring it to her door as soon as the next delivery arrived. Bessie knew the wagons usually came over three consecutive days and grudgingly agreed to wait another day for her supply.

Cal was in a truculent mood. His supervisor was a surly, short tempered man who barked out orders and made a point of never giving praise. It made for long difficult days for those working under him, especially for Calum who had suffered so much from his father's rough treatment. Coming home to yet more shouting and uproar was the last straw.

He took one look around the room littered with loose heather, rumpled bedding piled on the table, and disappeared down the stairs again.

Joe was eager to ask Sarah if she could shed some light on why Fiona was so angry with them but first they had to sort out the mess. So, it was some time later, with Ma and Rosie out in the street, before he could talk to her.

'Ah, dunno Joe,' Sarah was baffled. 'It was a long time ago, but Ah cannae think o' anything Ah did wrong.' She looked at him inquisitively, 'Ah did nae knaw you were sweet on her?'

'She's a bonny lass, ye knaw. Kinda ... unusual lookin'.' How could he describe the high cheek-boned, heart shaped face and sensual dark eyes without sounding like some pathetic love struck youth. 'Foreign lookin', ken?'

'Aye, she is that. She's also an awfy strange lass. D'ye want tae be wi' a girl who acts up so? We dunno where she's come fae or whit's happened tae her family, she could ha'e a madness inside her.'

'Ye could well be richt,' Joe sighed. In his present state of infatuation he cared little if she was a lunatic.

'Anyway, it is Glasgow Fair in a couple o' days,' Sarah continued, 'an' Ah think we should make a celebration of our one day's holiday and gae up tae Lanark and see the travelling show. They say it's arrived already! Tents, music... aw Joe, it would be lovely to tak Rosie and Calum.'

He agreed, but his heart wasn't in it and his mind tussled with ways to win over the Highland lass.

After sunset the evening grew cold. The streets of the village were soon deserted except for a few drunkards, heedless of the temperature, supping and nattering in the gathering dusk as they sprawled on the bank above the ale stall.

The valley was quiet. Bats fluttered and circled through the buildings, night birds flew down the river, calling plaintively. Tawny owls carried on desultory exchanges from the woods towards Corra Linn. Dusk moved smoothly into night.

Sarah looked up from her sewing and threw a couple of thin, dry sticks on the fire, hoping they would supply a few minutes of extra bright light so she could finish mending her torn hem. The room was dark and she was straining her eyes in low firelight and only two candles.

'Where's Cal?' she asked.

Joe was dozing in the chair; Rosie and Ma long since retired to bed.

They looked at each other in sudden alarm.

They hurriedly ran down stairs and out into the night. Nothing moved between the solid stone walls of the Rows. They enquired of the group of men if they had noticed a lad pass by, but their inebriated replies made little sense.

'D'ye think he's gaun upstream? Fishin'?' Sarah asked anxiously, as they walked all round the village.

'By hissel'? Ah pray he has nae. It's dark the noo, if that's where he's been, he should be back soon.'

He could see the worried frown on her brow and the way she was chewing slightly on her lip, a habit from childhood.

'Din nae fret,' he consoled her. 'Ah'll tak a walk up an' see.'

She looked at the looming black shapes of the trees and the hills beyond and then at the river, flowing like treacle below the mills.

'There's no moon the nicht,' she said quietly. It was not only a statement, it held so many concerns: poachers would be out, the game keepers and stewards would be out and Cal would be as good as blind in the woodland.

A figure darted out from the trees above Dundaff Linn, raced down the side of the lade and then veered up hill to vanish behind the bulk of David Dale's house. Sarah picked up her skirts and ran with Joe, both hoping it was Calum returning home.

To their immense relief he was standing by the fire when they burst into the room.

'Where ha'e ye been?' Joe demanded.

'Oot!' He was out of breath, leaves and grasses caught on his breeches; his dew sodden boots propped up by the grate.

'Ah ken tha'... were ye on Bonnington estate?'

'Mibbee...'

'It's dangerous, Cal. Dinnae gang by yersel. Whit if ye'd drowned?'

'Then Ah'd be deid' he cried emphatically, 'an' Ah wid nae ha'e tae gae tae the mill all day!'

'Listen, Cal, ye've only anither year or sae left, then ye can choose yer ane path. Ye've made it this far, din nae blaw it noo. Eh?'

Cal pressed his lips firmly together, tears smarting in his eyes, then without another word he pulled his shirt over his head and went to bed.

He wasn't going to tell them the terrible ordeal he had just been through, ducking and weaving through the undergrowth with two men hunting him down. He could still hear the rustles and snaps of their footsteps, their shouts and threats. Yet, even after this perilous episode, he liked the woods. Before the game-keepers arrived he discovered a peacefulness in his heart which he couldn't find anywhere else.

If, as Joe said, he could chose his own path when his indenture was up, then he would leave this dead, man-made landscape of stone, metal and machines and work on the land.

Perhaps as a game keeper?

A few hundred yards away, across the village, Fiona lay in the dormitory. She was wide awake. In this new mill, the beds were arranged in four rows, with two or three children in each bed. She no longer had the luxury of a bed to herself but her companion was a pleasant little girl so the arrangement was not uncomfortable.

Her attempt to find Joe had failed.

On leaving work, she hurried up to Dale's house to find the building work finished for the day. Undeterred, she ran on to Long Row and up to the door she saw Sarah use so many times. She was about to go inside, nervously wondering whether to knock at every door until she found him, when she was pushed aside by several men and children rushing out. A barrage of shouting and swearing sounded from above, hysterical high pitched voices of women, things being pushed and thrown about and then more profanities.

Whatever was happening? She lost her nerve and decided against trying to pass this ugly scene which sounded as if it came from the next landing.

Time was running out and she rushed back down to Mill Four just in time to take her place for Grace before the meal.

Tomorrow, she vowed, tomorrow I will talk to Joe and everything will be all right.

However, the next day it proved impossible to find a moment to slip away but an opportunity presented itself the following morning: Glasgow Fair.

Glasgow Fair was a traditional work free day for everyone in the west of lowland Scotland. For one glorious day even the most lowly factory worker could spend their time doing what their hearts desired and their pockets allowed.

Fiona dressed with care. The Mill provided a set of Sunday clothes, which, for the girls, consisted of a simple, high necked white dress with a sash. She brushed her hair and braided the front locks, drawing them back and securing them at the back of her head with a borrowed clasp. The style suited her, she thought, using the window panes as a mirror. She looked very pale and hollow eyed in the reflection so she pinched her cheeks to raise the colour and tried smiling at herself. It made little difference and she sighed in dissatisfaction at the sight before her. Well, she looked worse in her shapeless cotton tunic and yet he seemed to find her appealing, so...

Sarah and Rosie were also wearing their prettiest skirts, with light fitted jackets over lace trimmed blouses. The sprigged fabric was from the drapers stall and long evenings of cutting, pinning and stitching had produced outfits which they were justifiably proud of wearing.

Adorning their hair with sprigs of honeysuckle and wild roses, they carried shawls over their arms and gathered in the street with other villagers. Their mother was not going with them, pleading a sore head and that the climb up the steep hill 'would be the end o' me.'

Everyone was in good spirits, excited to have a day of freedom.

Flora and her family were also heading up to Lanark and as they passed the Scotts' door, Sarah noticed Flora looking at Joe.

Her brother seemed oblivious to the girl's interest.

'Flora!' Sarah called, 'Are ye goin' tae the toon?'

'Aye,' Flora was keen to strike up a conversation with Joe's sister. 'Shall we walk t'gether?'

As the Scotts were now assembled in the street, the two parties joined together, with Flora's father and mother taking the lead.

It was as they started at the foot of the steps that Fiona came hurrying towards them.

She was hoping to speak to Joe on his own and was taken aback to find him in company.

'Joe!' she cried, but her throat constricted with nerves and he couldn't hear her. She watched the party mount the steps, with Joe courteously allowing the girls to walk ahead of him.

'Joe!' she called louder, 'Can Ah speak wi' ye?'

He had one foot on the bottom step when he heard her and turned in surprise.

'Ah... jist want tae say...' Fiona stammered, despite rehearsing her lines for days, the words would not form. She gazed into his eyes, then, hungry to take in every feature, her focus flittered across his face and up and down his body.

He was appraising her in equal fascination.

'Ah'm sorry...' she whispered, blushing. 'Ah thocht ye were wi' Sarah...Ah did nae knaw she wis yer sister.'

The highland lilt and faltering speech made her apology even more bewitching.

For several seconds they stood in silence, the tender desire in their eyes telling each other all they needed to know.

'Are ye coming?' Flora's irritated voice called from higher up the stairs. She was annoyed by Fiona's interruption, the day ahead with Joe was promising and she was looking forward to having him to herself.

'Can ye join us?' Joe asked Fiona, holding her gaze.

Orphans were never allowed to leave the grounds unless in the company of a guardian and then only with express written permission from the manager. It took her less than a heart beat to reply.

'Aye, Ah can join ye.'

He reached for her hand to help her take the first step on the stairs up the hill. As their fingers met the touch gave such pleasure that they both gave an involuntary, nervous laugh. Aware of Flora and the others watching them, they let go of the grip, but not before the die was cast.

They were instantly and utterly besotted with one another.

The travelling show was parked on a field beyond the market but long before reaching it they were regaled by performers. Acrobats, stilt walkers and half naked young men dramatically swirling flaming torches and blowing flames in great gusts from their mouths.

A man in a bright yellow jacket and scarlet trousers jumped and cart-wheeled among the crowd, springing up in front of Fiona and Joe before bowing, presenting a flower to Fiona, and bouncing on his way.

Fiddles and pipes played for groups of dancers, drawing the crowds to join them, the girls throwing coloured cords around men as they wandered past, coaxing them to dance.

The day passed in a rush of excitement, laughter and dancing.

On her return to the mill that evening, Fiona was met by an irate Mrs Docherty. For an hour she reprimanded her and preached to her of the evils of society and the dangers lurking in the world for young women. David Dale, she was told, would not tolerate such behaviour in his workplace, however, nor would he countenance corporal punishment.

Therefore, Fiona would be penalised by a series of extra menial chores and would be excluded from meals. She would only receive a bowl of oatmeal, and, to hold her up as an example, she would sit separately from the other apprentices for the next month.

Had Mrs Docherty told her that she would be flayed alive over hot coals, Fiona would have accepted her fate. She now knew what paradise looked like, how it felt to be truly exhilarated and alive and everything else in life paled into insignificance.

Chapter Three

*'I am confident that not a single person in Scotland, who is able
and willing to work, has any occasion to leave their native country
for the want of the means of a comfortable subsistence.... the best
thing that can be done for them and this country, is to invite all
that cannot find employment to come here, and they will be
provided for.'*
David Dale (letter, published in the Scots Magazine 1791)

Anne Caroline leaned as far over the banisters as she dared,
straining to see the activity in the hall.

The house was in uproar. Renwick and Breen hurried about issuing
instructions, maids and footmen scuttled to obey their orders and the
clamour of dozens of voices filled the usually quiet hallway.

Her father was in his study with George MacIntosh and several
other important looking gentlemen. They all arrived with an
expectant air and, on seeing Anne Caroline hovering on the landing,
favoured her with bemused smiles and raised eyebrows.

The cause of this furore had started the previous day when Dale
received notice that a ship from Skye, bound for North America, had
just limped into Greenock. The victim of ferocious storms, it was
nearly wrecked during the first day of its voyage and forced to head
to a safe port. Aboard the ship were hundreds of Highlanders. Their
plans to start new lives abroad were in tatters and they were now
homeless and with no employment.

As soon as this fact came to Dale's attention he sent two friends to
speak with the Highlanders and to offer them jobs and housing in
New Lanark.

For years he had discussed ways of relieving the plight of those emigrating from the north and now he saw a real opportunity to give assistance. He firmly believed that ways should be found to keep Scotsmen in their homeland and feared the drain of skills and labour to the colonies would prove not only difficult for the men and women leaving the shores, but also disastrous for Scotland as a nation.

Many of his colleagues agreed with his point of view and MacIntosh was actively putting together a partnership to establish employment in the most seriously affected areas. This sudden influx of stricken families struck right to the heart of the matter and stimulated an increase in commitment from those merchants who had previously been unconvinced.

Two wagons bearing families were already on their way to New Lanark and there were another fifty or so individuals waiting for the wagons to return to collect them. As there was nowhere else immediately available to shelter such a crowd, Dale brought them into his own home.

Downstairs, the staff were horrified.

Renwick's first orders were for all the valuables in the dining room to be gathered and carefully stored in one of the rooms in the wings of the house. Then the furniture was covered and the rugs rolled up, leaving the room practically bare. For such a gracious house to be invaded by a rabble of country folk was astonishing. These were destitute strangers, "heathens" in the most part, Cook declared, and should not be trusted an inch.

Orders were sent to the kitchen for vast quantities of broth to be prepared, necessitating two junior footmen to run to the butchers and green grocers for extra provisions. Dale was famous for his good hearted gestures but this was far beyond the call of duty and shop keepers and businessmen alike wondered at the man's generosity.

Anne Caroline found the whole event thrilling. As soon as all the incomers had been ushered into the dining room, she crept down the stairs and peeped through the door.

A little girl was standing immediately in front of her. They looked at each other and Anne Caroline smiled; the girl smiled back.

Her face was brown from the summer's sun and smudged with dirt. She was holding a protective arm around an infant who was pulling the end of her shawl into its mouth and rubbing its sleepy eyes. Both the children had coal black hair, lank with sea salt and grime. An unpleasant aroma, akin to rotting vegetables, wafted from the room and, after a quick glance further inside, Anne Caroline gave the girl another smile and ran back up the stairs.

Their faces brought back memories of the night New Lanark's mill burnt down: helpless, dejected expressions of bewilderment and hopelessness. Some of the men, long haired and ruggedly built, their leggings torn and stained, were removing their boots and rubbing their sweaty stockinged feet. Their movements were awkward as if every muscle in their bodies was aching.

The older members of the group were sitting in crumpled heaps on Dale's elegant dining chairs which someone had arranged in a semi-circle in front of the leaping flames of the fire. Robert Adam's intricate plasterwork fire surround and mantelpiece had never before been admired by such an appreciative audience.

Around the sides of the room, women in brightly coloured fabrics knelt amid bundles of their belongings, arranging shawls and jackets into beds for the children on the floor. Babies cried and all the while there was the rise and fall of Gaelic voices.

It was an incongruous scene and one which Anne Caroline would remember for the rest of her life. She hoped they had been told that everything would be all right now: her father would take care of them.

Dale himself was presiding over an informal meeting.

George MacIntosh was proposing the formation of a new company to fund and manage a cotton mill north of Inverness, at Dornoch. He was promised support by eighteen colleagues, and Dale, while agreeing wholeheartedly with the idea of creating employment for the Highlanders in their own region, strongly advocated woollen mills as being the most appropriate industry.

'By all means, gentlemen, we should go ahead with a factory and surround it with housing, stores, smiths and the like, but surely it would be better practice to use the one raw material that is on their doorstep? Wool! In abundance!'

A lengthy, and at times heated, discussion followed and in the end they decided to sleep on the matter and meet again in the city before the end of the week. Dale bid them goodnight and, excusing himself from escorting them to the door, remained upstairs to write letters and prepare paperwork for the Highlanders' departure the next morning.

His colleagues descended the wide, curving stairs and gathered briefly in the hall, shrugging on heavy coats and retrieving their hats and gloves from Renwick. Beyond the dining room doors, the noise and smell of the shipwrecked Highlanders could not be ignored.

'I think I can say,' said Dempster, 'that in all the years I have known Baillie Dale, this is one of the most extraordinary examples of his philanthropy.'

One of the other gentlemen, Andrews, drew his gloves on and reached for his cane saying, 'I am sure the benefits from this 'rescue' will be mutual. With Blantyre, Catrine *and* New Lanark, Mr Dale is as much in need of labour as those poor unfortunates are in need of shelter.'

MacIntosh was quick to defend his friend. 'I would have you know, sir, that just as Mr Dale is a shrewd businessman, he is also a man of integrity. He is not someone who only gives lip service to charity. He sees it as his Christian duty to help his fellow man.'

'So long as there is profit in it at the end,' the man snapped back. 'This fine house did not build itself.'

'Now, now...' Dempster stepped in. 'There is no harm in making money and, if you use it to better conditions for others, why not also enjoy the rewards on a personal level.'

MacIntosh added, 'Not all Mr Dale's dealings are in business, ye know. Last year he became a director of the Glasgow Humane Society. How many of us have put our hands in our pockets for that venture? Have you?'

He turned to Andrews, who looked down his nose and said haughtily. 'I do not believe I am acquainted with it.'

'Probably not,' said Dempster, making for the door. 'You would not be interested in a Society which does not pay out returns. Its declared aim is to recover poor souls from the Clyde if they fall in and are in danger of drowning. Not a lot of profit to be made from that, I would say. Good evening to you, sir.'

A few days later, overlooking the hustle and bustle of the Trongate, the company reconvened in the piazza at the Tontine Hotel. To Dale's disappointment, it was decided by the majority of shareholders to build and equip the mills at Dornoch for cotton production. It was felt that the cotton trade would give a better return and with the continuing troubles in France now involving more countries in Europe, the American and Russian markets were the ones to develop.

The site which MacIntosh and his surveyors had identified was called Spinningdale causing George Dempster to roar with laughter and raise his claret glass to Dale.

106

'A fine pun!' he bellowed. 'I like it!'

'Unfortunately, I can take no credit,' replied Dale, smiling broadly. 'It has been known by that name, or similar, for hundreds of years. T'is just a happy coincidence.'

'There won't be many who believe that, ye know!' Dempster refilled his glass. 'Gentlemen! A toast to our new company, Balnoe, let us pray it brings prosperity to the Highlands!'

'I'll drink to that!' echoed MacIntosh, and they all raised their glasses and drank.

***

Before the autumn moved any further into winter, Dale wanted to visit New Lanark.

While he was keen to see how his half-brother was coping with the sudden addition of over one hundred people to the workforce, he had another more personal reason for the trip. His new house was now built and he thought it would be pleasant to travel there as a family and stay a few days, enjoying the country air.

Since Carolina's death, he discussed homely matters more with his brother, Hugh Dale, who lived in Glasgow. Margaret, Hugh's wife, was also supportive and helpful in giving a female point of view on Dale's family arrangements.

Margaret pointed out, quite rightly, that building the walls and covering the structure with a roof, did not mean the house was habitable. She offered her assistance in choosing furniture and all necessary linen and utensils which would turn the place into a comfortable cottage for the family to visit.

She set about discussing the matter with Breen who drew up lists of tables and chairs, cutlery, kitchen equipment and lamps.

In the end, it was decided that Dale would go first, accompanied by a wagon full of all the most basic requirements for living. Two footmen would go with him and attend to the cleaning and fitting out of the house, while Dale prevailed one last time on James' hospitality in Lanark.

107

When it was deemed in fair enough order, the coach and wagon would return to Charlotte Street to collect his children and further household goods.

When Anne Caroline saw New Lanark again, she was amazed at how much it had changed over the intervening years.

This was a real village.

As the carriage wound its way slowly down the precipitous, twisting road, long lines of rooftops came into view. Beyond them, the towering mills reached right along the banks of the river towards the mouth of the gorge.

'Look!' Anne Caroline cried out, 'The mill on the right... the one with the bell tower... that is the one which burned to the ground. It looks so perfect and clean, I can hardly believe this is the same place!'

To negotiate the final hair pin bend, the coach driver drew the horses to a near halt, working with the brakes and ordering the groom to take hold of the lead horses' bridles. With Mr Dale's daughters inside the carriage, he was taking no chances. Successfully round the corner, they made a slow descent beside Braxfield Row, the clatter of the horses iron shoes ringing against the tenement's high stone walls.

Dale's new house was situated in the centre of the village, with an open space stretching below it to the mill lade. Beside it, but far enough away to give privacy to each residence, sat the manager's house.

Dale was delighted to welcome his family to their new country home. He strode from room to room, throwing open doors and encouraging them to look around. On occasions he struggled to keep emotion from his voice when his thoughts turned to how much Carolina would have enjoyed the moment.

In his black jacket and breeches, wig secured beneath his hat, he was a solid, portly figure. In Charlotte Street, with its high ceilings and spacious rooms, he could move around freely. However, here, he bumped into unexpectedly close walls and as his daughters scampered around exploring every room, it seemed that a child blocked his path at every turn.

Breen and the small staff she brought with her, set about re-arranging the furniture and when the wagon arrived, she busied herself directing the rest of their possessions into their new positions.

Having his family around him was always a pleasure for Dale and he had eagerly looked forward to their arrival. However, the hub-bub of Julia crying, excited squeals and giggles and the general stream of exclamations and questions overwhelmed him. To keep out of the way, he adjourned next door to the peace of the manager's house, murmuring that he had business to attend to with Kelly.

It was true, in the main part.

The current housing stock was almost fully occupied, two whole blocks of which were now filled with the new families from Skye. If he wished to employ more people, which he did, it was becoming obvious that more building work would be required and he wanted to discuss where these houses should best be sited.

It was a fair weather day. Birds sang in the trees, late bumble bees buzzed among the last straggling foxgloves and above them, patches of bright blue expanded and shrank between rolling banks of clouds making their way leisurely across the sky. Having been cooped up on the long journey, Toshie decided to take advantage of the last hours of daylight and mustered the older children together for a walk in the village.

The children were dressed alike in dark blue jackets and gathered blue and white striped skirts. The younger ones sported matching ribbons in their hair, but Anne Caroline, conspicuously older than her siblings, wore a neat white muslin bonnet with a lacy brim.

Although New Lanark held over a thousand people, the streets were deserted. Dull rumbling sounds emanated from the mills, the river swished and gurgled, and every so often a wagon would rattle its way up or down from Lanark. Construction was still taking place at the furthest end of the Rows, giving rise to bouts of distant hammering and sawing from inside their walls.

The quiet, freshness of the valley cocooned the new village, cradling it among woods and meadows, absorbing its man-made lines into the landscape. The ugly scars of blasted rock and churned up mud were being naturally softened by Nature's invasion of green grassy spaces and plantations of young beech trees.

'Where is everyone?' Jean asked, as they admired Dundaff Linn's cascading, frothy water.

Toshie was not sure. She found the mills formidable and could not begin to contemplate what might be happening behind the hundreds of windows. Never had she seen such a place and she thanked the Lord that she was living in Dale's house and tending his children, not toiling in his factories.

When it grew too dark and cold for Jean and Mary to be out, they returned to the house. A fire burned in the grate and lamps were glowing in the front room, accentuating the growing darkness beyond the windows.

'My, you look a picture!' their father proclaimed. 'What rosy cheeks and clear eyes! The country air will do us all good.' He included Toshie in this statement, beneath her white cap, the maid's shining face was a pleasure to behold.

The Dales and their servants were not used to such modest surroundings but embraced the whole experience as they would a picnic.

Cook had brought provisions for the first few days but Breen, in consultation with her master, was eager to hire a house-keeper, and a maid as well. They would stay in the house when the family were in Glasgow and be there to serve them when they came to the village. Given Dale's appetite for good food, the housekeeper would have to be an excellent cook as well.

The table, placed in the front room in a space behind the chairs, was laid for a meal. As soon as the dishes were brought up from the kitchen, the older girls sat down with their father to enjoy dinner together.

Dale's opening Grace was longer than usual as he waxed at length on the subject of doing one's duty and ploughing back into society any good fortune you reaped. His children sat patiently, listening to him with a fond expression, but hoping he would draw to a conclusion before the broth congealed to a cold sludge in their bowls.

Breen, hovering below stairs, was also concerned at the seemingly endless prayer.

The stove was proving temperamental and would probably already have gone out, so goodness knows how long it would take to reheat their food. His prayer completed, she let out a sigh of relief on hearing normal conversation continue. Her master was not going to call on her to re-heat the dishes: she sent up her own silent thanks to the Lord.

It was an unusual experience to have his children with him at the main meal of the day and Dale found it pleasing and irritating in equal measures.

Anne Caroline was full of the sights on their walk, especially the beautiful waterfall.

'You must all see the great Corra Linn,' Dale declared. 'On an early visit here, Admiral John Lockhart Ross took me to view this astonishing waterfall. Alas, he passed away last year, but I will write to his widow at Bonnington House and ask her to favour us by allowing us to take a carriage to the house and walk down from there. It is much too far for you children to walk from here.'

'Is Corra larger than Dundaff Linn?' Jean asked. 'I hope we are not on higher cliffs for I could not stand to look down at the water from the rocks. My head was spinning and I was sure I would faint!'

'Oh yes, my dear, it is three, four or even five times as big as the falls you see here in the village. It is a tremendous sight!'

When they had all eaten sufficient of the cold meats and preserves, Dale called for the footman to clear the table. Giggs took Mary, who was nearly asleep, up to bed to join her baby sisters.

The rest of the family settled beside the fire.

'I wish we had the pianoforte here,' Jean said, 'Anne Caroline could play and we could sing.'

'You do not need accompaniment to sing!' Dale laughed. 'Sing with me, what better way to celebrate our first evening here.'

Their conversation was interrupted by the loud pealing of the mill bell.

'That is the bell to signal that the day is over,' Dale explained. 'In a few minutes you will see everyone returning to their homes.'

'Where is everyone?' Jean enquired, the matter had been preying on her mind since their walk.

'Inside the mills, at work.'

'So late?' asked Anne Caroline. 'We saw hardly a soul when we were out with Toshie.'

'You may think it a long day, but I can assure you, there are many factories where the machines do not stop. The employees work sixteen hours a day and then, when they leave the factory floor, another shift takes over. I do not believe in that practice, twelve is quite enough. Anyway, the orphans in my care will now have a good meal and attend their lessons.'

'Do they have a teacher, like us?'

'They have several teachers and yes, they are taught to read and write.'

Anne Caroline rose from her place by the fire and went to the window. She could make out a procession of lamps, rising and falling

111

with the steps of a dark mass of people pouring out from the lit doorways of the four great mills.

In succession, from the top of the buildings to the ground floors, the lights behind the windows dimmed then went out.

She soon became aware of the sounds of hundreds of clogs stamping on the street behind the house, punctuated by shouts and whistles, laughter and scraps of conversation. In the waves of noise came bursts of singing, much of it raucous and out of tune, and the gabble of Gaelic: fast words, rushed together, unintelligible to Anne Caroline but instantly reminding her of the rescued Highlanders.

Remembering the girl with the baby, she hoped they were happy now, or, if not exactly happy, that they felt safe and could climb into dry beds after eating a good meal. In her child's mind she imagined them all sitting down to eat as she had just done with her family. Perhaps they would sit by the fire and sing, or read some poetry?

In Flora's household there was maybe a semblance of similarity to the Dales' evening, but it was a poor imitation. Oatmeal from the morning was reheated, the stodgy lumps diluted with water, and bread, cold meat and hard cheese were laid on the table. Grace was said and after the food their father read from the Bible while his family tended to the chores.

Tiredness drained the fun from them and there was no thought given to singing. Flora and her brothers fetched clean water, emptied the dry closet, cleaned the crockery and carried in more coal, while their mother washed and mended essential garments.

As soon as their allocated tasks were done, the children undressed and rolled into bed, their eyes closing before the blankets had even settled over their weary bodies.

***

A few days later Dale received a letter in reply to his request for permission to view Corra Linn from the Bonnington estate. Lady Elizabeth Ross would like the family to come and dine with them the next day and if the weather was clement, they could take a stroll to view the great waterfall.

Toshie was immediately in a flap.

112

Both she and Breen knew that the daughters of David Dale, grandchildren of John Campbell, a wealthy and influential banker, would be rigorously, if surreptitiously, inspected from head to toe. The results would be discussed in country drawing rooms for weeks to come. Dale had already remarked in passing that the Admiral had been a Member of Parliament for the area and, no doubt, their hostess was still a guest at most of the grand local estates.

Their concern was with the children's wardrobe. Every piece of clothing from their trunks was examined, trying to find a suitable outfit for Anne Caroline and Jean.

By the time they boarded the carriage to go to Bonnington House the next afternoon, Mr Dale looked appreciatively at his two older daughters. He knew little of the antics with taking in seams here, letting them out there: he just thought they looked lovely.

The party was warmly welcomed by the late Admiral's wife, Lady Elizabeth Lockhart Ross. Under a thick covering of white powder and well applied rouge and kohl, she was a lady of indeterminate age, certainly a good deal older than Dale. Her stocky figure was tightly encased to the waist in embroidered green silk and the skirts of the gown billowed and swung around her on hoops, showing frills of black lace at her feet. A fashionably over-sized white wig, sprouting pheasant feathers, added more than a foot in height to her appearance.

After a short preamble, when Dale formally offered their condolences on the death of the Admiral, reciprocated by Lady Lochhart Ross for the loss of Mrs Dale, they took a turn around the ground floor rooms of the gracious old house. On reaching the dining hall, they were invited to be seated for a fine meal of rich roast beef accompanied by an array of vegetables.

Dale commented on the delicious buttered carrots, parsnips, green beans and potatoes and Lady Lockhart Ross told them of her walled garden. Sheltered from the elements, her gardener and his team of under-gardeners supplied the kitchen with an abundance of fresh produce throughout the year.

'We have the earliest peas and the latest strawberries! And all manner of herbs,' she enthused, 'It is such a joy to have these tastes in our garden.' She smiled at her guests. 'You live in the city and I am sure you can find all these vegetables and much more, right on your doorstep, in the markets. Alas, by the time it has travelled to Lanark, it is often bruised and past its best. The farmers here tend to grow cereal or potatoes, but I do so like to see colours on my plate. Don't you, Mr Dale?'

'Certainly. And do you also grow flowers?'

'Of course! I adore enormous vases of flowers to fragrance the rooms in the summer.'

'And what of game?' asked Dale, 'I dare say you have a good larder of pheasant and venison.'

'Indeed we do. On our Balnagowan estate in the Highlands we have a ready supply of venison and thousands of acres of grouse moors. However, there, as here, it is always a battle against the poachers. This area is very poor, as I am sure you understand, and it is often seen as an easy way to fill the pot. Our man, Grieves, hires more wardens over the winter months.' She shook her head, the extravagant high wig wobbling precariously. 'It is a constant battle. In fact we found one of your paupers on our land not so long ago.'

'One of mine?'

'Yes, quite so. A youth, small and nimble with it or he would have been caught.'

'And on what grounds do you believe he was one of mine?'

'He managed to evade Grieves and disappeared down the banking into New Lanark. He was keeping close to the river, not cutting up to town as many do.'

'And what had he poached?'

'As far as we know, he wasn't carrying anything. Perhaps he dropped it when they pursued him.'

The Magistrate in Dale rose up.

He presided over many poaching cases in the court and knew they fell into one of two categories, need or greed. If it was greed, and the perpetrators were usually well organised gangs making good profits, then he sentenced them harshly. However, if it was some man just trying to feed his starving family, then he tended to veer towards leniency.

'Perhaps he was not carrying anything and had just lost his way?' he offered, keeping his tone light.

'I see what they say about you is true, Mr Dale, you are a fair man! Well, best if it doesn't happen again.'

Dale assured her that he would make stealing, and the dire consequences of the act, the subject of his sermon on Sunday. Then none of his villagers would be in any doubt of the law, both man-made and from God.

Anne Caroline and Jean were both relieved when the meal finished. Having sat in silence and kept up suitably attentive expressions, they could relax a little on the walk down through woodland to the viewpoint for the waterfall.

The trees were mainly beech, chestnut and oak and their glorious autumn colours were a sensational sight to behold. Many of the lower branches were still a vibrant green, but the higher canopy, swinging and shaking where red squirrels sought out food, was ablaze with every hue. Deep bronze to bright yellow, copper to crimson, the leaves were shimmering in a gentle breeze.

Corra Linn did not disappoint them.

They felt the tremors of the pounding water long before coming into the clearing where they saw the fine mist of spray rising from the chasm below. Spontaneous gasps left their lips as they gazed in awe at the tumbling, pouring river, cascading down the cliffs in front of them. The previous week had seen little rainfall so the craggy shelves of rock were partially revealed on either side of gushing white torrents.

'I believe this is when she looks at her finest!' Lady Elizabeth shouted above the roar. 'Some of my guests say they prefer her when the Clyde is in spate...' she paused to catch her breath. 'But, to my mind, you have to be able to discern the cliff face to truly appreciate her beauty.'

A specially designed stone pavillion stood further up the path which allowed the best views from the safety of standing behind stout walls and large windows, but Lady Elizabeth took her party to the benches perched above the cliff.

Jean felt ill, she clutched her sister's arm and thought she was about to fall. The ravine before her seemed to be drawing her towards it and a sickening lurch pulled at her stomach. Fearful she was going to tumble to her death, she cried out, tears springing to her eyes.

'Jean, dear!' Anne Caroline took her by the hand and Toshie, standing well behind everyone, rushed forward to take charge, ushering her back along the path, away from the gorge.

Unable to stand from the weakness trembling in her body, Jean sat down on a fallen tree trunk and gulped in fresh air.

'I'm sorry. I... felt very sick and so... dizzy...'

'Don't fret, we will wait here for the others,' Toshie soothed, feeling the child's brow. It was clammy and hot, her hands visibly shaking. 'Just sit and rest awhile. I am sure it will pass.'

Any fever in the children fired anxiety and she was reassured when the colour began to return to Jean's face. She was recovered and standing again, with the maid brushing moss and lichen off her skirts, when the rest of the party retraced their steps.

Feeling foolish for causing a scene, Jean glanced sheepishly at them as they approached.

Lady Elizabeth smiled at her kindly.

'My youngest son used to take turns like that when he was confronted by cliffs. Vertigo, that's what it is. No one's ever died of it,' she said in her matter of fact way and led the group back to the house.

***

The villagers of New Lanark welcomed Dale's presence, and that of his family, with mixed feelings.

Those who lived through the great mill fire held the mill owner in high regard and watched his movements closely. They appreciated the sight of his short, plump figure inspecting the machine rooms and walking the grounds. However, newcomers felt under scrutiny and resented their employer living among them.

They felt unable to be loose with their language and act as they wished in their free time. There was always the nagging concern that he was within earshot and, especially as he was known to be a devoutly religious man, whether he would consider their behaviour blasphemous and banish them from the village.

So, when the Dales' carriage was seen to be packed up and the wagon arrived to carry his servants back to Glasgow, his departure was, again, met with mixed feelings.

The same was true for the servants and Dale's daughters. They all enjoyed the novelty of staying in New Lanark and the opportunity to explore new walks and meet new people, but they also looked forward to the warm, spacious comfort of Charlotte Street.

Dale was satisfied that offering work to the Highlanders was a good idea and had already spread the word that he would take another two hundred displaced families into New Lanark. Plans were being drawn up for an additional row of tenements to be built alongside the road leading towards Bonnington Estate, which would provide them with ample accommodation. He was also in correspondence with partners proposing the establishment of another new cotton mill, this time at Oban, on the west coast of Scotland.

There was a great deal to be done and Dale climbed into the carriage beside his children and waved farewell to Kelly and James with a more enthusiastic heart. Filling his mind and time with work went some way to quelling his grief and, in quiet moments, his Bible was always to hand.

Life went on.

'Tis strange no' to see lights at Mr Dale's windaes,' Sarah said to Joe as she came in from work that evening. 'Ah had grown used to them bein' there.'

It was a bitterly cold evening and Joe was kneeling, hunched over the stove trying to breathe life into the few sparks that glimmered among the ash.

'She's let the fire gae oot agin,' he muttered. 'She's gettin' worse.' He threw down the piece of kindling he was holding and pulled his tired body up onto the chair. 'Ah'm that vexed wi' her. Whit can we dae aboot her?'

Sarah took the chair opposite, shivering and drawing her shawl tight. They both looked across at the drawn curtain covering Ma's bed.

Joe was now apprenticed to Bill Ewing, a stonemason. He revelled in the work but while it offered the promise of a comfortable income in the future, the starting pay was less than he earned as a labourer, *and* he had also paid out a sum to secure the apprenticeship. Money had always been a problem, but now his mother was wasting more and more on drink.

'Whit's she done this time? It's no jist the fire, is it?' Sarah asked.

'Ever since those Irish women arrived and those two auld crones frae Skye, she's found drinkin' companions. Ah gave her the mony fae the butchers, same amount Ah always dae, an' fae the general store... an' whit does she bring in?' he reached over to the cupboard and showed his sister. 'A bag o' oats, some cheese an' a ham bone that a dug widnae thank ye fer!'

'Did ye ask her?'

'Oh Aye! She's bin rantin' an' carryin' on... Honest, Sarah, Ah knaw she's no weel in the heid these days, but she's reekin' o booze an' noo she's spent a' the mony...' he threw his hands up in despair and slumped back in the chair.

Sarah was worn out, her back hurt and the cold was making her teeth ache.

'We'll think o' summat,' she said. 'let's light this fire and at least ha'e a bowl o' meal to warm us. Cal and Rosie will be in soon... we can a' put oor heid's together.'

Once the fire was licking up the chimney they felt a little better. It gave both heat and much needed light; they were down to two candles, another thing Ma was supposed to have brought in that day. When Cal and Rosie returned, the porridge was still cooking so they sat round the fire and took the edge off their hunger with chunks of cheese and the last of some cold, cooked potatoes.

Their main problem was that the shops and stalls selling food were closed by the time they left the mill. More stalls were opening up in the village and a butcher now came once a week but again, they were all shut inside the mill, or in Joe's case, tied up on the building site or at the quarry.

'We will ha'e tae ask someone to fetch oor messages doon frae Lanark.' Sarah said. 'That's whit Bessie does.'

'Aye, but she pays fer it,' Joe told her. ' an' she's got seven wages goin' intae that hoose.'

'Mibbee, but then she's got seven mouths tae feed.'

Cal chewed on his potato and then blurted out. 'There's a job goin' at Braxfield, on the grounds. It's better paid than Ah'm gettin' here. Ah'm thinkin' o' asking McCulloch to let me gae fer it.'

They stared at him in surprise. Braxfield estate was just downstream from New Lanark, the property of an eminent Judge.

'Ye niver said anythin' afore?' Sarah cried. 'How did ye hear o' it?'

'Ah've been askin' folk fer a while... Ah heard aboot it today. Ah could bring in more.'

Joe put his hand on Cal's shoulder, 'Ah would nae count on McCulloch lettin' ye go, but it's worth the askin'.'

Rosie stood up, 'Weel, Ah think we should ask Bessie tae see if who e'er gets her messages would get oors too.' She went to the door, 'Shall Ah ask the now?'

Rosie was small for her age, but at nearly fifteen she was a forthright, sensible girl and could not abide indecision or, as she put it to Sarah, 'haverin' n' footerin'.'

The others shrugged.

'Aye,' said Joe, 'Why no'. Surely they can nae charge much more than Ma drinks!'

This arrangement worked well for the Scott family, however it almost immediately brought several issues to the fore. Mrs Jackson asked for a list of what they needed: none of them could write. On admitting to this, their neighbour kindly took down their requirements and promised to pass it on.

'Ye should gae tae the school!' she chided Rosie. 'A grown lass like ye, lucky tae be living in yon village, ye should knaw yer lettering by noo.'

Rosie did not tell her that they could not afford schooling. There were now six teachers in New Lanark and, while the pauper apprentices were taught in return for their labour, the lessons were open to all employees at the Mills, but there was a charge for the books.

The next biggest issue that came out of the new arrangement was, happily, a very fortunate one. When he paid for the first supplies, Joe queried the amount. Surely, they could not have purchased so much for such a small bill.

'Aye, it's richt enough!' the woman said indignantly, believing that he was accusing her of charging too much. 'Ah can buy ye rubbish if ye wish, but Ah thocht ye'd be wantin' the same quality as Bessie.'

Joe grinned at her and handed over the money. 'Naw, naw... ye mistake me, Ah'm well pleased wi' the basket. It's jist grand.'

'An' on Friday? The fishmonger's cart will be in, ye fancy some nice cod? Mibbee a wee treat, once a month? Ah'll see they pack it well wi' ice an' in this weather it'll keep as fresh as ye like.'

He agreed to all her suggestions, his head reeling with the sudden pleasure of being able to afford good food. Along with this realisation, his resentment towards his mother took a deeper dive. They had scrimped over everything, the younger children's education being only part of it. When he thought of the thin soups, woeful scraggy chickens and gristly meat his mother presented her family, saying the 'pennies would nae stretch tae better,' he could have shaken her.

A lump came to his throat when he remembered the family trying to find the money to pay for Meg's coffin, and Ma whimpering, 'Ah wish Ah could gie ma wee lamb a better send aff, but we ha'e tae eat an' there's jist nae enough pennies....'

When he laid the basket of goods on the table and told his brother and sisters the good news, his mother withdrew to her bed again.

They ignored her.

119

This was a good day and nothing was going to spoil it.

Her wild tantrums and weeping since the purse was denied to her, had forced them to allow her a few pennies each day to spend as she pleased. They knew full well that she was straight down to the grog shop with it, but at least they were spared the dreadful rages and moaning when the cravings for her addiction became overwhelming.

All evening they planned what to do with the extra money. Sarah and Joe both stated that the most important essential thing was for Rosie and Cal to go to school.

'An' if Ah get the job at Braxfield?' Cal asked.

'The schooling is in the evenings, so ye can still attend.' Joe said firmly. 'It's important Cal. Goodness, ye can nae be Heid Groundsman at the Judge's hoose an no' ken how tae read an' write.'

The idea appealed to Cal and he gave one of his rare smiles, his eyes lighting up. It completely changed his usually glum face.

'Ye've kept that hidden! Ye should dae it mair often!' Sarah said, laughing.

'Dae whit?'

'Smile! Yer a bonny lad but Ah never noticed it afore!'

His scowl returned, but the corners of his mouth curved despite his best efforts. 'Och, away wi' ye!' he muttered, turning his attention to the six piles of coins on the table.

Although the Scotts were unable to read, they could all count money. Each pile represented an expense the family had to meet before anything else was spent; rent, food, candles, whale oil, coal. The last pile represented their surprise weekly windfall.

'Ah need new winter boots,' pleaded Rosie.

'We all need new blankets,' said Sarah. 'We have turned and darned these until they're as thin as spiders' webs.'

'A new cookin' pot?' Rosie again. ' Ah'm fed up wi' havin' tae mind where the hole is afore Ah pour from it. Ah had porridge doon ma front one day!'

Joe placed the spare money in a rag and tied it up. 'First we find oot how much the lesson books are, then we'll get all these things bit by bit!'

'Can ma boots be first,' Rosie said. 'the sole's away frae the toe an' Ah keep catchin' it an' trippin'.'

'Ah dare say they can.' Joe patted her on the head as he passed.

He had other plans for his share of the money and they involved Fiona.

They had taken to meeting almost every day after work. These shared moments were fleeting, only a few minutes at a time, but they meant the world to both of them. They spoke of nothing and everything, intensely interested in the tiniest snippet of the other's life, holding hands and drinking in the sight of their beloved. He told her of his new apprenticeship, the skills he was learning, the way his master would talk to the men, any funny incident or dramas that might have happened during the day.

Fiona had tales of her lessons, the new teachers instructing them in art and music and the poetry she was reading. She would bring him pictures she drew and sing short verses of songs in her soft, highland way that made him yearn to take her in his arms.

He loved her more than he had known was possible. Before meeting Fiona, on the few occasions he was drawn to a girl, he would find her looks appealing, enjoy a flirtation and then lose interest. The lassies in the inn were different. They were there to have fun and although they were bonny enough, in their rough, loud way, they were as sweet and easy with all the lads as they were with him.

He wanted Fiona all to himself, as his lass, his special lass. More and more he wanted to be with her alone, away from prying eyes, where he could tell her and show her how much she meant to him.

If Fiona's father was alive he would already have asked his permission to marry her but, because of her position in the mills, he knew he would need to speak with McCulloch or possibly James Dale. His lack of finances was all that was holding him back, so now, he thought, the time had come when he should ask to see the manager.

However, it was Cal who spoke to McCulloch first.

'So, you are now thirteen years of age and you have taken a fancy to leave Mr Dale's employment and seek new employment on Lord Braxfield's estate? Is that so?'

McCulloch looked the boy over with apathetic eyes. He was used to these puny youngsters believing they were man enough to take on hard physical labour. They would knock on his door and ask to be released from their contracts.

'Yes sir.'

'Does mill life not suit you?' there was a sarcastic ring to his words.

'No sir.'

'And you would rather brush up leaves and dig soil, would you?'

'Yes sir.'

'You don't want to be a weaver then, I take it?'

'No sir.'

The manager walked over to a cabinet and pulled out a drawer to produce a ledger.

'1788, October... yes, Calum Scott.' he laid the book on the desk and pointed to an entry. 'What do you see there?'

'Ah can nae read...'

'There, boy, there... that mark on the paper...' he placed his finger at an exact point on the sheet.

'Ah see a ... mark? Sir.'

'And you put it there, did you not? Three years and three weeks ago.' He closed the ledger and replaced it in the cabinet.

'I wish you the best of good fortune following your chosen path. However, you are obliged to wait for another eleven months and one week before leaving New Lanark Mills. Now, hurry back to whence you came, you have wasted my time long enough.'

Calum was furious.

He ran from the office, now situated at the side of James Kelly's house, and turned up the hill, away from the mills. Anger blinded him and he kept running until his chest was bursting. Only then did he realise that he was beside the grave yard.

It was spitting with rain, gusts of wind shuffling the fallen leaves and rattling the bare branches of the beech saplings.

He went to Meg's grave, marked by a wooden cross, and perched on the headstone beside it. Slowly the rage seeped away. He turned his face to feel raindrops, like pin pricks, landing on his skin, and breathed deeply of the pure, fresh air.

Nature's scents of earth and grass soothed his disappointment and his attention turned away from the turmoil in his soul, distracted by movement in the top of a tree. The slope was so steep that he was at the same level as the upper branches of a stand of mature oaks. His eye had been caught by the brilliant red flash of a squirrel foraging in the bundled twigs of a rook's nest. He followed its quick, quirky antics, watching its agile paws clinging to the bark as it swung, upside down, along the tree's drooping limbs.

The longer he sat still, the more he saw. Field mice running by his feet, making tunnels in the dying, collapsed yellow grass, a flock of long-tailed tits swooping among the bushes; everywhere he looked, there was activity. A large black beetle tottered clumsily along the base of the gravestone he was sitting on and, on reaching the obstacle of his boot, made a difficult, exploring detour before resuming its path.

It seemed no time at all before the sound of the mill bell wrenched him back into himself.

He was cold to the bone. His legs, bare below his breeches, were blue. For a while longer he debated whether to go home, crawl into bed and say he was struck down with the pox. There were many workers off from work, struck down by a lurgy that was sweeping through the village. Much of the illness was temporary, mild discomfort, but a boy, recently arrived from Glasgow Town Hospital, was suffering from the pox.

When the diagnosis was confirmed, a shiver of panic ran through the locals. They all knew Mrs Dale and her son were among hundreds who had died of smallpox in the city and it was feared that this incomer would spread the disease to Clydesdale.

Cal thought better of pleading sickness. His wages would be docked and that would affect them all.

On cold unsteady legs, he stumbled down the hill, too late to eat the midday meal, but in time to be in his place beside the loom before the bell called everyone back to work.

'Tis less than a year to wait,' Sarah said, when he told her of his meeting with McCulloch. 'It will pass, all things pass,' she sighed wistfully, 'even those things ye want tae hang on tae forever.'

Joe's audience with McCulloch went a little better.

School books for Rosie and Cal were affordable and Joe enrolled them straight away. He then broached the subject of wishing to marry Fiona.

McCulloch's expression changed. The request for the younger Scotts to attend school was an admirable one but he could not countenance Fiona being granted permission to marry before the end of her indenture.

Joe pressed on with his argument that she would still carry out her duties in the Mills, but her board and lodging would no longer be a burden on her employer. He would take care of her and she would live with him in Long Row.

McCulloch was adamant. Marriage meant babies and babies meant long absences from work for the mothers. No, permission would not be granted. However, on looking up her records, he noted that she was one of the older orphans brought from Glasgow. Her period of apprenticeship was therefore for a shorter term than the standard seven years demanded of the very young: she was bound to the mill for four years.

This information gave Joe hope and he returned to work with a quiet smile of satisfaction on his face. He now had a date for her freedom, coincidentally the same as his brother and sisters.

Joe gave her the good news that evening, but told her in a way that made it seem he had found out by chance that her apprenticeship ended earlier than she thought. He wanted to ask her to marry him, but such an exceptional question could not be put to her in a few snatched moments sheltering from November's icy gusts in a doorway.

They both thought it miraculous that they had arrived in the village in the same week. It was an omen, Joe declared, and then spent the remainder of their short tryst explaining what he meant by an omen.

'I have tae go...' Fiona whispered, knowing she had already stayed too long.

He leaned towards her to put his arm around her shoulders, shielding her from the rain. She raised her face to his, her lips parted to say goodbye but the words were never uttered. He kissed her, tentatively and softly, then pulled her close against him in a tender embrace.

***

The knock on the door came as the Scotts were finishing their meal.

They had enjoyed several weeks of good food and were discussing the up-coming Hogmanay ceilidh which the Highlanders were planning for the whole village. Everyone was in good cheer, mopping up their bowls of beef stew with hunks of soft barley bread.

Joe opened the door to a swarthy, bearded man, his hat and cape dusted with snow. There was something familiar about the man, but Joe could not recall where or when they had met.

'Ah've tae collect the money on yer tab.' the man said, gruffly.

Joe smiled politely and started to shut the door. 'Ah dinnae have a tab, yer at the wrang hoose.'

The man rammed his foot against the door jamb, 'Aye, ye have, son. Joe Scott, Long Row. It's eighteen shillings an' threepence.'

'Whit! Ah have nae a debt in the world so away wi' ye and try it on wi' some ither body.'

'If ye cannae pay, we'll tak whit ye have for the noo and come back. There will be interest added, mind.'

Calum left the table to stand behind his brother and at the same time, Ma slipped from her chair and slunk into her bed, drawing the curtain.

'Who are ye?' Joe demanded.

'Rab Cook, Ah've been sent by Billy Struthers, proprietor of the liquor stall in the village.'

'Ye cannae be serious! Ah niver buy frae there! When have Ah ever....' the truth was dawning. 'Ma! Ma!' he shouted, shoving back the curtain and pulling her from the bed.

In a muddle of blankets and petticoats, her cap half off her head, he pushed her towards the door.

'Here she is!' he shouted at the man, aware that Bessie Jackson's door was opening. 'This is the person who owes ye yer mony. Take her!'

He held his mother by the shoulders and gave her another shove towards the door, all the bitterness he felt towards her was pouring out.

'She can clean bottles, scrub buckets...empty yer middens... ' he shouted. 'Ah dinnae care whit ye dae wi' her, but Ah'm no' payin' fer her booze an' ye cannae make me! If yon Struthers is stupit enough tae be duped by this auld woman then hell mend him!'

'Its yer name on the tab, son. Ye have tae pay or ye'll be up in the courts.'

'Ah've niver been near the stall! Ma name ye say... an' whit's tae stop me takin' yer name an' running up debts fer ye? Eh?'

'Ah'll wager Struthers will have witnesses...'

With that there was a cry from Bessie Jackson. She came across the landing like a ferret after a rabbit.

'Fer every paid witness he calls, Joe will have five mair willin' yins to swear he's tellin' the truth. Away frae here, Rab Cook!'

Rab left, hurling abuse at them all the way down the two flights of stairs; the Jacksons and the Scotts returning his threats with gusto. Other neighbours were joining the din, appearing on the landings in night shirts, the women pulling shawls around their undergarments, impatient to see what was happening.

125

They jeered and swore, shaking their fists and mocking his hurried steps, taking the side of the villager against the outsider, without needing to know the facts. Everyone liked the young Scotts and they also knew the old mother was a drunken burden on the family. If there was any trouble from that household, Marie was always at the centre.

When it all calmed down and the Scotts closed their door for the night, the excitement left them drained of energy. They took their seats at the table again to finish the meal, but they ate without relish. Their neighbours could close their doors on the matter, have a laugh at the disturbance and return to their evening. The Scotts had to deal with it.

'There'll be nae mair drinkin' Ma,' Joe said seriously. 'We're a' gettin' on here, life is gaun a'richt fer a change, so be part o' it, dinnae gae aff drinkin' an' causin' bother. There'll be nae mair o' that, do ye understaun' me? Nae mair.'

***

Mrs Margaret Dale and her three elder nieces were in the hallway of the Charlotte Street mansion preparing to go out, when Renwick opened the front door to Laverty.

'Good day, ladies,' he greeted them, noticing that they were all dressed in warm, hooded cloaks, waiting while Giggs knelt to retie the laces on Mary's boots.

Snow had been falling for several hours and Charlotte Street was covered in a dense white blanket. Their carriage was not outside, so he hoped they were not expecting to walk in the icy conditions.

'We are visiting neighbours,' Margaret said, her face partially covered by the fur trimmed hood. 'It is but a minute's walk from here, but the sight of the snow has chilled me before we even step outside!'

'It is indeed very cold!' Laverty smiled, suddenly recognising the lady infront of him. He knew Mr Dale's brother, Hugh, and had been introduced to his wife some years before.

'Mr Dale is with my husband in the drawing room.' Margaret was saying, 'He will not keep you waiting for long. A medallion has been struck of him and the artist is with them now. I have just seen it! Oh it is splendid, a true likeness!' she smiled. 'As you can imagine, my dear brother-in-law is finding the whole procedure faintly ridiculous. I have to say, I think it is a splendid idea!'

'A medallion! How extraordinary! I feel he should also be depicted in oils, his work with the Chamber of Commerce alone should warrant that! Perhaps he can be persuaded to sit for Raeburn?'

'Do not let Mr Tassie hear you!' she laughed, glancing up the stairs in case the artist was approaching. 'Do you know James Tassie's work?'

'Alas, I do not, but I am sure he must be very talented.'

'Please ask to see the medallion, Mr Dale will not originate any display, he would regard that as vanity, but I am sure he would be obliged to show you, if requested?'

'I certainly shall.' He stood aside as the group moved towards the door. 'Good morning to you!' he nodded in an avuncular fashion to each of the girls as they passed. 'Please take care on the snowy steps.'

The Stuart's house was only at the other end of Charlotte Street but by the time they arrived at the door the hems of their skirts were full of snow and their noses pink with cold. They were immediately shown into the smaller of the two drawing rooms where flames blazed valiantly to give a little warmth to the room.

To entertain a relation of David Dale was always an honour and Mrs Stuart glided about the room, ushering them into seats and offering refreshments. A side table was laid with an elegant silver hot chocolate jug and gold rimmed china. Their hostess lifted the lid off an ornate dish and, with a smile of satisfaction at her own thoughtfulness, offered warm toasted muffins to accompany their drink.

The conversation was dominated by the sad news that the brilliant young Viennese composer, Amadeus Mozart, had died. The Stuarts had travelled to Vienna only a year or so before and been ecstatic in their praise for his work. By the concerned, almost grieving manner in which Mrs Stuart spoke of the poor man, had Margaret not known better, she would have thought him to have been a close, personal friend.

'A tragic loss!' cried Mrs Stuart. 'The papers say he swelled up so much he could not move! Poor soul, just reaching the peak of his success... and he leaves a family...'

127

While her aunt talked and sipped hot chocolate with their hostess by the fire, Anne Caroline and her sisters clustered around the pianoforte with the Stuart girls. May and Lizzie were older than Anne Caroline but their age difference seemed less of an obstacle to their friendship now that they were all growing up.

In two day's time the Dales were throwing a reception for Hogmanay and it was thought a nice idea to have the children sing for them during the evening. Anne Caroline and Jean had no qualms about the event and were looking forward to it but Mary, at four years old, was nervous and felt sure she would forget her words.

'I am all muddled up!' Mary cried, when she, yet again, sang the wrong lines. 'It's easy with the other songs, they are new to me, but I am so used to Papa singing the old version of Old Lang Syne, that I cannot keep the new words in my head!'

Anne Caroline was losing patience, 'Oh Mary, you know, grandfather is very taken with his poetry and he heard this song last year in Edinburgh. It is not so very different...'

'Yes, it is! The old one goes,' she sang fluently, 'Should auld acquaintance be forgot, and never thought upon...' then turning to her sister, 'and Mr Burns writes "Should auld acquaintance be forgot, and *never brought to mind* ?"'

'Well, it is very similar, so why can you not remember it?'

'Because it is *so* similar! The verses that are different are easy but the chorus used to be,' she burst into song again, spitting out the words, ' "On old long syne my Jo, in old long syne, That thou canst never once reflect, on old long syne." and *now* I have to remember it's "For auld lang syne, my jo, for auld lang syne, we'll tak a cup o' kindness yet, for auld lang syne!"'

Her outraged little face made the others burst out laughing. Margaret listened to the repeated attempts to master the song and hoped the next few days would go smoothly.

The children's grandparents were travelling over from Edinburgh to spend New Year with them and over thirty guests were invited to the celebrations over the Bells. The party was supposed to help the whole family through their first celebrations after losing Carolina, but Margaret was already so fatigued with plans and lists and menus that she almost wished she had never suggested it.

Chapter Four

*'What is our life? It is even as a vapour that continueth a little
and then vanisheth away'*
David Dale
(letter to his father, after his daughter, Katherine, died, 1783)

'Ony meenit the noo...' Johnnie Logan cried out, his eye on his prize
possession, his pocket watch.

It had been a present to his father, fifteen years before, when he
went to the aid of a lady whose chaise and four over-turned on the
winding Hamilton road.

Few details were known of the incident, except that her grateful
husband rewarded Johnnie's father by giving him the beautiful time
piece. When Johnnie inherited it, he prided himself on keeping his
watch set to the right time, checking it against the Lanark clocks
every week. Unfortunately, it had a habit of running slow, so to be
sure of the exact moment of the birth of the New Year, Johnnie, one
of the oldest residents of New Lanark, had made a special trip up the
hill that day to make sure it was accurate.

'There!' He shouted, as the mill bell pealed the end of the day. 'Noo
we can a' enjoy oorsels!'

In his mustard coloured jacket, tall hat and red trousers, his bent
figure was a splash of colour against the snowy background.

He was standing beside a huge unlit bonfire set on a space above the
mill-lade. Although he was taking his role of time keeper very
seriously, his part in the evening was not strictly necessary. The
chimes from Lanark would be heard quite clearly in the valley but no-
one was going to point that out to the old man.

129

For days the villagers gathered fallen branches, old furniture, broken wheel spokes, anything that was flammable, and piled it on the fire. The whole operation was overseen by Big Lachie, Lachlan Macinnes, one of the new Highlanders. The Macinnes family ran to more than thirty in number, covering several generations, and Big Lachie was the self imposed head of the family.

When he first arrived he antagonised many of the men he encountered. At six foot four with long hair, a wild curly black beard and bushy eyebrows, his swaggering, belligerent manner caused contempt, and on a couple of occasions, bare knuckle fights.

However, like a stag who has secured his reputation and warned off any contenders, he settled down and set about making friends. A blacksmith by trade, his skills as much as his sense of humour soon earned him respect from the mill wrights and mechanics.

There was only one problem with Big Lachie, he was a Gaelic speaker and barely knew a word of Scots.

To mark the end of the old year and a clean, fresh start to the new, the Hogmanay ceilidh was welcomed by almost every resident. Flora's father and other strict Kirk goers renounced the celebrations as pagan rituals and would not take any part in them. Forbidding their children to leave the house, they would shutter the windows and pray for the souls of the heathens.

Clydesdale's snow covered hills and valleys shimmered like silver beneath a clear, star laden sky. The new moon, just a slender glowing crescent hanging amid glittering space, cast an eerily bright light across the icy landscape.

Paths were cleared for the horses and wagons, but the rest of the ground was carpeted with nearly a foot of snow. As soon as they were released from the mills, the village children, only clothed in light garments suitable for the humid work rooms, rushed to their homes for warm jackets and shawls. Moments later, they scampered out again to meet up and play in the frosty moonlight.

Hogmanay was always a great event but this year in New Lanark it was special. In the village's first, fledgling years, the residents either carried out small, family festivities or walked up the hill to join in with the entertainment in Lanark.

Now the community was large enough to start its own celebrations and Big Lachie seized on this with zeal.

To pass the Winter Solstice without being allowed to mark it with a festival was abhorrent to the Highlanders so they postponed their merrymaking on the twenty-first of December and transferred them to the New Year holiday.

McCulloch, deeply prejudiced against pagan practices, was fervent in his demands to his senior managers to ban the ceilidh and the proposed bonfire. However, he was over-ridden by both James Dale and Kelly.

So long as the fire was situated in a safe place, they thought it was preferable to keep the likes of the Macinnes clan content, rather than create animosity. The awful stories coming out of France were examples of the mayhem that could ensue if the lower classes were oppressed. There was also the Irish contingent to consider, around forty new employees at New Lanark, as a direct result of the troubles in their homeland: they too had sent representations to McCulloch requesting the ceilidh to take place.

In his own small way, James Dale did not wish to appear like a dictator over his domain. The community worked well together despite their different backgrounds and both he and his brother were of the mind that tolerance should be shown to foreign customs and beliefs.

The ceilidh was allowed to take place.

While children gambolled in the snow, pelting each other with snowballs, Big Lachie lit a flaming torch and set fire to the bonfire. A rousing cheer went through the gathering crowds, people running in and out their houses bringing food and drink, tables, presents and even chairs for the infirm. Many of the villagers owned musical instruments and soon there was a lively party atmosphere with singing and couples jigging and reeling.

Inside Mill Four, Fiona endured a full evening of classes and prayers. The orphans were not allowed to join the ceilidh. This, however, did not stop Fiona from telling Joe that she would meet him at the fireside.

'Ah will wait fer ye by the lade,' he told her as they parted earlier in the evening.

'T'will be late, Joe. You go an' be at the fire. Ah will find ye.'

He was doubtful, but she managed to persuade him. How could she tell him that she was not even sure if she could find a way of slipping out of the mill?

Long after everyone else was sleeping, she dressed and, carrying her clogs, tip toed to the dormitory door and put her ear against it. There had been no sounds for some time but two of the girls were ill and sleeping in a side room, causing Mrs Docherty and another woman to attend to them later than usual.

When she was sure there was no one around she lifted the latch. It clicked noisily in the silence and a girl in the end bed sat up, propping herself on her elbow. It was Susan.

A difficult truce had been formed between the two girls but they still harboured resentments towards one another. Fiona was annoyed that, of all the girls, it was Susan who saw her sneaking out.

'Whit ye doin'?' Susan whispered.

'Wheesht! None o' yer business!' Fiona hissed back.

'Yer goin' tae the ceilidh?'

Fiona pulled the door a little way open, the hallway was empty, lit by a candle near the sick room door. She was just drawing the door closed behind her when it was jerked from her hand.

It was Susan.

'Mrs Docherty!' Susan called. 'Mrs Docherty! Ah'm no weel!'

Fiona shot the girl a look of hatred and ran towards the stairwell, but before she could reach the top step she was caught in the beam of light from Mrs Docherty's opening door.

There was no point in Fiona denying her intentions, it was clear to see that she was dressed to go out, so she took the telling off and, murmuring apologies, turned to go back to her bed.

'I shall deal with you in the morning!' Mrs Docherty finished off in exasperation, turning to Susan. 'Now, whit's wrang wi' you?'

Fiona called over her shoulder, 'She wis taken bad, very poorly. Ah had tae clear up. Ah think she's taken whit Morag has...'

Mrs Docherty heaved a sigh. 'Come on then, let me dose you with that medicine the medic gave Morag, an' put you in the sick room. I hope this is not going to spread to any more of you.'

Fiona lay down on the top of her blankets, trying not to disturb Morvern who shared her bed, although several girls had been woken with the raised voices.

She had no idea what the time was and lay gazing up at the rafters, illuminated by pale blue moonlight. After some coming and going on the landing, it all went quiet again. She counted to twenty. Still no sound.

Carrying her clogs, she hurried to the door, out onto the hallway and then running, whirling round the corners, she descended the six flights of stairs and let herself out into the starry night.

132

'Fiona!' Joe pushed his way through the crowd towards her, catching her hands and twirling her round. 'Jist in time! Tis nearly midnight!'

'Ah'm here!' she laughed, feeling the exciting rush of delight the sight of him always evoked.

The crackling flames and loud fiddle music were deafening. All around them people were clapping with the music, dancing and spinning their partners, shouting to one another, clutching protectively at their tankards and food as children dodged and weaved between them, spilling ale and sending pies into the air.

Marie Scott moved around the shadowy edges, her steps unsteady, her hands shaking. Here and there, set down in the thick snow, were half filled tankards, put aside while their owners danced. The opportunity was ripe for the taking and she sipped a little from each as she made her way round the bonfire.

Joe drew Fiona away from the mob, clasping her hand fiercely.

'Ah want tae ask ye summat? An' Ah can barely hear mesel' think!' He grinned down at her.

She was so beautiful, he thought, standing in her cotton work dress with an old brown shawl around her shoulders. Her eyes were scanning over his face, reading his expression, trying to anticipate what he was going to say.

The music stopped and Big Lachie jumped up on to the make shift stage, a mound of snow cleared from around the fire, and held his hands above his head. Beside him, Johnnie Logan was peering into his watch.

'Fiona,' Joe swallowed hard, 'Ah ha'e never known such a bonny lass, wi' such a spirit and heart tae her as ye possess. Ah've loved ye since Ah first laid eyes on ye, an' would care fer ye and strive tae dae the best fer ye as lang as Ah draw breath. Ah knaw ye'll no' be free 'til the autumn, but, then, will ye be wi' me, as ma wife? Will ye marry me, Fiona?'

'Oh Aye, Joe... Oh Joe... *Tha gaol agam ort!'* She reached up and caressed his cheek, 'I love you.'

'Now!' shouted Johnnie. 'A Guid New Year tae us all!'

Lanark's church bells sounded through the still white landscape, Big Lachie roared out *'bliadhna mhath ùr* and the crowd erupted with cheers and whistles.

Amid the uproar of everyone turning to those around them, known and unknown, kissing and hugging and wishing each other good fortune in the year ahead, few noticed the rapturous embrace between Joe and Fiona.

The musicians struck up again and groups formed into ragged lines to dance in the warmth of the red waves of fire light.

When Joe and Fiona made their way back to the crowd, Sarah came rushing up to them. On hearing their news, she pulled Fiona into her arms and held her with all the fervour of a long lost sister.

'Ah am that happy fer ye both!' she stammered, tears coursing down her cheeks. 'Och, that's jist grand news!'

Cal and Rosie joined them and were as thrilled as their sister to hear of their betrothal.

'Wait here an' Ah'll fetch some ale!' Joe shouted, 'Dinnae move! Ah'll be richt back!'

On the other side of the bonfire, the Macinnes family were in high spirits. Big Lachie produced a ball of leather, soaked in paraffin, and tied to a length of chain. He lit it from the fire and, moving to an open space, whirled it around his head and body in fantastical arcs and circles. The light seemed to leave trails in the air, describing wheels and stars in the darkness, a stream of sparks flying in its wake.

His son Kyle, hot from throwing himself into the rhythm, laid down his fiddle on the makeshift table and admired his father's display. His attention was quickly diverted to two girls standing swaying and dancing together to the music, a boy at their side. The fair haired girl was pretty enough, but the other one was mesmerising. Her clouds of dark hair swung as she danced, her vivacious, expressive face was alive with a radiant smile.

He was drawn to her instantly and made his way through the revellers to where she stood. Why had he not seen her before? Was she just visiting for the ceilidh? A new tune was starting up, he would ask her to dance with him.

'*A bheil sibh 'g iarraidh a dhanns?*' he asked.

Fiona was caught by surprise by the Gaelic stranger.

'*Thank you,*' she replied politely in her native tongue, '*but, no.*' She softened the refusal with a smile.

The young man took the rejection well, nodding to her and returning the smile. He had curiously light grey eyes, she noticed, unexpected and arresting between thick black lashes.

He moved away but glanced back to catch her still looking at him.

She dropped her gaze immediately and resumed her dance with Sarah and Calum. He was a handsome man, older than Joe and more

134

slightly built. In another life she might have been interested to accept his invitation, but not now. Not with Joe in her life. No man could ever compare to her Joe.

Her heart leapt with happiness; she was going to be Mrs Joseph Scott.

Kyle collected another tankard of ale and watched Fiona from beyond the fire. She was worth another try, he thought, and she was also a Highlander. He sat down beside his cousin.

'Do you know who that girl is over there, the one with the brown shawl?'

'Aye, that's Fiona from Mill Four. She's on the looms.'

'I have never seen her before....'

'She's one of Dale's orphans, they lock them up in the Mill most of the time!'

'Is that right?' Kyle was pleased. So, this lovely lass lived and worked in New Lanark: he would look out for her and watch for a chance to try his luck another time.

* * *

The Dales' New Year's celebrations went very well.

Little Mary remembered all her words, only a few guests were unable to attend because of the heavy snow fall and the food and entertainment were acclaimed by everyone to be the best provided anywhere in the city.

Anne Caroline enjoyed every moment. All the reception rooms in the house were warm and comfortable, having had well stocked fires burning in the grates since dawn. They were scented by winter flowering jasmine, hyacinths and gardenias, specially ordered by her Aunt Margaret months in advance.

Before the guests arrived, the little girl wandered through the high, empty rooms, watching the servants, under Renwick's supervision, perfecting the flower arrangements, stoking fires and replacing spent candles.

She felt wonderfully sophisticated in her new pale pink muslin evening dress. It was of the same design as her aunt's with the exception of the neckline; where her aunt's was cut very low, it was not thought seemly for Anne Caroline at not yet fourteen years old.

So, the seamstress skilfully added a frill of matching lace to cover her modesty. The bodice was drawn into a tight waist with a white sash, flaring out in deeper pink outer skirts which were caught up in flounces, decorated with bows and silk flowers.

Several hours later, when the bells rang out across the city announcing the New Year, she looked around those same rooms, now packed with the cream of Glasgow's high society.

The ladies were bedecked with elaborate wigs, their necks and wrists dripping with jewellery, their faces powdered white, lips painted scarlet. Gowns with yards of silk of every colour, adorned with sequins, sea pearls, feathers and even sprays of real flowers, swayed and bobbed on wide hoops and petticoats. Gentlemen, in brilliant coloured waistcoats, stylish cravats and high, starched white collars, were immaculate in their cut away evening jackets and gleaming buckled boots.

Chatter and laughter blended with music from an accomplished trio performing in the hallway, altogether creating a sea of noise beneath the chandeliers.

It was after one o'clock in the morning before the last of the guests took their leave of the grand Charlotte Street house. Bleary-eyed maids and footmen set to work tidying away the debris and returning the rooms to order. Several of them, having taken too much to drink downstairs, struggled to carry out their duties, shattered by the long day.

Anne Caroline climbed wearily up the stairs with her ears still ringing from the music and excitement. As soon as she reached her bedroom, she wrestled to release the hooks and eyes on her dress. Forgetting to remove her necklace and the velvet ribbons in her hair and abandoning her gown where it dropped, she slid under the blankets beside Jean.

It was all she could do to blow out the candle before closing her eyes and falling into a deep, satisfied sleep.

David Dale changed into his night shirt and took a seat beside the fire in his bedroom. He was very tired but he was also pleased to have hosted a successful evening for which he was grateful to his sister-in-law for organising. A few doors along the corridor, in the largest of the guest bedrooms, the Campbells were hopefully sleeping peacefully. He hoped they were, because he knew Carolina would have wanted them all to be together, as a family, welcoming in the new year.

The last year had been distressing in the extreme.
He closed his eyes and prayed.

***

Ma lay in her bed shaking and shivering and apart from frequent and urgent visits to the closet, dozed and slept for two days.

'Come on, Ma,' Sarah urged, 'Jus' a wee spoonfu'. It's whit ye like... barley an' ham.'

'Ah cannae... tak it awa', the very smell o' it is churning ma belly...'

Sarah stood up from where she had been kneeling by the bed and drew the curtain across. 'Ha'e a sleep, then. Mibbee ye'll feel like it when ye wake.'

'She mus' ha'e eaten summat bad the ither nicht,at the ceilidh,' said Joe.

'Or drunk summat... she wis steamin' when she came in, an' as cold as ice.' Sarah doled out the barley stew for her brothers and sister. 'She's jist caught a chill, tis a'.'

However, the following evening Ma was even worse. Her family came in from work to find her delirious, feebly rolling on her mattress, her cap discarded and the blankets kicked away.

'We'll need tae fetch the medic,' Sarah said quietly, as she and Rosie braced themselves for the task and then stoically changed the bed sheets and started to pull off their mother's soiled clothing.

Joe hurried off to ask Bessie Jackson where to find the nearest physician and Cal, not wanting to stay in the room and see his mother unrobed, grabbed the bucket and ran down to the lade for more water.

It was only as the sisters removed their mother's undergarments that they became alarmed; her skin was yellow. In the dim light of the lamp it had been difficult to see, but on placing it near the bed to wash her, the strange colour of her palor became clear.

'That cannae be richt?' Rosie cried. 'Why's she yella?'

'Ah dinnae ken, but Ah hope Joe finds a doctor soon...'

They wrapped all the washing in a sheet and dragged it, bumping, down the stairs, with Cal behind them, carrying the wash basin and a bucket of water. In the dark, snowy street, with a lantern beside them on the ground, the girls rinsed and then washed the foul linen. It took many refills of water and their brother repeatedly running up and down the stairs bringing boiling water, before the job was done.

They were all worn out and hungry. Lost in their own thoughts, no words were uttered; they knew what they had to do and just carried on until it was done.

As Joe came striding back along the Row with a short, bearded man at his side, Sarah and Rosie were wringing out the last of the sheets. Holding on to an end each, they twisted it over and over until it was so tight it started to bunch up in knots.

'That'll ha'e tae dae...' Sarah said, and with Joe gathering up a frozen, damp bundle as he passed, they started carrying it back upstairs.

The stench of the sick room was still strong and the doctor's first instruction was to open the window.

'She is a drinker,' he stated, 'I've seen her with the O'Donnell women. How long has she been at the liquor?'

'Aye, she drank,' Sarah replied, 'but some while ago she had tae stop, well, more o' less stop.'

The doctor finished his brief examination. 'Your mother has all the signs of liver failure.'

'Whit can be done?' Joe asked.

'When it's gone this far? Nothing can be done, I am sorry to have to tell you. She is gravely ill.'

There was a long pause.

'How lang 'til it passes?' asked Rosie, breathing on her fingers, still frozen from doing the washing.

'It'll no' pass, child,' he rubbed his hand over his beard and then made ready to leave. 'The liver is now so damaged it can no longer function. She will not want to eat but if you can persuade her to drink a little water, it may bring some relief.' He moved to leave the room, eager to depart after giving such bad news, but he stopped at the door, turning to Joe.

'That will be one shilling, sir.'

Joe gave him the coin, 'How... how lang does she ha'e...?'

'I believe that she has less than a week to live.' He looked at the wretched, tired faces of the woman's family, 'My condolences to you all.'

Four dreadful days later, Marie Scott died.

***

Cook sat at the end of the long scrubbed table in the kitchen at Charlotte Street nursing a cup of tea. At the other end of the table, amid bowls, chopping boards, knives and a variety of ingredients, was a lean young woman in a long apron. Her dark hair was covered by a black bonnet which, with her plain, high necked black costume and drawn, frowning face gave a severe appearance.

This woman was the third applicant for the job of housekeeper at the New Lanark cottage. Each of them was given the task of preparing a simple dish for Breen to taste and, in Cook's opinion, they were all useless.

Outside, the rain lashed against the steamy window, inside, the heat was oppressive. It was a late March morning and after a few mild, spring-like days, a long spell of wet weather was soaking the west coast of Scotland.

The clock above the dresser showed Cook that the woman had only fifteen minutes left to complete the custard for her dessert, set the tray to be presented to the housekeeper and serve up the meal.

Toshie came into the room and, taking a cup from the dresser, sat down beside Cook. She poured herself a cup of tea and enquired how the preparations were proceeding for the formal dinner that evening.

'Och, Ah'm aboot ready wi' most o' it, if yon new lad brings me the last order from the dairy. Ah could be doin' wi' ma kitchen back,' she nodded towards the end of the table. 'This yin's takin' her time.'

Toshie felt Cook's attitude was unhelpful and would not be drawn into conspiring with her against the obviously nervous woman, sweat beading on her brow, struggling to do her best.

At last, the lamb and prune dish was ready to be served along with a close-textured sponge and custard. The hopeful young cook carefully wiped the rims of the plates, covered them with pre-warmed lids and set off towards Breen's study.

Removing the cover from the savoury dish, Breen surveyed it. The previous two cooks had been very disappointing, so she hoped to be pleasantly surprised. This one, Mrs Cooper, a widow with no children, came with good references and had only left her previous employment because the family was leaving for the West Indies.

To her relief, the casserole tasted delicious. The meat was soft and the prunes still held their shape, yet the carrots and other vegetables

139

were all well cooked. This was a favourite dish of her employer and the other cooks had served up hard carrots, tough lamb and the prunes were so over cooked they had dissolved into the gravy.

The sponge proved to be firm but light, the egg custard, smooth and delicately flavoured with vanilla. Mrs Cooper was called back into the room and her position confirmed.

They had found their new housekeeper and cook for New Lanark.

When the rains passed and milder, sunny weather bathed the country, nature took advantage of the conditions. Winter's monotone palette was swept aside, out with the greys and browns and in with pinks, purples, vibrant greens and yellows. Buds swelled on the trees and burst into leaf, bees buzzed between the early flowers and soon froths of pink and white blossom were blooming.

On a bright, warm day in late spring, Dale welcomed his family back to their house in New Lanark. He had not seen them for nearly two weeks and despite Anne Caroline pleading to accompany him, he had travelled alone, apart from his valet, to Ayrshire and then to Lanark.

In Ayrshire, he spent a few nights with his father in Stewarton before travelling on to visit the Catrine Mills. Once again, he stayed at Ballochmyle House as Alexander's guest and was very impressed with the progress he found in the village.

The second cotton mill was now in production, with another seventy or more spinning jennies, as well as the Corn mill, a brewery, stores for general goods and an inn. A new fire engine, personally ordered and paid for by Dale,was inspected and discussed. After the terrible fire at New Lanark, Dale felt it was money well spent although both gentlemen hoped it would never be needed.

Then he walked with Alexander to see the small holdings, allotments, he leased to the workers so they could grow their own fresh produce and finished the tour by calling in at the school.

Catrine, although smaller, was now as much a community as New Lanark. Yet only seven years before, neither had existed. Dale was filled with a pleasant satisfaction that he had been able to provide so many people with employment and, in so doing, give them better lives.

From Catrine he went to New Lanark.

Mrs Cooper, still rather solemn and reticent in her manner, had kept the house aired and comfortable. In the days before his children arrived, she provided him with excellent meals and seemed to accommodate the presence of Duncan, the valet, in a businesslike fashion.

Since her appointment, she hired a local girl as her maid and between them Dale felt the house was more comfortable than when his girls last visited.

So, when his carriage returned from Glasgow with his daughters, he was looking forward to giving them a lovely holiday in the country.

It did not take long to settle into routines of walks, meals and visiting local houses and the children especially enjoyed being outside in the fresh air.

One day Anne Caroline took a book to read while sitting on a blanket on the grass in front of the house. It was hot and the sun so glaring that she had to raise her parasol to shade the pages. She became engrossed in the romantic story, accompanied by only the gentle ripple of the mill lade and an occasional rustle from the breeze stirring the heavy foliage of a nearby chestnut tree. When the bell rang out, she jumped so violently her book slipped from her hand.

It was time for the middle of the day meal for the workers.

Within moments of the bell's chimes, the doors opened and hordes of people swarmed out, each set on their own determined course. Anne Caroline had seen this scene many times before and, not wanting to appear as if she was staring, slightly lowered her parasol and feigned reading again. She found the villagers extraordinary, all of them, from the tiny children, younger than Mary, to older men and women. In particular she was fascinated by the orphans who were under her father's care.

The orphan apprentices, boys and girls alike, were all dressed in white cotton tunics, and they made their own line through the throng, barefoot, directly towards the door of Mill Four.

Just before she reached the steps, an older girl, a long dark plait down her back, was approached by a young man.

Anne Caroline couldn't resist wondering if they were sweethearts. Her novel described such romantic exchanges, chance meetings between the beautiful girl and her dashing young man. The mill girl was certainly pretty and the young man? Oh yes, Anne Caroline smiled to herself, he was indeed very good-looking. His black hair was tied back in a ribbon and the loose blue shirt, tucked into breeches, showed him to be slim and strong.

141

The couple were talking earnestly; the girl using her hands in emphatic gestures, the man laughing and, hands on his hips, tilting his head to one side with a cajoling, appeasing look on his face.

Anne Caroline wished she could hear what they were saying, was it a lover's quarrel? It was wrong to eavesdrop, she knew she should not even be watching them so closely but she could not bring herself to stop.

Then the girl, catching up her skirts, ran up the steps and into the mill. The young man turned and leaned on the railings beside the lade, gazing into the slow moving water. His expression could not be read, but Anne Caroline felt that the pair had parted unhappily.

She returned to her book, where the heroine was undergoing her own misunderstandings with a bold young soldier. Sighing, she wondered if there was a man who, right at this very moment, was enjoying the sunshine as she was and would come into her life and make her heart sing.

The following day brought more sunshine and blue skies and Anne Caroline positioned herself in the garden with her book, hoping to see her sweethearts again. She was quickly rewarded with the sight of the black-haired man strolling slowly to and fro beside the mill lade. It was just before the meal-time bell, so, anticipating the forthcoming liaison, Anne Caroline kept a watch for the girl.

She was not the only person observing Kyle Macinnes.

Joe was working with a group of stonemasons further up the hill. They were preparing the lintels for the new row of tenements, hot dusty work. It usually held his attention and he enjoyed handling the stone and the camaraderie of his workmates. However, the previous evening, Fiona told him of the Highlander's advances. She wanted nothing to do with Kyle Macinnes, she said, and she assured him that she had told him as much to his face.

Now, Joe watched as Kyle waited for her outside the mill door. A nasty shiver of jealousy chilled him despite the heat of the day. Kyle was older than he was, better paid and, the one aspect he was most threatened by, he was a Highlander. Among the village it was often said that Highlanders only bred with other Highlanders: 'craws nest wi' corbies'.

Fiona came hurrying out with the other workers and Kyle slipped easily into step beside her, talking animatedly, never taking his eyes off her.

Joe dropped his tools into the basket and stood up.

142

'Oi, Joe!' called the foreman. 'It's no' break time the noo. We need twa mair o' these done afore we stoap.'

'Ah ha'e tae see tae summat...'

'No' in ma time ye dinnae.' There was a hard edge to his voice. 'Get that stane feenished an' then ye can see tae yer business.'

Fighting back a defiant reply, Joe took up his chisel and hammer again, but his attention stayed with Fiona. With her head held high, she did not appear to be saying anything: Kyle was saying a great deal. Only when she swung up onto the steps did he see her face clearly, she was smiling, nodding. Then she disappeared from sight.

Filled with fearsome emotions that seemed to reach down into his stomach, Joe resumed his work. His hands were shaking so violently he could scarcely hold the chisel straight. He could feel his pulse racing, his heart thumping.

As soon as he was free to take a break, he stationed himself at the head of The Row and waited for Kyle to pass on his way back to work.

'Kyle Macinnes!' he shouted, when the man came into view.

For a moment Kyle faltered, in front of him was a powerfully built man with a fierce glint in his eyes. He noted the aggressive stand, the balled fists and in a flash thought of the money he won at the gaming table the night before, the angry squabble and threats as he was leaving the inn....

In a reflex action born out of a life of fighting for survival, he swung a blow at Joe. It caught him on the temple and sent him flying off balance, staggering backwards and falling to the ground. Shaking his head and blinking hard to clear the dizziness, Joe launched himself up and straight at Kyle.

It was an evenly matched fight; Joe was taller and stronger but Kyle was an experienced fighter, taught by his father and as agile as a fox.

The commotion, taking place in the stream of people returning to work, brought villagers running to the scene. Sarah was passing by, averting her eyes from the brawl. Clashes among the men were common place, though usually after dark when drink had been taken.

Suddenly, she realised that it was her brother who was flailing around on the cobbled street.

'Stop them!' she screamed, seeing blood on Joe's face. She grabbed hold of Bessie Jackson's eldest boy, a huge lad. 'Get in there ye big lummock an' break it up! Whit ye gawping fer! They'll kill each ither!'

143

The lad just pushed past her to head down to the mills.

Throwing punches and wrestling each other to the ground, first Joe and then Kyle was on top. The tussle went on and on, falling and scrambling back to their feet, breathless and pausing for a few gasping seconds before piling back into one another, blow matching blow.

At last they came to a halt, six feet apart, arms hanging loosely at their sides, chests heaving. Kyle's long hair hung across his face as he assessed his opponent.

'Leave ... ma lass... alone...' Joe said, hoarsely.

He still had a poor understanding of Scots but Kyle knew enough to grasp what he was being told. So, that was what this was all about.

'Fiona? Ah have!'

'Ye have no'! Ah saw ye, mon! Talkin' wi her... no' half an hour ago!'

Kyle gulped for breath and swallowed. 'Aye... Ah wis tellin' her ...' he searched for the words, 'wishin' her well. She telt me... a day past, tha' she's tae wed.' He looked Joe up and down. 'Ah tak it yer the man she's tae wed. Guid on ye.'

'So... why did ye hit me?' Joe asked, still suspicious.

'Ah did nae knaw ye... ye looked awfy mad...Ah thocht...' Kyle broke into Gaelic. '*I thought you were here to take revenge for my winnings at the card game,*' he shrugged, struggling for the words in Scots and giving up. 'Twas summat else.'

A smile spread on Joe's face, 'Ye mean Ah've bust ma heid an' ripped ma troosers fer nuchin'?'

The street was empty, only Sarah standing with them, hopping from foot to foot, late for work but anxious for her brother. Now she started to giggle. The men glanced at her, suddenly aware of their situation.

Kyle nodded, starting to chuckle.

He raised his right hand, bloody and awkward. 'An' Ah've broke ma haun... fer tryin' tae be polite tae yer lass!'

Sarah's giggles were infectious. The animosity and tension diffused into the fresh spring air and they stood in the sunshine holding their sore sides and laughing at the absurdity of it all.

From the garden, Anne Caroline saw and heard only the start of the incident. Giggs, who had noticed the disturbance from an upstairs window, called her into the house but not before the first blows were struck.

Witnessing the raw, brutal fight unnerved the little girl. She had never been exposed to such violence and was horrified by the blood, the awful sounds when their fists made contact and their heavy bodies smacking on to the ground. It all happened so fast, bringing a harsh, bitter reality to the centre of the tranquil village.

Her romantic notion of the love-lorn young Highlander was shattered by this display of animal aggression. It was he who leapt forward and caught the other man with a terrible blow to his head.

She hoped she would never see such a spectacle again, but her mind kept returning to the subject, wondering what had caused the ferocious scene, were the two men fighting over the mill girl? If so, who had won? She determined to ask God to take care of them, all three of them, and bring about a solution which He, in his wisdom, would know to be the right one.

She would also pray for their forgiveness because, whoever was right or wrong, blood was spilt and injuries sustained: they had sinned.

News of the fight spread through the mills and came to Fiona's ears a few hours later. When she met Joe that evening she was appalled at his injuries, but before he would tell her anything, he demanded to know what passed between her and Kyle that afternoon.

Everything she told him confirmed Kyle's honesty. Following his overly persistent requests for her to be with him and her escalating annoyance and rebuttal, he came back that afternoon to make peace. As fellow Highlanders in the same Lowland village, he did not want her to bear him any ill will or have a lingering air of bad feeling between them, should they meet in the street.

Fiona chose not to tell Joe of Kyle's admitted regrets that he wished they had met earlier, when perhaps he could have won her heart before she was betrothed.

'He is no' a bad man, Joe, an' Ah cannae choose who taks a likin' fer me, so dinnae gae tryin' tae kill ony ither man who looks at me!'

Joe kissed her and then related the sequence of events, from his side, which led to the fight.

Watching her lovely face, he knew he had been a fool to behave so rashly but he also knew that his passionate feelings were so intense that he could not swear he would not be driven to do it again.

He longed for October, then she would be free and they could declare to the world that they were joined together in this life, as man and wife. Only five months to wait, God willing.

Their time together was always too brief but on that day especially, Fiona's hand gripped his tightly until the last possible moment, her eyes imploring him for one more kiss, one more whispered endearment.

He walked laboriously back home, his body aching from the beating and his head filled with images from the fight, snatches of Fiona's reassuring words.

'Are you all right?'

He looked out from his thoughts and directly into the eyes of David Dale's eldest daughter.

Immediately, he bowed his head, touching his forehead reverently. 'Aye, thank ye, Miss Dale.'

'I saw you fighting. Earlier.' She was on the grassy slope below her house and approached him with a concerned frown puckering her brow. Everything about her was spotless and shining, from the immaculate white frills of her skirt to her gleaming, neatly styled hair. 'Your eye looks very painful, have you been attended by the physician?'

He smiled at her naivety. 'Och, naw, Ah dinnae ha'e need o' a medic.'

Anne Caroline did not look convinced. 'Shall I ask Papa to call one for you?'

'Naw, naw, din nae dae tha' !'

Her deep brown eyes were scrutinising him. 'It was the other man who started the fight, I saw him. If you are worried that my father would berate you for the incident, I will tell him what I saw.'

'He may ha'e thrown the first blow but it wis me who started it. It wis ma mistake.' Joe rushed on, he did not want Mr Dale involved. 'Jist a misunderstandin' on ma part. It's a' done now, over. Ah ha'e no grievance wi' the man.'

Impressed by his honesty, Anne Caroline smiled at him. 'Very well, if you will heal without the attentions of the physician and your misunderstanding is clarified, you will only have God to ask for forgiveness.'

Her father's daughter, Joe thought a little uncharitably, but he bowed his head again, 'That Ah will, thank ye Miss Dale.'

She gave another sunny smile, 'What is your name? If you know who I am, should I not know who you are?'

'Joe Scott.'

'Then, good evening Mr Scott, I hope your eye is better soon.'

'Thank ye, Miss Dale.'

He set off up the hill, aware that she was following his movements. It was kind of her to be interested in his injuries and remarkable that she would speak to him. He recalled how clean she looked in her white skirts and knew Sarah and Rosie would ache for such a dress with colourful embroidery on the bodice. Feeling embarrassed at his dust ridden clothes and grazed, rough hands engrained with dirt, he wished he could provide more for his family.

One day, he thought, one day.

***

'That's the Dales packin' up tae leave,' Sarah said, standing knee deep in the washing tub tramping dirt out of their clothes.

Bessie Jackson sat on the door step, chatting with her. 'How'd ye ken tha'?' Bessie was usually the first with gossip.

'They store the trunks up in Mr Kelly's attic, an' they've jist bin movin' them o'er tae the hoose.'

'Och well, they've bin here a while noo, Ah daresay a gent like Mr Dale misses the city. Ye see the bairns cla'es? The brawest Ah've seen. As bonnie as ye like.'

'That Mrs Cooper is an odd yin, d'ye no' think?' the worst of the grime trodden out, Sarah climbed out the tub and Bessie got up to help her ring them out.

It was a warm, breezy evening and washing was rippling out from lines strung between windows right down the street. Little groups of villagers sat around, taking their chores outside to make the most of the light, enjoying the banter with their neighbours.

Life was easier in the summer months. The tedious working days were not as wearing when you could spend time outside in the fresh air in the long light evenings. Even the chores were less burdensome, laundry dried quickly, coal buckets only needed filling once a day and children could be sent out of the rooms to play.

'Mrs Cooper?' Bessie sniffed. 'She's an awfy douth bissom. Doon in the mooth aboot all an' sundry. Ah din nae ken she'll last here lang. No' through the winter, no' wi' the maister up in toon.'

They emptied the dirty water from the basin and while Sarah went for more water, Bessie climbed the stairs to get their kettles. They had

147

fallen into a routine of helping each other with many of the household tasks and Sarah enjoyed learning tips from the older woman.

These were often simple things. Things her mother should have shown her, like refilling the kettle and setting it to simmer on the fire ready for the rinsing water; it took the dirt out better and was kinder on her feet than plunging into cold water. Or like adding a liberal sprinkling of meadow sweet to the bedding in the summer to give a fresh, soothing scent.

Cal and Rosie were down in Mill Four at their lessons and Joe was up in Lanark with Tam. Sarah hummed as she trudged back up from the lade, a heavy bucket in each hand. Other women were doing the same and they would nod and pass a few words when they met.

After months of feeling guilty, Sarah allowed herself to just enjoy the evening routine. Her guilt was for her mother. With Ma gone, their life had improved in so many ways. After work she felt carefree and relaxed, there was more space in their room, they had a bed each, more money to bring in good food, pay for lessons and put by for treats, no wingeing and snoring from behind the curtains at night.

Ma brought about many of her own sorrows, her life had been blighted by Duncan but the path she chose to escape from dealing with Meg and constant drudgery, was her own path. It had led to her miserable, agonising death. There was nothing Sarah or any of her children could do to help her, more than giving her a home.

A gradual, quiet elation rose through Sarah; she let go of her guilt, released the oppressive weight of memories and regrets and let them flow away from her into the pale blue sky above.

She set the buckets down to rest her arms. The scent of hawthorn blossom was sweet in the air, pigeons cooing among the woods. It was calm, pleasant, snatches of singing and distant fiddle music wafted above the gentle gurgle of the lade's water. Low evening sunshine warmed her back and eased her mind; it had taken many years but she realised this light, comfortable feeling was happiness.

Her mind explored into the usually forbidden territory of her elder brother, as if it couldn't allow her to feel completely at ease.

She would often be reminded of him, wonder what he was doing, but it did not hurt so much nowadays. Sam was a grown man, his destiny was in his own hands and if he wanted to be with them again he would find them. Their old neighbours in Douglas would point him in the direction of New Lanark.

So, if he did not want to be with his family, that was his choice, she could do nothing about it. She picked up the buckets again, humming to herself.

It was a light-hearted tune to match her mood.

Later that evening, by the fireside in his house, David Dale was discussing arrangements for the next day with his half-brother, James, and William Kelly.

James was fourteen years younger than David. They shared the same father but James was the product of their father's second marriage, after David and Hugh's mother died. He was a sensible but fairly ineffectual man and while David wished him well and gave him employment, he rarely left him in charge of New Lanark without William Kelly by his side.

However, while his children and nursery staff would return to Charlotte Street the next day, Dale planned to travel separately to his Blantyre Mills before returning to Glasgow and he wanted Kelly to accompany him. This would necessitate leaving James in sole charge of New Lanark for several days.

Kelly's years of experience with the spinning machines and his skill as a clockmaker had been rewarded by the successful creation of his latest invention. He had cleverly devised a way of improving and altering the designs of Arkwright and Hargreave's jennies to massively increase their productivity. Driven by the ready supply of water, there was need for only one man to operate a machine, spinning more cotton, where several men had previously been required.

The patent for his machine was now granted and he and Dale were enthusiastically promoting and installing them into the other mills.

Dale was justifiably proud of his manager's genius but also relied heavily on him to keep New Lanark at the forefront of cotton production in Scotland. James did not have the same business acumen or drive as William Kelly, but while it would be foreseeable that Kelly would wish to move on to better things, James would be content to see out his days in his current role. He was competent, a member of the family, but not exceptional.

Kelly was exceptional.

Their business discussed, travelling arrangements confirmed, Kelly left to prepare for the morning's departure and James accepted a glass of brandy, settling back into his chair with a slightly perplexed expression on his face.

'I'll be forty years old next year, ye know,' James murmured.

Dale nodded. The subtle crackles and hisses from the low fire in the hearth, together with a rhythmic ticking from the clock, were lulling him into a doze.

'I have been meaning to tell you for some time... er,' James faltered and took another sip of brandy. 'Recently, I've been seeing quite a lot of a sweet girl, Miss Haddow, and I have decided to ask her to marry me.'

Dale was immediately wide awake. 'Why that's excellent news!'

'Never thought I was the marrying kind but... well, I now feel the time has come. Maybe the next time you are down here I can introduce you?'

'I shall look forward to it,' Dale raised his glass. 'Your very good health!'

James smiled warmly, raising his glass. 'When Kelly is back again I shall make a visit to Stewarton and tell the parents.'

'I am sorry to say that our father is looking quite frail these days but is remarkable for his age. I am sure they will be delighted and indeed,' Dale chuckled, 'surprised.'

His personal news delivered, James swallowed the remainder of his brandy and stood up.

'I'd best be off up the hill.' He started to button his jacket in preparation to leave. 'I hope the children enjoy a safe journey back to Glasgow tomorrow and that your visit to Blantyre goes well.'

Dale yawned, relaxing further down into the upholstered chair, his hands clasped across his large stomach. Nowadays, he rarely wore a wig in the country, particularly in summer, and his short grey hair curled on his brow. 'I have been invited to give the sermon there on Sunday, it will be a pleasure.'

'At least it is summer, so I am sure you will be comfortable at Monteith's house.'

They both had memories of a freezing winter night at Blantyre when the two of them had been driven by the discomfort of thin blankets and draughty windows to rise in the night to retrieve jackets and riding capes to spread across the beds.

'It will no' be Ballochmyle, but they are very hospitable. Ye know, James Monteith wishes to buy me out, dissolve the partnership. I have a mind to agree.'

James was surprised. 'I thought you were very satisfied with it?'

'Och, I am! I was full of enthusiasm to create the dyeworks, ye know how I felt about the first one at Barrowfield.'

'Dale's Red...' his brother reminded him of the nick-name for the brilliant red dye.

Dale beamed at him, creasing his double chins, 'The novelty has worn off now, t'will be back to 'turkey red' soon enough. I have Macintosh to thank for all of that, it was fortuitous that he persuaded that Frenchman to provide the formula.' For a moment, his attention went off on a tangent, wondering how the little man, Monsieur Papillon, was faring.

He could see him now, his narrow figure, prominent nose and the peculiar habit he had of polishing his glasses every few minutes. They were partners for a while, then Papillon left to establish his own works not far from Barrowfield, but they had lost touch. At least the Frenchman had not returned to his native land, the news from France was becoming more chilling with every passing week.

He returned to the conversation.

'Well, Monteith knows his own mind and he will continue the work. I have no doubt the mill will do well whether I am there or not. I also trust he will continue to provide for the children, I feel a responsibility for them. Their welfare is of great importance.'

James agreed. 'I'm glad you approve of how we are carrying out your instructions for the children here. You can see for yourself how well fed and full of energy they are, so you need have no qualms about your responsibilities here.'

'Aye, the uptake in schooling is heartening as well. Although the classes are now too large, sixty or seventy children in a group.' he sighed. 'We will hire more teachers. It is the orphans, the paupers, who most concern me, they must be cared for properly. The Lord has seen fit to allow them to be under my roof and I shall endeavour to provide a decent education. These wretched children have no one else to see to them.' He yawned extravagantly. 'At least I can provide a level of teaching which, God willing, they will benefit from and be able to live useful lives when they outgrow the mills. Were they not here, I dare say they would be begging or, in the worst cases, corrupted or already dead.'

Downstairs, Cooper was nursing a cup of lukewarm tea, waiting for the sounds of James Dale's departure. She could barely keep her eyes open but the presence of Duncan, Dale's valet, reading by a lamp at the other end of the table, forced her to stay awake.

151

The front door banged.

'That's Mr James away now...' Duncan snapped shut his book and headed for the stairs; Cooper followed.

Her master was retiring for the night so she hovered near the fireplace, ready to snuff out the lamps.

Just as Dale reached the staircase she ventured, 'I hope you have found everything to your liking here during your stay, sir?'

He turned back to face her.

'We have all had a very pleasant time, thank you, Mrs Cooper.'

The housekeeper was very relieved. Throughout the family's visit she had received no reports or instructions, except from Toshie about the children's routines and food. If there had been a mistress in the house she would have been given far clearer guidance.

Her main concern was with the new maid but she certainly was not going to bother Mr Dale with such a domestic problem. The girl was very lazy and seemed incapable of working without constant supervision. Cooper was also sure she saw her in the street with some young men and her behaviour was loud, to say the least.

With the fires made safe and the lamps extinguished, Cooper made her way wearily up to her attic bedroom.

The family were all leaving the next day so there was just one more final effort to put a good breakfast on the table in the morning and then she could rest.

A strange noise came from outside and she blew out her candle before drawing back the curtain. The road ran right behind the house and there, among the shifting shadows below the banking, was the house maid in the arms of a man.

Aghast, she let the curtain fall closed again.

What if Mr Dale glanced out the window and witnessed this outrageous scene? Such wanton behaviour could not be associated with this house. The girl must leave straight away.

***

It was a dull August day. Below shifting swathes of grey clouds, the Trongate was unusually empty, a few soldiers in their scarlet jackets, some earnest, fast walking clerks going about their errands and a chaise or two. The main activity was from a flapping, strutting crowd

152

of pigeons, scrapping over a pool of spilt oats in the middle of the street.

Inside the Tontine rooms it was lively with discussions on the down turn in trade and the growing unrest which was spreading out of France, across Europe and infecting even Scottish society.

Dale had just chaired a meeting at the Town's Hospital and sipped his glass of claret appreciatively, leaning over the Glasgow Advertiser to read more of the news from France. Things were not looking good. Jacobin masses had stormed the Tuileries Palace, massacring the Swiss Guard, and imprisoning the King. He read the accounts with a heavy heart.

''Afternoon, Bailie Dale!' Macintosh took a seat opposite him, surveying the faces at the nearby tables, nodding and raising his hand in acknowledgement to acquaintances. 'There's no end to the misery coming from France these days, eh?' he added, alluding to the newspaper.

'Such violence...' Dale sat back, pushing the paper to one side, away from his friend's overflowing glass. 'Now they have taken the King prisoner. They don't seem to know which way to turn over there, one minute there are food riots, the next they're invading Austria! There is a growing sympathy in our own land for the rights of the ordinary man, whether it be in France or closer to home. The Duke of Brunswick was calling for allies to invade France, but heaven knows how that would ease its starving people. We can only pray that any dissent against our government remains peaceful.'

'Ah, you mean the 'The Scottish Association of the Friends of the People' that are being advertised. They'll come to nothing, a few radical voices raised after Thomas Paine's publication. It is mainly the Edinbugh papers who are disseminating their ideas. That new Caledonian Chronicle won't last long and I doubt the readers of Tytler's Historical register amount to much.'

'Ye think so?' Dale's expression was grave. 'They have a very eloquent spokesman, a young lawyer, Thomas Muir.'

'The Edinburgh man?'

'He's a Glaswegian, born not far from here. I had occasion to know his parents, but at that time, it must be ten years ago now, he was a fresh faced lad, reading Divinities at the university. His father is a staunch Presbyterian.'

'Are you sure it's the same man? This Muir's a practising lawyer, earning himself quite a reputation for his outspoken conviction that many existing laws are criminally biased against the poor. That doesn't sound like a man of the Church to me.'

'Oh Aye, it's the same man. James Muir, his father, confided in me the disappointment he felt when Thomas changed his studies to follow the teachings of John Millar of Millheugh. He was the Professor of Civil Law up there at the time.'

Macintosh raised his eyebrows, his wig moving back on his head. 'Millar, that Republican Whig! Well, well, young Muir seems to have found his vocation, anyhow.'

'I have followed his progress over the years,' Dale said, thoughtfully. 'For all that he may be voluble on the matter of political reform and cause some headaches, I understand he's acquired a reputation as a man of principle, prepared to take on the most unrewarding and difficult cases and even occasionally foregoing a fee when petitioned by a destitute client. I would say that shows he retains the humility of a man of God.'

'You could well be right.' Macintosh conceded and changed the subject. 'I was sorry to hear of Richard Arkwright's passing. You were still doing business with him, I gather.'

'God rest his soul,' Dale nodded, taking another sip of claret. 'I received the news last week and unfortunately it was too short notice to travel south for his funeral. It was an honour to know him. He is one of our few fellow mill proprietors who grasped the need to provide decent working conditions. Too many look on the basics of good food and education for their employees as a luxury that should be cut from their accounts. Arkwright did not. May the Lord grant him everlasting salvation.'

'He upset a few carts while he walked among us, there's no denying it.'

'Perhaps, however, he also strove to do good in his life, there are many better off and living useful lives because of him. That can only be applauded.'

Macintosh agreed, and called for more wine. 'I hear you are selling Blantyre to Monteith?'

'The deal is done. The mill is his now.' There was a stubborn tenor to his voice.

His friend seized on it. 'So, the rumours are correct? I heard Monteith wanted out of the deal but you would have none of it.'

'We are all businessmen, George. We cannot gauge whether trade will dip or rise, gracious, if we could we would be vacationing with

154

our families, not still meeting with our brokers. Monteith is unhappy by the downturn in the cotton prices at present, however, it is the nature of our business and he will overcome these present difficulties.'

'Or not?'

'We are all in the same boat, are we not? A deal is a deal, and,' Dale gave Macintosh a wry look. 'The deal is done.'

Mcintosh smiled, ruefully. 'For all your philanthropic deeds, you are indeed, first and foremost, a merchant and a banker.'

'I beg to differ, I am a servant of God, in the first place. I am fortunate enough to be given the opportunity to create the means to provide for others. It would be a dereliction of duty to sway from the path, act irrationally out of pity, and put the stability of my own business in danger. I have plans for the capital coming from Blantyre, it will enhance the lives of many. I will not forego my plans.'

'My son has plans, ye know, he is looking to go into partnership with a young gentleman from Ayrshire, Charles Tennant. The man has been working all hours of the day in his bleaching fields but, he's a bit of a scientist and with Charles, my Charles, that is, they seem to think they've found a new method of bleaching cotton.'

'So, your son's finding his chosen path as a chemist rewarding?'

'Only time will tell, it is early days yet.'

Dale chortled, his bulky body shaking, 'In a way Charles has followed your trade, he's in the textile business. While we spin the cotton and dye it, he will be busy bleaching it!'

Macintosh enjoyed the wit but, smiling, said, 'If being closeted in a laboratory is part of the textile trade, then he will be!'

'In this changing world it may well become part of it!'

'By the by, how are the Highlanders down at your mills? I understand you are expecting hundreds more?'

With enthusiasm, Dale told him of the long, curved row of tenements he was having built at New Lanark to accommodate the newcomers. Advertisements were placed across the northernmost burghs and islands urging those who were considering leaving Scotland in search of work, to apply to Dale for employment in his lowland factories. The response was slow, but growing.

'Spinningdale is a little disappointing,' Macintosh told him. 'There is a definite unwillingness to work in a mill. These are folk who tend the land, rise with the sun and retire to their beds when the sun sets. I have heard many men are refusing to let their wives and children take jobs, even though they cannot earn enough to feed them.'

'If we build a place of work, houses and schools, we will pray the Lord will guide them to their shelter. Handing out charity is not the answer for this long term problem, we both know that. When the winter sets in and even those who travelled south to work through the summer have to return to empty tables and mouths to feed, they will see the sense of providing for themselves. We must persevere, my friend, persevere.'

Chapter Five

'... it gives me great pleasure to say, that by proper management and attention, much good instead of evil may be done at cotton mills.'
David Dale

Scotland's temperamental weather brought a sweltering, sun filled week to an abrupt end by dawning cloudy and cool for the Glasgow Fair holiday.

At the top of Mill Four, Fiona stood by the dormitory window and gazed down at the river, watching sand martins swoop and swirl across the water.

It was hard to believe a full year had passed since the wonderful first day she spent with Joe. Now they were to be married. Only two months to go! Every time she thought of it a pang of excitement shot through her, so fierce, it was painful. However, this year she would not be accompanying him to the Lanark celebrations. Mrs Docherty had sternly forbidden a repeat of her previous absence, citing her 'attempted' sojourn to the Hogmanay party as proof that Fiona could not be trusted.

Instead, a compromise was agreed. Mrs Docherty was not an unreasonable woman and with the knowledge that Fiona was to marry a resident in the village, she relented sufficiently to allow her to meet him for an hour while the other apprentices took their exercise and fresh air on the green.

'I shall be watching ye,' Mrs Docherty declared. 'I expect to have ye fully in view the entire time. No wandering off alone with this young man, do ye understand?'

So, within the hour, she would be with Joe again.

When she met him by the mill-lade, Sarah was beside him. Beneath a straw bonnet, liberally decorated with wild flowers, her expression was brimming with anticipation.

'Ah've brought ma measuring tape! Ah thocht Ah could size ye up fae a dress fer yer weddin'.'

'Aw Sarah, how can Ah ha'e a new dress? Ah can wear this?' Fiona held out the skirts of her plain white Sunday dress.

'Aye, weel, its braw enough,' Sarah regarded it critically, narrowing her eyes, 'but ye cannae be merrit in the Mill's cla'es.'

'An whit would Ah buy it wi'? Ah din nae even ha'e a farthing!'

'Och, din nae fash yersel' aboot tha'. Ah'm handy wi' a needle,' she spun round to show off her pretty fitted yellow jacket and matching gathered skirt. 'Ah sewed this, an' it's no' bad. Between us we can afford a few yards o' new cloth.'

She linked her arm in Fiona's and, with Joe on Fiona's other side, the three of them walked to a space on the bank above the lade.

Behind them was the massive, partially constructed new row of tenements; Caithness Row. Joe was keen to point out the stonework he had worked on but he also wished to discuss an idea Tam gave him the day before.

'Ye ken we were to be wed up in Lanark, at St Kentigern?'

'Aye,' Fiona looked at him with dreamy eyes. Joe had told her of how brave William Wallace married his sweetheart among the stone walls of that very church.

'Weel, Ah wis aboot to arrange for the banns to be read, an' Ah thocht, mibbee... shall we ask if Mr Dale would wed us?'

'Where? Here? He can do tha'?'

'Aye, ye recall a couple o' years back, Dale wed the MacCaskies? Tam minded me. Whit d'ye say?'

'Ah say tha' would be grand...' Fiona's face was the picture of adoration as she looked up into his sun bronzed face.

Sarah giggled, 'Aw Fiona, ye would say ony thing is grand if oor Joe suggested it! ' She mocked, putting on a lilting Highland accent, 'Aw Joe, eat deid mice an' wear bat droppin's in ma hair? Aw, tha' would be grand!'

'Awa' wi' ye!' Joe laughed, pushing his sister playfully on the back.

'Ah'm awa'!' Sarah cried, pleased to see that Fiona was also amused. 'Ah'll leave ye alane tae canoodle an' tak Rosie and Cal up tae the toon.' She suddenly hugged Fiona. 'Ah'll likely no' see ye again, tae talk like, until ye come tae live wi' us...'

Fiona returned the gesture with warmth. Surely she could not ask to marry into a better family?

Joe's request for David Dale to perform the marriage service, placed through McCulloch, was answered after a long delay. It was into September before he was summoned to the manager's office and told curtly that Mr Dale would be pleased to join them in matrimony on the last Sunday of that month, the 30th of September.

Joe was perplexed. 'Can it no' be the following Sunday? Did ye tell him tha' Fiona will no' be finished at the Mills 'til the 3rd o' October?'

'I informed him of that,' McCulloch said, irritated. 'There is only a matter of a few days in it, in any case. You are honoured that he has favoured your request at all!'

'Och an' Ah am grateful tae him, truly, 'tis jus' tha' she'll no' be allowed tae leave Mill Four so...'

'So?'

The two men glared at one another. They both knew exactly what this would mean for the newlyweds: they would not be allowed to be alone together until her debenture was complete.

The older man broke the silence first. 'If that is all, good afternoon!'

The disappointment of not being able to spend their first night together as man and wife was tempered by the fact that the wedding would take place a week earlier than either had expected.

Sarah threw herself into making Fiona's dress with renewed urgency. She had been relying on the thought that Fiona would be living with them before the great day, allowing the opportunity to fit the gown to her properly.

'Now whit am Ah tae dae?' she grumbled to Rosie.

'Ye could fit it tae me?' her sister replied helpfully.

'Yer half the size o' her from shoulder tae toe, an' yer all the wrang shape at the bosom.'

Rosie pulled out the cooking stool and hopped up on to it. 'Whit aboot that?'

Sarah yanked a drying cloth from the rail by the range, ' Push that doon yer front, bunched up like? here's anither yin. Aye... it might do, wait an' Ah'll fetch ma tape.'

It was late, with Joe and Cal already silently asleep, before the sisters were finished with cutting and pinning. By the dim light of candles and the dying fire, their eyes were red and bleary when they rolled the precious material in a clean sheet and fell, exhausted, into bed.

After that, every evening after work, they ate their meal, Cal and Rosie went to their lessons and Joe took over the chores to allow Sarah to sew.

Fiona's dress was not the only preparation for the coming wedding.

Fiona would often give Joe drawings; sketches of the waterfall, marsh marigolds on the river bank, a heron poised to strike above an unsuspecting fish. On some of these pictures she wrote phrases from poems or a title. One day, as he left her, holding a sketch depicting a view of the village, he realised that he had no idea of the meaning of the lettering along the top.

'Whit's it say?' he asked Rosie.

She took it from him and read, 'New Lanark by Fiona Macdonald.'

It bothered him. When they were married he knew they would sign a book. He felt ashamed, stupid. Beside his new wife's graceful signature, he would have to draw a cross.

'Could ye learn me how tae sign ma name?' he asked.

Having never written before, it took practice to learn the grip of the chalk, how to form the letters and let them flow together, but he toiled at it each evening. As he copied Rosie's example, time and time again, he appreciated for the first time how much he lacked in education.

Fiona could read and write, add sums, she knew the names of distant countries and could sing songs, not just church music. For four years she had attended Dale's classes every day, would she find him dull and boring, an illiterate manual labourer?

These thoughts brought more doubts to Joe's head and he was gripped by panic. Fiona was beautiful and intelligent, would she tire of him when they had lain together and the bodily desire for each other was satisfied? Could he hold her attention when she was set free from the confines of Mill Four and could discover the outside world?

There was talk of the hundreds of new Highlanders who were expected to take up employment at the mills as soon as the housing was habitable. How many more Kyle Macinnesses would arrive to take a fancy to her and, with him tied up in his apprenticeship, would she see a better life with one of them?

Plagued by these worries, he watched Dale's carriage arrive in New Lanark with despair.

Perhaps the best of his time with Fiona was about to end. There would be no more brief, joyous encounters, when they clung to each other in anticipation of exploring the possibilities of their union; hopes of sharing life together and having the opportunity to progress from pleasantries and banter and grow to have a deeper understanding of one another.

Among the daily grind, would they lose their magic?

For so long he had yearned to take her as his wife and be with her every day yet now, with the moment fast approaching, he was besieged with doubts.

When they met on the day before their marriage, he could bear it no longer.

'Fiona, Ah love ye mair than ye will e'er ken, but are ye sure ye want tae be ma wife?'

Aghast, Fiona cried out, 'An' why in heaven's name are ye askin' me tha' the noo?'

'Ah'm worried ye'll tire o' me... tha' Ah'll be a disappointment tae ye... ye dinnae ken much aboot life an' ye've no' had a chance tae live outside these walls... Ye've had a' this learnin' an' readin'. Ah have nae, mibbe ye'll come tae think o' me as a sumf...' She placed her finger to his lips.

'Wheesht! Yer naw stupit, yer no' a sumf! It's ye an' me, Joe. Look in tae ma eyes,' she looked intently into his. ''Tis tha' feelin'...' she searched for the right word, 'recognition. We've found one anither, Ah can feel it in ma heirt, jus' as well as ye can.' She moved her hand away, still holding his gaze, but there was a mischievous glimmer in her eyes. 'Any hoo, mibbee ye will bore me, an' who's tae say ye will nae tire o' me? But if Ah'm gaun tae be bored wi' any man, Ah wid wish it tae be ye, Joe Scott!'

**

The long assembly room was packed with a rustling, whispering congregation. All the orphans were present, dressed in their Sunday clothes, their hair neatly combed, faces newly washed. At the back of the room, seated, were other members of the village, followers of the Old Scotch Independents, of which Dale was a highly respected founder and pastor.

161

The Sunday services were a weekly event, compulsory for the residents of Mill Four in addition to their daily religious education, but today word had passed through the village that one of the mill girls was to be married. The Scotts' immediate friends and neighbours had long since heard the news and even those not usually drawn to a church gathering were there to witness the service.

At the head of the room, seated to one side, were David Dale and his older children, accompanied by James Dale, his betrothed Miss Haddow, William Kelly and his family and several other managers and supervisors.

It was not only their slightly segregated seating that set them aside from the rest of the crowd. The ladies' magnificent crinoline skirts of emerald greens, blues and startling pinks and their bonnets with expansive ribbons, shone like jewels in a sea of predominantly grey, black and white attire. To the paupers, especially the girls, they were an incredible spectacle.

Anne Caroline sat beside her uncle James and clasped her hands on her lap. She could feel the intense scrutiny of hundreds of pairs of eyes and was not quite sure where to look. On observing the very composed Miss Haddow, she took her cue and turned slightly in her chair, fixing her attention on her father at the lectern.

Almost every Sunday in life, she heard her father preach the word of God yet she never grew weary of hearing him speak. He would bring the words of the Bible to life, inspiring his listeners to lead their lives as the Lord intended, doing good to one another, enriching the lives of those around you, especially those less fortunate or in need.

While he spoke, enthusiastically, paternally, the congregation turned their gaze from studying the expensive outfits of their employer and his family and listened to his words.

As he drew to a close, entreating them to follow the scriptures and abide by the way of the Lord, he beckoned to a couple standing at the front.

Anne Caroline drew a sharp breath. Surely it was Joe Scott, the man injured man she exchanged words with in the summer?

Today his appearance was different, smartly turned out in a long jacket, dark breeches in knee length boots and a cream cravat, but his good looking tanned face and fair hair were unmistakable. Beside him stood the girl from the mill in a dress of sky blue. Her heart shaped face was pale, accentuating her large brown eyes and dark arched eyebrows.

162

She reminded Anne Caroline of a china doll, two spots of colour stood out on her cheek bones, belying her excitement at the occasion. When she moved, it was clear the dress was a little too small for her. It pinched in under her arms and stretched taut across her chest, which forced her to walk tensely, holding her head up and keeping her back very straight. The design of the blue bodice, cut deeply to the waist, revealed a high-necked white inset of white lace; appropriately modest for a church service.

The only adornment was a bracelet of shells, so tightly clasped around her wrist as to cause the shells to dig into her skin.

It was a plain wedding outfit, Anne Caroline thought. Yet there was something utterly striking about it when worn by this girl, with her long chestnut hair caught back from her face in a simple blue ribbon. She did not need hair pieces or flounces of sequinned taffeta to draw admiring looks.

Unexpected tears burned in the little girl's eyes prompted by memories of a warm sunny day, dust kicked up from scrabbling boots, two men punching and wrestling in the street, Joe's bloodied face. And now, the sweethearts were together and about to be married.   There was a calm serenity in the beauty of the young woman standing beside this tall, strong man who had fought for her....
Anne Caroline dug her finger nails into her palms; how ridiculous of her to cry!

During the summer, she had attended a high society wedding where the bride's voluminous white gown was appliquéd with exotic birds of prey, her head adorned with jewels cascading from her silver wig. Trumpets sounded after the ceremony and liveried footmen carried the couple on decorated sedan chairs to the assembly rooms at the Tontine.

For all its lavish expense, it lacked any romance or true emotion, being primarily designed as an expensively orchestrated exhibition of etiquette and a parade of wealth.

It paled in comparison to the service before her now.

After a short but rousing speech from Dale, Joe produced the ring and took hold of Fiona's hand.

His hands were shaking as he slipped it on her finger, his voice unusually deep, quavering.

Fiona squeezed his fingers and, looking reassuringly in to each other's eyes, supporting each other through the words of the ceremony, they took their vows. A great cheer went up as Dale

163

pronounced them man and wife, with a group of Joe's friends whooping and clapping from the back of the room.

Dale, smiling broadly, ushered the newlyweds over to a table to sign the register while he concluded the service.

'Congratulations,' James smiled at Joe and Fiona when, having signed the book, they passed close by on their return to the congregation.

Joe bowed slightly, his face flushed and perspiring, a lock of gold hair falling forward from the ribbon restraining it neatly at the nape of his neck.

Anne Caroline leaned forward in her seat, 'Oh yes, Mr Scott... and Mrs Scott,' she whispered, 'Congratulations!'

Joe beamed at her and Fiona glanced quickly up at the young girl, taken aback that one of Mr Dale's daughters should be speaking to them. She was greeted by a warm smile and glistening brown eyes which, through black lashes spikey with tears, exuded good will.

When the final prayers were said, the hall started to empty and Anne Caroline went over to look at the entries made by the bride and groom.

A wave of compassion seized her at the sight of the names. The confident sweep of 'Fiona Macdonald' and the wavering, deeply impressed lettering of 'Joseh Scott'; his nerves having caused the omission of the 'p'.

Two hours grace was granted to Fiona to accompany her husband back to his home and celebrate the marriage. When this had first been arranged by Mrs Docherty, Fiona received the news with a passive expression which masked an internal rage of injustice.

'Ah'll jist come an' be wi' ye!' she had declared to Joe, eyes blazing, waving her hands expressively and adamantly. 'Ah dinnae care whit onybody says tae the contrary! Ah'll be yer wife by then! 'Twa oors? Ah ask ye! Ah'll leave an' ne'er go back!'

It took him a long time to calm her down, partly because he agreed with her and wanted her with him straight away, but he also knew they could not afford to lose favour with the Mills. Many discussions had taken place as to whether she should continue in her work or find other employment. This dilemma also encompassed his brother and sisters. All of them were Dale's employees at present and yet all would be free to leave in the next week.

Decisions had to be made.

It was also a major concern that now that Joe was working for Ewing the stonemason, he was not personally entitled to a room in New Lanark. It was only due to his three siblings being employed in the mills that their lodgings were secure.

In the end, Fiona came round to understanding and quelled her fiery nature sufficiently to keep their good standing in the village intact.

So, two hours they had, and they were determined to make the most of them.

Tam's suggestion to Joe, to throw his family out the house and make the most of the time alone with Fiona, was met with a regretful grimace. It had crossed his mind, but to be rushed and nervous, fearful of the clock ticking, that was not how he wanted to spend his first intimate encounter with his beloved.

So, they all returned to the Row to enjoy an abundance of food prepared by Sarah, Rosie and Bessie with contributions from many others.

At the second landing on the tenement stairs, Sarah threw open the door to their room and stood back. Everyone cheered when Joe reached for his wife and caught her up in his arms to carry her over the threshold.

The table groaned with ham and chicken, bread, cheese, pickles, sugared cakes and clootie dumpling, still steaming in its cloth.

Soon, the room was filled with well wishers, kissing Fiona and slapping Joe heartily on the back. Tam's brother brought his fiddle and played on the stair way until there were so many people joining in that they all moved outside into the street.

Watery white sunshine filtered through a layer of cloud and gusts of wind picked up the dust on the road. It was cool and inclement but nobody noticed. There was music and dancing, clapping and cheering, the girls were breathless and shrieking as they were swung recklessly into reels by high spirited partners, clogs clattering on the cobbles. Laughter rang out amongst the stone tenements and neighbours hung out their windows, drinks in hand, singing along with the merriment.

For Joe and Fiona it was the happiest day of their lives.

***

Three days later, Fiona stood in front of Mr McCulloch and was formally discharged as an apprentice at the New Lanark Mills.

'Now then,' McCulloch steepled his fingers and fixed her with a steely look. 'A wee while ago, I believe Mrs Docherty asked you to give some thought to what you wished to do in the future. Have you come to a decision? Do you wish to stay on here? On the frames?'

'Naw, sir. But Ah ken whit Ah wid like tae dae.' Fiona cleared her throat. 'If ye wid be sae kind as tae consider me fer a job as assistant in the classroom, Ah wid be sincerely grateful.'

'Ah, yes, I had an inkling you would say that,' he picked up a paper on his desk. 'This is a note from Mr Lyme, he commends your work highly. You have risen from the bottom class to the top place of the top class, not only that, but you have achieved rewards for taking top place many times. I congratulate you. I understand you have discussed this with him and he feels your attendance would be useful in the schoolroom. Especially as you are a Gaelic speaker and have mastered the Scots language to a competent level, both written and verbal. As you know, we have many of your people here and are expecting many more.

'There is a sorry lack of translators at present and you could be of assistance to the teachers. Yes, I can recommend you to the Senior Managers to be engaged as a teaching assistant.'

Fiona could not wait to tell Joe and, as soon as the formalities were over, she ran back to the dormitory to collect her belongings in preparation to leave.

There was very little to take away with her. Her beautiful wedding dress, sewn with so much care and friendship, was wrapped in the white sheet in which Sarah delivered it on the morning of her wedding. She laid her parcel of mementoes from Mallaig on top of the bundle and wrapped the brown shawl from the Town Hospital around her shoulders.

The room was quiet, immaculate, the rows of beds neatly made up, their extra winter blankets folded in squares in the middle of each mattress. It was strange to know she would never sleep here again, strange and unreal.

There were things she would miss, the late night gossip, Mhairie and Islay to chat with in Gaelic and two new Highland girls who had cried on hearing that she was leaving. Still, she told herself, you will see them all everyday in the school room if the managers agreed to give her the position.

There was no-one there to see her leave so she checked the pile of tunics was complete and went to the door.

'*Tioraidh,*' she whispered, 'Goodbye,' taking a last look around.

Between these white washed walls, in this lofty, raftered space, she had sobbed and laughed, raged against the unfairness of life and revelled in the enchantment of being in love. It held vestiges of her hopes and desires, bleak moments of despair and times when she felt she would burst from the panic and frustration of not being free.

Now she was free and it was time to leave her old life behind.

While Fiona was making her way to her new home in Long Row, just a hundred yards away, Mrs Cooper was at her wits' end.

Mr Dale was next door at a meeting with Mr Kelly and was due to return at any moment. The fire needed tending, the dinner was only half prepared, bedrooms needed tidying, fires replenished... the list was endless. Her main problem was the new maid, Mary, who had been hastily engaged after the dismissal of the last one.

Not only had Mary taken to refusing to live in the house, but she was nearly always late coming down the hill from Lanark in the morning.

Although her first weeks passed dutifully enough, she was slipping into careless ways resulting in two breakages in the last week alone and now, the final straw, things had started to go missing.

On hiring Cooper, Breen gave express instructions regarding any staff or minor problems at New Lanark: she, Cooper, must deal with the matter.

It would be very difficult to swear that Mary was the one to blame but the coincidence in the timing could not be discounted. Who else would steal from the Dales? Certainly not the Charlotte Street staff and no-one else came into the house, so it could only be Mary who was the thief.

Half a dozen eggs disappeared from the larder, then a couple of days later, after looking high and low for the new bag of flour, only delivered on Wednesday, it was nowhere to be found on Friday morning. And now a knife, one of the smallest and most useful utensils in the kitchen, had vanished from its place in the felt roll in the dresser drawer.

Mrs Cooper braced herself and went through to the scullery.

'Mary, have you seen the little paring knife?'

167

'Naw, ma'am.' the girl, no more than thirteen years of age, turned wide innocent eyes to the housekeeper, her hands deep in suds, washing the table linen.

'Things are going missing, Mary. I am responsible for everything in this house and I will have to ask you to show me what you have in your apron pocket.'

There was no need to go any further, Mary's face suffused with crimson. For a few seconds they stared at each other then Mary spun round, pulling her hands from the wash tub and sending an arc of soapy water through the air as she fled to the back door and wrenched it open. Grappling in her pocket, she drew out the knife, causing Cooper to shrink back in fear.

'Ye can keep yer rotten knife!' Mary shouted, throwing it down to send it skittering across the stone floor before she raced away up the road.

When the Dale family came in from their visit to Bonnington House, Cooper asked to have a word with Miss MacIntosh: she couldn't bring herself to call her Toshie.

'Oh dear, how very difficult for you,' Toshie sympathised on hearing that there was now no maid in the house. 'Giggs and I are happy to help in whatever way we can while we are here but I suppose you will have to re-double your efforts to acquire a new maid. It is maybe just as well that we are leaving for Glasgow tomorrow but I am sure Mr Dale will want to return before the end of the month. I wish you good luck in having the household in order by then.'

Cooper nodded, her mournful face even more downcast than usual. 'Thank you. Your assistance and patience over the next few hours would be very much appreciated.'

It was all very well being told to find a new maid but, goodness knows, she had tried. Lanark folk were very suspicious of the New Lanark villagers. They judged them only by those they came into contact with in the town. These were, on the whole, the rowdy men, many who didn't speak Scots, who trailed up the hill to find entertainment by way of the card tables, cock fighting, badger baiting and drinking. Lanark women were propositioned, deals were reneged on, fights broke out and local girls with low morals were enticed in to earning easy money by offering them a good time.

So, it was little wonder that few families were willing to see their daughters go into service in a house in the middle of such a den of iniquity. Cooper rolled up her sleeves and hurried through the housework before providing the best dinner she could manage to prepare on her own.

Toshie, Giggs and even Duncan helped where they could but they had their own responsibilities and the five Dale girls were a full time job in themselves.

It was well past midnight before Cooper gave a last scrub to the kitchen table and emptied the dirty water, quietly, out into the street. She looked up at the starry sky and yawned, taking a moment to stand in the dark doorway and listen to the silence, interrupted only by owls and the distant rippling, rushing river.

If she could not find help to run the house in the next two weeks, she would hand in her notice.

***

Fiona slept in Joe's arms and woke to her unfamiliar surroundings with a blissful feeling of well being: her mind was clear, her body comfortable, her heart satisfied.

She could hear her husband's slow, peaceful breathing and feel the pressure of his arm around her shoulders. She wished they could lie like that forever.

The previous day she had prepared a simple meal for their return from work and sat at the table with her new family for the first time. There were no awkward moments. They were all good friends and easily familiar with one another, so the conversation flowed and when Cal and Rosie left for their lessons, Sarah excused herself, saying she had to visit Flora.

Alone together, in the privacy of their own home, Joe immediately left what he was doing and took her in his arms. Their first gentle, loving kisses became ardent, passionate. All their months of yearning culminated in that special loving embrace, releasing their inhibitions and allowing them to show each other how deeply they felt.

Fiona had no mother to pass on wise words for her daughter's first experience of being with a man. However, when Fiona's older cousin was to be married, she had overheard her aunt giving her advice. 'If you love a man, and he loves you,' she had told her, 'there is no need to fear the bed. Follow where he leads, lose yourself in the delight of

169

being with your loved one, desire feeds desire. Nature will do the rest, you will see.'

And Nature had worked its magic for Joe and Fiona. Never could she have imagined such delightful feelings, even the recollection of their shared pleasures sent thrills through her body.

When Joe opened his eyes, he drew back the bed's curtain to shed dawn light on them.

He kissed her and traced a finger tenderly down her cheek.

Finding wet tears, he whispered anxiously, 'Are ye greetin'? Whit's wrang?'

'Happy tears,' she murmured and nestled close against him.

Wanting to make herself useful, Fiona rose and dressed before the others and stoked the fire. After heating water and pouring it into the basin, she set the porridge to cook.

'Ah'll fetch some mair watter,' she whispered to Joe, kissing him on the lips and leaving him to wash and shave by the lamp light.

When she returned, the others were up and preparing themselves for the day ahead.

'Only twa mair days,' Cal muttered, watching his new sister in law doling out the breakfast. 'an' Ah'll be free.'

'Whit'll ye dae, Cal?' Fiona asked.

'Ah want tae work on the land, mibbee at a farm?'

'Wi' the winter comin' on?' Sarah sat down beside him, skilfully plaiting her hair, her hands behind her head. 'We've telt ye, they'll no' be hirin' till the spring. Ye would be best aff stayin' put at the mills, it's steady work....'

'Ah'll no' stay anither day! Ah hate it!' he rounded on his sister, 'ye din nae ken whit its like up in the top floor, wi' the grinding machines an' the men swearin' an' the never ending reels o' cotton tae be dealt wi'!' he spooned in his last mouthfuls. 'twa mair days an' Ah'm oota yon place!'

With that, he scraped back his chair, grabbed his cap and rushed out the door.

'An' whit aboot ye, Rosie?' Joe asked.

'Aw, Ah dunno. The mill's no' bad an' if Ah'm taken on a new contract they say Ah'll be payed mair than Ah'm on the noo. Did ye ken that, Joe? Sarah?' She looked from one to the other. 'Ah've bin doin' the same joab as Sally an' Flora who earn nearly a shilling mair a week than me. Ah'm bein' paid the same as when Ah started! They

170

dinnae change yer wages but they train ye up tae dae the harder work fer pennies.'

'Is tha' so?' Sarah was appalled. 'Ye mean, if Ah gae back tae the jennie wi' a new contract, Ah'll be earning mair wi' the same joab?'

'Aye,' Rosie helped herself to more porridge, 'D'ye think ye will? Gae back tae yer auld joab?'

'Ah'm no trained fer onythin' else, so Ah s'pose Ah will ha'e tae.'

Joe listened to his sisters and was relieved by what he was hearing. Only Cal caused him concern. He had suggested several alternatives to him, one being that he applied to the building supervisors, there was always work on the labouring teams busy in the village. His brother would not hear of it; he wanted away from New Lanark and would find himself employment where he could breathe fresh air and tend animals.

Joe wished him luck but felt he was setting himself up for disappointment. At least if he and Fiona were earning and the other two girls carried on at the mills, Cal would have a secure place to live until something turned up.

Joe was pleased at having provided a home for his family and immensely proud of his wife.

For the first time in a long while, his elder brother came to mind. He wished Sam could see them. Where was Sam? Was he happy and fulfilled? Did he have a woman to love him, a warm bed and food on the table?

Was he even alive?

***

In those darkening days of late 1792, the terrible violence in France cast a shadow over the whole of Britain. Reports of a massacre, ordered by Danton, of over a thousand Royalists who were being held in Parisian prisons, stunned the rest of Europe. The newly convened National Convention then took the outrageous step of abolishing the French monarchy, declaring themselves a Republic and instigating a new Republican calendar.

With Louis XV1 in prison awaiting trial, the French population were starving, winter was encroaching and after initial defeats the French army were now achieving victories in the military conflicts with their neighbours.

There was a sympathetic ground swell of unrest among the middle classes of Britain. Lesser merchants and traders were gathering together and forming a stronger voice against the injustices of high taxes and unequal rights. Friends of the People Societies were springing up in most of the larger towns, calling for reform to the government's oppressive policies.

In Scotland, Thomas Muir, although still in his twenties, was at the forefront of these calls for change.

His popularity, especially a growing support in Edinburgh, was causing grave concern to the hierarchy of Scottish politics. Lord Advocate Robert Dundas and the unforgiving judge, Lord Braxfield, found his views on law reform contentious and dangerous. Observing the collapse of society across the English Channel, these home grown Reformers brought real terror into the heart of the whole British establishment.

The troubles in France also impacted on trade affairs. Cotton prices were adversely affected and several mills were struggling. Monteith was hanging on at Blantyre, but times were hard.

Therefore it was with satisfaction that Dale returned from New Lanark to find the current figures from all his ventures were continuing in good health.

Also waiting at Charlotte Street was a letter from his father in law, John Campbell. They had spoken at length over the last year on the religious persecution of the French people and both shared a pessimistic view of the months and possibly years to come. However, it was the business of the Royal Bank of Scotland that the older man was mainly concerned in addressing.

David Dale and Carolina had made a perfect and affectionate love match, although Dale's critics had been known to comment that her father's influence, as a Director of the Royal Bank of Scotland, had been of considerable assistance to Dale's success as a businessman. It appeared a very happy coincidence that shortly after his association with John Campbell's daughter, Dale was appointed the first Glasgow agent to the Bank.

His friends argued it was a natural progression for such a respected and astute merchant. He had already proved his credentials as an excellent candidate for such a position of responsibility having close business relationships with all the leading bankers and trades people of Glasgow through the Glasgow Chamber of Commerce, a body Dale was instrumental in founding in the first place.

The Campbells lived in Edinburgh and they were proposing a visit to Glasgow for a short spell and wondered if they might prevail on Dale's hospitality while in the city.

Dale dipped his pen in the ink-well and replied that they would be most welcome and had only to notify him of a date, at their convenience.

Since Carolina's death, Dale was aware that he was not keeping as closely in touch with his late wife's family as perhaps he should. They were grieving as well and any opportunities for them to see their grandchildren should be acted upon and welcomed.

When his correspondence was complete, he was reminded of the time by several clocks striking the hour of two so, nearly late for an appointment, he made his way downstairs. Despite his hurry, he paused for a few moments beside a painting near the foot of the staircase.

Renwick was waiting in the hall holding his master's hat and cane. He averted his eyes, not wishing to intrude on such a personal moment.

The painting was a beautiful portrait of Mrs Carolina Dale with young Master William. Stavely, the artist, only completed it a few months before the little boy's untimely death.

Renwick could never quite decide whether it was a good thing to have such a striking and life-like picture of Mr Dale's recently deceased wife and child in such open view.

Was it a consolation to be able to gaze on their faces again or a painful re-assertion of what they had all lost?

***

The great day arrived. Sarah, Rosie and Cal Scott reported to McCulloch's office first thing in the morning to be officially released from their contracts. They were seen individually and the manager reviewed the comments from their Overseers, judging for himself whether he would wish to renew their employment.

Sarah was said to be 'industrious, neat in her work and reliable'.

'You are currently working on the spinning machines, are ye not?' McCulloch asked.

'Aye, sir.'

'D'ye wish to continue in Mr Dale's employ? In the same capacity?'

'Ah've bin dae'in' tha' joab the past twa years an' the girls at ma side earn more. Ah understaun' that wi' a new contract Ah get mair wages. Is that richt?'

'That would be correct. You would be taken under new terms for three years.'

Sarah bit her lip. She had been expecting it to be for just another year; three years was almost as long as the time she had already served.

'Ah wid like tae talk wi' ma brither, Joe, afore Ah say fer sure.'

'Very well. The offer of employment is open to you for one week.' McCulloch attempted a smile, this girl was already a trained and useful worker. 'Bear in mind the fact that New Lanark housing is for New Lanark workers. Your elder brother is no longer on the payroll and if perhaps it comes to being only your younger brother or sister working in the mills, it may not be to Mr Dale's advantage to offer a whole room to your family.' He tried another smile but Sarah's direct gaze seemed to see through it. 'Caithness Row will not take all of the expected new-comers, there will be a shortage of rooms again in no time at all.'

'Ah'll speak wi' Joe,' she said firmly, all too aware of the threat.

Rosie was next to be called into the office and, as an efficient and obedient worker, she was offered a new position in the mills.

She accepted her new contract with alacrity. It was the sensible thing to do, she thought. It was a guaranteed wage and she knew what the work entailed, which, at the end of the day was not so bad, so why try and find anything else?

McCulloch asked her to sign a contract and then instructed her to start in Mill Two on the following Monday morning.

Calum was barely in the room five minutes. Scowling at McCulloch, he stated that he would not be returning to the mills.

'As I told your sister...' McCulloch glanced at his papers to remind himself of her name, 'Sarah... if there is only one member of your family, and that being a child, working for Mr Dale, it may not be sufficient to lease you the room.'

The ramifications of this statement meant little to Cal. He had his heart set on leaving and nothing was going to dissuade him.

However, it was this thorny issue which the Scotts debated later that day.

'It's no' tha' Ah dinnae want tae be in New Lanark,' Sarah cried, 'It's jist the thocht o' startin' straight in tae anither three years!'

They talked round the table in the fire's glow. Fiona sat close to Joe so he could put his arm round her and she nestled against him listening to the conversation. Being part of a family again was a joy in itself.

'If baith Sarah an' Ah are workin' in the mills,' said Rosie, 'an' Fiona is at the school, Ah cannae see whit McCulloch is gaun on aboot. He's jist a bully, tryin' tae mak oor Cal dae summat he disnae want tae.'

Joe agreed but added, 'Ah dinnae think it's jist Cal he's bullyin', it's Sarah. He kens fine weel that she's handy on the frames an' he disnae want tae lose her.'

Sarah leaned back in her chair and stretched her arms above her head, yawning. 'Ah weel, Ah'll ha'e a whole week o' holiday afore Ah gae bak tae tell him Ah'll tak his job, sae at least that's summat.'

'Ah cannae gae back. Ye understaun' don't ye?' Cal said quietly, with none of the belligerent attitude shown to McCulloch.

His words were almost pleading. 'Ah wid rather die than spend anither week in tha' place. Ah need tae be ootside, tae see the sky an' no' ha'e that infernal grinding and clacking o' the machines ringing in ma ears a' day.'

Rosie put her hand over his and squeezed it. 'Aye Cal, we understaun'. Ye've helped us a' get this far an' ye've put up wi' it tae the end, we'll no' haud it agin ye tae leave the mills.'

'But it's no' jist me leavin' the mills, whit if McCulloch throws ye all oot o' here... it'll be a' ma fault.' He rubbed at his dusty fair hair, leaving it standing up in spikes.

'Naw, naw...' Joe spoke for them all. 'We've a' seen ye struggle wi' the work here. It's tae yer credit tha' ye've jist got on an' done it. If ye want tae dae work on the land then yer free tae gae. Ah jist worry for ye,' Joe paused, he didn't want to sound like a father preaching to his son. 'It's gie difficult tae get ony work in the winter, it'll be hard fer ye. Ye have a bed here an' food until ye can add tae the purse, dinnae worry aboot that.'

Pushing her chair back sharply, Sarah stood up and started to clear away their dinner dishes. 'Ah'm jist gonnae pop oot tae see Flora efter these are washed....'

Fiona leaned across and took the dishes from her.

'Awa' ye gae, Ah'll see tae these,' she said briskly.

She had been observing the emotions flitting across her friend's face. It was obvious Sarah was upset at having to remain in the same job, but, being the sweet-tempered person she was, she did not want to express the depth of her disappointment to the others.

Fiona empathised with Sarah, maybe even more than with Joe, and she could feel her distress as clearly as if it were her own.

Sarah accepted her offer and reached for her shawl. A moment after she had left the room, Fiona picked up the bowl of peelings and, murmuring that she was going to throw them in the midden, hurried after her down the stairs.

'Sarah!' she called, from the lower landing, 'Wait...'

She caught up with her in the street. As she had thought, Sarah was not heading towards Flora's house, she was walking down towards the lade.

It was a moonless night and the starry sky was brushed with wisps of cloud but, even in the gloom, she could see the glistening tears on Sarah's cheeks. Fiona linked her arm in her friend's and they walked for a while in silence.

'It's no' as Ah thocht it wid be,' Sarah said at last. 'Ah had these grand ideas tha' when the four years were up Ah wid be married, or seein' a lad or... well, Ah didnae think it would jist be anither three years o' the same.'

Fiona squeezed her arm comfortingly and they walked on, slowly, companionably. When they reached the steep bank above Dundaff Linn they stopped and leaned against the boundary wall to Bonnington estate. It was noisy with the rushing water from the lade's overflow adding to the splashing waterfall and on turning to look back at the village, a cold breeze whisked their hair away from their faces.

'Ye knaw,' Sarah said, raising her voice above the water's roar, 'this is whaur Joe an' Ah saw Cal comin' aff the Laird's land a while back.' She gazed at the black silhouettes of the four huge mills. 'He's always hated it here, Ah cannae blame him fer wantin' tae leave.'

'If ye did nae ha'e tae be in the mills an' could dae any work, whit would it be?' Fiona asked.

'Tha's an easy one! Ah would ha'e ma own dress shop an' make fine fashionable cla'es fer rich ladies!'

They giggled and started to walk back.

'An' if ye could nae do tha', whit else?'

'Mibee gae in tae service an' be a ladies maid, or a house maid...'

Fiona stopped and swung round to face her. 'Dale's efter a maid fer their hoose here! Ah heard it a day past.'

'But they have tha' lass, Mary Cleland frae the toon....'

'Naw, she wis stealin' so yon Mrs Cooper sent her packin' an' noo she's tae find anither yin.' Fiona's voice was rising with excitement. 'Ye wid still be in New Lanark, an' ye wid still be in Mr Dale's employ, sae auld Misery McCulloch could nae put us oot the hoose!'

They threw their arms round one another and danced around in the darkness.

'Whit's gaun on?' It was Joe, striding down the path towards them. 'Ah wis fair worried aboot you, lass? Ye've bin a mighty lang time puttin' oot the peelin's....' He took Fiona's hand, the concerned creases on his forehead disappearing as he realised that they were both laughing.

With great delight they told him about the possibility of Sarah working for the Dales as a maid.

'Ah ken it may no' happen,' his sister said, 'an' they may ha'e some ither lass already engaged, but its worth a try? Eh Joe?'

The next day Sarah dressed in her best outfit, the yellow dress and jacket she had made for the Fair holiday. It was of a thin material, unsuited to the chilly October morning and she managed to catch Bessie before she left for work to ask for the loan of her cream wool shawl. With Fiona's help she styled her hair neatly and presented herself at the back door of Dale's house.

Mrs Cooper opened the door looking haggard and pale.'Whit d'ye want?'

'G'mornin' tae ye Mrs Cooper.' Sarah smiled broadly, 'Ah heard ye were efter hiring a maid? Ah wanted tae offer ma services.'

'I have seen ye around the village,' the woman surveyed her critically. 'Ye work in the mills, don't ye?'

'Ma contracts o'er, an' Ah'm free tae seek anither job, if ye want me.'

'Come away in,' Mrs Cooper stood back and ushered her through the door.

After a barrage of questions, most of which Sarah answered by saying she was a quick learner, Mrs Cooper told her to come back the following morning to hear if she was successful.

'I will be requesting a reference from your manager,' she said as they were parting. 'I take it that will be Mr Kelly?'

'Naw, ma'am, that will be Mr McCulloch.'

'You will not require to be living in, will you? Not if you live in Long Row?'

'Naw, I live wi' ma family.'

'An' one last question, are ye seein' a young man at this time? Because we don't tolerate followers calling at the house.'

'Och naw, there would be nuthin like that.'

Sarah returned home flushed and eager to relate the whole interview to Fiona and Rosie.

It was strange to have no work to go to and the three girls made the most of this unusual time by taking their chores leisurely and enjoying frequent breaks to drink tea and get to know Fiona better.

Cocooned in the security of her new family, Fiona brought out her mementoes and unwrapped the little package on the table.

'Ah've carried these wi' me since leavin' ma hame in the Highlands...' her voice broke and she lapsed into a long silence, gently laying out the items in a row. 'The thimble wis frae ma granny, an' the wooden spoon... weel, Ah kept it by me sae Ah could sup, usefu' like?'

'An' the stanes? Why did ye keep yon stanes?' Rosie picked up one of the ordinary looking grey pebbles, rough and irregular and of no particular interest or beauty.

'Them's magic stanes. We a' gathered some stanes frae by the croft, an held them in oor hauns, rubbed them and passed them amang us... on the last mornin'... afore the soldiers came and burnt the hoose. Great flamin' torches, they had, held them high an' walked aboot, settin' alight tae the thatch and chasing us awa'. Ah grabbed a haunfu' o' they stanes frae the pile we made... together.' She sniffed back tears. 'Ah've lost some alang the way, but Ah feel a wee bit o' all ma family are on these stanes. They're special... rare... magic.'

Sarah was very moved, her own eyes smarting and her throat constricting so her words came out sounding high, unnatural. 'Ye wore the bracelet o' shells at yer wedding. Did ye mak it yersel?'

'Ma brither made it, Charlie, ma big brither.' Fiona took a shuddering breath. 'It's awfy small fer me noo, Ah wis jist a bairn when he gi'e it tae me. He wid mak these things an' gie them tae us fer wee gifts. He wis sich a kind lad. Tall an' strang, like Joe. He sailed wi' the rest o' them.'

She told the girls of the trek through the boggy glens and down along the trail beside Loch Lomond. How they sold their pony on the journey, earning useful money for the intended voyage to America, but had to pull their cart themselves the last miles into Glasgow.

'Ma mither fell ill, an' they widnae tak her on the ship. Ah could nae leave her, an' then suddenly... ma uncle got mad at me an' sed Ah wis tae mak up ma mind, fer they were sailin' an' they wanted me tae gae wi' 'em.' Fiona's dark eyes shimmered with tears and memories. 'Ah couldnae leave her... but she wis deid the next day, an' it wis too late, Ah wis left behind.'

'Yer ane Uncle left ye there?'

'Aye, but Ah understaun' tha' he hid a' his family tae be lookin' oot fer, an' he wis ma Da's brither, no' ma mither's...'

'Whit aboot yer Da'?'

'He wis a fisherman.' She reached for a pebble and rolled it between her fingers, the long sweep of her lashes hiding the loss in her eyes. 'He went tae sea yin day... an' his boat ne'er came bak. There'd bin a storm, an' they say they a' mustave drowned. It wis a lang time ago....'

Rosie filled the kettle and pushed the swee over the fire, stoking up the glowing coals. The mood was depressing and needed to be lifted. The other girls followed her lead, with Sarah giving Fiona a heartfelt hug before helping her to wrap up her things, keeping out the wooden spoon to add to their meagre selection of utensils.

Cal had left before dawn to go up to the market and ask around for any work that might be offered. It was dark and Joe was already home when he came back through the door.

There was a dejected air about him and he was tired and cold. The only paid jobs were for daily potato pickers and the season was well under way. Within a week all the local fields would be cleared so even if he was hired the next day, he would be out of work again before he knew it.

On the few occasions he plucked up enough courage to speak to the burly, bearded farmers they brushed him aside, saying he was too young and scrawny to be of any use. Some jeered at his request to be given a chance, sneering at him and cracking lewd jokes when he turned away.

One man, younger and garishly attired, suggested he tried for a position as a footman. 'Ye have the looks for it!' he'd quipped and nudged the man at his side. They had a nasty tittering laugh and Cal had touched his cap and moved away. For all their swearing and rough behaviour, he preferred the farmers' response to the ominous insinuations of the dandies.

'There's a' the big estates to ask at,' he said hopefully, 'Ah heard there's a new keeper at Carmichael, so Ah'll away over there the morrow.'

It was pouring with rain the next morning but, undaunted, Cal wrapped himself up with as many layers of clothes as he could manage to squeeze beneath his jacket and set off for Carmichael.

Sarah left the house at the same time. Wishing each other good luck, they parted outside Dale's house, both hoping the day would bring a new start to their lives.

For Sarah, the news was good. Mrs Cooper would engage her on a month's trial and if her work was satisfactory she would be taken on as the housemaid.

On telling Fiona and Rosie, they decided that a special meal should be prepared to celebrate. A lively, high spirited day was spent, so when Joe came home he was greeted by Fiona in her wedding dress and Sarah and Rosie in their brightest clothes. They had gone to great trouble to tidy and clean the room and cook a whole chicken in rich vegetable gravy.

Rosie was taking the week off from her schooling but accompanied Sarah to visit Flora, allowing Joe and Fiona an hour or so to be alone. This thoughtful gesture was greatly appreciated by the young lovers who made full use of their privacy.

'Ah hope Cal's found somethin',' Sarah said later, putting a lid on the pot and laying it to one side to keep warm. 'Ah'll keep this for him, it's gie cold t'night, he'll need summat warm tae eat when he gets in.'

They enjoyed their meal, but the jubilant atmosphere was tinged with a growing anxiety. Every time they heard footsteps coming up the stairs, they all looked expectantly at the door but each time they carried on past it. Eventually, the dishes washed and the fire stoked for the night, they pulled out Cal's hurlie bed from under Joe and Fiona's, and retired to bed.

In the early hours, just before dawn, Joe woke and drew back the curtain to check Cal's bed.

It was empty.

For days Joe asked his friends in Lanark to make enquiries and spread the word to all the farms and estate workers, had they taken on a new lad? If they didn't know his name, was he slightly built, with shorn, light coloured hair? Although Cal was fourteen years old, he could easily be mistaken for a lad two or three years younger: did anyone know anything about where he could have gone?

After nearly a week, Tam came down to work one morning with news that a boy fitting Cal's description had been seen sitting on a wagon among some other youngsters. The wagon, drawn by two well fed Clydesdales, was leaving the market and had turned off onto the Carnwath road. That was all that was known.

Joe was relieved. It would seem Cal had indeed found work, good on him. He hoped they would hear from him soon.

However, one week rolled into the next and there was still no word from Calum.

David Dale returned to New Lanark at the end of October to find his house warm and welcoming and the housekeeper in a brighter frame of mind.

The new maid was diligent and pleasant, she reported to her employer. However, there was more to Sarah's presence in the house than sharply ironed linen, squeaky clean cutlery and well-aired rooms. Cooper had found a friend.

Since her husband's death she had locked herself away in grief, taking each day as it came along, trying to keep going, concentrating on fulfilling her duties and relying on them to carry her through the day. Then, on coming to New Lanark, she discovered she was set apart from everyone else with little opportunity to mix with other people. In her previous employment she was part of a much larger staff which brought company at meal times and the noise and bustle of other bodies moving around the house. Here it was still, silent; she was alone.

She was neither part of the mills nor part of the village. Her position in the owner's household separated her both physically and socially. It left her to wile away tedious evenings sewing or reading by the little fire in her bedroom. Many times she just sat and stared into space, so lost in her own world of aloneness that she was oblivious to the room growing dark around her.

Her one consolation was her Bible and her deep belief in finding salvation through the word of the Lord.

She was a fervent follower of Dale's Scotch Independent Church and placed a disproportionate importance on the two hours she spent at the Sunday service each week. Not only did this give affirmation of her spiritual path but she drew comfort from being, at least for the duration of the meeting, surrounded by people.

Sarah's arrival came as brilliantly as drawing back heavy curtains to find bright sunshine streaming warmth and light into the room. This pretty, biddable girl changed everything for Cooper. Laborious tasks were made easier when accompanied by lively chatter and the girl's irrepressible giggle. Within days their routine included gossip over cups of tea and soon confidences were being exchanged, troubles shared.

Sarah was desperately anxious about the whereabouts of her little brother and not a day went by without them discussing the possibilities of where he might be working and why he had not contacted his family.

Having no family of her own, Cooper grew to involve herself in Sarah's worries and was genuine in her sympathy to their problems.

Likewise, she enjoyed the romantic tale of Joe falling in love with an orphan girl and having to wait to be married until she was free. Through Sarah, Cooper began to see the villagers as real men and women, suddenly they had names, little anecdotes associated with them of their struggles, loves or habits and as she learned about her neighbours she realised she had feared them out of ignorance.

Sarah revelled in her new life. Not only were her working hours shorter and her wage slightly higher but there were the delights of being out and about during the daytime. Twice a week she would accompany Cooper up the hill to shop in Lanark and, released from the daily twelve hour shifts enclosed in the Mill, even pegging out the washing in the middle of the day and chatting with passers-by, filled her with pleasure.

Only her nagging concern for Cal prevented her from being completely content.

Fiona was also worried about Joe's brother, but the delight of being married to her beloved and the satisfaction of being warmly included in his family had changed her life completely. She felt whole, as if the tortuous past four years were a dreadful nightmare and she had awakened to find herself free and cared for in a way she never thought possible.

Her new duties at the school were interesting and a blessed, almost frivolous occupation after the grind of the spinning machines. She slept in Joe's arms, holding his hand, delightfully aware of his presence, protective, affectionate, and would open her eyes to greet each day with pleasurable anticipation.

Every week more Highlanders were arriving to take up residence in the newly completed Caithness Row. It was a magnificent curved line of five storey tenements, beautiful in its simplicity. Joe looked on it with pride, as he did with most of the buildings he had helped to construct. Where others saw the finished stone work as merely part of the structure, his eye lingered on the lintels and details, critically assessing their lines, knowing which ones he had personally worked on, occasionally chiding himself for some perceived imperfections.

He was becoming skilled in his work, occasionally being taken up to his master's workshop in Lanark to be shown new techniques and see the array of precision tools he would acquire as he progressed. He was tasked to make a piece to be judged by Ewing. If it was declared competent he would be given more responsibility, delegated to carry out commissions outside New Lanark and this would have the added bonus of a raise in wages.

After discussion with Fiona and his sisters he chose a large block of sandstone and set about engraving a headstone for Meg.

***

Within the comparatively ordered, fair structure of Dale's mill village, the Scotts and the majority of the other residents were content with their lives. The work was hard, dangerous even, but within the community there was a sense of security. However, New Lanark was an exception.

Up the hill in the old market town of Lanark and most of the other towns across the Lowlands, membership of the local groups affiliated to the Scottish Association of the Friends of the People was gathering momentum. Even Joe's master stonemason, Bill Ewing, attended their meetings and spread the word of demanding better laws to represent the working classes. They wanted to remove the suppressive bias towards the landed gentry and aristocrats.

183

The issue of separating from England and taking back control of Scotland's own Parliament was also on the agenda and one that held wide and passionate appeal.

Thomas Muir arranged a General Convention of delegates from all the branches of the Friends of the People, including representations from the United Irishmen, calling for them to meet in Edinburgh before the end of the year.

Unbeknownst to him, this assembly was infiltrated by government spies who reported the proceedings to be anti-Unionist and treasonable. Muir became a marked man from that day on, but oblivious to the betrayal, he set about preparing his brief as defence counsel for his friend and associate James Tytler who, having carried Muir's words in his periodical, was charged with sedition.

Hundreds of miles away on a drab, cloudy Tuesday, early in December, a day to be spent like any other work-day for the Scotts, the French people were turning out in their thousands to witness the opening day of the trial of their deposed King.

Dale and his associates clustered round their tables in the Tontine Rooms, debating the merits of various outcomes for the wretched King Louis XV1.

Beyond the steamy windows, across Scotland's wintery land, the same discussions were taking place in drawing rooms, parlours, inns and workshops. The blustery sleet-filled winds rattling their windows were winds of change. Men in high places, instigated by Members of Parliament like the Scottish Home Secretary, Dundas, were moved to action. This was a dangerous time, they wanted Muir and his followers to be stopped.

Secluded in their little village down on the banks of the Clyde, the Hogmanay celebrations in New Lanark were once again arranged by Big Lachie, however this year there was double the amount of Highlanders in the village.

They were all keen to throw off their cares for a night of dancing and musical merriment and when the bell rang to release the mill workers, they found the bonfire already lit and tankards waiting for them charged with ale.

Sarah and Rosie persuaded Mrs Cooper to join them beside the bonfire to cheer in the Bells, but Joe and Fiona preferred to remain in the warmth of their room and experience the start of the new year in privacy.

'Ah dare say we'll hear the commotion frae here when it's gone midnight.' Fiona murmured, cuddling into Joe under the blankets. The room was softly lit by fire light and Joe placed a candle on the table, joking that he wished to see her beauty, not just feel it.

She had never been shy or embarrassed by her nakedness in front of her husband and it was a rare treat to be alone in the house together, not discretely closed in the dark behind the bed's drawn curtains.

She was waiting for that special moment, the moment of the bells. It would mark the minute he proposed to her twelve months before and she held it in a special place in her heart. Soon enough, there was a sudden halt to the music, followed by a silence.

Joe held his wife close and kissed her lovingly as a rousing cheer roared through the village. She returned his kisses with passion then pulled away from him, propping herself up on one elbow.

'Tis a full year that Ah ha'e bin yours, ma dearest. An' nigh on three month tha' we've bin wed.' A blush of pink swept up over her face, her huge dark eyes sparkling in the candle light. She smoothed away her tousled hair, lips quivering with emotion. 'Joe, ma darlin' Joe... Ah am wi' child.'

He was over-joyed by the news, hugging her and kissing her with a new tenderness. He knew little of pregnancies or babies but had gleaned along the way that girls took sick in the early months; Fiona showed nothing of these symptoms.

'Are ye sure? Are ye a'richt? Ye feel well?'

'Ah'm no' ill, ma dear, Ah'm havin' a babe, tis the most natural thing in the world!'

'Do the girls knaw?'

'Och naw! Wid Ah be tellin' ony one else afore ye?' She started to cry, the tears trickling down her face. She licked them from her lips, smiling at him, 'Ah'm tha' happy, Joe. Thankee...'

He found he was crying and too choked to speak, he pulled her down beside him and carefully arranged the blankets over her shoulders. She saw his wet lashes, understood the crumpled, compressed lines around his mouth as he fought for control.

'Happy tears...' she whispered, entwining her fingers in his and nuzzling his neck.

When Joe's sisters crashed through the door, giggling and red faced from the cold air and glasses of ale, they found Joe and Fiona sitting by the fire, hastily dressed to welcome them in and wish them New Year greetings.

The news of the expected baby drew more cries of delight and it was several hours later before the candles were snuffed and the room fell silent.

***

A few days into the new year, Archibald Paterson sat by the fire in Dale's study with a cup of strong coffee in his hand, his right leg propped up on a stool.

He suffered from bouts of gout and the rich food over the festivities had exacerbated the condition. The stricken foot was bound with red bandages which extended up to just short of his breeches and exhibited an expanse of his mottled, hairy leg. As he could only wear one boot and found walking with the stick slow and painful, he had decided to call on Dale, his neighbour, because it was only a matter of a few steps to the next seat.

The two men had known each other for over thirty years and been business partners selling imported yarns from Holland and Flanders in the '60s. Although their partnership was dissolved in the early '80s, Dale continued to trade from their shop at Hopkirk's Land and, on his appointment as first Glasgow agent to the Royal Bank of Scotland, he retained the premises for his new venture.

It was rumoured that Paterson felt snubbed at Dale's choice to trade alone, especially as it was uncannily close to the start of the lucrative banking appointment. However, whether the coffee room gossip was right or not, they remained friends.

Paterson was an exceedingly wealthy man. His collaboration with Dale had been just one of many, his real profits came when he branched out into property development. Indeed, it was he who saw the potential in buying a large tract of land in the Gallowgate and constructing a street straight through the middle. He called it Charlotte Street, in deference to the Queen, and set aside the end furthest from the city to be apportioned into generous plots, six on either side.

Dale, of course, bought the first plot, and Paterson took the one beside it for himself. The remaining ten plots were snapped up by tobacco merchants, architects and even James Jackson, the Postmaster.

It was now an exclusive and highly desirable address.

'Has the disquiet among the workers affected your mills?' he asked Dale now.

'Not at all! I hope I can place my hand on my heart and state that everyone in my employ is treated justly. They have no need to rise up and complain.'

'You have a considerable work force, I gather? Both locally and in the Highlands.'

'The northern mills are not going as well as I hoped. Even Dempster, stalwart that he is for the bettering of conditions up there, has to admit that Spinningdale is not producing as it should. Lack of labour... lack of willingness to leave the sodden, peaty land and even *consider* living in dry housing or working indoors! I ask you? What more can I do? It's the same story over at Oban!'

'And New Lanark and Catrine?'

'Ah, now, they are performing very well! You must come down and visit. I am very proud of them.'

'I doubt if I would enjoy a tour of a cotton mill, my friend, but your company is always good for my soul and Mrs Paterson might enjoy a sojourn to the country when the summer comes.'

A footman entered and set down a tray with fresh coffee and a bowl of boiled sugar sweets. He stoked the coal fire before retiring quietly from the room.

Paterson undid a couple of buttons on his jacket and loosened his silk cravat. It was pleasantly warm in the room despite the rain spattering against the windows. He cast an appreciative eye around the octagonal walls, this was a very comfortable and distinguished gentleman's study.

'Did ye read that Thomas Muir was arrested?' he asked, popping a boiled sweet in to his mouth and adding awkwardly, 'What d'ye make o' that?'

'Aye, he's made himself some powerful enemies.' Dale left his desk and took the chair on the other side of the hearth, easing his sturdy backside into the upholstery with care; was the chair growing narrower? Unfortunately, he knew this was not the case.

'An' now he's out on bail an' away to London.' Paterson sucked loudly on the solid boiled sugar. 'If I were him I don't think I would come back. Dundas and Braxfield have their knives drawn.'

'I dare say he feels he can ask for support from Lauderdale, after all he's a fellow Scotsman and seems to be a major participant in the English Society for reform.'

'I wager they are all running scared down at Westminster, I wouldn't count on any help from that neck o' the woods.' Paterson eased the cushion under his ailing foot, wincing as he moved. 'De'il of a pain, this!' He settled himself more comfortably. 'If the Advertiser's correspondent has it right, the Frenchies are about to cut the head off their king, that'll embolden the Republican troops!'

'It is a black, ungodly regime that holds power over there, I pray for the citizens. If they would just take heed of the Lord's words and care for each other, work together to overcome the unjust laws that have led to this turn of events! Goodness, they now have civil marriages, forbidding even a word from the Lord's teachings to guide them on their way!' Dale's jowly cheeks shook as he spoke.

Two days later, Dale was reminded of their conversation when news came through that Louis XV1 was to be executed.

There was a footnote to the article to say that Thomas Muir was no longer in London but was believed to be sailing across the Channel to plead on the sovereign's behalf in the hope of a stay of execution.

The efforts of Muir and many other supporters of the French King were to no avail. Louis XV1 was guillotined on 21st January.

Even as society tried to come to terms with the enormity of this act, there were further developments to talk about, developments which involved everybody.

France declared war on Britain.

Chapter Six

"Gentlemen, from my infancy to this moment, I have devoted myself to the cause of the People. It is a good cause. It shall ultimately prevail. It shall finally triumph."

Thomas Muir – High Court
Edinburgh 31st August 1793.

On a bright morning in early March, Joe sought out the team of labourers working at the foot of the village.

'Tam,' he shouted up to his friend, 'can ye gi'e me a haun?'

'Whit fae?'

'Ah need a haun wi' puttin' the heidstane up on Meg's grave.'

'Ah can nae come the noo but mibbee o'er dinner break?'

'Grand! Ah'll meet ye by ma hoose.'

Joe hurried back up the hill to ask to borrow a hand cart, waving to Sarah as he passed her pegging out washing beside Dale's house. She was singing, enjoying the fresh spring air, her golden hair drawn back under a neat white muslin bonnet.

'Tam can come up aboot dinner time. Can ye be free then?' he called.

Sarah had already discussed the possibility with Mrs Cooper and called back that she would keep an eye open for them passing and join them.

The beautifully carved stone was covered by a sack wrapped with thick leather straps. It was immensely heavy and took all of Joe and Tam's combined strength to lift it onto the hand cart. With the wheels beneath it, they manoeuvred it carefully up the hill, beside the steps, with Sarah walking ahead. In places, the rise was so steep that Joe

189

was forced to crouch among the new green shoots of woodrush, digging his heels amongst brittle brown leaves of last season's ferns to get purchase on the slope and dragging it towards him, with Tam shoving it from behind. Eventually, puffing and sweating, they trundled it between new graves to its position. Joe had spent some time that morning excavating the hole and with his friend's help they lowered it off the cart and into place.

It was only then that he untied the straps and lifted off the sack. The top of the stone was carved to form an arch and beneath it was the silhouette of a child kneeling in prayer, encircled by an intricately chiselled ribbon and bow.

'Aw Joe, tha's the brawest thing Ah've iver seen!' Sarah exclaimed, reaching out a hand to touch the finely hewn inscription. 'Whit does the letterin' say?'

Joe traced his finger along the lines of letters, "Here Lies Margaret 'Meg' Scott 1783-1788, At Peace'.' He stood back, his eyes still on the stone. 'Ewing says it's guid enough tae be passed as his ane, an tha's his highest praise!'

'How did ye ken whit tae write?' Tam asked, incredulous. 'An' the picture?'

'Fiona drew it a' oot fae me. She's the only ane who's seen it. Ah wis worrid incase Ah made a stupit mistake, bu' she ken's its a'richt.'

He smiled to himself remembering her genuine admiration of his efforts.

When the earth was filled in around the stone and securely stamped down, Sarah laid a bunch of snowdrops beneath it and spontaneously they all bowed their heads and stood for a moment in silence.

'Ah's best be gettin' back,' Sarah said, 'Thank ye fer helpin' us Tam!' she kissed him on the cheek and swung away down the hill, stopping from time to time to pick more blooms from the pools of white snowdrops.

'My yer Sarah is awfy bonnie, Joe.' Tam said, watching her until she was out of view.

'Why don't ye ask her fer a walk? Ye've known her a while noo an' ne'er said anythin' tae me aboot fancyin' her!'

'Och, away! A lass like tha' is no' fer me! She wid laugh an' tell us tae jump in yon river!'

Joe smiled at him, seeing Tam as his sister might see him: rough, wiry with curly brown hair and an angular face. It was his sound character and exuberant love of life that made him so popular, but were these the attributes a girl would appreciate?

'Ye can ask her? Ye ne'er know!'

'Naw, Ah've bin thinkin' o' daein' summat else though. Ye ken they're recruitin' fae the army up in toon this week? Ah ha'e a mind tae gae.'

'Tae join up? Gae tae France?'

'Ah cannae stay in Lanark fillin' barras a' ma life! Tis different fer ye, Joe. Ye have a wife an' a wean on the way, a home and...' he gestured to the headstone, 'a trade. Ah'm jist a labourer. Ah want tae see mair o' the world, foreign lands....'

'An' ye can get yersel' killed an' a'! Gi'e it plenty o' thocht, Tam.'

'Aye,' Tam grinned and winked at him. 'Ah will.'

The next day, Tam signed up to three years in His Majesty's Armed Forces.

By May, many young men from Clydesdale had been seduced by the promise of an exciting life and the idealised notion of protecting their homeland from the dangers of invading French troops.

One of the men who worked at William Kelly's house left a few weeks after Tam. He had also attended to much of the heavy work in Dale's house so, until a replacement was found, Sarah and Mrs Cooper took on the burden of emptying the coal sacks and replenishing their water butt from the lade.

Tired and slightly annoyed at having soiled her newly laundered white apron with coal dust, Sarah left her work one evening brushing ineffectually at the offending grey smears. Her mind was on the contents of her cupboard and what would be the easiest meal to prepare for that evening.

As a housemaid, her hours were shorter than any of the rest of her family and it usually fell to her to make the dinner.

She did not look on it as a chore, it was the sensible routine to follow and meant that food was on the table when the others came home. Since being with Mrs Cooper, an accomplished cook, she was enjoying learning new recipes and methods of combining ingredients in ways she would never have imagined.

So, her thoughts were on domestic matters when she entered their room and found a figure slumped in the chair by the fireside.

The noise of her opening the door startled the figure who jerked upright and Sarah, caught unawares, let out a cry.

It was Calum.

191

After her initial shock, Sarah rushed to take him in her arms and he stood up to welcome the embrace.

'Aw Cal! Calum... let me see ye? Where ha'e ye bin a' this time?' She hugged him and clutched him tightly against her. 'We've a' bin tha' worrid!'

At last she released him and stood back to see him properly. He was a lot thinner, his deep set eyes dark rimmed with shadows, his cheek bones jutting out of a hollowed, sallow face.

'It's gie guid tae be hame...' he said hoarsely, his voice in the stages of breaking to a man's deep timbre.

'Where ha'e ye bin?' There was anxiety in his sister's question, she was horrified by the sight of him. 'Where e'er it wis, there wis nae ony food. Yer skin an' bone!'

'T'were bad, bad... but Ah could nae leave afore now...' he burst into a fit of coughing, doubling over to hold his sides and sinking down onto the chair again.

Sarah laid a hand on his forehead. 'Yer burnin' ! Ye ha'e a fever! Cal, whit's wrang wi' ye, d'ye ken?' As she spoke she was feeding the fire and swinging the kettle over the flames. 'When did ye last eat?'

'Ah dinnae ken, mibbee a day past...' another bout of coughing, leading him to wretch.

She helped him undress and discovered his body was infested with lice, his hair running with them. Throwing his clothes in a heap in the wash basin ready to cut up and burn, she took out some of their precious soap and washed him down, trying to be gentle where he had open sores from scratching himself. Like a small, trusting child, he let her tend to him, meekly lifting a hand or moving this way and that as she dried him and dressed him in one of his old mill tunics before settling him to rest in her bed.

It was only right, she thought, that he should have the comfort of the large inset bed while he was ill.

'When did ye get yon cough?' she asked, handing him a bowl of porridge.

'A while back, winter, it's bin bad since the snaw. Ah got awfy chilled... ' he shivered as memories threatened to crowd in upon him. He spooned in the oatmeal.

'D'ye ha'e pain wi' it? Ye haud yer ribs like they're sair? An' yer shoulder? '

'Aye, Ah ache doon ma back as weel. Och, Ah'm jist sair.' His eyes told her more: he was seriously ill and needed help.

Joe was the first to come home and decided to fetch the doctor right away.

The diagnosis was swift: pneumonia.

For weeks they nursed him, hurrying home from work to give him company after his long days of lying alone in the bed. Physically he began to gain strength and the racking cough subsided a little but he was a different boy from the one who left them on that rainy day last autumn.

There was a hard, bitter streak festering inside. He would not be drawn about where he had been for all those months and a shutter would clamp down if they pressed for information. Sometimes, his cries and shouts would wake them in the middle of the night but when a candle was lit and they went to his side, they found him in a deep sleep, sweating, tears running down his face.

For Calum the dreadful experiences of being worked almost to death on a remote estate were too terrible to express. He was ashamed to have allowed himself to become such a victim; a servant to a heartless, demanding master who treated him, and the other lad on the steading, like vermin.

Many's the time he was punished, beaten or forbidden his daily bowl of oatmeal. His apparent crimes were petty, spilling a bucket of feed by mistake, leaving a rake in the wrong place, taking too long to muck out the stalls.

How could he tell Joe that he took on such a job rather than enter the mills again?

The mills were dreary, noisy and dusty but in their own way he now realised that they were safer than the outside world. Even the Overseers, who he hated when they roared at him and chased him not to dally, might raise a hand to him in threat but never struck him.

Far the worst part of his time away was pining for his family. Even at nearly fifteen years old he often cried himself to sleep, curled up in the hay barn, miserable beneath a tarpaulin.

Now, when he woke to find himself back in his home, the events at the farm seemed unreal. It was as if those ghastly memories came from another boy, in another life. It was best to leave them separate, for to even talk about them brought them into the light and acknowledged they happened.

193

He wanted to blank it from his mind, wipe the past away. So he refused to speak of them, leaving his brother and sisters frustrated.

By the hot days of summer, he was well enough to take care of the lighter tasks around the house. This was a blessing to Fiona who was imminently about to give birth.

Her teaching work was sedate and undemanding so she agreed with the new teacher she was working beside, Mr Hardy, that she would carry on assisting with the classes until the baby arrived.

Conveniently, she started to feel the first dragging, squeezing pains, not in the school room but while taking a stroll, arm in arm, with Sarah. Excited and nervous, the girls returned to the house. With Bessie popping in and out to give advice, they prepared for a long vigil.

However, it was barely a couple of hours before Fiona was gripping Joe's hand and screaming unintelligible Gaelic oaths as she summoned every ounce of strength to deliver her first baby.

Whether they could understand her words or not, it was clear to them all from her vicious tone that she was in a fury.

Bessie laid down her knitting and went to join Sarah and Joe at the bedside.

'It'll no' be lang noo,' she said wisely. 'When they get a' angry at ye it's a sure sign the babbie's on its way.'

Her words were borne out when, after a final, tremendous effort, the baby was born.

'It's a wee boy!' cried Sarah, wrapping a square of clean linen around the tiny, screaming infant and laying him in Fiona's arms.

Everyone clustered round the bed with Rosie and Sarah hugging each other. Even Cal, who had been keeping out of the way beside the fire, was grinning from ear to ear and peering over their shoulders to catch a glimpse of his new nephew.

'Donald,' said Joe, unashamedly weeping with emotion as he gazed in awe at his dark haired, red faced son. 'We will ca' the bairn Donald, after yer faither, ma darlin''

'Donald,' Fiona murmured, exhausted yet utterly elated. 'Aw Aye, Joe. Ah wid like tha'. *Fàilte,* Donald Scott, welcome.'

***

For the Scotts, the long summer which followed was spent becoming accustomed to the new member of their family. The escalating horrors of the French situation seemed a long way away.

Robespierre, now a dictator and declaring himself a 'Supreme Being', was becoming paranoid and turning his attention to beheading anyone he perceived might attempt to stand in his way or overthrow him.

Thousands of men and women, many of them no more than peasants, were being sent to the guillotines in groups of fifty or sixty at a time.

Dale read the newspapers avidly and met with his colleagues to discuss the possible dire consequences of the war. When Robespierre was eventually brought to book by the Convention and arrested, it was the talk of the Tontine Rooms.

Having thrown himself into work and current affairs since his wife's death, Dale was busier than ever with his duties as a magistrate. He was also taking an active role in the Glasgow Chambers of Commerce. The war with France brought many and varied implications to the merchants of the city and along with his other businesses, he had to attend more meetings with his partner, Robert Scott Moncrieff, at their branch of the Royal Bank of Scotland.

On his return from a short visit to New Lanark, he found that Thomas Muir was once again in the news and his situation had worsened.

Chiding himself for neglecting his old friend in a time of need, Dale penned a letter to James Muir, asking if it was convenient to call on him at his home at Huntershill.

A few days later Dale's carriage drew up outside the Muir family home, an attractive white house on the old post road to Stirling, lying just north of the city at Bishopbriggs.

James Muir greeted him in the hallway. He was haggard and stooped, appearing much older than Dale recalled and having lost a great deal of weight, his dark jacket and breeches hung loosely on his tall frame.

It was a warm late August day so they seated themselves in the garden in the shade of a magnificent old oak tree and drank tea, served by his butler.

'I read of your son's trial.' Dale said after the preamble of social niceties. 'I gather he was arrested on returning from France.'

'Aye, he never intended to evade the law, ye know. It has all been a terrible series of misadventures. Had he not sought to plead on the French king's behalf last winter, he might not be in the position he is now.'

'He actually believed he could prevent the king's execution?' Dale asked.

'Oh Aye, but he arrived in Paris on the eve of the execution so he was denied the opportunity. While there, he was given warm hospitality and even met and conversed with Thomas Paine. Having been an ardent admirer of Paine's publication, the Rights of Man, he was delighted with the association and through him met like-minded men.' James sighed and took a sip of tea.

'This must all be a very difficult time for you,' Dale said sympathetically.

'It is, my friend, it is. Ye know Lord Braxfield has used him as an example, don't ye? The trial was a sham! When Thomas returned to Scotland in the spring, he came from Ireland and unfortunately was immediately recognised and taken to Edinburgh's Tolbooth jail.'

Dale nodded, he knew Robert MacQueen, now Lord Justice Braxfield, having purchased land from him to build New Lanark. Indeed, recently appointed to the position of Lord Justice Clerk, Scotland's leading Judge, his cruel, unsympathetic practices knew no bounds.

'It was reported in the newspaper.'

'The conditions were *dreadful*! I visited him... no man wants to see his son, his intelligent, God fearing son, in a place like that. They struck him from the Register ye know! While he was abroad! He cannot practise in a court now.' Muir swept a hand over his face in an effort to control his emotions. 'He cannot practise anywhere now! Transportation... fourteen years in Botany Bay! That's what that devil of a Judge has done to my boy!

'Now they have him locked up on an armed cutter, the Royal George, at Leith...' His voice was cracking, 'I'll not live to see fourteen years, Dale, I've seen the last of ma boy...'

Dale waited until the other man had composed himself again before offering comforting words and drawing his attention to relevant portions of the Bible.

They were both religious men and for a long time they sat talking together in the garden. Birds sang in the trees, the sweet scents of newly cut grass and privot hedging stirred in the air. It was not for

196

them to understand the ways of the Lord, they had only to trust in Him and pray for justice and the safe keeping of young Thomas.

It had been a harrowing afternoon but as Dale's carriage rolled back through the countryside towards the Merchant City, he looked at the spires on the horizon and hoped he had given Muir a little comfort.

Preaching God's word gave him solace. As much as he hoped it was enlightening for his audience, he found it a balm to his own soul. What was life about if it was not to spread the word of God and give others the hope of salvation and life everlasting?

There was such misery and hardship to be found in every corner of society, everyone had their problems to bear. James Muir's heart-breaking predicament was just one of thousands of men and women dealing with challenges through their lives. Dale was convinced that embracing the Lord and believing and trusting in Him brought a relief and purpose to it all.

He knew personally of the terrible pain inflicted by loss and tragedy. Not a day passed when he did not feel the ache of missing Carolina or pray for her and his departed children.

Now he must take care of their daughters and strive to maintain his businesses through the turbulent months ahead. It was his duty to look out for all the workers who depended on him and ensure their employment and living conditions were not damaged by the War.

As the horses trotted past a corn field his eye was caught by a group of colourfully dressed women throwing sheaves of straw into stooks. Ahead of them a line of men were steadily scything across the golden crop.

Dale's mind lingered on using the theme of harvesting for his next sermon and he was so wrapped up in the composition that before he knew it, the carriage was passing through houses and he was among the city streets.

He sighed, praised God for delivering him through the darkest hours and looked forward to spreading the Lord's word on Sunday.

***

197

The golden days of autumn drew imperceptibly into the shorter, grey days of winter. Just as the woodland animals took refuge underground or bundled into dreys and nests to cope with the lean dark months, so did the villagers of New Lanark.

The empty streets no longer resounded to music and gossip. During the few hours of daylight it was only housewives who scuttled to the middens and coal stores, hunched under their shawls, their faces screwed up against the cold. When the Mill bell tolled the end of the day, there was a rush from the mills to every tenement door-way, seeking warmth around the firesides, behind shuttered windows.

Rain and wind battered the trees, ripping away leaves and branches and sending torrents of water foaming and swirling through the gorge.

There was hardly any snow that winter and only the occasional sparkling, frosty morning. So rare was it to see the sun that, despite the accompanying bone-chilling temperatures, these were welcomed as a departure from the monotonous gloom of thick cloud.

Little Donald Scott proved to be a contented baby. Disturbed nights in the Scotts' room soon passed and by the spring he was sleeping through the whole night.

It was Cal who was causing concern.

His rattling cough persisted, leaving him shattered and weak. At Joe's insistence, he returned to his school work but would come home to fall onto his bed, exhausted. He was certainly not fit enough to do a day's work but it preyed on his mind that he was becoming a burden on his family.

Every morning he watched Rosie rise and light the fire, preparing herself to leave when the mill bell sounded. As she was going out the door, Fiona would be up and about, making porridge and heating water for Joe to shave while she was feeding Donald. Then Sarah would draw back her bed curtain and step over him on the hurlie bed and then she too would get ready for a full day's work in her smart black dress and white apron.

And he, Calum?

He looked on their activity from under his blankets, hearing their chatter, the bell and their called cheerios as one by one they left for work. From outside on the landing came the familiar trampling of dozens of footsteps descending the stairs, workers, folk earning their living. When the last clatter of clogs and resounding slams of the tenement doors died away on the morning air, only Fiona and the baby would remain.

He felt useless. He was among the women with their babies, decrepit old people and the sick.

Fiona was sweet and kind to him and Joe kept telling him not to fret, he would be stronger soon. They were all so loving and forgiving, which made it worse.

Days ran into weeks, the weeks into months and when the thorn bushes foamed with white blossom in May, Calum admired their blooms with a sinking heart; it was a full year since he had escaped from the farm and trudged back through the hills to New Lanark.

Time hung heavily and he spent whole days lying in his bed wrapped in dismal thought, with little energy to rise and dress until evening came and it was time to eat and leave for his lessons.

He was no longer a part of the gang of mill lads who he worked beside for four years. They looked on his departure from the village as a personal rejection and excluded him from their street games. One of the most popular boys, Ewan, lead the gang in calling insults to him if he happened to be passing.

Hunching his shoulders and pretending to cough and wheeze, Ewan played to his audience, exaggerating Cal's laborious gait in a hurtful parody, earning boisterous laughter from the others.

Calum had always found it hard to make friends and took their abuse and mocking sniggers to heart.

It was a hot day in early summer before he summoned the strength and courage to knock on the office door at Kelly's house. He could see no alternative but to ask for a job in the mills. McCulloch had left his position due to ill health so he was seen by a clerk who was brusque and efficient.

Although he was fifteen, Cal's obvious, debilitated condition meant that he was offered a task more usually given to a five or six year old. It carried a very low wage.

He asked for a day to reflect on signing the contract and returned to the Row with his head low. A dark despair whispered in his ears, the pointlessness of his day to day life spread out before him: years of toil, for what? Along with the voice in his head there was confusion, an unbearable longing to rid himself of the torment of futility that shrouded his every waking moment. This was immediately followed by panic because he could see no way out.

He was trapped in a life he hated.

Half way to his home he turned, as if in a daze, and walked back down into the village. As he passed Dale's house Mrs Cooper was coming out the door. She smiled at him demurely, giving a little wave and he glanced towards the movement of her raised hand.

For a second their eyes met and the housekeeper felt a startling rush of terror. The boy's deep brown eyes held a look she had seen before, an expression so agonised it was etched in her mind for all time: hopeless, lost and desperate.

Cal walked past her towards the Highlander's new housing and then down the hill to cross the bridge over the lade. Mrs Cooper had never ventured to that part of the village before, except to attend the bonfire at Hogmanay. She was still fearful of the swarthy, foreign speaking people who inhabited those rows of tenements. Yet, without a moment's hesitation, she was impelled to follow this stricken, round-shouldered lad as he wound his way towards the river.

Her skirts kicking out around her neat little black boots, Mrs Cooper broke into a run to hold him in her sight. Her heart was thumping, her breath loud in the still summer air. At the bottom of the village, upstream of the mills, were the iron foundries. This was unknown territory to her, terrifying with roaring furnaces and men in their rolled up shirt sleeves and leather aprons, but she pressed on, her eyes fixed on the boy's awkward, plodding figure.

She came to an archway between two buildings where the noise and heat were tremendous. Two work horses were tethered by the forge door and she edged past their massive hind quarters, holding herself clear of their tails as they swished at annoying clouds of flies. Through the open door she glimpsed some men inside, illuminated by the red glow of the fire. They were shouting to one another and hammering at metal, sending sparks flying into the air.

None of them noticed Calum, but she could see him. She started to run, shouting his name, over and over.

He was clambering up the rocks above Dundaff Linn and though she was sure he could hear her, he never so much as paused. Hand upon hand, his bare feet gripping the slabs of stone, he ascended the cliff.

She couldn't let him carry on, what would it do to Sarah if her brother jumped to his death?

Realising that she was not capable of following him up the rocks, she swung round and ran back to the forge. The men stared at her, open mouthed, as she pleaded with them to save the lad on the cliff top.

Big Lachie strode to the door way and, seeing Calum stretching up for the last few hand holds, the huge man threw down his tools and ran to the cliff.

He made the climb appear effortless, swinging from rock to rock until he was within reach of the boy. Heedless of his cries, he caught him up and hoisted him on to his shoulder, then slowly retraced his steps down to the ground.

Ross Macinnes, Big Lachie's brother, joined them by the waterfall.

'Whit's a' this aboot?' he demanded, turning from Cal's stoney face to Mrs Cooper.

She was suddenly at a loss as what to say. Had she imagined the gravity of the situation, made herself appear foolish? Then she looked at Calum again and knew she had not been mistaken. Even the Macinnes' men, complete strangers to his life, were grasping the seriousness of what they witnessed. They too, could read the turmoil in his face.

'He has not been well,' she said simply. 'A prolonged illness...'

'Ah'm done wi' a' this!' Calum blurted out, not meeting their eyes. 'Ah'd be better aff deid. Ah'm useless...'

'Ye climbed them rocks, laddie,' Ross said quietly. 'If yer lucky enough tae ha'e life in ye tae tackle tha' cliff, ye should nae be takin' it fer granted. There's plenty poor souls up in yon graveyard who could nae keep a haud on it, an' there's ye aboot tae throw it a' awa'.'

Mrs Cooper couldn't help admiring the gentle, firm tone of the Highlander. She looked afresh at his weather beaten face and thick curling grey hair. He was not a giant of a man like Lachie, who stood beside him, but the craggy features and square jaw were of the same mould.

Calum was taken by a fit of coughing but when it passed he said bitterly, 'Och, ye dinnae un'erstaun' ... Ah need tae work, tae dae summat...'

'Work is it?' Ross shot a look to Lachie and there was a rapid exchange in Gaelic before he continued. 'We've jist lost twa men tae the war, if it's work yer after, ye can clean the harness fer us. It'll be everyday, mind, excepting Sundays.'

Calum blinked hard and rubbed at his nose, dubious, 'Fer truth? Wi' pay?'

'Aye,' Ross spat on his hand and held it out. 'An' when ye're weel agin ye could be handy wi' the horses.'

Calum pushed back his shaggy mass of hair and attempted to spit on his own palm, but his mouth was dry. Self-consciously, he grasped the man's hand.

'Start t'morra.' Ross said firmly.

After the drama of the incident, the group became ill at ease standing by the riverside and Big Lachie barked something to his brother and strode back to the forge.

'Ma brither disnae speak a word o' Scots,' Ross said with a grin, 'but, he can understaun' jist aboot every word ye say, sae dinnae gang thinkin' he cannae!' he gave Cal a slight push on the shoulder, a friendly gesture, but saw the instant fear on the boy's face.

With a stab of protective maternal instinct, Mrs Cooper also noted him flinch: it wasn't just his lungs that were damaged.

In the absence of any words from Cal, she thanked the Macinnes men on his behalf and walked back up through the village, Cal at her side.

'Dinnae tell ma sister, eh?' he said, when they were crossing the bridge.

'Very well, if that's what you wish.'

He nodded, 'D'ye think they mean it? Aboot the job?'

'Aye, of course they do! There are good people in this world as well as bad, Calum. I hope you can discover that for yourself.'

He shrugged, coughing again. 'Well, tis better than the mill.'

Much later, when she turned the wick of the lamp down and rested her head on her pillow, Mrs Cooper relived the episode.

It brought back such unpleasant memories that she lay long into the night wrapped in the past, reliving another time, a time with her husband.

That last fateful embrace goodbye, when she saw the pain in his eyes, the same expression she recognised instantly in Calum. Only then, she did not act upon it. Her dear Robert was so down at heart about life and unable to deal with the daily knocks and injustices it delivered, no matter how hard she tried to console him.

He left her arms and walked straight to the Clyde, where he jumped from the bridge and drowned. In taking his own life he had sinned against himself, against God, and her almost fanatical religious beliefs would not allow him forgiveness.

Calum only informed his family of his new job when he rose from his bed early the next morning.

They were startled at the news, exclaiming that he was not yet well enough and firing questions as to how he had heard that there was work available at the forge. Who had he spoken to? what would he be doing?

He didn't reply, not wishing to raise his own hopes that the offer had been made in good faith. Part of him still wondered if he would turn up that morning just to be ridiculed and sent away again.

However, he was greeted with a nod from Ross and taken into a shadowy barn where, when his eyes adjusted to the gloom, he saw an assortment of harnesses, bridles and saddles on hooks and racks around the walls.

Left alone to get on with it, he immediately set about fetching water and dragging a bench to the doorway so he could work in the sun light. Swallows swooped over his head to their nests in the rafters behind him, the over-flow from the mill lade splashed nearby but otherwise he was left alone. He liked that, just being allowed to work at his own pace, take his time. It didn't matter if he paused to watch the birds, or if he was overtaken with a coughing fit. He could recover in his own time with no one there to see him, fussing, bullying or jeering.

Soon the pleasant scent of saddle soap and the rewarding pleasure of polishing the buckles in the warm sunshine began to ease him out of some of his initial anxiety.

In the middle of the day Ross came in, pulled a newly cleaned bridle from the hook and brought it to the door to examine it.

'Guid enough,' he said, his manner less abrupt than with his other workers.

There was little response from Calum and Ross went back to the forge.

'*He's an odd one, that new lad.*' he said to Lachie in Gaelic. '*Troubled. We had best keep an eye on him, the river's a mere step away.*'

***

Anne Caroline dried her eyes and squared her shoulders. She was feeling very upset and knew that any display of her sadness would not be appropriate.

203

The family were staying in New Lanark for a special reason, a celebration: David Dale was presiding over the baptism of his new baby nephew. It was not yet a year since James and Marion were married and his youthful wife was brimming with happiness. The infant was a boy and the reason for Anne Caroline's tears was the choice of his name, William.

No one could ever replace her little brother and although she knew that her uncle discussed their choice of name with her father, it brought back the pain of her brother's death.

'Of all the names they could have chosen,' she confided in Toshie, 'I do wish they had decided on another. And look, to make it even worse, it is June...' she glanced out the window. 'even the day appears the same as the day he died...'

'Come now, dear,' Toshie spoke firmly, 'There will be many, many babies christened William, and you cannot blame the wee mite for being born in the summer-time. Stop that crying and praise the Lord the child is healthy. This is a happy day, a family gathering when we can all rejoice, so be grateful for it.'

Her words could not be repeated a week later when the same family members donned mourning clothes for the funeral of Dale's other brother, Hugh.

***

The rustling instability in Britain's chattering classes was again making itself known. There was an upsurge in demand for parliamentary reform right across the country. Far from succeeding in stamping out calls for change, instigated by Thomas Muir and his fellow activists, the harsh sentences of transportation meted out to these men only strengthened their cause: they became martyrs.

In London, uncomfortably close to the heart of government and the monarchy, a very organised and eloquent group of men were taking over the reins from the comparatively gentile Friends of the People Societies.

This new London Corresponding Society soon became the target of the government's efforts to suppress free speech.

Thomas Hardy, a Scotsman, was among the main players in the Society and was the first to be put on trial for treason. After being

204

ruthlessly arrested earlier in the year and held in the Tower of London, his case was finally heard in October.

Public sympathy was with him, not only for his views but also because his wife died in childbirth amidst the uproar of his arrest. After an unusually long trial of nine days, he was acquitted, but there were several more of his colleagues to be brought before the courts in London and the newspapers were filled with accounts of the proceedings.

Dale followed the trials closely.

While young Muir had been sent to Botany Bay, Hardy and his colleagues were being charged with Treason which carried the death penalty.

As they discussed at length in the Tontine Rooms, where would all this end? If France could fall into such chaos, was England, and therefore Scotland, going down the same path? And the ruthless means in which their own leaders were proposing hanging, drawing and quartering these men for their ideas, were they so far removed from Robespierre and his bloodied guillotine?

Robbespierre's brutal regime was brought to an end during the summer when he was put to trial and found guilty of his extreme, unjustifiable slaughter. Sentenced to death, he discovered for himself the decisive finality of 'Madame Guillotine.'

It was a turbulent, disturbing year.

However by the end of December a little light was coming through the darkness on the continent; Christians in France were to be allowed to worship again, openly, in their churches. This piece of news, more than any other from across the Channel, brought hope to Dale and his fellow churchgoers in Britain.

On Old Year's Day, Dale spent several hours writing letters and attending to his many ledgers.

For Hogmanay, the Dales were invited to a function at Patterson's house, next door, and the older girls were spending the afternoon in their bedrooms preparing for the occasion. Their Aunt Margaret was with them which not only gave Anne Caroline and her sisters the benefit of feminine advice but also provided Hugh's widow with a useful distraction in an otherwise empty day.

Dale left his desk, his joints aching from sitting too long in the same position, and walked over to the study window to look out at the frozen garden.

A week ago a severe frost had taken a grip on Scotland and far from releasing its hold, it was becoming more intense. Every blade of grass, twig and stone was encased in ice, sparkling to the top of the trees and rooftops. It was a wonderful sight to behold, a miracle of nature brought about by sudden plummeting temperatures freezing a thick fog. Today the air was crystal clear, the view startling in white sunshine flowing down from the fathomless deep blue sky.

He remembered a similar day from his childhood. The memory of a walk taken with his father in the dazzling landscape was as clear if as if it had happened yesterday.

Just before the freeze set in he attended an important meeting, sharing a carriage with his colleagues MacIntosh, Alexander and Scott Moncrieff. It was the culmination of many months, years, of planning and it was a charitable project which was dear to his heart.

At the meeting, the mighty new Glasgow Royal Infirmary was finally established and along with renowned professors and surgeons he was now a Director of this great hospital.

It had long been acknowledged that Glasgow's Town Hospital was struggling to cope with the demand of the city's diseased and injured inhabitants. Glasgow needed somewhere that was wholly given over to ministering to its rapidly growing population and could no longer carry out ad hoc operations or adequate nursing in the present building.

It was unacceptable for the loud sufferings of patients undergoing the agonies of amputations or internal procedures to be experienced in wards shared by watching paupers and lunatics.

As a Magistrate in the city, Dale was involved with the venture from the beginning. He had greatly appreciated the care given to Carolina and little William, so he knew personally of the importance of having a place to turn when loved ones took ill. He was in the fortunate position of being able to pay for physicians to attend his home but the Infirmary, funded by the Council and public subscription, would open its doors to even the poorest. By attracting high calibre surgeons and practitioners it would provide the best possible service.

Building work was now underway on a large plot close to the cathedral. The land had previously held the ruinous remains of the 13th century Bishop's Castle and a Royal Charter was obtained granting this Crown-owned land to the hospital. It was hoped that the doors would open within the next year.

It gave Dale a certain amount of satisfaction to be a Director of such a worthwhile project and he personally pledged five hundred pounds.

'What was the point of making money if you don't put it to good use?' he told Claud Alexander.

Alexander, and possibly MacIntosh, were among the few in his circle who understood his principles.

When others mocked his 'wasted expenditure' on school teachers for the New Lanark school, the stipend for a resident doctor in the village or the extra clothes and bedding he procured for the Boarders, he would shake his head and pray for them. It was as if the lesson of France's impoverished people rising up to demand better conditions meant nothing to some of his wealthy colleagues.

Dale followed his own course and, happily, Alexander was of a similar mind. Both Catrine and New Lanark were making them satisfactory profits even in this depressed market, but it was not at the expense of their workforce.

To mark the arrival of the New Year he arranged a day of celebration for his young Boarders in Mill Four. After talks with the local magistrates in Lanark, his brother James, and Kelly were very much in favour of the idea and, on surveying the icy scene beyond the window, Dale hoped it would pass enjoyably.

So, on the first day of 1795, all three hundred and seven orphaned children from Mill Four walked up the frozen white hillside from New Lanark in an orderly, but excited, procession.

They were dressed in specially made new outfits, the boys in blue suits, their caps trimmed with fur, the girls in white muslin with little black hats. They made a wonderful spectacle moving out of the mill and streaming up the steps, their breath floating in puffs above their heads, noses and cheeks pink.

Many villagers came out to watch them and from an upstairs window in Dale's house, Mrs Cooper and Sarah looked out on the parade. They hoped that this heart warming sight would persuade the people of Lanark that drunkards and womanisers were but a minority in Mr Dale's mill village.

Among the crowd, wrapped up warmly in her brown shawl with her baby on her hip, was Fiona. She waved and called out to many of the children as they passed, knowing them well from her time in Mill Four or from helping them in the schoolroom.

'Aw, Ah wish we'd bin taken up tae the toon when Ah wis a' the mills.' she said to Rosie, as the last of the children disappeared from sight up the silvery, shimmering hillside.

'Ye jeelous?' Rosie teased.

'Awa'! Ah would nae change one thing in ma life noo! Not fae a' the money in Scotland!'

'Aye richt!' said Rosie, yawning; it had been a very late night at the Hogmanay ceilidh.

'Ah ha'e the brawest man in a' the land... and the finest babbie!' She hugged Donald and kissed his forehead. 'Whit mair could Ah wish fae?'

'Anither yin?' Rosie glanced pointedly at Fiona's stomach.

'An' tha's anither reason Ah'm the happiest lass i' the village!' laughed Fiona, placing her hand on the prominent bump under her dress. The new baby was due in the spring.

The girls went back to the fireside to prepare food for Joe and Cal's return. A crowd of the men had left early that morning for a game of curling on the common ground outside the town.

Curling was one of the benefits brought to them by the long freeze. There were several local ponds where curling games took place if the water iced over, but when it was as cold as this winter, they extended the places to enjoy the game by covering areas of flat grass with water and letting it freeze.

Most of the local estates took advantage of even occasional bitterly cold nights in the winter and made curling rinks on their lawns, sprayed by servants during the night and frozen and ready to play on by first light.

However, if the icy weather continued long enough, it was also easily and quickly achieved by ordinary townsfolk. Men and women were carrying buckets of water to any handy, flat piece of land in villages right across Scotland during those freezing days, creating impromptu sheets of ice and hastily organising matches.

Old rivalries reared their heads, new champions were crowned, the games were rounded off as darkness fell with music and dancing by the light of braziers and a feast to keep the chill at bay.

There were two teams from New Lanark and Joe was with several men he knew from the village but he missed Tam. It had been Tam's father who taught him the basics of the game the first winter the two boys met, back in the days when they were labouring together on the foundations for Mill One. Joe took to it easily, he had a good eye for

208

judging distances and a strong swing to send the stone rumbling across the ice.

Now, as a stonemason, he had made his own stones. He chose two lumps of granite over a year before and whenever he had time he'd fashioned them to be almost perfectly round and set a metal handle into the centre with a lump of lead. The design of the handle was copied from the one belonging to Johnny Marshall, a carpenter in the village, who was a real enthusiast for the game.

Joe was proud to place his stones on the sledge beside Johnny's two polished beauties, and haul it up to the town on that shining New Year's Day.

The wide expanse of ice was bustling with players and onlookers and Johnny, in his element, soon took charge. Sliding about directing the divisions of the rinks, he called to Joe to fetch his two metal rods and string from his satchel, so he could set about making the Tee hole. Then, tying the string to the central spike, he scratched perfect circles around it.

The rinks ready, the games began and with much calling and laughing, bickering and cheering, Old Man Evans and his brothers won the competition. Johnny and Joe's efforts were rewarded by coming an honourable third in the scores.

The children in Mill Four also enjoyed a memorable day.

Dale's plans for them went smoothly and they were greatly admired by the town's folk. After being toasted from a bowl of punch donated by the local magistrates, they returned to the village for an evening of music and merriment.

The snow started to fall a few days later, tiny flakes steadily building up to blanket the entire country and making roads impassable. The steep road leading down to New Lanark was indiscernible from the rest of the hillside, just the steps were cleared by teams of men to make a route for provisions to be carried down from Lanark.

Only a few of the usual stallholders ventured down to sell their wares and were besieged by waiting customers, hungry for bread, cheese, oats and anything else they could purchase to fill their store cupboards.

By the third day there was a let up in the snowfall. The skies cleared and with the night temperatures dropping to seventeen degrees below zero, Kelly and Dale took the decision to buy large quantities of coal and basic food supplies and have them brought to the village. There was a ready group of strong men to deploy on this errand and a clerk was sent round the houses, knocking at the doors of all the construction workers and requesting them to report to Mr Kelly.

Joe was among the men called upon and with Fiona hurriedly insisting that he wore two jackets and his thickest scarf and cap, he joined a small army of husky men to receive his orders.

They were all pleased to be doing something because the hard winter weather forced them to be laid off from their jobs for nearly two weeks. Two weeks without a wage in the most gruelling months of the year was making for fractious, difficult relations with their wives and families.

Their task was simple but arduous.

The supplies had already been ordered and were waiting to be collected in the stores and merchants' yards in the town, but because of the depth of the snow and the slipperiness of the underlying ice, no horses or wagons could be used. All the bags of coal and food were to be carried by hand or dragged on the sledges which Kelly had cleverly arranged to have made the previous day.

Remembering the struggle that he and Tam had been faced with when they man-handled Meg's headstone up the hill, Joe chose not to be part of the team pulling the toboggans.

In spite of the freezing air, they soon worked up a sweat and Joe was not the only man to pull off layers of clothes and tuck his scarf and cap in his belt. With their eyes half closed, squinting against the brilliance of sunlight reflecting off the dazzling white snow and crystallised trees, they brought the goods down the hill.

It was dusk before the last load of coal sacks were thrown wearily into a pile at the foot of the steps, but there was little to show for all their efforts. As each relay of supplies arrived, the managers dispersed allocations to the never ending queue of waiting residents. With nearly fifteen hundred mouths to feed, the food and fuel disappeared like snow before a fire.

Never ones to let the chance for a ceilidh pass them by, the Highlanders pooled what food they had and took advantage of the fine, moonlit night to bring out their tables, light torches and dance and sing to the music of their fiddles.

Hearing it from the Row, Fiona begged Sarah to care for Donald and hustled Joe back into his heavy outdoor coat; the same trench coat that once belonged to his father. She did not want to dance or drink with her native people, she just wanted to be alone with Joe under the stars on this magical evening.

'We'll no' be lang!' she told her sister in law, winking at her. 'Ah ken ye want tae gang tae the ceilidh, sae we'll no' tarry.'

Sarah giggled and bounced Donald on her knee. 'Och away wi' ye, Ah'm no' tha' bothered.'

The truth was she was very keen to be among the revellers, Sean would be there.

She had met this cheeky Irishman on two occasions since they were introduced at the Hogmanay ceilidh and he asked if she would be going along to Caithness Row that evening. She'd answered with a haughty, 'Mibbe aye, mibbee naw...' but fully intended on dressing in her most becoming outfit and joining them as soon as possible.

Fiona and Joe wandered down past the dancing, hand in hand, saying very little but feeling each other's presence with every step. When they reached the cleared path towards the bottom of the village, Joe put a steadying arm around his wife's waist.

'Tis gie slippery, an' ye ha'e yon metal heeled clogs on. Ah'm feart ye'll slip wi' the bairn.'

'Then ye'll jist ha'e tae haud me tight then Joe,' she smiled up at him, her eyes teasing.

Down by the riverside they paused to look at the frozen water. More than half of the Clyde's surface was covered with thick snow, lying on a layer of ice. At the far side, the water gushing down from Dundaff Linn showed as a sparkling black streak, the current breaking off chunks of ice and whisking it down stream. All along the sheer rocky banks the water running from the hillside had formed into hundreds of icicles, some twelve or fifteen feet long, some so long that they were attached to the rocks below like silver pillars.

'Aw, tis the bonniest sicht!' Fiona sighed.

Joe hugged her to him and kissed the top of her bonnet.

'Ah niver thocht ma life would be sae guid,' she said softly. 'Some time's Ah worry tha' such happiness as we ha'e cannae last.'

'An' why wouldnae it last?' Joe asked, tilting her face up to look into her eyes.

'Aw, Ah dunno, Joe. Tis just tha' there's sae much sadness an' sufferin' a' aroond, an' Ah find mesel' feelin' guilty tha' we are sae lucky.' Her expression was serious, her dark brows drawn in a frown as she gazed up at him with melancholy eyes. 'As Sarah says, everythin' passes... we must nae tak oor love an' oor guid life fae granted...'

'Ah niver tak ye fer granted ma darlin', nor wee Donnie,' he kissed her again, this time on the lips, firmly and with deep feeling.

She closed her eyes and felt his touch, aware of the distant music and the rustling of the river running beside them.

'Remember this nicht...' she whispered when they parted, 'we must baith mind this nicht fer a' time.'

They stood holding each other, drinking in the unique sights and sounds in the frozen night air.

It was only when they turned to walk home that they saw a crouched figure further downstream; it was Calum. He saw them and beckoned, putting his finger to his lips.

'Whit ye daein'?' Joe asked quietly as they approached.

'Ah'm watchin' the otters... see?' he pointed to the river bed and as their eyes followed his directions, they saw the dark, round-backed shapes of four otters bounding across the ice.

'There's a holt on tha' island,' Calum said. 'Ah've bin here a while an' they keep comin' and goin' frae under yon trees. They've catched no end o' fish!'

Joe was smiling at him, not because of the animals frolicking in the icy water, nor because Calum was covered in snow from where he had been pressed into a drift. He was smiling with relief.

There was a light, enthusiastic tone to Calum's voice, his face was transformed by genuine pleasure. Joe had not seen him look so well in years and, after the profound sentiments he shared with Fiona, he felt a lump in his throat.

Everyone was well, everyone in his family was content. Surely that was all you could ever ask for in life? And he had it, in abundance.

It was only as he and Fiona ambled back up the hill that an unbidden thought sprang to mind. Was Sam happy? Would they ever know what became of their elder brother?

***

Anne Caroline admired her reflection in the mirror.

Her father was entertaining important guests, Directors of the Royal Bank of Scotland, and, for the first time, he asked her to assist him in hosting the meal. For this special event she was trying on an array of dresses and was particularly taken with her final choice.

It was of deep rose coloured muslin and very simple in design, being modelled on the latest fashion from London. Following the modern French trend to shed the obvious trappings of wealth by flaunting yards of silk or taffeta on hooped crinoline skirts, this dress had a high waist and a narrow skirt.

The plainness of the gown was part of its charm, although it did have the pretty detail of an attractively scooped neckline, trimmed with a dainty white ribbon drawn through lace and tied in a trailing bow at her cleavage. Attached to the back of the dress was a long fold of the same material, hanging straight to the ground, the hem edged with the same delicate lace and ribbon as her bodice.

Toshie, who now attended her, was a little nervous of the amount of bosom it showed but both Anne Caroline and Jean over-ruled her, saying it was not unbefitting for a girl her age. Anne Caroline was, after all, sixteen, they cried, nearly seventeen, and she should wear something sophisticated and stylish.

Her gown and jewellery chosen for the afternoon, her hairstyle discussed at length and now decided, Anne Caroline changed back into her thick linen day dress and woollen stockings. Although each separate room of the Charlotte Street mansion was warm, the hallways of the high ceilinged house were cold and draughty, especially during the recent freezing weather.

During the last two days the fearful cold eased and now the snow was thawing. All the piles of snow cleared from roads throughout Glasgow and beyond were lying in wilted, discoloured heaps, oozing streams of water into puddles. The bare branches of the trees were no longer resplendent in icy shrouds, but were dripping and plain on that dull February morning.

By midday, brooding clouds were spilling a curtain of rain over the city.

While the raindrops spattered at the windows, downstairs in the kitchen Cook was wrestling with the stuffing for a rolled fillet of lamb. Breen sat in a chair by the fire, a cup of tea in one hand and a list of preparations for the evening in the other.

Since their mistress died, Cook and Breen had taken over many of the domestic responsibilities regarding menus and provisions for the household. Mr Dale was easily pleased but, having great respect and even affection for their employer, they catered for both his appetite

213

and appreciation of fine food and took a pride in serving him the most satisfying and varied diet they could devise.

A door slammed in the back hallway and one of the footmen came in, water running in rivulets off his cap and jacket.

'Camlachie Burn's burst its banks, Miller's puttin' oot sand bags.'

Miller was the head gardener and his efforts with the beautiful lawns and flower borders in the back garden had been seriously damaged a few years before when the nearby stream was in spate.

'Ye'd better tell Renwick right away, he may wish to look at the cellar in case it's showing any water.' Breen advised him, sipping her tea.

Her mind was full of the linen they required for the evening's table settings and whether, if the weather continued to be so wet, some of the guests from further afield might be invited to stay the night.

On inspecting the cellar, Renwick discovered that water was already gathering on the floor. Unfortunately, if the cellar was filling with water it would mean, as it was still raining heavily, that the kitchens would no doubt be affected within the hour.

'How very inconvenient,' Dale said, on hearing the news. 'I do not wish to postpone the dinner this evening.'

He visited the cellar with Renwick and while they were watching the slow rise of brown, welling water, a cry went up from the kitchen. Water was already spreading though the back hall and across the flagstones.

After some thought and discussions on the options available, he penned a letter to one of his neighbours, David Black, a tobacco merchant, relating the unfortunate circumstances of his basement being flooded and an important social engagement to cater for that day. Would it be possible to request the use of their kitchen? He would be indebted to their generosity in a time of such urgent need.

Within minutes of sending the letter, a reply was received; they would be honoured to be of any assistance to Mr Dale and put their kitchen at his Cook's disposal.

The next few hours were spent salvaging what was required for the evening and transporting Cook with her kitchen maids and all the paraphernalia she needed to complete the meal, across the street to Mr Black's house. Relays of footmen splashed their way to and fro, with Renwick (smart and dry under an umbrella) directing the operation.

214

Dale stood at the cellar door and surveyed the water rising around his racks of wine.

He owned a considerable amount of wine and it was one of his indulgencies to procure only the finest, smoothest vintages. The guests that evening were important colleagues and as the Glasgow agent for the bank, as well as being the son in law of one of the Directors, he wished to serve them the very best.

He issued orders to Renwick who dispatched a footman to the Clydeside in search of a sea-faring man who, for payment of his services, would wade into the water, already several feet deep, and retrieve the bottles. However, the sailor who arrived at the door had all the brawn and height required for the job, as well as his tarred canvas trousers and boots, but was unable to read.

All the labels on the bottles would look the same and as it was pitch dark in the cellar, he would also have to carry a lamp in one hand, leaving only one hand free to pick up the bottles.

The simple task of selecting the right wine took on a challenging aspect. Not to be out done, Dale turned to Anne Caroline, who was hovering beside him, eager not to miss any of the drama.

'Climb on the man's shoulders!' her father instructed, hands on hips, his large, waist-coated stomach becoming proudly prominent. 'I will tell you which bottles to pick up. You will be quite safe and, apart from your feet, perfectly dry.' he smiled at her with twinkling eyes.

So, this she did. Perched on the sailor's shoulders, she clutched his black, slightly sticky hat to find her balance and he took a firm hold round one of her ankles. Then he plunged down the steps, up to his waist in running water, and, holding the lantern high, waded to where Dale directed.

Amid much laughing and cheering, the task was completed successfully. Renwick bore the bottles away to decant the treasured red wine and Dale shook the seaman's hand and pressed a shilling in to his palm.

When the guests were assembled around the dining table that afternoon, Dale regaled them with the story of the near calamitous flood. The gentlemen roared with laughter at the recounting of Anne Caroline riding on the sailor's shoulders and the ladies gasped in astonishment at her bravery. Some were shocked at the idea of Dale allowing an uncouth stranger to have such intimate contact with his daughter.

From her seat at the other end of the table, Anne Caroline observed her father's genial face as he elaborated on the tale. Beyond the candelabra and arrangements of ivy, forced lilies and holly, he was extolling the virtues of his kind neighbour, David Black, and the lengths his gardener was taking to make sure Camlachie Burn could not destroy the garden again.

The day's events had been an adventure and she wondered, fondly, how many times in the future she would hear him retelling the story.

Only one of the four older ladies in the party adopted the new fashion for simplicity in her attire. Like Anne Caroline, her white gown and gracefully up-swept, natural hair-style appeared naive and underdressed when beside the richly coloured velvets and wide hooped skirts of the others. However, it became a topic of conversation which allowed for some lively debate, with Anne Caroline feeling sufficiently confident in her knowledge of ladies' wear to be able to take an active part.

When everyone had eaten sufficient of the various delicious platters, Dale and the gentlemen retired to the library and Anne Caroline escorted the ladies through to the drawing room.

She was not in the least nervous of her role as hostess, having known most of the guests by acquaintance since she was a small child. So, she invited them to make themselves comfortable, opened the lid on the piano and proceeded to play a selection of music. This allowed the other ladies, all well known to one another, to engage in conversation.

Comfortably aware of his eldest daughter entertaining his colleague's wives, Dale passed around the brandy and settled into a discussion about the government's attempts to thwart their growing opposition. This serious subject moved to one closer to home, the provision of more police officers for Glasgow's streets now that most of the soldiers who were usually on hand in their sentry boxes, were deployed in the war.

The whole afternoon passed very pleasantly and when the carriages arrived at the front door to carry their guests away into the gathering darkness, the ladies in the party praised Anne Caroline's demeanour.

'Mr Dale,' cried one lady, grasping her host's hand and peering earnestly at him from under her riotously curling wig. 'Your daughter is a delight! And so accomplished at the pianoforte! She must accompany you when you next come to our home. She is growing into a fine young lady, a credit to your dear late wife. You must very proud! You must also make sure she gains experience of society and bear in mind that you have *five* daughters to find husbands for, arrangements cannot be made soon enough!'

Dale accepted the complimentary remarks about Anne Caroline but demurred over the need to rush into finding suitors for his daughters.

There would be time enough for all that, he thought. Anne Caroline was barely more than a child and anyway, he thoroughly enjoyed having her beside him to share the occasion.

It was still raining when the carriages left Charlotte Street with the horses splashing, fetlock deep, through puddles, throwing great sprays of water up from the wheels.

'My, the Falls of Clyde will be looking grand,' Dale mused, 'There will be plenty water running the mills today.'

He placed an arm around his daughter's shoulders and they returned to the warmth of the drawing room fire. 'Why don't ye fetch your sisters, I feel a damp evening like this requires a song or two. What say you?'

***

The drastically low winter temperatures with the ensuing frozen earth and consequent flooding, ravaged the entire British Isles. It was the coldest winter ever recorded, reaching minus twenty one degrees even in the south of England. Its short term benefits of ice markets, curling matches and beauty, did little to outweigh the long term damage wrought on the land.

On a mild, hazy day in April, Fiona gave birth to another baby boy. This time, there was only Bessie at her side, everyone else being at work. She lay with her new son in her arms and thanked God she survived the ordeal.

Not wishing to alarm Joe, she had secretly dreaded the confinement, fearing an inner premonition that something would go seriously wrong. There had been nights when she woke in a sweat, clutching at him, gripping his hand and trying to see the outline of his profile in the darkness.

Life was so precious, but having found this joy she was filled with the horror of losing it.

217

Now, the dangers of childbirth behind her, she nursed her baby and scolded herself for fretting so much.

When Joe came home he was thrilled to find his wife lying peacefully in their bed holding their new son.

'He's no' like Donnie, is he? Ah can see he has hair but... it's gie fair!'

'An' tha's a surprise?' laughed Fiona, 'You wi' all yon golden locks! Wee Sam will be the image o' his faither, ye can see it a'ready.'

'Sam?' Joe touched her arm tenderly. They had discussed many names, both for boys and girls, but not mentioned the name of his brother as a possibility. 'Are ye sure yer happy wi' tha' name?'

'Aye, Ah'm sure.' Fiona kissed the baby and turned to Joe, 'Gie me a kiss tae seal it?'

A myriad of thoughts and memories from his childhood flashed through his mind. The name Sam meant only one person to him: his brother. The hurt and loss he felt by Sam's sudden desertion were too painful to burden this tiny, sleeping infant.

'Ah can nae,' he told her. 'Ony ither name, but no' ma brither's. Ah'm sorry, darlin'.'

For a few moments she was non-plussed, then she asked, 'Whit aboot David? Like we talked aboot, a while bak? After Mr Dale?'

This brought a genuine smile to Joe's face, 'Aw aye, David. If it had nae bin fer Mr Dale we would nae be t'gether.

'We can ask him tae christen the bairn when he's here next time. An' tell him the reason fer the name.'

Joe leaned towards her and kissed her firmly, sealing the decision.

A few weeks later Sarah brought them news of Dale's imminent arrival in the village.

'He'll be comin' wi' a' his lassies. Aw, dear me, there's sich a load o' work tae be done afore they a' arrive! Mrs Cooper is in a fair state aboot it.'

Sarah was also concerned about her employer being in residence. When he travelled on his own to visit the mills he would only stay two or three days but if the family were with him, this was usually extended to several weeks. The previous year she had not minded the extra hours of work, enjoying the tittle tattle from the Glasgow staff and learning new dishes to prepare. However, nowadays, her attention was almost exclusively on Sean.

From opening her eyes in the morning, he was never far from her thoughts. He was all she dreamed of as her perfect man, playful yet hard working, romantic but not too earnest. Interested in her and listening to what she said to him as well as happily entertaining her with funny stories. All the while, his playful light eyes emanated his obvious feelings of attraction.

They would meet after work and, with the lighter evenings, enjoyed strolling up the hill to sit among the bluebells and look down on the village. In recent days he would hold her hand as they talked, caressing it lightly with his fingers. One day soon, she knew, he would kiss her. She would day dream of that moment while she dusted furniture and scrubbed floors, eager for the time when Mrs Cooper would say to her 'that'll be you done for today, Sarah' and she could leave.

Now the Dales were arriving and she would be expected to stay much later in the evenings. She found herself worrying about this and realised it was because Sean had many admirers; most of the village girls would watch him from beneath their lashes as he walked past. The more brazen ones openly called out to him and she knew of two who lived close to his family in Braxfield Row who would seize any chance to woo him away from her.

'Ah will nae be free till nearly dark t'morra,' she told him as they sauntered up the steps to their special place on the hill. 'Mr Dale will be stayin'.'

'Ah well, we can make the most o' just now, ma dear,' he said in his sing-song Irish accent.

They sat down on the fallen log they always sat upon and she slipped her hand in his, leaning closely against him. There was a mist rising from the river and from their viewpoint it could be seen hanging in a gauzy ribbon down the valley, tracing the curves of the riverbed.

'Yer lookin' awfy lovely the day, Sarah. Ah can't hardly take me eyes off ye! Sure an yer the prettiest girl in the whole village an' yer here with me! Tis a wonderful day!'

She giggled, squeezing his fingers.

'Give me that smile again?' he teased, 'ye just don't know what a gorgeous sight ye are when ye smile. Ye have the sweetest face and the...' he bent his head close, lowering his voice, 'most kissable lips...'

219

She melted inside as his lips met hers. Reaching up to touch his strong dark hair she lost her balance and they tumbled backwards off the log and fell together onto the grass. With a wry smile, he asked if she was all right but made no move to take his arms from around her.

'Aye, Ah'm no' hurt...' she murmured, enjoying the closeness.

He kissed her again and took her in a much firmer embrace.

It was a long time before they made their way back down into the village.

Sarah was giddy and light hearted as she called goodnight to him. He backed away from her in the dusk, mischievously blowing kisses and miming sweeping bows.

It was mid afternoon on a beautiful, sunny spring day when four bay horses drew Dale's carriage slowly down the hill beside Braxfield Row.

The village was busy with wagons and workmen. Young women with babies and the old folk of the village were also out and about. They were making the most of the fine weather to do the washing or sit on the grass to do the mending, chatting, while infants toddled among them. A wagon, piled with sacks of coal, was discharging its load into the bunker for Caithness Row, its horses munching contentedly in their nose bags.

Work was starting on cutting into the hillside to make way for another row of tenements near the entrance to the village, an extension to Braxfield Row. These new buildings, Mantilla Row, were just part of the next phase in the ever increasing size of New Lanark.

It was a bustling, noisy scene and as Anne Caroline climbed from the cocoon of the upholstered carriage, she took a moment to steady herself after the long swaying journey and survey the colourful activity. She remembered her earlier visits and, taking in the changes, felt proud to be part of this growing community.

Inside the quieter hallway she said to her father, 'I am sure there are few of our friends who realise what a town this is becoming! I believe they think you have but one mill here... sitting alone in the countryside!'

'I have invited them to visit, all and everyone, and there is a growing interest. I should be delighted to show them around.'

Mrs Cooper welcomed them nervously, wringing her hands and helping Giggs and Toshie to usher the younger children into the house. Every year the house seemed more cramped as the girls grew older and more boisterous, and they were always tired after the long journey, requiring a meal straight away. Cooper was prepared for this and had a table already laid with several sweet and savoury dishes to start their holiday off on an enjoyable note.

Sarah ran up and down the stairs from the kitchen, an excited, warm feeling inside her: she was in love. Sean had declared his love to her the night before as they lay among the bluebells, telling her he wanted her more than any girl he had ever seen in his life.

She glowed at the memory; she had found her true love.

One of her duties was to be at the disposal of the Glasgow servants and over the years she had grown to know Toshie and Giggs quite well. They were very exacting, expecting her to provide hot water or a needle and thread at a moment's notice. If they sent clothes to be washed they would inspect them in detail when she returned them, lifting the cuffs and turning the collars to make sure they were properly ironed. Duncan, Mr Dale's valet, kept himself to himself and would attend to all the master's personal effects without fuss or demands.

It was late when Sarah placed the last washed dish in the cupboard and, stifling a yawn, asked Cooper if she may leave.

'Be sure and be here for six o'clock tomorrow,' she was told. 'I will need your assistance with the breakfast... eight more people to feed and all from this wee kitchen... and then there's the main meal. Mr Dale will be out but Miss Anne Caroline and the rest of them....'

Sarah assured her she would be there punctually in the morning and left before Cooper could engage her in further conversation.

It was already dark but by the light of a waning moon she could see a figure standing by the entrance to the Rows. Immediately, all tiredness left her. Her pace quickened and she ran the last few yards, straight into Sean's arms.

'Ah thought ye couldn't be making it this night,' he laughed, holding her close and kissing her neck.

'T'were awfy busy, but Ah'm here noo!'

He took her by the hand and started to walk towards the hill steps.

'Aw, Sean, its as dark as a chimney up there. We can talk an' be here for a while, can we no'?'

'With all the village keekin' out their windows at us?'

'So, let'em see us! Whit's wrang wi' that? Ye ashamed o' me or summat?' She said it lightly, keeping a smile on her face. Last night, in the dusk she allowed herself to become too carried away. She knew she would find it hard to resist him if they were alone together and decided, for her reputation as well as safety, she would behave with more decorum from now onwards.

'Oh no! Sarah, ma heart's desire, I would rather die than have ye thinking that! I just wanted to return to our most special place... in the moonlight... to have ye to meself, just for a wee while?'

'Tae talk? Nuthin' more, Sean. Ye are the most beguilin' man...'

He took her hand and placed it on his arm in a courteous, formal manner. 'May I ask ye tae walk wi' me, me darlin'?'

Smiling, she let herself be led up the steps and off to the side, through the shadowy woods. When they sat down he put his arm around her and they gazed out over the rooftops and smoking chimneys in the darkness below. Sean's soft words, gentle kisses and handsome, earnest face, flattered by the moon's gentle light, soon won her over. All her resolutions dissolved into the scented evening air.

The next morning, struggling to rise and dress when Rosie left the house, Sarah was regretting her lapse of resolve.

It was a sin to lie with a man before you were married, she knew that, and yet when she was with him it seemed so right, so natural. In the cold light of dawn, she knew she had done wrong and the joyous feelings of love were tinged with bittersweet regret.

Sean was a carpenter, good at his trade and earning a decent wage. They had been seeing each other for over four months and in the last few weeks they saw each other nearly every day. However, if he wanted to be as intimate as that again, she would wish to be betrothed to him and have his support secured, should she fall pregnant.

Brushing her hair vigorously, as if she was brushing away the guilt that besieged her heart, she made up her mind to be more forceful in rebuffing his advances.

By the end of her working day, Sarah was worn out. Once again it was late and the mill workers were already released from their toil when she met Sean.

He made no attempt to draw her away from the street, instead, after a few minutes of idle talk, he looked at her with concern.

'My but they've worked ye like a slave, me poor darlin'. Ye look like ye need yer bed. I have to go up to Lanark this eve, so I will bid ye good night and sweet dreams.' He kissed her hand, flashing his brilliant smile.

222

Sarah returned his smile but felt a chill of disappointment as she watched him striding away up the hill. It was one thing for her to wish their relationship to be less demanding, but quite another for him to just walk off and leave her after only a couple of minutes. All day she had been longing to be with him... and now?

She realised she was being unreasonable, of course he had other things to attend to in his life and hadn't he stayed in the village long enough to see her before he left? How absurd, she told herself, to be upset, but she was, indeed, upset.

It was not the fact that their evening was cut short, it was something else. It was a look in his eyes, or rather the lack of a look in his eyes....

Near to tears with exhaustion and hurt, she pulled herself up the two flights of stairs and, finding Fiona alone with the babies, told her all about her worries.

'Well, we'll jist ha'e tae pray yer no' wi child. Whit e'er were ye thinkin?' Fiona was more amazed than shocked. Sarah was so practical and sensible, it came as an uncomfortable surprise to discover this wild side to her friend.

'An' whit if he no longer wants me noo! Och Sarah, Ah've been an awfy fool. When Ah'm wi' him Ah jist gae daft, there's nae doot aboot it.'

'D'ye care fer him, though? Or is it jist his bonnie face an' laffin' eyes?'

Sarah shook her head. 'It's a' o' him. He makes me laff, an' when we've talked aboot things, serious things, mind, he has a clever mind, quick. Ah like that, an' aye, yer richt, he has a bonnie face.'

The sad expression that came over Sarah's own pretty features, caused Fiona to say, 'Och, yer makin' a muckle oot o' a mickle! He's away tae be wi' his friends, an' yer aboot deid on yer feet frae yer work. Once ye meet agin, ye'll see, it'll be richt as rain.'

'Ye think?'

'Aye, Ah think.'

When Sarah was sufficiently comforted to retire to bed, Fiona went across the landing and asked Bessie for a sheet of paper. By the fire light, drawing two candles close to her on the table, she wrote a note to Mr Dale to say that they were now the proud parents of another little boy. They wished him to be named David in respect and gratitude to their employer and would be very grateful if he would

223

baptise the infant. On reading it through several times, she threw it in the fire and begged another sheet of paper from Bessie.

David was whimpering and crying again. Unlike her first child, her newborn baby was rarely peaceful. She had to write between calming his cries by rocking or feeding him, only managing to put down a few words at a time.

On this attempt, she added a line to remind Mr Dale that he presided over their marriage three years before.

When Joe came in, she read the letter out to him for approval and he added his signature, neatly, beside hers at the bottom.

First thing the next morning, Sarah laid the letter on the silver salver for Dale to receive when he came downstairs. It was several hours later, when she was in the middle of peeling potatoes, that Cooper came to the scullery and told her Mr Dale wished to speak with her.

Dale was in the parlour with his two elder daughters and Sarah curtseyed to them and clasped her hands behind her back.

'I understand from Cooper that you are the sister of Joseph Scott?' Dale looked at her with a pleasant, inquisitive raise to his voice. 'I have here a letter from Mr Scott, requesting a christening performed for his new son. Please inform your brother that I would be most pleased to officiate and look forward to meeting the child on Sunday.'

'Thank ye, sir.' Sarah bobbed another curtsey and hurried back to her chores.

Anne Caroline gestured to the letter, 'May I read it, Father?'

'Certainly.' He handed it to her and continued attending to his other post.

Anne Caroline turned to Jean. 'I thought it might be the same person! I was correct! Do you remember some years ago, when we were staying here, we witnessed a lovely wedding? The groom was tall, with pale gold hair and the bride wore a blue dress with a ribbon in her hair?'

Jean wrinkled her nose, trying to recall the event. 'I am not sure...'

'Well, the new maid is the sister of the groom.' She glanced down at the letter again. 'And the couple have two babies now! How lovely!'

'Was that the wedding where the bride was one of father's orphans?' Jean asked.

'Yes,' Images came back to Anne Caroline of even before the wedding; the orphan girl emerging from the mill in her cotton tunic, the slim dark-haired young man pacing beside the mill-lade, the fight. 'Look though, Jean, this letter is penned by the girl from the mill and it is beautifully written.' She noted the signatures and how Joseph had spelt his name correctly this time but did not mention that to Mary.

It would seem scornful to draw anyone's attention to the man's previous illiteracy. She liked what she had seen of Joseph Scott and his family and would never intentionally hold them up to mockery.

When Sean was not waiting for her after work, Sarah was desolate. How could he use her so? He told her he loved her, took advantage of her love for him and now she was abandoned.

'Whit's wrang wi' ye, oor Sarah?' Joe asked her when Cal and Rosie were down at the schoolroom. 'Ye've bin near tae greetin' a' eve, whit's happened?'

In a rush, sobbing as she spoke, Sarah told her brother how deeply she felt for Sean and how he had abruptly stopped seeing her. She did not tell him how close their relationship had grown and was grateful to Fiona for remaining quiet on the subject.

Joe was angry, he did not like to see his sunny little sister so heartbroken. 'Ah'll ask aroond.' he told her, 'ha'e a word wi' him. Ah'm no' havin' yer feelings trampled upon by the likes o' an Irish incomer.'

'If he does nae want tae see me, Joe, ye cannae mak him! That would spoil it a' ! Love is only true if it's gi'en wi'oot being asked fae, wi'oot bein' forced... Ah'll jist ha'e tae bear it.'

When they were lying in bed that night with baby David, blessedly quiet while she nursed him, Fiona whispered to Joe not to interfere.

'Yer no' her faither, Joe. An' Ah mind whit happened when ye went aff an sought oot poor Kyle Macinnes?'

In the dim light she saw a wide grin spread across her husband's face. 'Aw, ye mean Ah cannae enjoy anither battering?'

'Ye ken fine well whit Ah mean!' she whispered back, nudging him in the ribs.

He squeezed her hand, 'Sae lang as he doesnae tak a swing at me first! But, Ah will ha'e a word wi' him.'

When Sarah came home from work the next evening, Joe was sitting by the fire with Donnie on his knee and, without any preamble, she asked him if he had spoken with Sean.

'Naw, Ah have nae, but no' fer the want o' trying. He's no' in the village.' Joe set the restless child down on the floor and steadied him until he found his balance. Donnie was able to walk now but still with a wobbly, rolling gait.

'Whit d'ye mean, he's no' in the village?' Sarah demanded, hands on hips.

'He's in the jail.'

'Whit!'

Joe's mouth set in a firm line, he had been dreading telling Sarah his news. 'He's a skellum, Sarah, a bad lot. Nigh on everyone Ah asked had the same tae say. He's fair-farrant, gi'es his smile an' charms his way wi' folk, but he's a wild yin.'

Sarah sat down at the table, her legs suddenly losing their strength. 'Whit's he done tae be in the jail?'

'Talk has it, he caused trouble a' the inn. He's known fer his strong views agin' the king an' the English rulin' his homeland. When Ah wis askin' aboot him, Ah wis telt he has bin in the jail afore, in Ireland.' Joe gave her a sympathetic smile, 'He's trouble, lass. Tis best he's no longer here.'

For a while, Sarah seemed to be taking the revelations well. After sniffing back tears, she changed out of her uniform and pulled a shawl around her petticoats.

The rest of the family were relieved. They set about rolling out the hurlies, listening to Rosie relating a long tale of how one of the little boys who swept up behind their looms had nearly been crushed, and, but for the bravery of the Overseer, would surely have died.

She had no sooner stopped talking when Sarah asked, 'Which jail is he in?'

They turned to her, their faces blank, still lost in the near tragedy of Rosie's story.

Sarah stared directly at Joe and asked again, emphatically. 'Which jail is Sean in?'

Joe knew the answer but he also knew his sister and he definitely was not going to tell her that Sean was just up the hill in Lanark.

'Ah dunno,' he lied. 'They said he wis taken awa'... mibbee Hamilton or even Glasgie.'

With a helpless cry, she climbed over Cal's bed and fell onto her own mattress, yanking the curtain closed.

Although she was out of sight, her sobs and wails were loud in the small room. Cal looked at Rosie and raised his eyes to the ceiling.

'As if it's no' hard enough tae sleep wi' the wean bawlin' a' nicht!'

Fiona was apologetic. There was little she could do to quieten wee David when he started to cry. No amount of milk would appease him and his little face would screw up into an angry crimson square, mouth gaping, eyes tight shut as he put all his might into whingeing and screaming.

The whole family were losing sleep, making them irritable and quick to snap. Now, with Sarah already so upset, Fiona cradled David to her breast and went to Bessie's.

Bessie understood her plight, having been plagued by the infant's screams from across the landing from the day he was born. She measured a small amount of brandy into a cup and stirred it well with a spoonful of honey.

'Now, dinnae gae feedin' a' this tae the wee mite a' at once! Tis jist tae see ye through the nicht. There's plenty here fer yon christenin', if ye want tae be able tae hear Mr Dale's words.'

'Ah'll no' tak it through by, Ah'll gi'e it tae him noo.' Fiona dipped the tip of her finger in to the mixture and let the baby suck the sweetness. At first his eyes opened very wide and he took a lusty breath to carry on crying, but when she offered it again he took it. After a few more mouthfuls, he seemed quieter and by the time Bessie offered Fiona a wet cloth to clean her fingers, David was asleep.

'Ah dare say he's as tired oot as the rest o' ye!' Bessie chuckled. 'Awa' tae yer bed, hen, an' get some sleep while ye can.'

Fiona was careful to wash her hands thoroughly and wipe the baby's face before going back to her room. She knew Joe would not approve. His years with his mother, and the damage wrought by his drunken father, made him fearful of strong alcohol.

She need not have been so concerned because, like the rest of the family, Joe was already asleep when she returned. He merely grunted an affectionate 'night night' when she blew out the candle and climbed in beside him.

Chapter Seven

"Man's inhumanity to man makes countless thousands mourn!"
Robert Burns

Sarah made every effort to be stoical about the situation she found herself in with Sean. It was through no lack of love for her that he was not with her, he certainly would not have chosen to be arrested and held in prison. She clung to this knowledge, repeating it to herself when her feelings of yearning threatened to become overwhelming

The christening passed without event and, with a little help from Bessie's 'medication', baby David slept throughout the service.

The Dales' house was always in a state of preparation or tidying up while the family were in residence. The constant activity was due not only to the demands of the Dales and their servants, but also because they were receiving guests.

Every few days another grand carriage would roll down the winding hill and deposit its occupants beside Mr Dale's house. These were friends and acquaintances from Glasgow who, taking advantage of a fine spell of weather and the knowledge that Dale was staying in the village with his daughters, had decided to accept his invitation to see New Lanark for themselves.

Their interest had been aroused earlier in the year, during the severe ice and snow, when an article appeared in the newspaper describing the procession of Dale's orphans when they went up to Lanark on New Year's Day. The journalist was obviously greatly impressed by the proceedings and sang high praises for the 'heart-warming spectacle'. For many years Dale had offered his fellow mill owners and merchants a tour of his cotton mills to show them the healthy working conditions he provided for his workers. However, he had been sadly disappointed by their apathy, or in some cases, open

228

hostility towards his commitment to provide basic comforts and schooling.

It now seemed that across the country there was a growing awareness that peasants, paupers and workers alike, should be treated with more consideration. The French Revolution was a stark lesson to any ruling class that they neglect their workers at their peril. With the rise and rise of Societies calling for more rights for the common man, outbreaks of violent opposition to the government were becoming more numerous.

Dale had just finished reading the autobiography of the black slave, Olaudah Equiano, a Christian convert who managed to buy his freedom and was now living in London. His poignant yet powerful tale of life as a slave clearly illustrated the needs of all men to be treated as God's children.

Equiano's words were read by thousands, his story having a profound effect on the majority of his audience, but there were inevitably those who only read them out of ghoulish curiosity.

It was simply unconscionable to Dale to treat one's fellow man contrary to the teachings of the Lord. Many long winter afternoons were spent around the tables in the Tontine debating just this point. To emphasise his argument, he always threw open an invitation to his colleagues to observe for themselves how manufacturing could be achieved on a large scale *without* causing suffering to the workforce.

His closer friends, like MacIntosh and Alexander, shared Dale's views, but many railed against them. To invest in factories and offer them any job of work was sufficient charity, they said, because anyway, these wretched, poverty-stricken men and women would only drink or gamble their wages. They were the useless flotsam of society and there were plenty more beggars who would be grateful to take their places if they did not want to work.

'So,' these wealthy men would say with a flourish, draining their wine glasses and preparing to return to their mansions, 'If they don't like doing the job and think they can do better elsewhere, they can just leave!'

Their attitude incensed Dale, but he felt that the best way to persuade them of his case was to provide them with the evidence. It had taken ten years, but at least a few of them were boarding their carriages and coming to see his venture in action. He was proud of New Lanark and thoroughly enjoyed showing them around.

For their part, the merchants and bankers, surgeons and fellow magistrates were filled with admiration for the mill village.

They could barely believe the stark beauty of the architecture and the astonishing setting, deep in the gorge below the old market town of Lanark. It was clear to see the vast scale of Dale's cotton production, but what also impressed them were the light buildings and healthy workforce.

When they were shown around Mill Four where the orphans were housed, the aroma of wholesome broth or meat stew greeted them in the hallways, as delicious as if prepared in a good gentleman's club. The sight of the dormitories, sleeping sixty or more in each, drew cries of surprise from the ladies when they saw row upon row of neatly tended beds. Boys and girls were segregated and all were provided with scrupulously clean bedding, the windows thrown wide to fill the space with fresh country air.

It was the school rooms which provided the biggest contrast to other Mills. Dale was employing sixteen teachers, along with further assistants, to teach over five hundred children every week. If the lessons were underway when the visitors arrived at the door, they were welcomed inside and invited to watch the class taking place.

Some of the children took turns to read poetry to the guests, or if it was a music lesson, they would sing a newly learnt song, or perform a dance. There were eight separate classes, divided by ability, some of them with upwards of eighty children in them, and the teachers arranged displays of the girls' sewing work along with colourful drawings by even the youngest pupil.

Without fail, the comments to Dale were favourable and even at times loud with effusive praise. He waved them all on their way, hoping that they might have understood a little more that what he was doing should not be exceptional, it should be the normal practice.

He prayed that in some small way he might make a difference to their attitude towards those who were less fortunate than themselves.

If other employers would only look to their own souls and follow the path of Christian benevolence in bettering the lot of others, perhaps more lives could be improved.

While Dale and his managers were delighted with the attention, Cooper was not so pleased with the burdensome task of organising the house and providing refreshments for so many people. No sooner had she unpacked the provisions for one meal, prepared it and cleared away, than the next delivery was arriving at the door.

Becoming rapidly overwhelmed with so much to do and so little staff at her disposal, Cooper asked for assistance from Toshie.

So a routine was put in place whereby Toshie would consult with Mr Dale and Anne Caroline every evening and draw up requirements for the following day. Cooper also requisitioned a clerk from Kelly's office to act as errand boy.

In the mornings, Toshie would stand in the little kitchen and address them all, while Sarah cleared up the servants' breakfast table. 'There will be a party of four tomorrow, who will be taking tea with Mr Dale and his daughters, so we will require sweet biscuits and a platter of cold meats and cheeses, sufficient for ten. Then the next day, let me see,' she would consult her notebook, 'A lecturer from the university is arriving. He will be staying overnight in Lanark but we are to provide his main meal here... and he has two companions with him so, we will need...' and on she would go....

Cooper rolled up her sleeves, called on Sarah to skivvy for her and longed for the day when the trunks would be brought over from Kelly's house and the family would return to the city.

After a month of entertaining, the Dales finally left the village.

As the sound of their carriage receded into the distance, Cooper walked back into the house and, shutting the door, leaned against it and let out a long sigh of relief. Then, calling Sarah up to the parlour, she surveyed the crumpled cushions, dying fire and untidy table and sat down on a nearby chair.

'Are ye a'richt, Mrs Cooper?' Sarah asked anxiously, she had never seen the housekeeper sitting so casually in the front parlour before; it seemed disrespectful.

'Aye, I am well enough but I am very tired. And you, Sarah, you have been looking very peeky the last few weeks, your eyes are ringed with shadows. There are chamber pots to be emptied, bed linen to be washed, floors to sweep and scrub and all the breakfast dishes to clear.' She stifled a yawn. 'These things will all have to be done, but not today. Today, I am going to rest and you, Sarah, are to go home. If you are wise you too will rest.' She levered herself to her feet, brushing a piece of thread from her long black skirts. 'I will see you in the morning.'

Although the Dales were no longer in the village, the steady stream of visitors continued to arrive.

William Kelly and James Dale took over the entertaining, restricting it to a glass of wine with the gentlemen, a tray of tea if ladies were present, and then a tour of the mills and the school room.

The building work on Mantilla Row created a great deal of noise and bustle, taking up most of the flat area at the entrance to the village. There was a clear road through the piles of materials to allow the wagons access to the mills for deliveries, but coupled with the market stalls, there was little space left to accommodate the visiting carriages and gigs.

On one occasion, a sudden load crash from the half built tenement caused a horse to bolt and the gig nearly overturned, causing great concern. James Dale decided it would be safer if all the visiting traffic allowed their occupants to alight beside Dale's house, but then removed themselves to the far end of the village.

Calum was one of three lads instructed to attend to these vehicles, and if the visitors had driven themselves, the boys were to take charge of the animals until the tour was complete.

This suited Calum very well. He had a way with horses and relished his short role as a groom to each of these beautiful animals. The other lads would fit the horses' nose bags and then, a rein held loosely over their arm, prefer to sit on the wall playing dice. Calum would groom the striking bay geldings, grey mares, matching chestnut pairs and pick out their feet, talking to them and polishing up the harness while the horses ate their feed.

He felt a lot better these days. In the warmer months of the year his chest was not so tight, his cough less troublesome and he enjoyed going for long walks on his own in the lighter evenings.

Sometimes, he would carry his fishing rod and a jar of worms and treat himself to a bottle of ale, wedging it among rocks in the shallow water to cool. He enjoyed his solitary pursuit, not caring if he caught a trout or not by the end of the evening. Contented, he would lie back on the riverbank and watch the water for any tell-tale circles of a rising fish as he sipped the cold ale and munched on a hunk of cheese and bread before heading back in the dusk.

He came home late one evening and proudly laid two brown trout on the table.

'My, Cal! they're beauties!' Joe praised him.

Fiona was settling Donnie in his new high-sided wooden cot, a surprise gift from a neighbour. She immediately admired her brother-in-law's catch.

'They're that big we could dine on them a' week!'

It was a wild exaggeration but Cal was pleased and set to work gutting them. Sarah, murmuring her own congratulations to him as she sewed by the fire, suddenly bundled the cloth away and hurried to the door.

The smell of the fish entrails turned her stomach.

She ran down the stairs, holding her hand over her mouth and just made it outside and in to the street before throwing up. Her insides were heaving, the stench still in her nostrils. Shaking from the exertion of vomiting and the violence of her reaction, she walked falteringly down to the lade and drew up a bucket of water to wash her face.

It was no good, she would have to admit it to herself, but the longer she pretended it wasn't happening, the longer she could ignore what the future held.

It was late July. Sean had been gone from her for over three months and her moments of folly with him on the hillside were taking their retribution. She was in no doubt that she was carrying his baby, yet she chose to shoo the reality from her mind and continue with her every day routine. It would be a long time before it showed and so, until she was forced to tell anyone, she held onto her secret.

Fiona, however, knew already.

It mainly fell to Fiona to do the household's washing and she had noticed a distinct lack of Sarah's personal laundry for three consecutive months. It left her with a quandary, but as they hardly spent any time alone together these days, she never managed to broach the subject.

It was Sarah's strange behaviour when Cal brought in the fish, which finally gave Fiona her opportunity. Amid much weeping, Sarah admitted to her condition, making Fiona swear on her babies' lives never to tell anyone.

'Och, Sarah! Ye'll ha'e tae tell Joe an' the ithers! Dinnae be stupit!'

'But Joe will be mad a' me! He did nae tak tae Sean anyhoo, sae noo whit will he say?'

'Aye, he'll be mad, but it'll pass. He's yer brither, he'll want tae look after ye.'

'Anither mooth tae feed... an' whit will Mrs Cooper say? She's gie churchy, ye ken? An' ma work....' Sarah could feel a new feeling, fear, trickling down her spine. 'Aw Fiona, Ah'll lose ma job. Ah love ma job...'

'Mibbee fer a wee while, but Ah could tak care o' yer babbie an' ye could gae bak tae work richt awa'.'

'Would ye do tha'? Or... mibbee, Ah should stay an' mind Donnie an' wee Davy?'

Fiona put her arms around her friend. 'We'll find a way, din nae fret.' She smoothed Sarah's fair hair away from her crumpled, tear-ravaged face. 'Ye've a family tae see ye through, lass, we'll tak care o' ye.'

Joe was furious. It was not his sister who he raged against, it was 'that Irish bastard', and every blasphemous word he could call upon to vent his anger. Fiona had never seen him so irate, and soothed her sons as they became agitated by his shouts.

'Yer scaring the babbies!' she cried. 'Ah ken yer vexed, Joe, but it's no' helpin' tae upset us a'!'

He stopped abruptly and looked around the room.

Cal was staring at him, his face ashen, eyes dark and unsettled. Rosie sat on the stool by the fire, her cheeks flushed, her lips set in a line, nervously twisting the dish cloth between her fingers. Fiona and the babies, looking at him, aghast, and Sarah, his little sister... tears rolling down her cheeks, hugging herself and rocking backwards and forwards as she perched on the edge of her bed.

He was acting like their father. Perhaps he had good reason to be as mad as hell, but he should have known better than to exhibit the full force of his wrath in front of members of his own family, fellow victims of his father's temper.

It might be seven years since Duncan Scott was killed, but the wounds he inflicted were too deep to ever heal. They had soon re-opened, raw and sensitive, when Joe paced around the room, bellowing and swearing.

'Ah'm sorry,' he said quietly. 'Ah should nae ha'e roared at ye a'... Ah'll gae oot fer a bit an' cool doon.'

Joe went straight up to Braxfield Row to the lodgings where Sean used to stay. No-one had more news of him. The last report was that he had been removed from Lanark, possibly to Hamilton, but the other men in the room had no further information.

Sarah insisted that her family keep her secret to themselves. Somehow, she felt, if she just carried on with her daily routine she would come to terms with her problem before having it made public.

With her skills in dressmaking, she managed to adapt her two black housemaid's dresses to allow for her growing proportions. Tying her apron loosely, she would check her appearance in the Dales' mirrors and delude herself into believing that no-one could tell what she was hiding beneath the folds.

Then, one blustery September day, Nature conspired against her subterfuge.

Mrs Cooper wanted all the heavy bedding aired before Mr Dale's next visit and, seeing it was a fine windy day, instructed Sarah to peg it out on the line. Autumn leaves tumbled about in the air, caught in updrafts and swirling through the village between the tall tenements and mill walls.

On the drying-green beside Dale's house, Sarah was struggling with flapping blankets, the wind catching at her skirts, pushing them this way and that. As she stretched up to secure a corner, a gust blew against her dress, pressing it tight to her body. Resting for a moment, she felt the baby kick and instinctively laid a hand on her stomach.

From an upstairs window, the housekeeper was watching her and stifled a gasp of shock. It was clear to anyone that the girl was pregnant. If any proof were needed, Sarah's subconscious movement to feel the baby confirmed Mrs Cooper's worse fears.

Cooper was waiting for her when Sarah came back into the scullery. The girl was windswept and smiling but the smile left her face as soon as she saw the housekeeper's expression.

'You are with child!' she snapped. 'Sarah, you are having a baby!'

Sarah bit her lip, lost for words and horrified to see that Mrs Cooper's usually friendly attitude towards her was now one of hostility.

'There is no need to try and deny it. I have seen your condition for myself.' Cooper's words were clipped; she was livid. 'I told you there were to be no followers, no men hanging about... you assured me that was not the case. You are in service, girl, you have been employed to do a job of work and...' She pursed her lips, her face contorted with distaste. 'I relied on you, Mr Dale took you on in good faith, a mill girl with no experience and you have let us all down!'

Sarah stared at the floor. There was a ferocity to the woman in front of her that she would not have thought possible.

'You are not married! You have never even mentioned a man... I cannot... *just cannot,* tolerate this sinful behaviour. Leave! Leave at once! You have sinned against God, against all that is right and proper!'

235

Sarah was startled into speech. 'But Ah can still work, Mrs Cooper! Ah am fine an' fit, Ah can work until the babbie comes...'

'You will do no such thing! I will not have this house contaminated for one minute longer by someone with such loose morals! Go!' She snatched the laundry basket from the girl's hands and opened the back door, her body shaking. 'Get out!' she hissed, 'And do not ask for a letter of reference from Mr Dale, you are leaving in disgrace!'

***

David Dale's round, black-clad figure with his tricorn hat atop his wig, was a familiar sight on the streets of Glasgow.

Rolling along on his sturdy, stockinged legs, he would raise his gold topped cane in greeting to acquaintances, a placid, approachable expression on his features. His usual path wound between the lush gardens and parks behind the Gallowgate and Trongate,

Turning into the Merchant City, he knew most of the proprietors of the businesses and shops he passed, many of which had arranged loans through his branch of the Royal Bank. In the alleyways and roads he recognised faces. Some from illustrious dinner tables and others, sheepishly tugging their caps to him, from the court room when they had appeared before him in his capacity as a magistrate.

There was always business to attend to, whether with Scott Moncrieff at the bank in Hopkirk's Land, at Mary Brown's, his cotton broker or as an Elder at his church. More casually, with other merchants in his club in the Trongate. It was not in Dale's character to take time away from work, every day was filled with meetings and letters.

On entering the Tontine Rooms one blustery day, he hung up his heavy woollen outer coat and zig-zagged between the crowded tables. His progress was slow, pausing to pass words with friends and pat others on the shoulder in greeting. Everyone wanted to be noticed by him, favoured with a brief exchange: even being seen to be associated with Dale was a feather in their cap.

A haze of blue pipe smoke hung above their heads, glasses chinked and gold and silver buckles and watch chains flashed against the flamboyant waistcoats of these rich businessmen.

From a table near one of the fireplaces, he was hailed by a company of gentlemen and encouraged to join them. Among the group was his neighbour, Archibald Paterson.

'We have been hearin' about your mills in Lanarkshire,' Paterson said, pouring Dale a glass of claret and heaving himself along the settle to make room for his corpulent friend. 'When are ye down there next? I have a mind to see this place myself.'

'You are welcome whenever it is convenient for you. My doors are open.'

'I hear your Poor House waifs can put on a show,' quipped one of the other men, younger, not one of their usual circle. 'Ye have them singin' and dancin' for their supper as well as spinning your cotton!' There was a sarcastic ring to his voice.

Dale bristled at the remark, recalling the anxious little faces of the Highland twins as they earnestly took turns to sing a duet in front of a University professor. He would not tolerate their innocent efforts to better themselves being ridiculed by this ignorant dandy.

Removing his hat, Dale sat down and opened the buttons of his jacket, taking his time to get comfortable. The young man with the powdered face and artificially curled hair was waiting for a response, his eyebrows, lined with kohl, raised theatrically.

Dale did not dignify the comment with a response, choosing instead to raise the subject of the newly proposed compulsory conscription to the military.

Paterson noticed the deliberate snub and smiled to himself, finding Dale's nature a tonic in this back-stabbing, criticising world.

Most of the men he knew would have risen to the jibe, justifying and arguing their point of view, but Baillie Dale had no need. He was highly respected in Glasgow and would not lower himself to be drawn into a spat with someone who clearly knew little of his business practices.

From the heavy British losses being incurred in the war, the conversation soon turned to the new Glasgow Infirmary. It was on schedule to open before the end of the year and would greatly relieve the beleaguered Town's Hospital.

There were too many male patients there, they were told by Dr Leonard, a surgeon from Edinburgh, riddled with syphillus, their brains addled and their bodies diseased. These crazed, dangerous men would be kept on the upper levels and it would still remain open and function as a Work House. It would provide basic shelter and work

237

for the destitute, but any new patients requiring medical intervention would be taken into the Infirmary.

Venereal disease was becoming a major concern in the city and while the male victims were housed in the Town Hospital, the females, believed to be the perpetrators of the plague, were locked up in another building, hidden from society. As these women were in the main prostitutes, few had any pity for them, and they mouldered there until the ravages of their disease finally killed them.

Religious evangelicals, Dale included, were growing deeply concerned by the level of drinking and debauchery in the city. The previous few decades of wealth and therefore wide spread employment, had attracted tens of thousands to make their home in Glasgow. Unfortunately, this included a large element with scant regard for the Bible.

Dale continued to give generously to the British and Foreign Bible Society in the hope that the Lord's word would be widely available to all who sought its guidance. Every week he, and his fellow pastors, preached passionately on choosing the way of the Lord, abiding by the Holy Commandments and living a wholesome, industrious life. Yet the prisons were full and thieving and violence were rampant, especially in the poorer areas.

'With the soldiers away in the south or Europe, we are being left unprotected in our own neighbourhoods.' A thin, elderly member of the group complained.

'Well, if this new tax is levied we may soon have a Chief of Police,' Paterson said, helping himself to more wine and offering it around the table. 'and a dozen more officers patrolling the streets.'

'It might improve matters,' Dale agreed. 'I heard that about seventy watchmen would be hired, it will be an expensive project. However, it would be money well spent if God fearing citizens could cross the city in dark evenings without fear of being molested.'

'In my opinion,' added the elderly gentleman, 'it will be the new street lighting that will make all the difference. If the robbers think their faces will be seen, they'll think twice before committing their crimes.'

Dale hoped that was the case. The winter evenings would soon be upon them again, restricting the hours of travel for most residents and forcing them to seek the safety of their homes before night fall.

September's autumnal chills were cooling the air and the chestnut tree at the bottom of his garden was already showing a crown of gold.

Altogether, he thought, there had not been much of a summer this year and the reports of the disastrous harvest made depressing reading.

Wheat shortages were causing riots as far afield as Devon and Cornwall. In Scotland the militia had been called to a furore in Perth where women, desperate to feed their families and unable to afford the rising prices, resorted to just seizing goods from stall holders.

Despite the cosy fire near their table, Dale felt cold from the thought of militant reformers, a failed harvest and the worsening events of the war with France consuming the lives of young Scotsmen.

It had a terrible resonance of the building storm which overwhelmed France eight years before.

***

Thursday 29th October 1795 was an overcast, normal working day for the villagers of New Lanark.

Rosie threw her shawl around her shoulders and left home when the bell rang out into the darkness at six o'clock. Hurrying along the Row, her heavy skirts rustling round her legs, she joined hundreds of others before disappearing through the door way to Mill Three. She was in charge of one of Kelly's water driven mules, spinning hundreds of spindles. Kicking off her clogs outside the door, she entered the warm, humid room and settled in for the day.

Joe met Ewing's team at Mantilla Row and set to work sorting stone and mixing mortar, while Cal joined the Macinneses in the lamp lit workshops, rekindling the fires in the forge.

Over four hundred miles away in London, an enormous crowd was walking through the shadowy, dawn streets towards Westminster.

After being tried and acquitted of treason, Thomas Hardy and his partners in the London Corresponding Society had gained huge support. Their membership was open to all and this mass demonstration was bringing together nearly three hundred thousand weavers, traders, dockyard workers and common people to make their dissatisfaction known.

These were ordinary people who were driven to breaking point by the poor harvest, severe shortage of wheat, rising prices and men being laid off or their wages cut because of the recession.

239

As well as these difficult conditions the government's new policy of compulsory conscription for the war against France was hitting directly at the poorest in the country. Those with money could buy their way out, forcing only those who lived hand to mouth to leave their families unsupported and take up arms.

The people wanted a change. They demanded parliamentary reform, and this was an unprecedented show of unity. In all, one third of London's entire population surged to the meeting.

On that chilly autumn day, the King emerged to find himself the target and was hissed and hooted, with the more militant among the crowd throwing rubbish and stones at his carriage. The Corresponding Society's well organised leaders provided slogans to brandish, demanding lower bread prices and the end of the war. Along with this sea of waving banners came angry cries, 'Down with Pitt! No war! No king!'

The newspapers carried detailed accounts of the day's events and it was the subject of great debate the length and breadth of Britain in the following week.

'The Tory's will be terrified!' MacIntosh bellowed over the table to Dale.

They were sharing a pot of coffee at the Tontine Rooms and the place was loud with discussion and scraping chairs, the doors constantly opening and closing behind new arrivals. It was raining outside and the gentlemen's heavy wool coats dripped pools onto the floor boards, adding another strong odour to the colognes, tobacco and sweat.

Despite being only mid-afternoon, it was a gloomy day and the coffee house's whale oil lamps caste their golden light over the tables.

'Aye, the King too, no doubt.' Dale replied. 'We must pray for an orderly containment of this situation. There is true concern on the part of those who are causing all this agitation and it must be addressed, but goodness only knows how they will go about it.'

'I understand there may be talks to try and end the war.'

'War... so much violence and unnecessary suffering.' Dale shook his head, his large cheeks trembling. 'It would be a mercy if an end to the fighting could be achieved. However, there are serious matters close to home and those will not be helped by bringing our soldiers back. Jobs are scarce enough for the men who are here.'

'Thomas Hardy is a brave man, flying in the face of Parliament's displeasure. He should remember his fellow Scotsman, Thomas Muir, your friend's son, mouldering away in Botany Bay.'

'Perhaps Hardy can continue what his predecessor started, it is fitting that he is also from Scotland.'

'Pitt is rushing through new powers to prohibit any more of these huge gatherings. His gagging Acts may bring a superficial silence, but for how long?'

'That is the danger,' said Dale. 'These young men believe in what they are doing, they are driven by what they see as injustice. That is a powerful force, not so easily laid to rest.'

'Now,' said MacIntosh, 'Spinningdale.'

It was the main reason for them meeting that day.

Dale leaned forward so that his words could be heard more easily above the din, without having to shout his business to everyone's ears.

'The figures are not good.' he said. 'We require more investment or the mills will fold this winter. It is as simple as that.'

MacIntosh's brows drew together and, resting their arms on the table, the two men spoke privately, their faces only inches apart.

'We have already put in £2,300...' said MacIntosh.

'And we need another £2,500 or we will surely lose our first investment. I know our partners will not be happy but this is, after all, more of an exercise in charity than production of profit.'

'I cannot see them giving more... not in this climate.' MacIntosh was grave. 'Personally, I do not think I would be minded to pour more of my own capital in to the venture either.'

'I propose we borrow from the bank.' Dale stated calmly. His astute business mind had been working on the problem since reviewing the figures in his study the previous evening. 'We have achieved a certain success in that we give gainful employment to a great many Highland families who would otherwise be destitute. We cannot fail them.' He looked earnestly at MacIntosh. 'A fine mill is now built and the housing stock forming the village around it is occupied. The two weaving houses have over twenty looms producing the handkerchiefs... and they have a steady market, but these are hard times and they are not reaching the expected prices.'

'Very well,' MacIntosh was relieved he was not being asked to provide the funds out of his own pocket. 'I am as committed as you, Dale, in keeping these Scots in their homeland but I wish they would

241

grasp the opportunity we have supplied more wholeheartedly.' He sipped his coffee, thoughtfully. 'If you can arrange a loan through the Royal Bank, I agree that we should borrow enough to support our original investment.'

Dale was satisfied with the response.

They were fulfilling their aim to provide jobs in the most impoverished parts of the north, but it was yet to be seen whether Spinningdale would ever be viable. His mill at Oban was faring better and he was pleased to acknowledge that his example was being followed by others and more factories were springing up in the area.

One great triumph, rising like a counterweight to the depression and war, was the giant stone bulk of the Glasgow Royal Infirmary.

The opening was a grand affair, attended by the Lord Provost in his chains of office and many other city dignitaries.

Anne Caroline was delighted to accompany her father on the occasion, being invited on a tour of the completed building and also to the meal which followed the ceremony.

Persuaded by Toshie that it would not be suitable to wear anything daringly modern, she chose a high necked dress with a fitted cream bodice and a wide skirt of matching cream and russet stripes over hooped petticoats. Pinning her wavy brown hair back from her face, she styled it to fall in a cascade of curls down her back.

It was a bitterly cold December morning so she wrapped up warmly in a cape and, mindful that it would be removed for the meal, carefully placed a pretty bonnet at a jaunty angle on her head. She looked, she thought, sophisticated and older than her years. This pleased her and she plucked at the long skirts to raise them sufficiently for Toshie to buckle on her new high heeled shoes.

The Infirmary's architects, Robert and James Adam, guided the admiring group around the five main floors, including a vast basement: eight wards in all, holding one hundred beds. These two men, in immaculate black jackets and breeches, with colourful brass buttoned waistcoats and frilled cravats rippling at their throats, escorted the Lord Provost at the front of the party. Behind them gaggled twenty or so eminent merchants and surgeons with their wives: the ladies' formal day dresses bringing soft waves of colour into the clinical lime-washed walls and flagstones of the interior.

Describing their reasons for designing this window or that corridor as they passed through the rooms, the architects brought them all to a circular room on the top floor with a glazed dome ceiling.

'The operating theatre! This glass ceiling will allow as much natural light as possible to flood the room. I am sure you will agree that a surgeon must be able to see what he is doing!' Robert Adam quipped, but his audience was so full of awe at his brilliance that there was no polite laughter. The men and women who were gathered around the room were beginning to understand the forethought and importance of every carefully assessed detail.

The new hospital was magnificent.

In her fur trimmed cape and bonnet, Anne Caroline stood at the doorway of the round room and an involuntary chill prickled her skin. She did not wish to imagine the pain that would be inflicted in that room and turned away, telling herself that such medical operations would only be carried out if strictly necessary and were surely preferable to death? She did a poor job of convincing herself.

The celebratory meal was a much more pleasant experience. Seated between her father and a young surgeon, she followed the conversation and enjoyed the beef and scallop pie, delighting in the formal atmosphere and elegant guests.

The surgeon on her left was a gaunt young man with bushy eyebrows. His shock of light brown hair sprung out from his head and swung untidily above his collar as he turned his attention from Anne Caroline on one side to an elderly lady on the other. He was very talkative, preferring to expound his views rather than ask for, or even allow space for, responses from those listening to him.

Anne Caroline was not impressed, much to the chagrin of Mrs MacIntosh, who way laid her in the corridors as they made their way to collect their capes.

'Is he not the most intelligent man?' she beamed, taking Anne Caroline's arm. 'I thought the seating plan exceedingly well thought out. He was by far the most eligible man there and also the youngest, it was fitting that you were placed together.'

'That may be,' Anne Caroline said, sighing, 'but I am quite exhausted by his monologue! He would also have been more attractive company had he taken the time to chew his food and swallow it before he spoke.'

'He is exuberant though, is he not? And a surgeon? With a brilliant future ahead of him?'

Anne Caroline laughed, 'Mrs MacIntosh, I am only seventeen, I am hardly yet introduced into society! And you are already trying to persuade me of a good husband!'

'Humour me, my dear.'

'Perhaps when I am another four or five years older I will ask for your introductions...'

'Four or five years! You have Jean and Mary coming up behind you, you must open your eyes to all possibilities immediately!'

Anne Caroline just smiled at the well intentioned lady. She was in no hurry to marry and leave her father's house, quite the opposite. She adored her father and enjoyed her new role in accompanying him to functions. If she were to ever consider an attachment for a man he would have to be as good and kind as her dear Papa and that would be very difficult to find.

***

It was a month later, in late January of the new year, when Sarah gave birth to her daughter.

Fiona sat by the fireside nursing Davey, with Donald playing on the old rag rug at her feet and watched her sister-in-law-sleeping. Sarah's arms were cradled around the new born infant, her flowing fair hair fanned out on the pillow. They both looked serene in their slumber, with no tell tale signs of the trauma they had just endured.

It was a long, difficult birth and Fiona was aware it was a miracle both mother and baby were alive. The physician was called upon in the end and even he had struggled.

How different from the arrivals of her own babies. Her lips curved into a smile as she recalled Joe's wide-eyed wonder when Donald was born. How she clung to him during the final moments, drawing strength from his support, from his love.

Poor Sarah did not have that, she did not even know where Sean was, let alone whether he cared for her or would acknowledge his own child.

They had all talked endlessly about what would happen after the baby arrived. Now she was here.

Sarah's immediate reaction to being a mother was disinterest. She was so tired and sore that she barely seemed to look at the baby's face; grudgingly allowing the doctor to finish attending to her. Then, before he left, he encouraged her to hold it to her breast while she lay back and closed her eyes.

It was agreed by the family that Sarah would stay at home and look after the children and, as soon as possible, Fiona would return to work. Since Sarah was dismissed from Dale's service, money was tight and it was hoped that she would be able to feed both Davey and her own baby and allow Fiona to earn again.

The few savings Joe had put by in the New Lanark Savings Bank were very depleted but in the coming spring he was due for a raise in wages. If Fiona was back at the school, the extra income would make all the difference. Joe had come to terms with his sister's predicament and, as dependable as always, dealt with the practicalities of looking after her and providing a home. Unlike with his mother, Joe did not resent supporting his sister but sometimes in quiet moments, he wished that he and Fiona could live in their own place: just the two of them, with their children.

He dreamed of earning enough to lease a small house in Lanark where they could grow their own vegetables, the boys could play at the door and he and his wife would have the luxury of a separate bedroom. Private. Quiet. There was only another year and a half to go before he was qualified and he already had plans of what he wanted to do when that great day arrived.

However, it was still some time away and with Sarah's new child there would be more unexpected expenses.

'Whit are ye callin' her?' he asked his sister when he came home to find his little niece had finally made an appearance. Two whole days of living through Sarah's painful labour had been hard for all of them sharing the cramped room.

'Ah thocht o' Catherine?' Sarah murmured, her eyes heavy, a weary tone to the words.

'Aye, that's bonnie,' Joe pulled the blanket away from the sleeping baby and looked on her neat little head. 'She's a'richt?'

'Ah ken frae the doctor tha' she's a'richt.' Sarah tucked the cover around her child again and closed her eyes. She had hoped it would be a boy and felt nothing for her sleeping daughter. She longed for her old life back again, to be working at Dale's house, walking up to Lanark with Fiona, making new clothes... Everything was spoilt and it was all Sean's fault.

Her feelings were the same when the day came for Fiona to take up her position at the school.

245

'Ye'll be fine.' Fiona said firmly, excited to be returning to work but anxious about leaving her sons.

She had left Sarah in charge of them before on a few occasions and gone out for an hour or so at a time. Apart from wee Donnie crying when she first left the room, there were no problems with the arrangement.

Davey took to Sarah as a wet nurse and she was coping very well caring for both the babies. Fiona's own body was finding it more difficult, but on the days when she was required to work during the daytime, rather than just the evening classes, she could still return to the house in the middle of the day, which eased matters.

When the light spring days returned, so did the visitors to New Lanark.

William Kelly was used to the upheaval of arranging tours of the mills and welcoming guests. However, as the numbers increased, he delegated most of the hospitality to his clerks, or if James Dale was available, he would entertain them.

Fiona had noticed the carriages arriving in the village throughout the previous summer and enjoyed watching the ladies with their parasols and silken dresses. This year she was in the schoolroom and in much closer contact to these refined strangers who exclaimed at the children's achievements as if they were miracles performed by another species.

So many changes had taken place since she last worked in Mill Four that it took her a while to learn the new routines and become accustomed to the team of new teachers.

Mr Lyme was still there but now he was just one of a dozen or more. There were special teachers for arithmetic and others for reading and writing. Two music teachers, art teachers and two women specifically charged with instructing the girls in sewing.

David Dale's programme of lessons took his five hundred pupils up through the eight classes, depending on ability and the individual child's progress, which made for large and varied lessons.

It was rewarding work and Fiona was thrilled to be back among many of the orphans she knew from before she was married. It was also an unusual treat for her to be able to speak in Gaelic and she would return to the Row with sparkling eyes and flushed cheeks, relating her experiences to the others before they retired to bed.

In late July, the sad news spread across Scotland of the untimely death of the young poet, Robert Burns. He had been unwell for some time and, never having a strong constitution, he succumbed to heart failure.

His work was admired across the broadest spectrum of society. Even the poorest peasant could relate to his heartfelt pieces relating to simple, everyday life, as well as his outrageously bawdy poems fit only for the ears of men. In the great houses of Edinburgh and Glasgow, the wives of wealthy merchants recalled his vivacious personality at their soirees. The ordinary folk who knew him as a farmer, exciseman, friend or neighbour, all shared a sorrow at his passing.

Anne Caroline's grandparents were among those saddened by the poet's death. They purchased copies of his latest works and sent them to Glasgow, encouraging their grand-daughters to learn the ballads.

'Oh, I do think it is terribly sad that Mr Burns died before seeing his baby son,' sighed Jean, reading from the newspaper. 'It says here that the baby was born on the day he was laid to rest. He and his wife had nine children! My goodness!' She laid the broadsheet on the table and looked wistfully out of the window at the summer garden. 'His poems are so romantic... Grand-mama was greatly taken with him and said he was such a handsome, delightful man.' She turned to her sister. 'You attended one of the gatherings where he was present, did you not?'

Anne Caroline was working on a watercolour painting of a vase of moss roses arranged on the table in front of her. She dabbled her brush in a little pot of clean water and sat back.

'Yes, I remember him. He was... enchanting! I wish I had been older, I am sure I would have had more appreciation for the occasion. He exuded an importance, not in a bad way...' she narrowed her eyes, recalling the evening. 'You could not help but be drawn to gaze upon him because he had an air of excitement, an interest for all around him.'

'I wish I had met him,' Jean said, picking up the newspaper again. 'His work is so well known it would have been wonderful to tell people that I had met the great poet. Ah well...'

'He wrote a poem for Wilhelmina Alexander you know? But it has not been published in his collections.'

'Wilhelmina knew him?'

'I believe he used to live near Catrine. Anyway, he left for Edinburgh and then to travel around Scotland long before I visited Ballochmyle.' Anne Caroline surveyed her paint-box of colours, assessing which shade of green to mix with a deep blue for the shadows on the rose leaves. 'He left Ayrshire, didn't he? Was it in Dumfries that he lived?'

'Yes, he died in Dumfries, working for the Customs and Excise. Do you think the newspaper is accurate?' Jean returned to the article. 'I would not imagine a creative gentleman of Mr Burns' talents to be a clerk?'

'Perhaps his income from poetry was not sufficient? Which would be a shame, because his words brought such joy and entertainment. He should have been amply rewarded.'

Jean completed reading the obituary which confirmed that Burns could not live by his writing alone. Then she grew bored of current affairs and joined her sister in a little painting.

The following week, on a glorious summer afternoon, Mrs MacIntosh arrived in her stylish little gig to collect Anne Caroline from Charlotte Street.

In an effort to ensure Anne Caroline mixed with young people of her own age, Mrs MacIntosh was taking her to her son's home for a party on the lawns. Charles MacIntosh's career was blossoming and his wife was keen to show off their new home which, while still modest, indicated their rising status.

Musicians played under an awning and servants, hired for the day, mingled with the guests in the garden, providing trays of sweet meats and flutes of sparkling wine.

'Gracious, it is hot!' cried Mrs MacIntosh, flicking open her fan and vigorously fanning her rosy cheeks. 'I think I will repair to the shade of the drawing room, my dear. Let me see who I can leave you with...' she looked around the little clusters of guests admiring the herbaceous borders and chatting in the sun. 'Ah, Rosemary MacCall is over there, she may be a little older than you, but very well connected...' she took hold of Anne Caroline's arm and propelled her across the grass.

The introductions performed, the older lady excused herself and, perspiration beading on her powdered face, glided away to the open French doors.

Anne Caroline was grateful for Toshie's advice to carry a parasol and, raising it over their heads, suggested to her new acquaintance that they take a stroll around the grounds.

Although she was small and plump, Rosemary was wearing a low cut, daringly flimsy gown, which was the height of fashion. She was happily aware of the admiring glances from the young men in the party and keen to take the opportunity to parade in front of them.

Anne Caroline found her to be very good company and the two struck up a friendship amidst the melodious music and flower perfumed garden. Rosemary seemed to know everyone and would pause beside guests, her round face dimpling with smiles, introduce them to Anne Caroline and then move on to the next group.

As they approached the group containing their hosts, Rosemary whispered, 'You know, Charles and Mary already, but do you know the Tenants? Charles and Margaret have only been married a year but they are the happiest couple in the world! He is quite brilliant! Papa says he is a little too outspoken regarding Parliamentary Reform and should be more wary to whom he speaks. But oh! he has the clearest eyes and most charming way to him.' She sighed, theatrically, 'How lucky dear Margaret is. I do wish there were more men as well favoured as Mr Tennant.'

The man in discussion turned at that moment and seeing the girls approaching, stood aside to allow them to join the group.

'I am delighted to make your acquaintance, Miss Dale,' Charles Tennant smiled. 'I have enormous respect for your father. He was a weaver from Ayrshire and so am I. If I achieve half the success he has, I will be a contented man.'

His comment could not have been more endearing to Anne Caroline and when his wife added how they planned to visit New Lanark, she decided she liked the Tennants, very much.

'My Grandfather lives in Ayrshire still, at Stewarton. Are you from there?'

'I was raised in Ochiltree and return to visit my family from time to time, but I was apprenticed in Kilbarchan.' He placed an arm around his wife's shoulders, 'I had the good fortune to set up business beside a farm near Barrhead, which just so happened to belong to Mary's father.'

'Are you still a weaver?' Anne Caroline asked innocently.

The company laughed, but not unkindly.

'I started out as a silk weaver, you know,' said Tennant. 'But it is the bleaching side of the textile industry in which I am engaged.'

'Mr Tennant is in partnership with my Charles,' Mary MacIntosh put in sweetly, wishing to draw attention to her own husband who was content to let the conversation pass over him. 'He is the Chemist behind the process, isn't that right, Mr Tennant.'

249

'Indeed, it is...' Tenant's words were overtaken by the musicians suddenly striking up into loud renditions of old Scottish Ballads.

Mary clasped her hands together. 'I do hope everyone will like this, I asked for a medley of the best known pieces from Robert Burns' work. Charles and I felt it would be fitting, so shortly after his passing.'

The assembled guests were moving closer to the musicians, some of them swaying with the music, smiling to one another.

'We knew Mr Burns, he was a good friend of my father's.' said Tennant.

Anne Caroline looked at him in amazement, 'How extraordinary, I know a lady to whom he dedicated a poem! A very beautiful poem...' she added hurriedly, seeing the raised eyebrows in her audience. 'She is a refined and modest lady but did not wish her identity to be published.'

'Oh, Burns was a prolific writer,' Tennant said. 'My father is immortalised in his epistle 'James Tennant of Glenconner' and I am even given a mention! As 'wabster Charlie'! due to my weaving at that time.'

Mary MacIntosh was delighted with the response to her entertainment and slipped her hand through her husband's arm. She was so proud of him and had every confidence that this garden party would be the first of many as they took their place in Glasgow Society.

The air was cooling and midges danced in the slanting rays of evening sunshine when people began to give their thanks to their hosts and drift from the house. When the senior Mrs MacIntosh appeared, suggesting that she take Anne Caroline home, it was with a feeling of reluctance that Anne Caroline accepted her invitation. The men had withdrawn to the house, but she could have stayed and talked to Mary MacIntosh and Rosemary all evening.

The fame and wealth of David Dale was known to most of those present and as Mrs MacIntosh had anticipated, his eldest daughter's appearance on the social scene was noted with interest.

Chapter Eight

'Our minds must be convinced that everything we do is present duty and in discharge of it we aim at glorifying God and doing good to ourselves and others.'
David Dale (sermon 8th January 1792)

At the beginning of August, a week of constant rain seeped from the Lanarkshire hills and poured into the Clyde, bursting its banks and spreading out across pasture land.

The Falls of Clyde roared through the gorge, ripping off overhanging branches and turning the waters into peaty, thundering cascades, sending up clouds of spray that could be seen from miles away. Great mounds of white, foaming flocculation floated past the New Lanark Mills, catching onto the otters' island and careering off towards the fourth massive waterfall at Stonebyres, several miles downstream.

With this plentiful supply of energy all the water wheels beneath Dale's mills were running to full capacity. Occasionally, in long dry spells, some of the wheels could not be worked, so Kelly was in a buoyant mood when he saw the high water.

'Give us that wrench!' he shouted above the din of clattering machinery as he worked on the pipes in Mill Three.

The two little boys at his beck and call jumped to fetch what he needed, watching the manager with owl eyes.

For years now, Kelly had been tinkering with the heating system in the mills. He was a familiar sight to the workers, pushing his thick wavy hair behind his ears, sleeves rolled up, his jacket thrown aside, down on his hands and knees peering beneath the floor boards. Or down in the workshops at the bottom of Mill Four, pouring over specifications for new brass fittings or pipe joints.

There was nothing he enjoyed more than creating new parts for machinery, expertly designing and over-seeing the moulds for replacing or repairing used pieces of the wheels or the gearing mechanisms.

To allow the cotton to run smoothly it required a warm, damp heat in the work rooms but, so far, his attempts at installing stoves were met with severe disapproval from the insurance company. Cotton mills were notorious for being fire hazards at the best of times, therefore the source of the heat had to come from a location far from the flammable cotton fibres.

So, he turned his attention to an arrangement of pipes to conduct steam, generated far away from the jennies, through a series of pipes and vents running around the buildings.

He was adjusting one of the new valves when a piercing scream went up and the Overlooker pulled violently on the handles to disconnect the gears.

Rosie, who was close to where Kelly was working, jumped back from her station, peering around the long room. The dreadful cries were coming from under the frames and as Kelly ran to the machine, she saw the spindles at the far end filling up with red thread: blood-red thread.

In a flash, he was stooping low and reaching beneath the network of flying cotton to haul out a shrieking, shaking child.

The little girl was no more than five or six years old, her head a grisly mass of blood where the hair had caught into the threads and been wrenched from the scalp.

It was the first serious accident Rosie had ever witnessed and she crumpled to the floor feeling very sick and dizzy. She was not the only one affected but little attention was paid to the weeping and horrified whispers of the other workers.

At Kelly's instructions, the Overlooker picked the girl up and took her straight to Mrs Docherty.

She was one of the Boarders so she was Dale's responsibility and Mrs Docherty would be called on to attend to her injuries.

'Och, it wer' jist dreadfu'...' Rosie told Sarah that evening. 'Ah cannae tell ye! Her wee heid wis covered i' blood... an' a' doon her frock wer' bricht red wi' blood!'

'That's why ye must tie yer hair back! They telt as a' at the stairt. It's gie dangerous!'

'Ye see these wee mites crawlin' aboot 'neath the thin layer o' threads, brushin' awa' a' the dust an' pickin' up the broken threads, an' they seem tae be sae wee that there's plenty o' room fae them. Bu' mibbee she pu' her heid up? Aw... Sarah, Ah'll never forget tha' as lang as Ah live.'

'Whit did ye do wi' a' the bloodied cotton?'

'Kelly pu'ed it aff the spindles, an' then he telt us tae get on wi' it.' Rosie was still pale from the memory of the horror. She had never had much to do with William Kelly and understood his need to put them back to work straight away, so, too shy to say anything, she carried on at the machine. For the rest of the day she fought off waves of nausea and a light headed, trembling feeling. It was a relief to be back home.

'Ah'm no' goin' tae the fields the nicht,' she said, unhooking her work pinafore and stepping out of it.

She shook it out, sending up a cloud of white specks of cotton, then, folding it neatly at the end of her hurlie bed, she lay down in her loose shift and stretched luxuriously.

'Why no'?' Sarah asked, busy with the babies at the table. 'It's bin sae wet the past days, noo the sun's oot again they'll be lookin' fer mair hands tae turn the hay.'

Many of the villagers earned a little on the side when it was harvest time. James Dale turned a blind eye as long as they either went to the farms after work or took no more than a couple of days away. This was usually covered by a lie about being unwell, although the tell tale sun-burnt faces and scratched forearms told a different story.

'It's guid money an' a', but Ah feel sae bad at whit happened the day... Ah jist want tae lie here an' do nuthin'.'

'Ah would love tae gi'e a haun wi' the harvest.' Sarah muttered, laying baby Cathy in the cot and starting to gather up her soiled linen to wash. 'Cal's fair enjoyin' it. Ye would nae think he'd bin a' work a' day when he came in fer his dinner an' wis oot tha' door afore it wis even swallowed.'

'Is Fiona no' hame yit?'

'Aye, she wis in fer a wee minute an' then oot agin wi' Joe. They're still sae sweet on one another... if Ah wisnae sae sore heartit mesel' Ah wid be happy fer them!' She ended with a laugh at herself. 'Listen tae me! Ah'm turnin' in tae a bitter auld woman!'

253

'Aye, ye are.' Rosie said solemnly. 'Ye'r a richt crabbit thing these days, Sarah. Yon bairn's yer ane doin', sae dinnae gae takin' it oot on the rest o' us.'

Shocked by her sister's outburst, Sarah fell silent. She thought she was keeping her inner turmoil hidden, but obviously not successfully enough.

Quietly, she picked up the coal bucket and made for the door. 'Can ye mind the weans till Ah fill the bucket?'

Rosie waved her hand at her. 'Aye, but Ah'm half asleep as it is, sae dinnae be lang....'

Out in the fresh evening air, Sarah toiled down to the bunker, picking her way between the sharper stones with her bare feet. When the bucket was filled, she paused to breathe in the scents of late summer and gaze along the Row towards the woods of Bonnington estate.

The nationwide recession was not evident in this little village, clinging to the steep banks of the River Clyde. More buildings were being constructed, new buildings, with the simple name of New Buildings.

The foundations of these narrow, tall tenements were already in place, cut into the hillside behind Dale's house. They were to provide more housing but also to give a larger meeting room for church services and it was proposed that the bottom rooms, on street level, would be leased to the stall holders as permanent shops.

As the evening was dry and warm, the grassy area above the lade was scattered with families and groups of men, purchasing ale from the stalls and lying on the banks to chat and relax.

She was not sure when she became aware of him, but her eyes focused on a figure meandering between the villagers.

It was his walk, the distinctive rise and fall of his body with every stride, the way he held his head, the set of his shoulders: it was Sean. Despite the beard, loss of weight and straggling hair, she recognised him. He was heading towards her, his direction taking him to the foot of the steps leading up and out of the village.

With a gasp she ran across to intercept him, calling his name, heedless of the pain in her feet as they were sliced on the stony street.

He stopped and stared at her, then a slow smile spread across his features and he opened his arms wide.

In three quick strides she was up in front of him and with all the force she could muster she slapped him hard across the face.

He staggered backwards with a look of utter shock.

'What was tha' for?'

All the pent up fury and pain inside came flying out as she rained blow after blow on his chest, until he caught hold of her wrists.

'What the hell's the matter with you woman?' He shouted.

Unable to speak, Sarah glared at him, tears streaming down her face.

'I've been in the jail...' he cried, 'I thought you knew? I was told your brother asked about me and I thought you wouldn't want to see me any more... but I didn't think you were that mad about it!'

'So...' she swallowed hard, trying to steady her breath. 'Why are ye here?'

Seeing she was calmer, he released her, but took a step away. 'Business.'

'Business? No' tae see me?'

'As I said, I didn't think you would want me.'

'Ah wanted tae see ye a year past... more... Ye've disgraced me... ye've ruined ma life! Ah've lost ma joab, folk dinnae look a' me i' the street... Sean... ye can ha'e no idea wha' Ah've bin through...'

He was watching her intently, his mouth slightly open, eyes flicking across her face, trying to catch every contortion, every frown and emotional expression.

'What's happened?'

'Ah've had yer bairn!' she spat out the words. 'Tha's whit's happened!'

His whole body relaxed, 'Aw Sarah, I didn't know...'

She was holding his gaze steadily, aware of the effect he was having on her. There was something about his features that combined to make him almost beautiful, yet, even in the smooth symmetry, there was nothing effeminate about him. She still felt a powerful attraction to him, like a moth to a flame, drawn to him in spite of everything. However, she was cautious now, fully conscious that she was letting down her guard. Surely, she had learned her lesson?

'Sarah...' he said, kindly, in his Irish lilt. 'Are ye all right? Is the babe all right...' he took a step towards her, again reaching to take her in his arms. 'Come now, tell me about it...'

'Ah'll gie ye 'tell me about it', Sean Rafferty! Dinnae touch me!'

A girl's voice came from behind her, 'Sarah! Whit's goin' on?'

It was Fiona. She looked at the unkempt man, a hand print of coal dust smeared on his face and suddenly realised who he was and what must be happening.

255

'Leave us be, Fiona!' Sarah snapped. 'Sean's jist here on 'business',
he's no' here fer onythin' else. Sae he'll be awa' noo!' she pushed
him roughly on the shoulder. 'Awa'!'

With a haughty shake of her head, Sarah turned and stalked towards
the Row, leaving Fiona and Sean speechless.

After a few moments, Fiona gestured to the low walls of the New
Buildings' foundations and they walked over and sat down.

Sean buried his head in his hands.

As Sarah stumbled back into the room, she collided with Rosie who
was walking about, rocking Cathy in her arms.

'Where ha'e ye bin! The wean started creatin' afore ye wer e'en on
the street! How lang does it tak ye tae fetch the coal?' She looked
again at her sister. 'Where's the bucket? Whit's up wi' ye?'

'Sean's back!' Sarah staggered to the table and sat down heavily on
a chair, lifting her feet to examine the cuts and grazes.

'Sean? An' whit's he got tae say fer hi'self?' Rosie shifted Cathy
onto her hip and carried on pacing the room to quieten her. Donnie
trotted over to peer at Sarah's feet, concern on his little face.

Sarah started to cry.

'Aw Jesus!' Rosie cast her eyes up to heaven. 'In the name o' the
wee man, will ye whisht! If yer no' greetin' cos he's left ye, yer
greetin' cos he's bak!'

It was quiet and dark in the room when Fiona, and then Joe,
returned. They found Sarah sitting sullenly by the red light of dying
coals. Rosie had already retired to bed, stating loudly that she needed
to sleep and was taking Sarah's bed so that she could draw the
curtain: it had been an eventful day.

Fiona pulled a shawl round her, chilled after sitting so long talking
to Sean in the gathering dusk. Between heating some broth and
settling her sons, she related her conversation with Sean.

Joe sprawled in the big chair by the newly stoked flames, listening
to the tale and observing his sister's reactions. It was clear from all
Fiona was telling him that Sean genuinely had not known of the
chaos he left behind him when he was arrested. It also became
apparent that Sean now wanted to take responsibility for Sarah and
Catherine.

'D'ye still care fer him?' Joe asked his sister.

She squirmed and fidgeted in her chair, then raised her eyes to look
at him.

'Aye, Ah do. But...'

Fiona and Joe looked at her expectantly and after a long pause she said, 'Aye, Ah do.'

'An' whit wis the 'but'?' Joe asked.

'Nuthin.' She clammed up, pushing her fears away.

There was a nagging doubt eating away within her but she couldn't voice it. She couldn't even properly form what she felt so confused about whenever she thought of the handsome, roguish Irishman. He unsettled her, that was all she knew and what reason was that to put forward in the cosy, domestic surroundings of their room? The man was prepared to marry her and own his child. Wasn't that all she had dreamed of during the months before Catherine was born? What was holding her back from seizing his offer and embracing it with all her heart?

She couldn't pin-point it, it was beyond reason, so she remained silent.

The following day, Fiona met Sean as they had arranged and told him Sarah was waiting for him in the Row.

'Treat her kind, Sean?' Fiona whispered to him as she turned away to go to work. 'It's bin a hard time.'

'I will,' he nodded, seriously. 'I didn't mean to hurt her, ye know?'

'Well, mak sure ye dinnae hurt her agin... or ye'll ha'e ma man efter ye, an' ye'll no be wantin' that!' Fiona smiled at him to lighten her words and saw a sparkle in Sean's eye.

He had dangerous eyes, the sort of eyes that made a woman weak. Even she felt the force of his sexuality and so it was little wonder Sarah was under his spell. Anyway, she told herself, he will do right by Sarah and the baby, so I should be pleased.

A breeze whipped at her skirts and she tucked her hands into the warm folds of the shawl, assuring herself that the chill she felt was caused by the onset of autumn.

***

'How many?' Dale asked, incredulous.

'Five hundred and forty three,' the clerk replied.

'Jings! Well, would you credit it! nearly five hundred and fifty visitors since last spring. That's what, sixteen months? Well, I'll be blowed!'

Kelly passed the visitors' book across the desk and pointed to several entries. 'They are coming from all over... Edinbugh, Manchester, London and look here, Belgium and,' he turned some pages, 'America.'

They were all seated in Kelly's office in New Lanark on a rainy autumn afternoon. Dale and his daughters were staying in the village for a week or so because he was keen to see how the new building work was progressing. This unexpectedly cheering news regarding the visitors touring his works was a delightful surprise and he sat back in the chair, causing it to creak under his weight.

'And the comments are good?' he enquired.

'They are excellent. No-one leaves here without a true affirmation that your practices on improving working conditions are anything but an inspiring experience.'

'And the schooling? What say they to the schooling?'

'The same, indeed some of the ladies become quite lyrical concerning the children's efforts. We have a very good team of teachers now, confident and enthusiastic in what they are achieving.'

'I hope they also note that our production is high. That is the key! A healthy, contented workforce will produce more on the factory floor. That, and following the Scriptures. If we live by God's ways we will gain more from life, I cannot stress it enough. Ye know, I have just been in correspondence with Thomas Bayley from the Manchester Board of Health. I know him from old, from work with the Chamber of Commerce. He is a good man.'

Dale paused to reflect for a moment. 'He and his colleague Dr Percival have long been lobbying Parliament for healthier working conditions in factories and... d'ye know what he sent me?'

Kelly and the clerk shook their heads.

'He sent me a long questionnaire. It was all about the running of the village, everything! From how we keet the rooms clean to how we deal with outbreaks of typhus.

'I replied with full details, but I would have thought it common practice to scrub and air the rooms regularly. Perhaps our yearly wash down with new flecked lime will be noted. There was even a question regarding what kind of food we give the children in Mill Four. I have to say, it was extraordinarily satisfying to be able to report a mere handful of deaths in our mills for I feel we take their safety and well-being very seriously.'

'You received my letter concerning Millie Walker?' Kelly asked. 'The orphan who had the misfortune to be scalped in an accident in Mill Three?'

'Aye, I read your letter. You said she was recovering, though. Is she?'

'Yes, except, of course, she will have no hair and the shock of the incident has brought out a nasty rash, lesions all over her body. Mrs Docherty has been applying calamine, but the doctor says it is a nervous disorder. I fear she may not work again for a while yet.'

'I would be grateful of you keeping me informed of her progress.' Dale picked up a sheet of paper with expenses for the machines. 'How is the new heating system performing?'

'The workshops are making new vents, but the stoves are working very well. That's nearly a year they've been running without any insurmountable problems.'

By the time the meeting adjourned, Dale was pleased to know his plans were on course.

He donned his hat and a heavy overcoat and strolled down through the village to look at the Clyde. As he walked, villagers would pass by, the men doffing their caps and bowing their heads, the women dropping curtseys. He gave them all a cheery smile and the ones he knew by name, he would pause in the drizzling rain to exchange a few words.

Even on this dreary day there were four horses belonging to visitors tethered down by the forge. He watched as a small, stooped young man moved between them. The saddles were covered by cut pieces of tarpaulin to keep them dry and the boy was carefully tucking any stray flaps back around the leather where the wind dislodged them.

It was heart warming to see such diligence from his employees and as Dale walked past, he raised his cane in acknowledgement of the lad's nod and bow.

Anne Caroline enjoyed being in New Lanark.

Even on wet days there were things to see from the windows and the exciting novelty of staying in their country cottage made even simple pastimes more fun.

Jean and Margaret were collecting wildflowers and pressing them between fine sheets of tissue paper with the intention of making a scrapbook. After country rambles they would consult reference books to find the names and inscribe neat nameplates, painted with butterflies or leaves, to include below the specimen in the finished book.

Mary brought her embroidery and Anne Caroline's love of reading meant they could all spend hours peacefully engrossed in their favourite hobbies.

Only little Julia needed entertainment and Giggs kept her amused with stories and specially chosen toys brought down from the city.

Cooper's new housemaid was a local girl from outside the village. She was small and neat, with a long nose and narrow face and while she performed all her duties immaculately, she barely had a word to say for herself. Much against her high moral standards, Cooper often found herself rueing the day she sent Sarah from the house.

Sometimes she would see her in the road. Embarrassed at having been so aggressive towards her but still dismayed by her immoral conduct, Cooper would avoid all eye contact. If possible, she removed herself to the other side of the street. She saw for herself how depressed and fragile the girl appeared and even after the baby arrived, she wore a grey, sour countenance, discouraging gossip or pleasantries with other young mothers.

However, Cooper always remembered the pretty, fair haired girl in her prayers, fervently asking God to forgive her for her weak and sinful nature.

She begged Him to show Sarah compassion, yet it never crossed her mind to reach out her own hand in forgiveness.

***

When the farm horses began toiling in the fields, ploughing the earth for autumn crops, and the daylight hours drew shorter, there was a gradual falling away of the flow of people visiting New Lanark. The community drew back into itself, driven by the need for light and warmth few ventured far from their firesides.

Brisk winds stripped the leaves off the trees and bleached the grassy slopes, making the village as grey and stark as the rocky river bed.

Sean found employment on the New Buildings and arranged a room, as a lodger with an old lady and her spinster daughter in Braxfield Row. Neither Joe nor Sean broached the subject of Sean joining his wife and child and staying in the Scotts' room, but the notion of living away from her family was strange and frightening for Sarah.

After their hasty marriage inside the ancient stone walls of St Kentigern's Church on the hill outside Lanark, they moved into their new place with Cathy.

It was not a good start to their married life, both of them awkward with each other and constantly in the company of old Mrs Hayes and the prickly, middle aged, Clarinda Hayes.

Clarinda worked as a Twister in Mill Two, where both her brothers had been employed but they had been called up to the army and the elderly widow's impoverished circumstances forced her to rent out the second set-in bed. Both mother and daughter were disapproving of Cathy's presence, especially as they knew her parents were just newly married, but 'needs must' as Mrs Hayes pointed out and the rent was agreed.

When Sean left for work every morning, Sarah would dress and hastily follow him out the door, running down the hill and along the Row to return to her old home.

Complaining to Bessie one Sunday afternoon when Sean was up in Lanark with his Irish friends, Sarah was suddenly struck with an idea.

She was kneeling on the floorboards, pinning up the torn hemline on Bessie's best dress, when she stood up very abruptly with a shocked smile on her face.

'Ye ken ye said Mrs Connelly would fancy a new dress?'

'Aye, she was gie taken wi' the last yin ye sewed fer me.'

'Bessie, de ye ken she'd pay fer it, if Ah made it fer her?'

'She's tight, tha' yin, but she cannae dae onything wi' her hands, they're tha' bad wi' the rheumatics. Aye, Ah ken she'd pay.'

'Then that's whit Ah'll dae! Ah can earn money agin! Ah'll ask aboot and find ither folk who need cla'es an' soon we'll ha'e enough tae rent oor ane room!'

It was a special moment, a moment Sarah would look back on as marking the start of her new life. The miseries of becoming pregnant, losing her job and being abandoned by Sean had crushed her self confidence. She had felt worthless, sinful, as Cooper told her, but these burdens were over.

That was all in the past.

Now she had the means, with her own hands, to create a better future and with Sean beside her and Cathy to care for, there was a wonderful feeling of hope. Things would be better; she could actively contribute to the family purse, yet still look after her little nephews.

The warm feeling of happiness which had eluded her for so long, filled her heart and shone through her eyes. Sean noticed it immediately and in her change of attitude, it affected his mood and he felt lighter and more comfortable with his sudden new circumstances.

Being a husband and father did not come naturally to Sean Rafferty, but he was trying his best. He took Sarah's plans as a means to improving their accommodation and in so doing, their relationship.

Dress-making and fashion were on Anne Caroline Dale's mind as well. Invitations to the winter season of house parties and theatre outings were now arriving and sat in a growing line along the mantelshelf.

Three new gowns were being made and she spent hours with Jean and Mary, trying to perfect different hairstyles. With Toshie's expertise, this was now being achieved to great success and attractive adornments of ribbons, seed pearls and brightly coloured glass beads lay in her jewellery box alongside the beautiful cameo brooch her father gave her on her eighteenth birthday.

Rosemary McCall was a regular visitor to the Charlotte Street mansion during the stormy winter of 1796. The gusty winds and torrential downpours that persisted through into the new year made even walking short distances an unpleasant task. So, her mother would arrange for her to be taken there by carriage and a few hours later, collected again.

The two girls were now firm friends but Rosemary, being three years older, took a much more serious view on presenting herself to the possibilities of meeting a husband.

'You are still young,' she would say to Anne Caroline, 'I have already passed twenty one years, I need a husband!'

'Oh now Rosemary, most of the ladies we know were not wed until they had reached twenty and five years. You have plenty of time.'

Rosemary's round face and button eyes looked anxious. 'Oh, how I would like to have a household and entertain, like dear Mary MacIntosh or the Tennants. By the by, I understand that Mrs Tenant is with child!' Again, the anxious look. 'I would so love to have a child. I would dress it up in the finest clothes and the nursemaid would wear a smart uniform...'

Most afternoons were spent in these idle conversations but when they attended a dinner together Rosemary became more serious. She spoke knowledgably about the latest news of the war and Glasgow's own local current affairs. For all the world, she appeared unconcerned in finding a gentleman to marry.

When Anne Caroline queried her friend's different personality among company, Rosemary disclosed how she learned from a book that a young lady should keep herself abreast of all topics on which a gentleman might wish to converse. To that end, she read the newspaper avidly the day before an engagement.

'I have no interest whatsoever in that sort of thing,' she admitted. 'It is very tedious, but easily learnt.'

'And if a gentleman is attracted by your knowledge,' mused Anne Caroline, thoughtfully, 'and enjoys your discussions so much that he wants you as his wife, what will you do after the wedding?'

'After the wedding? Well, there will be no need to try and impress him, will there?' Rosemary gave one of her sweet dimpling smiles, 'We will be married and I will have children and servants to talk about.'

'Is that not using deceit? Tricking the poor man into believing he is marrying one sort of person, while you are actually quite another?'

'What does it matter? At least I am not doing what Louisa Fitzgibbon did! Enticing, or as she told Moira Willoughby, *allowing* Walter to lie with her and then going all pathetic and vulnerable when she fell with child so he *had* to propose marriage.'

'I would think it matters a great deal,' said Anne Caroline, vehemently. 'If I am ever to marry, I would wish to know that my husband cares for me, as I am. My father is very strict in these matters. We must be honest with ourselves and others, it is the only true course to take in life. God has made us as we are and so long as we strive to do good, we should not apologise or pretend to be anything other. I have to say I agree with his views.'

For a few seconds they sat in silence by the drawing room fire, the wind buffeting the windows.

'Let us not fall out over this?' Anne Caroline murmured, laying a hand on her friend's arm and being rewarded with a smile. 'We will enjoy all our engagements and just see what transpires. For myself, I hope to have a pleasant time and if you wish to meet your future husband, then I hope you are successful... and I am sure it will be for your own charms, Rosemary, and not your discourse on Pitt's policy on whatever new topic is in the news!'

Throughout the darkest months of the winter the two girls enjoyed the sumptuous dining tables and dancing halls of Glasgow's upper class circles.

While the foot soldiers of His Majesty's regiments were wading, thigh high, through freezing mud in Europe or being blasted by canon at sea, violins played in drawing rooms, carved meats and fruit were set on silver salvers and laughter rang out beneath many candle-filled chandeliers.

Although most of the guests at these fine occasions were happily oblivious to their good fortune, Anne Caroline was made aware of her privileged position.

Every Sunday she and her sisters accompanied their father to church and listened to his long, thought provoking sermons. When their mother was alive, they would, on occasions, walk further through the streets of Glasgow to the Baptist Church, where Carolina worshipped. However, nowadays on a Sunday if the family were in residence in the city, they were always to be found in the front pews of the Old Scotch Independents, the church Dale had helped to found.

David Dale was unique among his fellow Christian evangelists by his love of the good things in life, while also succeeding in remaining mindful and humbled by the hardships that beset his fellow man.

He took great pleasure in his wine cellar, fine cheeses and meats, knowing that he could do so with a free conscience. He worked honestly and relentlessly to balance his wealthy lifestyle by improving the lot of those less fortunate.

The Church was a constant and fulfilling part of the Dales' life and there would often be ministers arriving at Charlotte Street to have discussions on religious and community matters. Anne Caroline would hear the distant ringing of the doorbell and Renwick's measured footsteps across the hall but, unless she was expecting a friend to call, she took little heed of who was ushered up the stairs or into the library.

Until one sunny February morning when she was crossing the hallway just as Renwick was opening the door to a visitor.

The man who entered was swathed in a black knee-length cape and as he gave his name and started to unbuckle the clasp of his cape, his gaze fell upon Anne Caroline.

She felt a start of delight as their eyes met and graciously inclined her head, before forcing herself to continue to the library.

Assuming the stranger's sombre black jacket, breeches and waist-coat with a high starched white collar was the attire of a minister, she guessed he must be a cleric from out of town. Certainly, she would have noticed him had they met before.

There were several handsome young men at the parties over the new year festivities but not one of them provoked such a sensation. His hair was raven black and cut short, his face angular with a clear cut, square jaw and his eyes a light grey with thick black lashes. Their silent exchange, mere moments of connection, caused her heart to race and she went to the mirror beside the fireplace to quickly survey her appearance. Sleeking any stray hairs smoothly into place, she hoped the gentleman's fleeting appraisal of her had not been too disagreeable.

Disappointed to realise that Renwick was immediately escorting the visitor upstairs to her father's study, she hovered in the library waiting to contrive a meeting when he took his leave.

For over an hour she lifted this book and that, unable to settle and telling herself how foolish she was to be wasting her time waiting for the opportunity of another brief encounter.

At last, she heard voices, her father's and another, coming down the stairs. Bracing herself, she grasped a book in her hand and walked, casually, out into the hallway.

'Ah! This is my daughter, my eldest daughter, Anne Caroline.' Dale said, beaming. 'Mr Aleksey.'

'My pleasure to make acquaintance,' Aleksey took her hand and bowed.

'Good day to you, Mr Aleksey.' Anne Caroline tried not to stare at the man but his exotic good looks and foreign pronunciation were enthralling.

'Mr Aleksey is from Russia. He visited New Lanark in the summer and wished to meet me.'

Aleksey was retrieving his cape and fastening it at his throat. On closer inspection, Anne Caroline could see that he was most probably not a man of the church because the clasp was encrusted with jewels. The cape and also the jacket beneath, were of the finest yarn.

'I took him for a minister,' Anne Caroline said, when Aleksey had taken his leave.

'No, he is an agent for a yarn importer in St Petersberg and is looking to do business with me. I have gained a favourable enough impression of him and await his instruction.' Dale was smiling at her, noting her heightened colour. 'I can see you also thought he was agreeable.'

'He was a very... remarkable gentleman.'

'Indeed. He is returning to Russia in a few days but I am sure there will be other 'remarkable' young men for you to meet in Glasgow. I cannot say I would be delighted if you were to become attached to a foreigner and sailed to a new life overseas. There are plenty good Scotsmen and plenty time to meet them, eh?'

She slipped her arm through his and cuddled against him.

'Oh Papa, I would never be with anyone who did not wholeheartedly meet with your approval, you know that!'

'A good Scotsman, Anne Caroline, an honest, God fearing man is what I wish for you and all your sisters.'

'As you say, there is no hurry. I am not like Rosemary, who desires to be married this year!'

'I am glad to hear it. Now, I must attend to some letters.' He squeezed her hand and then made his way up the stairs, seizing the bannister rail to aid his climb.

His weight and girth were increasing and he no longer felt fit enough to take the long walks he had been accustomed to over the years. Age was creeping steadily through his bones.

He knew it when he woke in the mornings with aching joints and in the afternoons, after a large meal, when he was troubled with dyspepsia. There was much to do and his many ventures required constant vigilance but he was starting to feel a lack of energy. Sometimes be was forced to leave his desk in the middle of the day and fall asleep in the cushioned chair by the fire.

During the last year both his father and step-mother had died. Both in their eighties, it was hardly unexpected, but after the loss of his brother Hugh, he was now very aware of being on his own at the head of the Dale family.

When he reached his study he set about opening the ink well and drawing a new sheet of paper from his bureau. He was replying to a letter from his old friend James Muir, who had written to him relating news of his son.

Thomas Muir was reported to have escaped from Botany Bay and sailed to California. From there his whereabouts were unknown, with some accounts saying he was in the hands of the Spanish and being moved on to Mexico.

Dale dipped his quill in the ink and composed a letter which he hoped would give support and comfort to its reader.

***

A few months later, Anne Caroline received an invitation to dine at Rosemary McCall's house. Weeks of anticipation and planning had gone into organising this event and Rosemary's excitement knew no bounds. Her mother extended invitations to a group of her daughter's younger acquaintances and added a well researched number of eligible batchelors to the list.

Anne Caroline arrived early, having arranged to stay the night with her friend, and found their beautiful townhouse bustling with last minute activity. A maid took her overnight bag and showed her up to Rosemary's bedroom.

'I can hardly breathe with nerves!' cried Rosemary, in a state of undress with her hair in tightly bound rags. 'To think! Gilbert Morris has accepted! He is truly wonderful, do you not agree?'

Anne Caroline recalled the man in question and wondered how Rosemary could describe him as wonderful. He was from a rich and established family, which ranked high with her friend, but was inclined towards being portly even at his young age and was exceedingly quiet.

'That is good news,' she replied, then changing the subject, 'It is past five o'clock and your guests will be arriving at six o'clock yet you still have your hair in curling rags?'

'Oh, I know... my hair just will not curl! I have even combed a little lard on the strands before binding and wished to leave it as long as possible to take effect.'

'When did you tie them up?' Anne Caroline asked, admiring the high bed, draped with pale yellow fabric and piled with pillows.

'Yesterday afternoon... do you think I should risk taking them off now?'

'No,' said Anne Caroline, in a serious tone. 'I think you should leave them in for the entire evening.'

A quickly stifled titter came from the maid who was attending to the girls' evening wear.

267

'The entire evening?' Rosemary cried.

'No.... of course not... You should unwind them right away! If they are not curled now they never will be!'

The maid, struggling to keep her face composed, was called upon to undo the rags. Not only were the desired ringlettes curled but they were so tight that they sprang out at right angles from her head.

'Oh Anne Caroline...' Rosemary's voice was low with concern as she watched the unfolding hairstyle in the dressing table mirror. 'I look like a *spaniel*...'

The maid was shaking with mirth and when Anne Caroline joined her in a fit of silent giggles it became too much to contain and they both exploded into uncontrollable laughter.

Half crying, half laughing, Rosemary swung her head about, astounded at the sight of the clubby rolls of hair bobbing above her ears.

'What am I to do?'

Wiping tears from her eyes, her friend attempted to stem her hilarity. The sight of Rosemary in her shift and stockings with such an outraged face and ludicrous hair-do, was too much to control.

'It is *not* amusing! What can be done?' Rosemary kept looking from the mirror to her friend and back again with panic-stricken eyes. 'How can Gilbert fall in love with a *spaniel!*'

Anne Caroline burst out laughing again, clutching at her sides and then patting her chest in a desperate effort to calm herself and attempt to focus on helping her friend.

The maid's face was twisted with the effort of remaining respectful, her eyes wet with suppressed giggles. She offered to light the fire to see if the heat would melt the cold lard enough to relax the curls.

'It is too late for that...' Rosemary whimpered, 'By the time the fire is lit and giving heat, the carriages will be here! Oh dear, this is the worst night of my life!' She jumped to her feet and paced about the room. 'Fetch my mother! perhaps she will know what can be done!'

Mrs McCall suggested the curling irons to be heated and then used to soften the ringlettes. This was undertaken and by the time the clock in the hallway sent six chimes ringing through the house, order had been restored in Rosemary's room.

Still pink and nervous from her ordeal, Rosemary descended the stairs with Anne Caroline and took up her position in the drawing room, ready to greet her guests.

The party all assembled, they moved through to the dining room and Anne Caroline found herself seated opposite a Mr Cambridge who smiled at her with an openly appreciative expression on his face.

'I understand you are visiting Glasgow on business?' she ventured. 'Have you travelled from afar?'

'From London, Miss Dale.'

'And is London your home town, sir?' she asked, noticing how the powder from his hair was leaving a dusting on his black velvet collar.

'My family home is in Kent, but I am practising law in Westminster.' He took a sip of wine and continued, 'Am I correct in surmising that you are the daughter of Mr David Dale, the magistrate and merchant?'

'Why, yes! Are you acquainted with my father?'

'Alas, no. Although, I have heard his name in the upper circles of the city's society. He is a progressive thinker in the area of social betterment, I understand, and an astute business man to boot.'

'If by 'progressive' you mean he believes that all men and women should be treated fairly, as God prescribes, then, yes, he could be described as such.' She watched the man's face while she spoke and saw his brows raise, fractionally.

'It would be an ideal world if all masters of manufacturing could also be bankers. Philanthropy is so much easier when one has a deep wallet.'

His words were said lightly but Anne Caroline did not like the offensive inference. She was about to speak up in her father's defence when Cambridge, oblivious to her reaction, continued; 'Your father's house is that superb mansion at the far end of Charlotte Street, is it not?'

'Yes, indeed...'

'My own father's house, our townhouse that is, is similar in size and style. It is located near to Westminster, in a gracious area of trees and gardens....'

Cambridge's voice trailed on, boasting of his family's wealth, their country estates and his own aspirations, being the eldest son, of inheriting the bulk of the riches.

The more he spoke, the lower Anne Caroline's opinion of him grew. Yet he took her silence as a sign of enthralment and in the few moments when he drew breath, would favour her with admiring and flirtatious glances.

269

Rosemary noticed nothing of the interaction between her guests, all her attention being focused on Gilbert Wilson. It seemed that her disastrous curls were not the catastrophe she imagined and when they all adjourned to the drawing room he settled himself in the chair beside her and was very attentive to her conversation.

When the carriages arrived at the door and guests began to make their farewells, Cambridge took up a position beside Anne Caroline to walk to the hallway together.

It was a warm spring evening with moths spiralling around the carriage lamps. The perfume of dew from the privot hedge wafted into the house.

'Good night, Miss Dale,' he said, bowing excessively low over her hand so his lips nearly touched her skin.'It has been a great pleasure to meet you.'

'Good night, Mr Cambridge,' she said firmly, withdrawing her fingers from his grasp.

'Perhaps, I may call on you in the next few days. I do not return to London until next week.'

'We are going down to the country so I am afraid it will not be possible to meet again.'

'Perchance when I return?' he did not believe she was rejecting his offer and flashed a churlish smile. 'I am sure we shall meet again, Miss Dale... at a time when a country visit is not so pressing.'

Anne Caroline returned a composed smile to his slightly arrogant phrasing. She preferred to remain silent rather than allow her impatience to show through a reply.

'Oh, what a wonderful evening!' Rosemary enthused, as they undressed and prepared for bed. 'My head is giddy with memories of Mr Wilson's compliments!'

'Or maybe the porter you were taking at the end?' Anne Caroline suggested. 'It is very strong, both in taste and the effect it has on one's senses, I could only manage a taste.'

They climbed into the wide feather bed and Rosemary blew out the candles and flopped down into the pillows.

'Did you enjoy the evening, Anne Caroline?' she asked, into the darkness.

'Oh yes, it was most agreeable.'

'And tell me, did you find Mr Cambridge good company?'

'He was unrelentingly boorish and very pre-occupied with advertising himself as a 'good catch''

270

Rosemary yawned and turned on her side, closing her eyes.

'Oh dear, we knew little of him before this evening,' she said sleepily, 'but as he is a friend of Mr Johnson and was to be staying with him over this date, Mama presumed to include him on the invitation.'

'No matter, despite Mr Cambridge, it was a lovely evening and I am sure all your guests will remember it with pleasure.' Anne Caroline whispered back, knowing how important the success of the evening was to Rosemary.

There was no reply and after a few silent minutes the sound of steady breathing told of Rosemary's slumber. Anne Caroline lay on her back gazing up towards the dark ceiling until her eyes became accustomed to the dimness and she could trace the lines of the bed curtains and the moonlit window.

'Maybe one day,' she thought, remembering snatches of the evening, 'I will meet a new gentleman attending one of these soirées. Someone fine and interesting with whom I could share a lively conversation and look upon with the same delight as Rosemary looks upon her Mr Wilson.'

***

A fresh, sunny day greeted the Dales when they set off for New Lanark a few days later.

The family travelled with Toshie in the coach and four, leaving no room for anyone else, so Giggs and Duncan followed them in the wagon with their luggage, grocery provisions and the many portfolios filled with Dale's business papers.

The wagon was to take the usual route, staying on the moors and higher ground running through to Carluke. However, Dale instructed his coachman to take the family on the riverside road to Hamilton and then through the deep, winding Clyde valley towards Lanark.

He knew the area well from both his early trips to New Lanark and also from his youth, when he was a journeyman traipsing between the Lanarkshire towns.

Famous for its fruit growing climate, the Clyde valley came into its own in the springtime, providing a wonderfully scenic drive. The colourful spectacle was a novelty for his daughters and they were so taken with the beauty of it that the horses were reined in to a halt several times when the girls clamoured to alight and take a closer inspection.

Hundreds of fruit trees were heavy and bowed low with thick pink and white blossom, bobbing and swinging in the breeze.

Sugar-pink and white flowering apple orchards clustered on the fertile hillside, mixing with cherry, damson and plum trees. Their leaf buds burst behind the petals to show brilliant greens and reds of the different hues of emerging foliage. Woodlands of beech, elm and oak, decked out in their light green leaves, sheltered swathes of bluebells growing densely on the shady slopes.

The twisting road followed the river upstream through Rosebank and Hazelbank, dipping and turning at every corner, until Julia became sick with the swaying motion.

They stopped on top of the cliffs overlooking Stonebyres Linn so she could climb from the carriage and recover in the shade of a group of beech trees. Anne Caroline sat on the grass beside her, enjoying the stillness and birdsong after the rumble and clatter of their journey.

Higher up on the hill, above the steading of Linnmill, women in large bonnets and colourful petticoats were working among rows of new strawberry plants; weeding and laying straw beneath the flowering shoots. Movement in the dappled shadow of a nearby orchard showed a bee-keeper tending his skips, a veil of fine netting tied over his broad brimmed hat.

Fearful of the sheer drop at their side, Jean remained in the coach with her father and despite being urged by Toshie to do so, refused to join them in the fresh air.

'It is so beautiful in this valley,' Anne Caroline said, when they were all packed into the carriage again. 'I shall try and catch its charm in watercolours so the memory of today is captured for all time.'

'It may be very pretty,' Julia declared, her face pale and pinched, 'but I never want to come this way again!'

When they arrived at their destination, the wagon with Giggs and the others was standing by the house, most of its contents already unloaded. Mrs Cooper greeted them and, as she did every time, hustled all the children through to the front room where a delicious array of food was set upon the table.

For weeks she had been planning and preparing for the family and it was a personal achievement for her when they took their seats and enjoyed the fruits of her labour. Being the housekeeper for Dale's occasional, country residence was very demanding in ways the other servants could not understand.

The house was limited in its size and the capacity of the ovens and larder restricted her scope for menus. However, during the weeks and sometimes months when the family did not visit, it was depressingly large and quiet within its walls. Then, all of a sudden, there was a flurry of overwhelming activity and organisation to be accomplished.

Sarah watched their arrival with interest. In particular she noted the Miss Dales' clothes as they climbed from the carriage.

Since the warmer days arrived, she was enjoying the stream of wealthy visitors to New Lanark. The ladies, in their fashionable dresses, modelled the latest designs from some of the country's leading designers.

If the weather was fair, as it was that day, she would take the children out to the grassy slope below Caithness Row and spread a blanket on the ground. The little ones played around her and she could see the carriages and riders arriving while she sewed, all the time observing the cut of the gowns and the new shapes of sleeves and bodices.

It had only taken a few months for the demand for her skills to become such that, together with Sean's wages, they could afford to rent a room of their own.

The longed for intimacy of having their own room had not brought the marital bliss she hoped it would.

Sean still went out nearly every evening to meet his friends and was sometimes very much the worse for drink when he returned.

When she spoke to him about the long hours she spent alone sewing by the fire, he told her that it was good for her to have peace and quiet to work. One evening, he came home to find her tearful with the weariness and loneliness of the still room, with only baby Cathy, asleep in her cot, for company.

'You wanted us to have a place of our own and now you're complaining!' he shouted, his mouth in an angry line. 'I work all day and cannot just sit by the fire with you at night! I have people to see, things to discuss...' he picked up a folded piece of material on the table and flung it down again in a rumpled pile. 'I am a man, I am not about to waste my free time watching you stitching away, dressing the village women!'

273

His harsh tone and bitter words were a shock to Sarah. She bit back her responses and let him calm down, trying to appease him and win back the amiable Sean she loved. Inevitably, their privacy also brought more opportunities to share the marital bed, which produced the not unexpected result of discovering another baby was on the way.

So, when the Dales were in residence over the spring, Sarah was experiencing a productive but emotionally stressful, period in her life.

After three weeks holiday, the Dales' carriage and the sturdy wagon were brought to the door to be loaded up for the family's return to the city.

Sarah was walking up from the river, where she had been washing clothes with some of the other housewives, and paused for breath near the four gleaming, carriage horses. A boy was holding the head of the lead horse but the huge beasts were dozing, flies buzzing around their eyes.

Donnie and Davey could totter along beside her but little Cathy still needed to be carried and Sarah put her on the ground for a minute to rest her arms. The sun glinting on the polished brass of the horses' harnesses and the splendid coach was a sight to behold and she was admiring the lamps and glimpses of rich red velvet upholstery on the seats when Mrs Cooper came hurrying round to place a picnic basket inside.

She saw Sarah and abruptly turned her face away with an audible sniff of disapproval.

The woman's deliberate snub made Sarah take a step towards the open carriage door.

'Guid mornin', Mrs Cooper.' she said brightly. 'Ah dinnae ken why yer still sae snippy wi' me. Ah'm a merrit woman noo.'

The older woman pulled herself up to her full height, 'And have you made your peace with the Lord?'

'Aye, Ah have,' Sarah replied flatly, disliking the house keeper's tone. 'Ah hav the Church's blessin' on ma marriage an' a'.'

'And have you asked forgiveness for your sins?'

'Aye! ' Sarah cocked her head to one side, 'An' ha'e ye?'

'I have not sinned against the word of the Lord!'

'Aw, ye dinnae think sae? An' whit de ye ca' throwin' me oot the hoose an' gi'eing me yon evil looks when Ah had nae ony work? Ah thocht ye were ma friend, an' ye jist shunned me.'

Mrs Cooper's face was the picture of outrage, 'How *dare* you talk to me like that!'

'Ah'll talk in ony way Ah choose! We're baith women in this village, an' Ah'm a respectable wife an' mither. Ah earn fer ma family an' keep a guid hoose... sae mind how ye talk tae me!'

They glared at one another until the footman came out of the house with more luggage. Cooper dropped her eye contact first and turned away in a swirl of black skirts, the long ribbons from her cap floating out behind.

'If the meenister can gi'e me forgiveness...' Sarah called after her, hurt by the woman's haughty attitude, 'an' he's closer tae God than ye, then mibbee ye can see me as Ah am today... no' as Ah wis two year ago!'

The horse nearest to Sarah swung its huge head round to see her and she laid a hand on its nose. 'She's a gie silly auld bat,' she muttered to the animal. 'But Ah wish we could be friends agin.'

It took Cooper a while to settle down.

Once the Dales were gone, the stifling stillness of the empty house engulfed her and she went up to her room to pray.

She was not proud of her display of hostility towards the mill girl, especially under the watchful eyes of the three tiny children at her skirts. Sarah had been such a sweet girl, so pleasant to have in the house. She still missed her cheery laugh and wide smile. The little bits of tittle-tattle from the village which they would share used to bring a warmth and companionship into her life. Now, the endless days spent alone or chivvying the new, quiet maid, were sometimes unbearably boring.

More than boring: she was lonely.

She reached for her bible and sat on the edge of her bed reading it until the mill bell pealed out, signalling the two o'clock break for the workers. For several minutes she gazed unseeingly in front of her, lost in thought.

Then, decisively, she closed the bible and laid it on the bed-side table. God had seen fit to place Sarah back on the road to salvation and provide her with a husband and a healthy child. No doubt, the girl must have suffered for her sins. So, perhaps it was time to embrace the path the Lord prescribed and make peace with her.

Chapter Nine

"... I wish much to retire from business but I am afraid that I will not get the works easily disposed of. I would not wish to dispose of them to any person that would not follow out the plan I have laid down for preserving the health and morals of the children."

David Dale (letter to Dr Currie 1798)

Dale stepped out of his front door and struck out along Charlotte Street towards the Gallowgate. It was spitting with rain and he grimaced against the discomfort of the droplets. Despite the shower, he felt well today.

On those days when good health favoured him, he would make the most of them and throw his energy into attending to his affairs. All morning there had been paperwork for the Chamber of Commerce, mainly because of the continuing down turn in trade due to the war with France. However, new markets were now being identified and opened up. It was looking a little more hopeful for those merchants who had invested too heavily in Europe and had been in danger of collapsing due to those outlets being either closed or seriously restricted.

Dale was heading to the Tontine rooms to meet with his colleague at the Chambers, Gilbert Hamilton.

Hamilton was a good friend and being only a few years older than Dale, was one of his contemporaries. They had a long association, both having been founding members of the Chamber of Commerce for the city. Also, being like-minded in most matters, they were the founding members of the Glasgow Humane Society.

'You are looking in better fettle today than the last time we met,' Hamilton declared, slapping Dale on the back and offering him a chair.

Dale squeezed into the armchair and propped his stick at the side.

'Aye, Ah'm grand today! I don't know about you Gilbert, but my old bones are getting weary. I was just writing to my friend Dr Currie, saying how I have been feeling quite under the weather the past few months.'

'Och, ye know what they say, 'ye'll ne'er be younger than ye are today'!'

They both laughed and Hamilton poured him some coffee.

'That is very true,' Dale chuckled, 'but the day is coming when I will not have the life in me to deal with all the business that crosses my desk.'

'Ye certainly have a great many factories to your name. How are they? In this difficult time?'

'I cannot complain, but they must be constantly assessed and the managers guided. I feel I shall be disposing of them in the near future.'

Hamilton was taken aback, 'Sell out? Retire from business?'

'Aye. It may take many years so I am prepared to let my intentions be known.'

'It'll be a sad day when you are not at board meetings and in the thick of it with the other merchants. You're one of the main men in the establishment, my friend, I am sure you have many years left. Don't be too hasty.'

'Kind words, but I cannot see me doing so much in a few years time. Perhaps at the Chambers, aye, I grant you, I would miss that. But the running of the factories?' He took a drink of coffee, swallowing hard. 'No, I will be retiring from all that. My concern is to find buyers who will follow my practices where the working conditions are concerned. I feel a responsibility for the children.'

'And ye have a good few of them, I gather.'

'Aye, at New Lanark alone they number more than five hundred and these poor infants have good food and are provided for with shelter and instruction under my care. In recent years they have been sending more from Edinburgh than this city, but if they do not come to my mills they might be farmed out to unscrupulous masters. The problem I am faced with is not only selling the businesses, which are returning profits, but securing a sale where the children will not suffer.'

'We are living in a more enlightened time now. There will be masters out there who will wish to accept your methods along with the mills.'

'And pay for teachers out of their profits? Buy good meat? See to it that they are clean and clothed with all the expense that entails? I am afraid I do not share your optimism. Money, greed, it is too prevalent in this world. We must take care of those less fortunate, educate them so they may read the Lord's word and learn a skill. I am proud to say that all my Boarders will have the means of earning a living when they leave my mills and that is how it should be done. Every man should be given the tools to better himself.'

He drained his glass and Hamilton refilled it.

'So, you believe every man, even the paupers, have Rights, eh? You have sympathy with the reformers?' Hamilton asked. 'We hear little of them these days. Most of them are gagged by the new laws.'

'Pah! Their calls are merely muffled, which is far more dangerous. Like putting a pillow over a wild animal; you will not hear its roars until it has bitten its way out and then it will be twice as fierce!'

'Ye know that there has been word of Thomas Muir?'

Dale was immediately interested, 'No, what is the news?'

'He's in Cuba! Alive and well and heading to Europe. Possibly France. No doubt he will be held in high regard in Paris. There are whispers among his sympathisers, seeking separation from England, and they are secretly growing in momentum.' Hamilton leaned across the table, lowering his voice, 'And, of course, we now have the United Irishmen coming across the sea to find a safe haven in Scotland. Goodness knows what will happen with all these underground radicals!'

'Well, it is certainly a worry. What with this new General Bonaparte taking victories down through Italy and all...' Dale wiped a hand over his face. 'Well, my Lord Provost...' he said using his friend's title from '92, and scraping his chair back to straighten his legs. 'I hope there is an end to this war soon and not a victorious one for the French!'

They settled down to discuss ongoing trade matters before Dale, feeling drowsy, took his leave and walked home. His cushioned chair by the fire was beckoning.

While Dale was relaxing in his study, Anne Caroline was entertaining a friend.

Miss Spears was from Manchester and when she travelled north to visit friends and relatives she stayed at Charlotte Street. Anne Caroline was only a few years her junior and the two girls always enjoyed their times together.

'The rain has passed,' Anne Caroline cried, looking out at the sunshine sparkling off wet foliage in the garden. 'Let's go out for a walk?'

They changed their flat satin house shoes for sturdier boots, collected shawls from their rooms and donning summery bonnets, set off towards Glasgow Green. Chattering as they strolled along, they were soon among others, making the most of the break in the showery afternoon.

'My goodness!' Miss Spears suddenly exclaimed, raising her gloved arm to wave. 'There's my brother's friend! What a coincidence!'

Walking towards them, a surprised smile lighting up his face, was a slender young man with short dark hair.

'Good Afternoon, Miss Spears!' The man doffed his hat. 'I would never have thought to see you in Glasgow!'

'Nor I, you! Let me introduce my friend, Miss Anne Caroline Dale.'

'Good afternoon, Miss Dale,' he took her hand and gave a polite bow of his head. 'Robert Owen.'

'I cannot believe this! I did not know you came to Glasgow!' Miss Spears cried, gaily.

'This is my first visit. I am here on business and only just becoming familiar with the streets of Glasgow.'

'Mr Owen is a partner at the Chorlton Twist Company in Manchester.' Being accomplished as a hostess, Miss Spear's social skills immediately came to the fore and she rapidly found a mutual interest between her two friends. 'Mr Owen is in textiles and knows a great deal of the cotton industry. He has owned his own factory, have you not?'

'Yes, some years ago.' Owen nodded.

'Miss Dale's father is a mill owner, you know.'

Owen turned his dark, soulful eyes to Anne Caroline, 'Ah, yes, of course, David Dale. I believe he has several spinning ventures right across Scotland.'

'You are quite right, sir. We are newly returned from the largest and I believe, the most charming, New Lanark. It is thought to be a splendid example of cotton production and lies just below the Falls of Clyde.'

'It is a famous beauty spot, Mr Owen,' Miss Spears said excitedly. 'You should see the waterfalls! Breath-taking!'

'Many people come to New Lanark nowadays just to see the mills,' Anne Caroline told him.

'I would very much like to see the mills,' Owen's words were imbued with genuine interest and Anne Caroline was struck with the intensity of his gaze.

His features were delicate and although his nose was long in proportion to his oval face, it was not overly so and contrived to make him look quite artistic and intellectual. He would, she thought, be more suited to being a composer of great music or a writer than a cotton merchant.

'Oh please, do visit them whenever you would find convenient. Either Mr William Kelly or my uncle, Mr James Dale, would be more than happy to show you around. And please tell them that I have extended the invitation.' She smiled sweetly up at him, 'I am sure you would not find it a wasted journey.'

Owen was very grateful and thanked her profusely.

'Are you walking this way?' Miss Spears asked, indicating the Green ahead of them.

'Unfortunately, I must return to my hotel and prepare for a meeting, but it has been a grand surprise to meet you both!'

'What a nice man,' Anne Caroline said, when Owen was out of earshot. She linked her arm in her friend's, 'He has a slightly unusual accent, but I cannot place it.'

'Mr Owen is Welsh. My brother has known him many years and thinks very well of him. He is a tremendous reader, I understand, and loves to debate deep issues with his friends.'

Tilting her head on one side, Anne Caroline sighed. 'What a shame he lives in Manchester, he makes a refreshing change from the gentlemen I meet here.'

Miss Spears patted her on the arm, 'Manchester is not all that far away, my dear. If he has come here on business then he may well have need to return at some point?'

Anne Caroline chuckled, a mannerism reminiscent of her father. 'That would be pleasant, it would be very agreeable to meet Mr Owen again, and maybe not just for a fleeting moment on the street!'

After spending hours in the company of young men who tried to captivate her attention, she found the few minutes of meaningful, open exchange with Owen had made a much stronger impression. His words and the memory of his youthful, vivacious face replayed many times over the coming days.

A week or so later, after Miss Spears returned to Manchester, Anne Caroline and her sisters were upstairs preparing for their morning walk, when the doorbell sounded through the house.

'Excuse me, Miss Caroline?' Breen enquired, from the open bedroom doorway. 'There is a gentleman to see you? Are you receiving visitors?'

All five girls were immediately attentive, pausing in their various states of undress to find out who was downstairs.

'Who is it?' asked Anne Caroline, suddenly cold with the thought that it might be the haughty Mr Cambridge.

'A Mr Robert Owen.'

The pleasure of hearing his name caused a flush of pink to glow on her cheeks.

'I shall be down directly, please ask him to wait in the library.'

Her sisters hovered around her, asking questions, suggesting additions to her outfit, giggling and clamouring to be allowed to accompany her to meet the young man.

'What about our walk?' Margaret piped up, scowling.

'He may only be here for a few minutes, I will find out.'

After fussing with her hair she wondered whether to change out of her modest, pearl-grey day dress.

'No, no,' Jean told her impatiently, 'You look lovely, it is very becoming and you must not keep him waiting too long.'

Taking a last look in the mirror at the high-waisted *Directoire* style gown, Anne Caroline flicked her long hair behind her shoulders and went downstairs.

Having feared that he might not appear so attractive to her on a second meeting, she was not disappointed by Mr Owen.

The moment their eyes met she sensed the same heightening of her senses and delight at feeling the full force of his personality shining back. His slim, boyish figure was stylishly attired and in his choice of greys and dark browns for his jacket and breeches, only his cravat, a deep red paisley pattern, had any colour. It gave him a modest, serious appearance.

'I shall not detain you, Miss Dale,' he started, slightly flustered. 'I have just returned, last night, from a very pleasurable journey to the New Lanark Mills. It is certainly a considerable and highly productive enterprise. I just wished to give my thanks to you for your introduction.'

She accepted his thanks and enquired about his journey. After the first few minutes of awkwardness they found that conversation came easily between them and they sat down on the window seat. There was a delicious mix of awareness of each other as strangers to be explored and an uncanny sense of friendly familiarity.

Suddenly, Anne Caroline remembered her sisters and seeing her start and her eyes flit to the carriage clock on the mantelshelf, Owen stood up.

'I am so sorry, I called unannounced and I am sure you have other matters to attend to...'

'Oh no, not of any real consequence,' she smiled, but rose to stand beside him. 'My sisters and I always take a walk in the morning, unless the weather is particularly unkind. That is all.'

'Then, I will leave you to your walk, I would not wish to deny you and your sisters this lovely morning.'

'Might you join us?' she asked, on an impulse. 'I mean, you probably have business in the city, but if you are free for a short while...?'

He had an endearing way of raising his brows and slightly dipping his chin when he smiled at her.

'I would be honoured to accompany you all, thank you.'

They made a cheerful party, leaving the house in a rustle of petticoats, the older girls opening parasols against the brilliant sunshine and the younger ones running ahead, laughing and calling to one another. Giggs followed a few paces behind.

Mr Owen walked between Anne Caroline and Jean, engaging them both in conversation but his eyes lingered on Anne Caroline when she spoke. Often she would glance towards him to find him watching her.

Glasgow Green was bustling with people. Little dogs ran amongst the children and there were groups of boys playing hand ball or crouched on the hard pathways playing marbles.

'I gather from Miss Spears that you are originally from Wales,' said Anne Caroline.

'I grew up in Newtown, a wonderful little place. I knew everyone and they knew me, it was a happy time.'

'Why did you leave?'

'I had learned all I could learn at the school by the time I was eight or nine years of age and was an inquisitive child so I went to London. It was a great adventure because I journeyed alone, but my brother lives there so I stayed with him until a position was found for me.'

'An apprenticeship? In what line, Mr Owen?' She was not aware that she was asking a lot of questions and Owen appeared completely at ease answering.

'I spent a year in a drapery store while I was at home in Wales and it was in a draper's, with a good and honourable Scotch family, the McGuffogs, that I found employment.'

'That must have been a very big change for you, having only known life in a rural town in Wales and then suddenly living in London!'

'The McGuffogs were in Stamford in Lincolnshire and I was lucky to have such a fine teacher in business matters.'

They walked and talked, until Jean, realising that she was intruding, subtly moved ahead to be with Margaret and Mary. When a large circuit was completed and Julia was complaining of being thirsty, Mr Owen wished them all a pleasant walk back to Charlotte Street and bid them farewell.

'Well!' cried Jean. 'You two never stopped talking! My goodness, dear Anne Caroline, you were like the Inquisition itself! Poor man!'

'Oh, I wasn't! was I?' she was mortified, until, remembering Owen's delightful laugh and the sparkle in his eyes as he took her hand to say goodbye, she knew he had not objected to her interest.

Later that day, she sat down to write to Miss Spears. As well as hoping that she passed a smooth and uneventful journey home to Manchester, she told her of the second meeting with their mutual friend, Mr Owen, and described their most pleasurable walk on Glasgow Green.

'He really is a very charming man,' she wrote, adding, 'I hope he feels able to call at Charlotte Street again when he is next on business in Scotland.'

Owen had not mentioned when he would be returning and Anne Caroline was consumed with a terrible restlessness at not knowing if she would ever see him again.

***

On a wet, gloomy day in September, Joe put down his tools and turned away from the work bench. It was dark inside the wooden shed despite two lamps with their wicks turned up high and the space was loud with the incessant pattering of raindrops on the roof.

He was now a fully qualified stonemason. This meant he could charge more for his work and had the confidence in his skills to accomplish the important jobs which Ewing was passing on to him.

Ewing lived on a small holding on the edge of Lanark consisting of a two storey, slate roofed house surrounded by a collection of low barns. There was an enclosed area of land at the back where he kept a cow, a highland pony to pull his cart and a crowd of noisy ducks and hens. For any fine carving Joe would walk up the hill and avail himself of the small, sheltered barn which was fitted out as a workshop.

He owned quite a few tools himself and was saving up for more but they were expensive. At present it was easier to use some of Ewing's and then give him a cut of the finished price in return.

He was just pouring himself a beaker of water when the latch lifted on the door and Melanie, Ewing's daughter came in with a basket of apples. Melanie was a shy little girl who had formed a loyal attachment to Joe since their earliest acquaintance.

When Joe was first apprenticed to Ewing, he rarely went up to the workshop. However, he slowly struck up a friendship with his master and over the last few years he was treated more like one of the family than an employee.

Ewing's wife died shortly after Melanie was born and it was his spinster sister who ran his house and took charge of Melanie. Miss Emily Ewing was a quiet woman, older than her brother by several years and undemonstrative of any affection towards her young niece. Her attention was directed almost exclusively to baking, reaping high praise from local hostelries and shops which she supplied on a daily basis.

Ever since Joe had known them, Melanie would help her aunt with the baking, even when she was so small that she needed to stand on a stool to reach the table. As well as teaching her to bake, her aunt took it upon herself to impose a strict program of lessons, so before the child was eight years old she could read and write as well as her father.

Being without brothers or sisters, Melanie was starved of company and on his first few visits Joe made a fuss of her, joking and swinging her around so fast her feet would leave the ground. It was a favourite game with Sarah and Rosie when they were young. She was the same age as Meg would have been had she lived, a poignant reminder to him of what could have been.

At every opportunity, Melanie would come to the barn, offering him food or suggesting she might brush up the dust for him: anything that gave her the chance to pass a few words with her new friend. She was never a nuisance and Ewing took to calling her 'Joe's wee shadow'.

It was thought of as a bit of a joke, so when she appeared with the apples, Joe laughed and said, 'What d'ye ha'e fer me the day, Mel?'

'Apples.'

'Away! those are no' apples! they're plums!' he said, picking one out of the basket and sinking his teeth into its crisp, white flesh. 'Aye! Ah were richt, plums!'

'Aw... yer a funny yin...' she put down the basket and hauled herself up into her usual position, sitting on the end of the high work bench with her feet dangling below her long skirts. She was a podgy little girl with a round plain face. Her large cheeks were accentuated by the way her aunt insisted her hair was severely scraped back into two long, thin plaits and wound tightly into a bun: well out of the way of the mixing bowl.

Joe finished his apple, took a last swig of water and then bowed to his chiselling again.

Mel would rarely say a word, only offering to fetch a tool or turn up the lamp if she saw it was required. Sometimes she would bring a book or pamphlet with her and read to him, but more often than not, they enjoyed a companionable silence.

Simply being in the same space as Joe and being able to watch him work seemed to be enough for her and he accepted her presence as others might let a pet dog lie at their feet.

As he worked, his mind was on Fiona.

Only a few days earlier she had told him that she was expecting their third child. He was delighted, of course, but there was always a cloud of fear attached to a new baby arriving; the uncertainty of the dangers of the actual birth, would the infant be healthy and also the future responsibility of yet another mouth to feed.

There was already to be a change to their circumstances; Rosie was betrothed to be married and would be leaving home before the New Year. Her intended, Gerard MacAllister, was a skinny, baby-faced young man who worked in one of the offices under Mill Four. Fiona confided to Joe that she thought the poor boy had been given little choice about the engagement, although he seemed content enough with the arrangement.

Several of her friends were already housewives and Rosie was eager to move on to this stage in her life. So when MacAllister's mother suddenly died, she wasted no time in moving their occasional 'walking out' relationship to one of official betrothal.

It was an ideal opportunity to take over the household and with only his two younger sisters still living at home, she was looking forward to more space in the MacAllister's larger, airier room in Double Row.

Among the pools of gold lamp light, Joe worked on his intricate stone carving, mentally calculating how much money he would need to earn in the coming months, without either Fiona or Rosie bringing anything into the house. It was frustrating, just as he achieved a better status in his trade and was hoping to start seriously saving up for a place of their own, now they would be back to a hand to mouth existence.

Cal would be the only Scott still on Dale's payroll, although with on-going construction work, Joe supposed that he would be considered to be a New Lanark worker for a good while into the future.

Cal's job was erratic. The past two winters had seen him struck down with many bouts of illness, causing him pains in his chest and shoulders and wheezing so badly he was unable to draw breath. The Macinnes' only paid him for the days he attended to his tasks, so the approaching cold months might again bring spells of no wages from that quarter.

The dream of giving Fiona a proper home of her own was drifting out of sight again, somewhere beyond the horizon of the foreseeable future. As always, Joe would just have to knuckle down and work hard if he was to provide for his growing family.

He blew away the chiselled stone dust and Melanie sneezed loudly at his side.

'Aw, sorry, lass!' he cried.

She smiled happily back at him, rubbing at her nose and wrinkling it up.

He returned the smile with a friendly wink and set back to work, wondering if his next child would be a girl.

It would be nice to have a daughter, like Ewing's little Melanie.

***

When Mrs Carolina Dale was alive, she insisted that all the rugs in the house were taken outside twice a year and beaten thoroughly to clear all dust and dirt. This usually occurred in the first fine days of spring and then again at the end of September or early October, when it was thought the winter was approaching.

Breen made sure that these instructions were continued after her mistress's demise despite the great upheaval within the house being disliked by everyone.

Dale would conduct any business affairs away from Charlotte Street over those days and his daughters took walks and called on friends. Although their bedrooms were hardly affected, the small rugs by the firesides being easily enough removed, the footmen and maids filled the corridors moving the larger carpets.

The one which created most disruption was of a fine silk and wool mixture which ran the length of the dining room, beneath the grand table. It was immensely heavy and cumbersome, even when rolled up, and took six men, with added assistance from Renwick and the maids, to manhandle it outside.

It was during this operation that Mr Owen rang the front doorbell.

Hurriedly adjusting his jacket and smoothing his hair into place, Renwick answered the door.

When Anne Caroline was advised of her caller, she ran downstairs and met him in the library.

'Mr Owen,' she greeted him, closing the library door behind her to block out the sounds of the servants manhandling furniture. 'What a very pleasant surprise.'

Owen was admiring the book lined walls and swung round as she entered.

'Good morning, Miss Dale. I appear to have arrived at an inconvenient time. My sincere apologies.'

'It is of no matter,' she waved a hand at the bare floor boards in front of the ornate fireplace. 'As you can see, they have already emptied this room of rugs.'

'I have a letter here from Miss Spears. She heard that I was travelling to Glasgow and begged me the favour of delivering it to you.' He held out an envelope.

'Thank you, Mr Owen, that is very kind. I hope it did not cause you to come out of your way.'

'Not at all.' He was looking at her in his strange, intense way. 'Your father owns a most superb library. There are all manner of books here, such a rich collection.'

'You enjoy reading, sir?'

'It is my favourite pastime. Every day, I would honestly say that I read for more than four hours. I have done so since I first learnt to read.'

'Oh, it is my greatest pleasure, as well. And while I cannot own to spending so much time in its pursuit, it must be said that when we visit the country I can take a chest full of books and yet it is never enough!'

They moved to the window seat, where they had sat together on his first visit, and continued an animated conversation. They exchanged views on many shared, favourite titles, from Robinson Crusoe to Paradise Lost and discussed works by philosophers and travellers.

His eyes gleamed with interest and she found she could hardly resist staring at him when he spoke. There was a calm energy to the young man, as if he was devouring the experience and, from his questions and responses, there was a sharp intelligence behind his sanguine exterior.

There was a sound at the door and Mary entered.

'Forgive my intrusion,' she smiled at them. 'We are leaving for our walk now, Jean asked me to inform you...'

Owen had jumped to his feet when Mary came in and now Anne Caroline also stood up.

'Do please join us?' she asked him, remembering their last, very pleasant, stroll together. 'The house is in such an uproar that my sisters will be keen to be outside.'

Owen agreed readily and once again escorted the Dale girls on a promenade around Glasgow Green. His knowledge of the trees and shrubs, plants and birds was a constant amazement to them all, especially Anne Caroline.

'I have a great love of Nature,' he told her when she enquired as to how he knew so much. 'In Newtown I rambled all over the countryside as a small boy. My uncle farmed nearby and my cousin, Richard, and I spent many hours together exploring among the hedgerows and woods. I was fortunate in Stamford to have a park, Burleigh Park, just close by and would take my books there in fine weather.'

'That was when you were employed in the Drapers?'

'Yes, at the McGuffogs. The days, of course, were spent in the store but in the summer I took enormous pleasure from rising at four in the morning and reading or walking until eight o'clock when the doors opened.'

Anne Caroline was enchanted but refrained from repeating her 'inquisition', as Jean had called it, on this outing.

Over the next few weeks, while Owen was in Scotland, he met them by the Green on several occasions and would join them for a while. All the girls were pleased to see him but for Dale's eldest daughter, when she saw his distinctive figure walking towards them, arm raised in greeting, these became memorable and eagerly anticipated mornings.

On their last walk together before he left for Manchester, Anne Caroline gave him a letter for Miss Spears.

'I do hope this finds her in good health.' she said, quietly. 'She is a dear friend and I wish we lived closer.'

Owen took the envelope and tucked it into his inside pocket.

It was a cool day, the first frosts nipping at the autumn leaves and a sharp breeze whisking them off the branches and swirling them into piles against the garden walls. The time had come to say goodbye and Anne Caroline was reticent to be the first to end their morning interlude. Owen, too, was quieter than on previous meetings and when she raised her eyes to his, she saw an earnest, slightly pained expression.

She dropped her gaze, but unable to stop herself, looked directly back into his eyes again. This time the look lingered until they both made the effort to break contact.

'Well, I wish you...' she said, at exactly the moment he said, 'With regret, I must be leaving...'

They laughed, aware that their feelings were reciprocated. It made for a hurried, nervously spoken farewell, but a wonderful feeling of elation for both parties.

***

In early December, Rosie Scott became Mrs Gerard MacAllister.

With much partying and music in the Row, the villagers lit braziers to cheer the freezing, dark evening. Then, dressed in their best clothes they took advantage of the chance to drink and carouse until early into the small hours of the next morning.

So by that evening, after a full day's work on little sleep, the Scotts sat at the table, tired and feeling the anti-climax of the excitement.

Fiona ladled mutton and barley into bowls and handed them to Joe and Cal.

'It seems gie strange wi'oot oor Rosie,' she remarked, prodding the fire into more heat before taking her seat for dinner.

'Well, there's still the five o' us here,' Joe said, 'an' it'll no be lang afore there's six.'

'We've got used tae Sarah livin' oot,' Calum muttered through his broth. 'An' its a mighty mair peacefu' place wi'oot that wean o hers.'

'Och, wee Cathy wis nae ony trouble.' Fiona put in kindly. 'Ah pray her next wean is as guid. It'll no' be lang comin' noo. Ah hope tha' Sean pays her a bit mair care, she's gie doon aboot him, an' Ah have nae seen the man in weeks.'

She was concerned about Sarah, who was heavily pregnant and barely stayed an hour at Rosie's celebrations, before trudging away up the hill. Sean was notable by his absence from the family gathering.

Cal carried on spooning in his food.

'Ah wonder how Rosie's gettin' on,' Joe said thoughtfully. 'She's al'is had ye an' her sister tae help her wi' things.'

'Rosie will manage jist grand,' Fiona patted her husband's arm. 'Ah've ne'er known onybody sae guid at dealin' wi' things, she jist gets doon tae it, sorts things oot.'

'Aye, Ah ken.' Joe still looked dejected.

'Its a change fer us a', no' jist Rosie an' Sarah gaun awa' wi' their men.' She was going to add that Calum would be the next to go but refrained from saying more.

Calum was nearly twenty years old but he never showed interest in any of the girls in the village and his downcast eyes and reclusive nature did not encourage friends.

Many of the young men in New Lanark were being called up to the war but the Scotts prayed Calum would be spared. He was not only small in stature for his age, but his body was thin and growing more bent with every passing year. It hurt Fiona to remember him as the fresh faced boy who had set off in search of farm work, only days after she married Joe and moved to the tenements.

The lad at the table was a ghost of his former self, with black shadows beneath his eyes and hollow cheeks. Sometimes, when he did not know he was being observed, she noticed a heart-rendingly desolate expression on his face which gave her a physical stab of sadness.

Now that Rosie was away and Sarah was occupied with her dress-making while watching the children, chores in the Scotts' room were falling to Fiona. Joe and Cal were helpful with the heavy tasks but keeping on top of it all, with her job as well, was going to be a struggle.

Seeing the worn out faces of some of the other village women trailing small children, she determined not to become the same. They sloped along in ill fitting clogs, their greasy hair caught up into caps, trudging between emptying the closet, collecting coal, filling water buckets and all the other daily jobs, with a down trodden look of abandonment.

Excepting her sons, Joe was the most important person in her life and she loved him more with every waking moment. They still shared a deep desire for one another which had not been reduced by the mundane grind of family life. Their first exciting passion had grown naturally into a deep mutual love.

She made a conscious effort to style her hair and dress prettily, not because he demanded it or for any concerns that she might lose his interest, but for her own sake. His smouldering look of appreciation was her reward. It still gave her such a thrilling sensation that no matter how tired she was, it was this special relationship that made her simple life so happy.

Up in Glasgow, surrounded by all the luxuries money could buy, Anne Caroline and Rosemary did not feel the same contentment.

'Mr Wilson has not visited for over a week now,' Rosemary complained. 'And our last conversation was a stilted, difficult affair. Oh, I fear he is tiring of me.'

'Or are you tiring of him?' Anne Caroline suggested, remembering her friend's list of criticisms regarding the gentleman following a dinner they all attended.

Rosemary fiddled with the lace cuffs of her dress, 'I am sure I would not be if he would just... well, if he would just stop *prevaricating* and propose marriage. He will go on so about his estate in the highlands and the collection of porcelain his mother procures, or other meaningless subjects, rather than his feelings towards me.'

Anne Caroline tried to be understanding and soothed Rosemary as much as possible, telling her to be patient. Patience was a virtue she was endeavouring to cultivate in herself.

Mr Owen was constantly in her thoughts. The winter's social calendar and the usually eagerly anticipated Hogmanay celebrations held little attraction if he was not going to be among the guests. She dressed for each occasion with a bittersweet longing that one day she would be preparing for their next meeting.

The inner wheels of Dale's household turned methodically, with Anne Caroline assisting her father to entertain or accompanying him to formal dinners in the city.

While Breen would meet with Anne Caroline to discuss the finer points of menus or requirements for overnight guests, she, Renwick and Cook took charge of downstairs responsibilities.

Renwick and Duncan attended to their master's affairs with their usual efficiency and having worked together for so long, it made for a comfortable working atmosphere.

It was a smooth running, peaceful house, often filled with the laughter and singing of the younger girls and the sound of Jean and Anne Caroline's melodious practice on the piano. Mary, Margaret and Julia were not yet so accomplished and the servants gritted their teeth as they polished and laid fires to a background of bickering and repeated, discordant phrases of jarring notes.

Throughout the days of frost and snow, long candlelit evenings were passed gathered around the drawing room fire. Sometimes the furniture was cleared away to allow space for the younger girls to practice dances. Or with one of them playing the piano, hymns and ballads were sung, with their father often leading the singing.

Anne Caroline's state of pining for Mr Owen was relieved by an infrequent but heart-felt exchange of letters with Miss Spears. In her letters she confided to her friend how deeply she felt for the young gentleman and how much she missed his company.

For her part, Miss Spears assured Anne Caroline that whenever the opportunity arose, she was extolling her virtues and encouraging Mr Owen to take the relationship further.

However, by early spring, Mr Owen seemed unforthcoming about his feelings towards Anne Caroline.

'Mr Owen may be bold and confident in all matters to do with trade and industry,' Miss Spears wrote, 'but I fear he is struck by the great wealth and high standing of your dear father and does not feel he should aspire to hopes of a future with the daughter of such a man.'

Noting the tone of frustration in the letter, Anne Caroline felt that gentle enquiries and hints regarding her feelings were not having the desired result. She implored her friend to make it clear to Mr Owen that she, personally, would be delighted to share the future with him.

There was, however, a serious barrier to the young lovers hoped for union.

Dale had passed few comments regarding Owen after hearing he toured New Lanark the previous year. Despite not having met the young man, he was not in favour of his daughter's involvement with him.

'I am sure Mr Owen is a pleasant enough fellow,' he told her when she raised his name one morning at breakfast. 'But I understand from others that he does not attend church and is not given to religious belief. I find that a difficult aspect of his character, Anne Caroline. You know my Christian views and more importantly, I know that you share them as deeply as I. How could you be content in a relationship with such a gulf of understanding and belief between you?'

When she remained silent, he continued.

'The journey through life is hard enough even with the Lord's guidance, but if you were sharing it with someone who shuns the word of the Holy Bible, takes no heed of His teachings, how could that be endured?' He could see her skin grow pale and the little changes to the set of her lips and the lines around her eyes told of her disappointment.

'You have asked me for my opinion, my dear,' he said gently, 'and in my love for you, I must be honest in my reply. It would appear that Mr Owen, who is also a land louper, not a native of this country, is not an admirer I can welcome.'

Her eyes implored him. 'If you met him, Papa, and talked with him more fully you would think differently, I am sure...'

'Mr Owen lives in Manchester, does he not?'

'He does, at present, but is a partner in the Chorlton Twist Company which occasions him to come to Glasgow frequently....'

'There are fine God fearing Scotsmen on your doorstep, Anne Caroline, and you are a lovely young lass. Do not settle for the first gentleman who pays you attention. I am sure you will soon meet someone far more suitable.'

With that, he put a hand on the dining table to push himself upright. 'Whoever marries you will be a very fortunate man. Be in no haste, my dear.'

A terrible frustration and misery came over Anne Caroline and she wished she could relieve its effect by crying but the problem was too serious to be easily solved with a few tears.

She could not dismiss this wonderful man yet nor could she bear to override her father's wishes. Something had to be done and she spoke at length to Rosemary of her concerns.

'I am absolutely convinced that if Papa could just talk to him, he would change his views. They have so much in common in their backgrounds which surely would strike a chord? And in their shared business knowledge? Mr Owen is a genuine believer in my father's passion for the need for better conditions in the factories and was hugely impressed by what he saw at New Lanark.'

'And what of the Church issue?' Rosemary asked, perceptively.

'I will raise the subject with Mr Owen at the earliest opportunity, for it is a subject dear to my own heart as well.'

Then, in April, Owen wrote to advise her of his forthcoming journey to Glasgow and a request to allow him to call upon her at Charlotte Street.

The day of his visit fell during the week her father was travelling on the west coast, visiting and preaching to the Old Scotch Independents congregations. She was disappointed that the two men would not have the opportunity to meet, but also thought it was opportune that she would have a chance to discuss Owen's religious views more fully before taking their relationship any further.

On the day of Owen's arrival, Anne Caroline was overcome with nervous anticipation and prepared for his visit with shaking fingers. However, when he was shown into the drawing room by Renwick and the initial pleasantries were exchanged, all her anxieties melted away.

There was something so intangibly pleasant about Mr Owen, that even before they were settling back in their chairs, the intervening months of separation seemed like no time at all and they were engaging in easy conversation.

'Lest I forget,' he produced an envelope, 'Miss Spears has made use of my services and denied the Postmaster General his revenue once again!'

Anne Caroline laughed and took the letter as he continued.

'I feel no guilt, although perhaps I should, for while my father is in business as an ironmonger and saddler, he is also the Postmaster at Newtown. I fear he might frown on my being called upon as an unlicensed postman!'

Then his voice changed to a more serious tone.

'Miss Dale, I cannot tell you how much I have looked forward to being with you again. I hold you in the highest regard and, as I am sure you realise, have deeply affectionate feelings for you.' He leaned towards her, 'I have spoken on many occasions with Miss Spears and she has advised me that you... well, that you have those same feelings for me. If this is incorrect, please tell me now and I will say no more.'

'Oh, yes, Mr Owen,' Anne Caroline assured him, 'You understand correctly. I too have longed to see you again.'

'Oh Miss Dale, I would dearly love for us never to be parted again. Would you do me the honour of being my wife?'

Her heart racing, Anne Caroline gave him a wide smile, her eyes showing her acceptance.

'I would gladly be your wife,' she said with feeling, 'but, I could never marry anyone without my father's consent. If you can find the means to overcome my father's objections it would go far to remove any I may now have to the request you have made.'

'Please, inform me of his objections, so I might address them right away.'

'My father is of the understanding that you are not a church goer. Which Church do you attend, Mr Owen?'

'I do not care for organised religious services, Miss Dale. So, I cannot pretend to be a member of any congregation, either here or in Manchester.'

She was aghast, 'Do you not believe in God? Or the teachings of the Holy Bible?'

'I neither believe nor disbelieve, however, I was a devout Christian in my childhood and hold firm to the belief in doing good to one's fellow man. I have studied the religions of the world and find that they all proclaim to have the true meaning of life and each, fanatically, denies that the others could be worthy.

'I find it unacceptable that, in such a nebulous and spiritual matter, each demand complete faith, without question or tolerance towards differing views.'

'I am a practising Christian, sir. Do you find that offensive?'

He was shocked, 'Oh Gracious no! I would not presume to judge you for your beliefs or hold them against you, if they are sincerely held.'

Anne Caroline was immensely satisfied by his answer and smiled up at him, urging understanding.

'I have been raised to hold the Lord's words in respect and to abide by the Holy Scriptures. It is an especially important and comforting element in my life,' she was trying to convey more to him and from the intense way he was holding her gaze, she knew he took her meaning. 'I would never wish to be reprimanded for my religion, or restricted in my worship.'

'My dear Miss Dale, I can assure you that I would not take any part in such suppression of an individual's liberty. Just as I would respectfully ask to be allowed to follow my own course, and continue to abstain from religious meetings.'

'While I would wish that you might embrace the word of God, I would not presume to preach or lecture to you on the subject.'

Anne Caroline found that she was trembling.

Their short, honest exchange spoke of more than religious tolerance. They were stating to one another how much they respected each other's views and in so doing, laying bare the fact that their feelings were sufficiently deep that even differences in faith could be freely admitted without repercussions.

Now, all they had to do was persuade David Dale of Owen's worthiness for his daughter's hand in marriage.

Chapter Ten

*'Riches are one great object... And if these are obtained by
oppressing the poor, or withholding from the needy what his
wants demand of us, the consequence is awful...your riches are
corrupted.'*
David Dale 'Substance of a Discourse'

Pacing the floorboards of her room in Braxfield Row, Sarah kept
pausing by the window to look up and down the street for any sign of
Sean returning home.

Four months earlier, in January, she gave birth to a healthy little
boy. The infant, who they named Stephen, was noisy and fretful.
Cathy had become quite jealous of his presence, clinging to her
mother and crying at the slightest provocation. Her children's
constant demands were draining Sarah of both the energy and will to
continue with her dressmaking and Sean's behaviour did not help
either.

The New Buildings were complete and the only work he could find
was at Stonebyres estate, several miles down the Clyde Valley. For
most of the week he was choosing to sleep there in a bothy with some
of the other workers, returning briefly to see his family when he
brought back his wages.

He told her it was because he was too tired after work to make the
trek home, but she was sure it was due to the chaos of the baby's
screaming and her own unkempt house-keeping.

Wrapped in a lethargy of depression, she missed the last two wagon
loads of heather and straw for re-stuffing the mattresses. Now, the
bed was uncomfortable and lumpy and there were moths and mites in
the dirty blankets. The angrier Sean became with her for her
slovenliness, the worse she felt. This lead to long spells when she

would sit in a daze, nursing Stephen and letting Cathy run around the room unattended.

The place was a shambles, scattered with pans, clothes pegs, cutlery or anything else the inquisitive little girl's fingers could find of interest. Adding to the untidiness was a layer of dust and cobwebs.

During the hours when Fiona worked in the schoolroom, Sarah would try and gather herself together enough to take her children down to the Row and watch over Donnie and Davey. Knowing her own room was in a terrible state of disarray she made sure her sister in-law, and also Rosie, never visited.

It was becoming increasingly difficult to keep them away but her confused state of mind preferred to leave the mess and struggle on trying to hide it from her family, rather than tackle the problem.

In an effort to relieve the gnawing anxiety inside her, she had taken to pacing around the room, Stephen at her breast, her cheeks wet with tears.

Suddenly there was a loud knock on the door and Bessie burst into the room.

'Sarah, ye'll ha'e tae come... Fiona's babbie's on the way an' yer needed...' She stopped, staring at the filth and disorder all around. 'In the name o' God, whit's gaun on here?'

'Och Bessie...' Sarah started to sob and the sobs grew to a wail until she could no longer stand and sank on to a chair.

'Lass... Och now... calm yersel'...'

The old woman looked from the piles of dirty linen to the stained, dried pots beside the ash-filled fireplace. Everything was covered in grime, even little Cathy was smeared with food, her once white tunic, grey and soiled.

'Yer no' weel. Ah telt yer sister t'other day, Ah sed, yon Sarah's no' bin like hersel' since the wean. Ye should ha'e sed summat, lass.'

Bessie took stock of the situation and decided that now was not the time to start to tidy up.

'Ye ha'e yer ane problems,' she said quickly. 'Ah'll chap at Rosie's door tae gie me a haun wi' Fiona. As soon as she disnae need me, Ah'll be back up an' we'll see tae this.' She turned to leave but asked. 'Where's yer man?'

'Workin' awa' at Stonebyres. He can only mak it back when he brings his wages o'er.'

Bessie's eyes narrowed. 'How lang's tha' bin gaun on fer?'

'Two, three months past, since he stopped at New Buildin's.'

Bessie opened her mouth to say something but snapped it shut again. She left Sarah and hurried down the steep road in the gathering dusk.

She had heard that Sean Rafferty was no longer on the building teams in the village because her middle son used to work beside him, but she also knew he was at the tavern in Lanark almost every evening.

Just a few hours later, Fiona was delivered of another baby boy. After making sure that she was comfortable, Bessie left her with Joe and went across the landing to her own room.

It was late but her eldest son was still awake, lounging by the fire, a tankard of ale in one hand, his pipe in the other. There were only three sons at the mills now, her two younger lads having left the village, one to the war and the other as an apprentice weaver in nearby Nemphlar.

Keeping her voice low so as not to disturb the rest of the family, Bessie asked him if he knew anything of Sean Rafferty, young Sarah's man.

'Ah would nae ask, Ma.' he whispered. 'he's wi' a crowd o' Irishmen.'

'He's workin' at Stonebyres, eh?'

'Naw, he's no' in work at a'. Always aff up tae Paisley or o'er tae Cambuslang. Ah dinnae ken whit fer, but one o' yon men he's thick wi' is anither stirrer. Tis best no' tae ask, Ma. Leave it be.'

'Whit d'ye mean a 'stirrer?'

'Agin the king... agin the English, ye ken? They're a shady bunch.'

Bessie knew little of politics and was virtually unaware of anything that happened outside David Dale's village, so she just tutted under her breath.

'Weel, he's bringing doon the rent tae his wife, sae he must be workin' someplace.'

'Aye, at the cards, that's where he's makin' his money. There was a scuffle t'other eve, wi' that Kyle Macinnes, Big Lachy's son? He reckoned Sean was cheatin' but could nae prove it.'

'Och, the poor wee lass,' Bessie murmured, thinking of Sarah's distraught face. 'That man's been naught but trouble since she took up wi' 'im.' She swung the kettle over the glowing coals. 'That's Fiona wi' anither bonny wee bairn. Ah'm that tired, Ah feel Ah've gi'en birth tae him mesel'!'

While the water boiled for tea, she poured herself a dram of whisky.

'Here's tae the Scotts!' she whispered to her son, who raised the remnants of his tankard in a toast. 'There's rarely a day when a' that family are content. Ah'll see tae Sarah the morra... Weel, Ah'll gie her a haun tae clean the place, but the Lord alane kens whit can be done tae help the poor lassie.'

Despite burning to tell Sarah of her son's revelations about Sean, Bessie held her tongue. She offered her all the practical aid she could manage, given her own commitments, but was shocked to realise just how desperately sad the situation was between Sarah and her husband.

It was only a few days later, by way of a chance meeting, that matters came to a head.

Joe was on his way up to Lanark when he reached the bottom of the steep steps to find Kyle Macinnes only a yard or so ahead.

As there was no-one else around and a good fifteen minute walk ahead of them, they could not ignore each other's presence.

Kyle spoke first, 'Guid day tae ye, Joe Scott.'

Joe returned the pleasantry and they started to climb the hill together.

'Ah hear ye ha'e a new bairn.' Kyle said, politely. He had taken to wearing his hair in the new short style, cut back from his face, which showed his fine features to full advantage.

'Aye, a boy.' Joe plodded on, step by step. 'How d'ye ken tha'?'

'Yer brither, Cal, doon a' the forge.' There was a strangeness to the way he said the Scots words and Joe recognised the Highland inflection from Fiona's accent.

It gave Joe the familiar pang of anxiety: Kyle was still, in Joe's eyes, a threat to his marriage. He nodded to himself, of course, a lot of the Macinnes family worked at the blacksmith's workshop.

'Yer brither's a hard worker,' Kyle continued, 'he has a way wi' the beasts an' never complains at his job, even when he's gie troubled wi' his chest.'

'Cal's a guid lad.' Joe agreed.

'No' like yer brither in law! Tha' Rafferty has it comin' tae him.'

Joe bristled. Although he did not care for Sarah's choice of husband, he did not take kindly to Kyle's insulting tone of voice.

'Whit ye mean by tha'?' he asked, sharply.

'He's a cheat! Ah caught him mesel'! he took near on twa pounds aff me afore Ah saw his game. He's sae quick wi' his fingers, sleight o' haun they ca' it. He's practised at it an' damn near fooled me!'

'Tha's a serious thing tae accuse a man o' dae'in!'

They had reached the brow of the first hill, where the steps gave out onto the road high above the village.

'An' it's a serious crime tha' he's done agin me!'

The two men stood facing each other, hands on hips, breathing heavily from the steep ascent.

'Ma grievance is no' wi' ye, Joe.' Kyle said, pleasantly. 'Ah have nae a fight tae pick wi' ye.'

Six eventful years had passed since their public brawl over Fiona. Throughout those years they had spoken, briefly, on a handful of occasions, civilly, but warily.

Joe started to walk on and Kyle fell into step beside him.

After a while, Kyle broke the silence. 'When ye next see Rafferty, ye should mibbee warn 'im tha' Jamie Bryson is efter 'im. He took Jamie fer a gie lot mair than me, an' he's swearin' tae kill him.'

Joe knew of Bryson, he enjoyed a feared reputation as a gambler and loan shark. Many still connected him to the unsolved murder of a local man who tried to renege on repaying a debt and was found with his throat cut in the neighbouring Mouse River gorge.

'He's workin' awa', Ah hav' nae seen him fer weeks, months.'

'Naw! He's in yon tavern a' the time, mon! It were only last nicht Ah saw him.' Kyle said vehemently.

'Last nicht?'

'Aye, an' he'll be at the tables agin the nicht, fer he telt ma cousin he would meet 'im there.'

They said little more on the subject and parted at the head of the Wellgate, merely nodding to one another and turning different ways.

Rafferty played on Joe's mind all day. By the evening, he was so unsettled that he told Fiona about his conversation with the Highlander.

'Ye spoke wi' Macinnes?' she cried, with an expression of amusement. 'Ah'm tha' glad! Tis time the two o' ye buried the past.'

However, when he related Sean's gambling habits and explained what dangerous company he was keeping, she became alarmed.

'Tha' cannae be richt? Sarah says he's doon the valley an' is hardly ever hame?'

'Ah'm gaun tae tak a walk up an' see fer mesel'' Joe told her, then seeing the panic growing in her eyes, he added hastily, 'Dinnae fear, ma darlin', Ah'm no' gonnae dae onythin', jist see if he's in the toon.'

'An' mind ye come back safe, noo.' She looked fondly down at their tiny new son. 'Yer a faither tae three, an' wee Robbie has nae even met ye proper yit.'

There was only one tavern in Lanark where serious gambling took place, so Joe made his way there and seeing a couple of the lads from the village, joined them in a drink.

It was a small establishment, with trestles down the middle and set-in booths on either side, cramped, smoky and filled with the din of rowdy men's voices. The card games took place in rooms at the back and it wasn't long before Sean came in from the street and headed towards the back of the inn.

Joe was outraged at the sight of him.

Sean was dressed in a new smart jacket, a garish cravat at his throat and shining leather boots, but it wasn't the expensive outfit that disturbed Joe, it was the two blousy women who trailed beside him, hanging on his arms and fawning over him. All three of them were the worse for drink and heedless of the exhibition they were making of themselves.

It was enough to have seen his brother-in-law in Lanark, when he was supposed to be elsewhere, but for him to be flaunting these loud, coarse women of the street was more than Joe had expected.

Sean handed the girls some money and disappeared through to the back rooms. Squealing with giggles, the younger of the two women, a hard faced girl with a darkly rouged mouth, tossed back her mane of hair and ordered ale from the inn-keeper.

Some men called out to her and invited her over to join them, which she did, pulling her friend with her and climbing provocatively onto the men's knees.

Joe had seen enough. Abruptly, he set down his glass and, saying curt farewells to his friends, made for the street. It was a mild, light evening and he stood by a group of tethered horses, collecting his thoughts. How could he tell Sarah what he had just seen? He had warned her that Sean was a bad lot, but had not realised the depth of the man's cruelty to his sister.

Why did he keep her in such poverty, alone for days on end with two tiny children when he could afford to spend money on clothes and prostitutes? Initially, Joe's misgivings about Sean were caused by the rumours of his involvement with insurgents, but now he knew there was far more to it.

A great crash came from behind him.

The door of the inn flew open and figures came tumbling and staggering out. Punches were being thrown and one of the men fell to the ground with the others kicking at him as he rolled from side to side, covering his head with his hands.

Joe knew immediately that it was Sean.

Instinctively, he moved forward to stop the onslaught and was drawn into the thick of the blows. Being taller than most of his assailants and with the power of a man used to handling great weights, he was holding his own until a blade was drawn.

He saw its metallic flash a moment before it arced through the air towards his chest. Dodging it, he blocked the blow and kicked out at the man in front of him, sending him flying back between the agitated horses.

As he pushed back into the fray, he was suddenly gripped by the shoulders and dragged backwards into a vennel.

'Leave him! The officers are on their way, they'll arrest everybody!' Kyle's voice hissed in his ear.

'They'll kill him!' Joe bellowed, yanking himself free.

Kyle grabbed him again, twisting his arm into a lock behind his back.

'Think, mon! It's no' yer fight! He'll ha'e tae tak whit's due tae him. Those are Bryson's men, they know whit they're aboot. If they were oot tae kill 'im they'd ha'e done it far awa' frae prying eyes.'

The sound of clattering hooves on cobbles rang out down the street and within seconds soldiers were storming towards the inn.

Joe stared in horror as Sean and his attackers were swamped by the uniformed Guard. He gasped and struggled to release Kyle's hold on him.

'Ah telt ye they'd be here...' Kyle muttered, letting go of Joe's arm. 'Come... let's get oot o' here afore they take us along wi' them an' a'!'

Running through the back streets, they made it to the top of the hill above Braxfield estate before relaxing into a walk as they hit the road to New Lanark.

Joe glanced at the shorter man at his side, 'How did ye ken the Guard were on their way?'

'Ah telt them,' Kyle stated flatly. 'Ma cousin knew there was gaun tae be a fight, about ten o'clock, that was the time he heard.'

'Why did ye tell them?' Joe was incredulous.

'Tae get rid o' Bryson an' his lads. Then Ah got tae thinkin' an' Ah thawt ye might ha'e taken it intae yer heid tae visit the inn an' see if Ah wis tellin' ye the truth.' There was a note of humour creeping into Kyle's voice.

Joe stopped in his tracks. 'Ye came tae keep me awa' frae the fight?'

'Aye, in a way.'

'Whit way?'

'Ah felt kind o' guilty cos Ah've been warnin' everyone tae keep awa' frae the tavern this nicht, but wi' ye... Weel, Ah guess Ah made ye curious aboot Sean an'...' he shrugged. 'Ah didnae want it on ma conscience if ye were caught up in it all.'

'An' am Ah supposed tae be gratefu'?'

'Naw, Joe, yer supposed tae be free tae gang back tae yer wife an' weans, an' no ha'e me worked up wi' guilt 'cause ye've been seized by the Guard on account o' my words tae ye this mornin'!'

Kyle was grinning at him and Joe could not help but smile back. There was a frankness to his words that could not be dismissed.

'Yer a mean bastard, Kyle Macinnes,' Joe said, laughing. 'Ye've made it sae Ah cannae e'en hate ye ony mair!'

They carried on down the road to the gorge, talking confidentially about what they would say to their friends and families about their whereabouts that evening. There were bound to be questions and they needed to have their stories straight.

As they neared the village, Kyle pointed out that Joe was bleeding from a cut above his eye. There was also dust and horse muck caked on the knees of his breeches and down his back from when he was wrestled to the ground at one point.

'Aw hell! Fiona will be mad a' me!'

'Ye can wash a guid deal aff at the river afore ye gang in tae the hoose, but yer eye? That'll tak a deal mair explaining!'

'Ah'll gae tae oor Sarah's first. Tha's whit Ah'll dae...' he pulled some grass and started to rub at the dirt on his legs. 'ye can come wi' me, an' a'.'

'Whit fer? She's yer sister....'

'Aye, but she kens Ah dinnae care fer her man an' willnae believe the story frae me. Ye tell her.'

'Aw mon!' Kyle spun round on his heel, looking up to the stars. 'Ah've done ma guid deed fer the day...'

'Then ye can dae anither.'

'An' break a habit o' a lifetime?'

'Aye.'

When they reached the Rafferty's door, Kyle was still grumbling about not wanting to be drawn into the Scott family affairs and his reluctance to tell Sarah of her husband's sins.

'Jist tell it as it is, will ye, an' quit yer moanin'!' Joe told him, but added an appreciative smile. 'She's no gaun tae tak it weel, but Ah wid rather it were ye than me who she'll hate fer tellin' her the truth'

Sarah did not take it well.

She was sitting alone by a dying fire in the dark, sour smelling room. Her eyes were swollen and red from crying all evening, her hair loose and hanging in tangled strings about her shoulders. She was appalled to have them enter her room unbidden, finding her in such a state. Then further distressed on hearing their tale.

Joe mended the fire and lit the stumps of two candles to give more light before setting about washing his face, leaving Kyle to speak to his sister.

In the dim, flickering light, he watched Sarah's ravaged face as she realised the lies her husband must have been telling her over the last few months. There was no mention of the town girls. Kyle had not seen them that evening and, if he knew of Sean's entanglements, he did not include it in his account: Joe was certainly not going to say anything.

A horrible awareness of how low his sister had fallen slowly dawned on Joe.

Where was the pretty young woman who twined flowers in her hair, sang at the fireside and took a pride in her dress and cleanliness? Her face was pinched and creased with frown marks, her lips torn where she chewed them nervously, her nails bitten to the quick.

She had made no attempt to change from the shapeless maternity gowns after Stephen was born, covering her heavy body with one of the long loose aprons from her time in Dale's house. It was now worn and grey, tattered at the hem and stained from the children.

His heart went out to her but he also felt a dread of what he saw before his eyes. There was a look to her, an attitude and deadness about her eyes that reminded him of their mother.

It made him cold inside, almost nauseas, and he knew he had to stop his sister from repeating their mother's mistakes.

'Where's Sean now?' Sarah asked, when she had heard the worst.

'In the jail, Ah wid think.' Kyle told her. He had drawn a chair over from the table to sit beside her at the fire. He was shocked by the change in Joe's sister, barely recognising her as the same person when he entered the room.

'If he's put awa', whit will Ah dae? The rent's due at the end o' the week an' Ah have nae ony money tae pay it.'

The image of Sean in his rakish clothes, dropping coins into the prostitute's hand, swam before Joe's eyes.

'Ye'll come tae us. Move bak in tae the Row.' he peered into the shadowy corners of the room where the babies were sleeping. 'Why don't ye pick up the bairns an' come wi' me, richt noo?'

'Aw naw, Joe! Whit if Sean comes hame an' find me awa'? Ah cannae dae tha'! Poor man will be needin' me if he's released by the Guard.'

'Poor man!' cried Joe. 'Dinnae gi'e me a' that... ye owe him nuthin' lass, yer worth mair than this, much mair. Let's pick up the weans and gae hame.'

'Naw, naw... leave me alane, Joe!' she cried. 'he's ma husband... Ah'll stay here till he comes back!'

Both Kyle and Joe tried to make her see sense but eventually Kyle threw up his hands and, reeling off a string of curses in Gaelic, turned to Joe.

'Ah'm oota here! Guid luck tae ye!'

Joe could do no more, so he also took his leave, impressing on Sarah that she was welcome to return to the Row at any time. She was adamant that she would stay in her own room.

Out on the street, Joe and Kyle parted with a curt pat on each other's shoulder and a 'cheerio': not quite friends but no longer foes.

Two days later, with no sign of Sean and her efforts to be allowed to talk to him at the jail refused, Sarah presented herself at Joe's door.

'They'll be callin' fer the rent, an' there's nae money sae... can Ah stay here until Sean sorts it oot?'

Joe hugged her and ushered her inside but kept his lips pressed firmly together.

Sean could be weeks, perhaps months before returning and even if he did, he was only a burden and source of heart ache to his family. In his mind, and privately with Fiona, Joe could give vent to his disgust for his brother in law, but with Sarah he knew it was wisest to keep quiet and let her find out for herself.

When they settled down to sleep that night, there was a sombre mood in the room. Cal moved from his inset bed to the hurlie again, giving up his own wider, more private mattress to Sarah and her two children. With eight of them rustling and snoring, and the babies' intermittent cries, they all suffered a fitful, disturbed night.

Before dawn, Cal was roused from sleep yet again by Sarah tending to Stephen, only feet away from him, behind the curtain. He clasped his hands behind his head and lay on his back looking up at the ceiling.

In the shafts of moonlight coming through between the shutters, the heavily laden pulley loomed pale above his head. He felt it crowding down on him. He was suffocating; trapped beneath the burden of sharing the cramped space with five demanding infants and all the paraphernalia, noise and noxious smells that went with them.

How could he bear this?

He loved his family dearly but these were not his children, and his life was being invaded by the tiny creatures who tottered about the room, clambering and nattering like animals, demanding attention.

There was no longer any choice or excuse for delay, he had to move out before they drove him insane.

***

Owen returned to Glasgow at the end of the summer.

During his time in Manchester his thoughts were rarely far from the lovely Miss Dale and he set about finding a way to meet her father and, when infront of him, making a good impression.

There was a very fortunate piece of information which came his way obscurely and then was confirmed during a conversation with Miss Dale during one of their walks: Dale was looking for a purchaser for the New Lanark Mills.

Plans began to formulate and before leaving Manchester he wrote to Mr Dale asking for a business appointment. This was granted and on his first day back in the city, Owen duly presented himself to the Charlotte Street mansion, five minutes before the prescribed time.

Anne Caroline knew of his intention to speak with her father but did not know either when or on what topic. He just assured her that he would do all he could to make himself known to the great man and be seen in a suitably agreeable light to allow further meetings to take place.

Renwick opened the library door, paused for a moment to allow his presence be known and then said, 'Mr Dale will see you now, sir. I will escort you to the study.'

Owen followed the butler up the grand staircase, silently admiring the portraits and finely turned banisters as he strove to appear composed and calm. It was not that he feared David Dale, nor that he felt at a loss at what to say at the meeting, it was the overriding high regard which he held for the man that made him nervous.

The name of David Dale was known to be synonymous with astute business sense, strong religious morals and an expansive philanthropic nature. This was the man who would judge if he, Owen, was good enough to marry his daughter.

It was a daunting thought, but he had taken on ambitious tasks in the past and knew he would try his very best to show himself to be worthy.

Dale was standing by the window, a short, rotund figure in silhouette against the day light outside.

'Mr Robert Owen,' Renwick announced, then withdrew, closing the door behind him.

'Come away in,' Dale boomed, walking towards him, hand outstretched.

Their eyes engaged for the first time as they shook hands.

Owen was instantly aware that for all Dale's appearance as a benevolent, cheerful, old Glasgow worthy, here was a man who should not be underestimated. The older man's frank, open gaze told of a self confidence which immediately demanded respect.

'Take a seat.'

'Sir, it is an honour to meet you at last.' Owen sat down where he was indicated.

'So, ye wanted to see me?' Dale eyed him with interest from the other side of the desk.

'Yes, sir. I had the pleasure of meeting your daughter about a year ago and she kindly suggested I visit your mills at New Lanark.' Owen was speaking slowly and precisely, determined not to rush or stumble through his request.

'Aye, she mentioned it to me at the time. I gather you used to own a mill?' His face showed he was sceptical.

308

'Indeed, I did, sir. It was my good fortune to experience the business for a short spell and then I enjoyed an association with Drinkwater, at Bank Top Mill.'

'Peter Drinkwater, eh?' Dale knew of the mill owner. 'He has been utilising Watt's steam engine to great effect, has he not?'

'Quite so, the very fine yarn the mill produces has gained the factory a good reputation.'

'And you work in Manchester now?'

'I am a partner in the Chorlton Twist Company, with the position of managing director. It is in this capacity that I travel twice yearly to Scotland to meet with our Scottish customers.'

Dale leaned back in his chair and asked amiably, 'And what is it that you wish to see me about then?'

'I understand that you are looking to sell the New Lanark Mills and I am here because I am interested in buying them.'

A look of total astonishment crossed the older man's face. 'You? Buy New Lanark? But you are only a boy!'

Owen did not take offence, with a deferential manner, he said, 'Mr Drinkwater said the same when I applied to be his manager and I was but twenty at that time, and proved satisfactory. I am twenty eight years old now although, I grant you that I appear younger. However, I can assure you that my partners Mr Barton and Mr Atkinson are considerably older and wealthier than I.'

'Mr Atkinson? Of Borrodale? And Atkinson in London?'

'Yes sir, I joined these gentlemen over four years ago and we formed the Chorlton Twist Company. Since then I have overseen the building of our new factory, installed the machinery and presided over all stages from import of the raw cotton right through to the sale of the product. The enterprise is doing well.' He finished on a firm note and waited for a response.

Dale was still looking at him in puzzlement.

Owen was young, probably the same age as his nephew, Hugh's boy, David, but Owen spoke with the poise of someone comfortable with their subject, secure in the knowledge of their chosen trade. Dale was pleasantly surprised.

'There is more involved with New Lanark than merely cotton production,' Dale said slowly. 'As you will have seen from your visit, it is the home of hundreds of pauper children and I take their welfare very seriously. They receive good food, clothes and an education at my expense; the mill's expense. It is the right and proper Christian way to treat these poor orphans.'

'I am a strong advocate for better working conditions, as are my partners. We are all on the committee of the Manchester Board of Health which was formed two years ago. Our aim is to devise remedies for the evils of factory employment.'

This was an encouraging piece of information. Dr Percival, who was a leading light behind the Manchester Board of Health, was one of Dale's most respected colleagues. He was known to be currently pushing for parliamentary reform to establish laws for regulating humane and healthy conditions in factories.

'If you are agreeable, sir,' Owen suggested, 'I would ask for your permission to make a detailed survey of the mills.'

Dale agreed to his request and the meeting drew to a close.

When Owen walked out of the house into Charlotte Street, he felt satisfied that he had made a good first impression and was keen to travel to New Lanark as soon as possible.

***

A long dry spell reduced the waters in the Clyde to a level where Kelly was forced to stop production in Mill Three for several days, diverting what flow there was to the other wheels. This gave rise to an unexpected holiday for the mule supervisors and the women, like Rosie, who tended the jennies.

Corra Linn laid bare her giant steps of rock, with only a stream trickling down the hillside. Dundaff Linn, beside the village, could be walked across, so low were the waters. The workers from the west bank could use the easily forded, boulder strewn river bed to take a short cut to the mills.

It was rare for the river to run so low but gave no great concern because in Scotland it is never dry for long.

One evening during this time, Sarah and Fiona were taking it in turns to tramp the washing in the big tub.

With their hair pushed up under kerchiefs and their arms bare in sleeveless bodices, they ploughed their way through the job. While

310

one girl tucked up her skirts and climbed into the tub to work the dirt from the cloth, the other held baby Robbie and watched over the three lively scrabbling infants playing around them in the street. Sarah's youngest, Stephen, sat propped up in the wash basket, gnawing on a clothes peg, one brilliant red cheek showing the cause of his teething pains.

The whole of New Lanark was a hive of activity, taking advantage of the warm evening to tend to chores or relax and play on the green. The shops, several now housed in New Buildings, were doing a good trade, with rowdy queues outside the liquor store.

Long golden rays from the setting sun slanted across the gorge, turning the lines of tenement roofs a deep orange, illuminating the rising, vertical plumes of smoke from hundreds of chimneys and flashing off the window panes. As the sun dropped below the hills beyond Corehouse, pigeons cooed in the surrounding woodland and the cries of oyster catchers mingled with the villagers' blethering voices.

'Och, here she comes! Try an' be friendly,' Fiona told Sarah, spying Rosie bustling along the Row.

Since marrying, Rosie was full of her own self-importance. No-one ran a better home, was married to a more attentive husband or enjoyed such well-appointed lodgings as Mrs MacAllister: or so she led them to believe.

It was true that their room was equipped with a splendid oak dresser, an oven and good quality furniture. This was because the late Mr MacAllister, Gerard's father, had been a carpenter and his uncle, now also deceased, a blacksmith.

Her family were pleased for Rosie's good fortune but the constant reminders of how much better off she was than they were, was a source of irritation. Especially to Sarah, who was still living with her brother while Sean languished in prison.

Rosie's tiny figure, neat in a white bonnet and pink and green patterned dress, picked its way through the ball games, squealing toddlers and gossiping neighbours to join them outside their doorway. She was holding two small boxes tied with string, which dangled from her fingers.

'Wait till Ah tell ye whit ma Gerry telt me the day when he came hame fer his dinner!' she cried, as soon as she drew within earshot.

Sarah jiggled Robbie in her arms to keep his complaining to a whimper.

311

'There's a man comin' doon next week tae inspect the mills! An' de ye ken why he's comin'?' She didn't wait for a reply, 'Mr Dale's sellin' up! He's sellin' the mills!'

'Naw! Tha' cannae be? Aw, tha's awfy bad news if yer richt!' exclaimed Sarah.

'Oh course Ah'm richt! Ye sayin' ma husband would be makin' it up?'

'Och, Rosie,' Fiona said, soothingly, dismayed by the news. 'O'course she's no'. Its jist sich terrible news. Who's buyin' the place?'

'Ah dinnae ken, but Gerry's heard tell it's an Englishman.'

'Away! Oh dear, whit will happen tae a' o' us?' Fiona's dark eyes were wide with alarm. 'Mr Dale is sich a grand master, sae guid tae us, an' fair wi' his demands.'

They looked at one another in horror.

'Weel, Ah jist wanted tae pass it on as soon as Ah could, seein' as Gerry hears everythin' that goes on aroond here.' She raised one of the little boxes and held it out to Fiona, Sarah's arms being occupied by Robbie.

'Ah wis bakin', an' thawt ye'd like a cake. Tis like a Fair holiday t'day, wi nae work tae be gaun oot tae. Ma oven works a treat sae Ah've had a grand efternoon!' She gave a little laugh, 'Ah'm awa' tae tak tea wi' Mrs McGuffy afore Gerry leaves the office.'

She tripped away back down the Row, one hand plucking at her long skirts to keep them up out of the dust, the other swinging the second little cake box.

Fiona, knee deep in suds and left holding the box, looked at Sarah and pulled a face.

Sarah scowled, 'Tea wi' Mrs McGuffy? Ah'll gie her tea wi' Mrs McGuffy! She's sae fu' o' herself Ah'm surprised she can force a dish o' tea doon her throat!'

When Joe came in he was no sooner through the door than Fiona was telling him about the sale.

He was as shocked as she was and the evening was spent discussing the possible changes that might take place without their present benevolent owner.

Calum took the news to heart, a sickening fear welling in his stomach. Having disliked New Lanark on arrival as a little boy and yearning for his release from the mills, the trauma of his months away from the village completely changed his mind.

New Lanark was home. New Lanark meant security. Under the management of such a deeply religious and kind man as Mr Dale, Calum felt safe from the cruelties he endured while abroad in the countryside.

'We dinnae ken yit if there will be ony changes, dae we?' He asked Joe anxiously.

'Ah dinnae ken, Cal. Ye ken as much as Ah dae, an' tha' does nae amount tae a handfu' o sand.'

The news of Mr Dale's intention to sell the mills spread like wild fire.

Everyone would be affected by the possible changes that a new owner would bring, whether they were aware of it or not. From little five year old Ben White, the newest orphan to arrive from Edinburgh Poor House, struggling to adjust to Mill Four, to Big Lachie, settled in and established at the forge.

Most of the villagers never noticed Robert Owen's quiet arrival and subsequent detailed survey of the equipment and buildings. His presence was only felt by those in the office, otherwise he was just another of the now commonplace stream of wealthy strangers who strolled between the mills and marvelled at the beauty of the lade and river.

The weather broke a few days before Owen came to the village so the river was high and all the water-wheels and jennies were working at the time of his inspection.

Kelly was relieved to show the mills at their best but made no secret of the fact that when the river ran low, the power and therefore production was also affected to their detriment.

Calum, however, did note the presence of Robert Owen but was unaware of his identity.

On taking charge of the cream coloured mare Owen hired while in Lanark, Cal removed its saddle to groom it and noticed that the horse's girth was rubbing a sore patch behind its elbow. The hair was worn away and the animal's skin was raw and weeping from the chafing leather. There were various pieces of sheepskin kept in the store room and he cut a long rectangle and sewed it into a sleeve to cover the girth strap where it lay across the wound.

When Owen returned at the end of the day, not only did he admire the well turned-out horse, its mane and tail now brushed and floating in the breeze, its coat gleaming, but he immediately spotted the sheepskin wrap.

'I do not recall seeing this when I mounted this morning? Has there been a mishap?' he asked of Calum.

'No sir.' Calum explained, warily. Was the stranger going to berate him for interfering? He looked pleasant enough and was a young man not much older than himself, but any interaction with outsiders filled him with trepidation. 'Ah jist saw there wis a wee sore bit under there... an' thocht it might be comfier tae mak a pad fer it?'

Owen stooped to inspect it more closely.

'Good.' he said, turning a smile to Calum. 'I will instruct the stables to take further care of her when I hand her back.' And then, to Calum's amazement, he took the reins, mounted and said, 'Thank you,' before riding off up the hill.

It was so rare for anyone to thank Calum for his work that his mouth was hanging open as he gazed after the narrow, impeccably dressed figure.

***

'I leave for Manchester tomorrow,' Owen informed Anne Caroline, as they strolled across Glasgow Green. 'My visit to New Lanark was very productive and I will relate my findings to my partners on my return.'

'Father will not be drawn with any views on your proposal to purchase the mills. He has a way of avoiding all mention of the subject, even though he is aware of my feelings for you.'

'We must keep up high hopes, my dear. At least I will have another opportunity to converse with him when I return and who knows what may lie ahead.'

She squeezed his arm and looked affectionately at the young man at her side. She had grown very fond of the sight of him, the sound of his voice and his quick-witted, entertaining conversation. She could never imagine growing tired of looking at him or being in his company. They were so attune in personality that any differences of opinion they might have were easily discussed and overcome.

On the day she knew Owen was leaving Glasgow, she felt an emptiness which threatened to consume her so she arranged for Rosemary to join her for the afternoon.

314

Rosemary was also in need of consolation due to Mr Wilson, the object of her affections, having made a proposal of marriage.

'After all this time! After months and months of calling on me, talking with me in the most intimate terms, and now he proposes... to Isobel MacPherson!' Rosemary dabbed at her eyes with a lace 'kerchief. 'It is so humiliating! I hate him with such a passion that if he was before me now, I am sure I would strike him!'

'Did you know he was seeing Miss MacPherson? Did he ever speak of her?' Anne Caroline asked, concerned by the depth of feeling in her friend's voice.

'Oh, he might have told me about the MacPherson *family* before, because they own the neighbouring estate to the Wilson's in the Highlands. He did not say *anything* regarding having a relationship with one of the daughters.' She snivelled into the kerchief again. 'Hateful man! He wrote to me... not even having the decency to tell me to my face!'

'And what did he say?'

'He said, ' it is with regret that I am writing to inform you that my father desires me to be joined in matrimony to the elder daughter of Thomas Macpherson.'' She shook her head, ringlets bobbing. 'I remember every ghastly word as if it were in my hand now. Apparently, this understanding was struck between the two families years ago! And yet the brigand had the audacity to woo me while in the city. I feel ... used...'

'Perhaps his true affections do lie with you, dear Rosemary, and he is being forced into this union by his father. I am sure he held you in respect and cared for you very much. I have witnessed his behaviour when we were all together and he appeared genuine to me.'

'Do you think so?' Rosemary tried a wavering smile.

'He may feel as badly about this affair as you do, but has to do his duty by his family.'

'That may be true, but he is a man, not a little boy. Why does he not make his own choice for a wife?'

'I daresay money is involved, if the arrangement was made between the parents. You know how Felicity Douglas married her cousin, just so the estate could remain in their family?'

'It is beastly. Simply beastly! And now I am without any admirer.' She raised her teary eyes to Anne Caroline. 'And how goes it with your Mr Owen?'

'He has left, today, for Manchester. We will have to be patient until his next journey north, although I fear that may not be until the spring. We will have to be good friends to one another, Rosemary, and keep each other's spirits up over this period of uncertainty.'

Anne Caroline rose and went to the bell pull by the fireplace.

'Let's have some hot chocolate,' she said firmly. 'It is such a damp and miserable day, and with our emotions at a low ebb, I fear we feel the chill more than usual. Hot chocolate and sweet cakes... that will help to cheer us up!'

Early snow in November brought disruption to the start of the winter season of luncheons and afternoon entertainment usually enjoyed in the city to combat the tedium of Glasgow's darkest months.

To her delight, at an afternoon party of poetry reading at the MacIntosh's home, Rosemary was introduced to a bookish gentleman, Mr Peckham. Although nearly twenty years her senior, he became her close companion at every dinner they both attended.

Mr Arthur Peckham was a widower, without children, and a Professor of Chemistry at Glasgow University. He knew the MacIntosh's due to having taught their son, Charles, and had kept up the acquaintance. He knew many of their circle of friends, being more of the older generation than Rosemary and her contemporaries.

After several of these occasional meetings, he called upon Rosemary's father to ask for her hand in marriage.

'When I think of all those wasted months, years, with the hateful Mr Wilson, I am soon to be Mrs Peckham!'

Anne Caroline tried not to let her amusement show. After pining miserably for her lost love, poor Mr Wilson had instantly been renamed the 'hateful Mr Wilson' as soon as Rosemary's betrothal was announced.

The wedding was arranged for the spring and the girls set about all the preparations required to ensure it would be an outstanding social event.

***

There were no such joyful events to look forward to for the Scotts in New Lanark.

After six months in prison, Sean Rafferty was released.

He returned to the village amid a shower of sleet and on discovering that Sarah was with her brother, braced himself and went to their door.

It was mid afternoon, murky and cold, the streets empty of people and Sarah was alone in the room with the children. It was Donnie who ran to the door and opened it, with Sarah coming behind him, carrying Robbie.

'Hello Sarah,' Sean said, simply.

He was drenched and his long hair hung around his shoulders, dripping and dishevelled.

'Sean...' she gasped, suddenly overcome with dizziness at the shock.

Leaving the door open, she returned to the chair by the fire, reaching for the table to steady herself as she passed. Her legs were giving way and with Fiona's baby in her arms she was conscious that she must not drop him.

Sean came into the room and closed the door behind him. Looking closely at Sarah, he took the other fireside chair and leaned towards her, saying, 'That's no' wee Stephen? Is it?'

'Stephen?' she stared back at him with wild, disbelieving eyes. Some of the confusion was lifting and she could focus on her husband's face.

Nodding towards the cot she said in a dazed voice, 'Naw, yer son's o'er there.'

She watched Sean as he bent over the sleeping baby, gently stroking his downy dark hair, a serious expression clouding his face.

Then he went to where Cathy was sitting on the bed and picked her up, hugging her close. The child wriggled away from his rough, wet coat, holding up her damp hands and examining them as closely as her father was examining her own little face.

When he placed her back on the bed to carry on playing among the bedclothes, he returned to sit beside Sarah.

There were tears in his eyes.

'Ah've missed you all so much,' he said hoarsely. 'I love you, Sarah.' he placed his hand on her knee. 'I may not have shown it, or been a good husband but I do, I love you... and our little children.'

She listened to his words and looked searchingly into his eyes.

'Ah ken ye love me, darlin'. And ye must ken how much Ah love ye. Ah wisnae weel efter Stephen wis born, Ah wis kind o' mad...

everythin' wis a trouble an' Ah couldnae think richt.' She rearranged the baby on her knee to free a hand and grasped his hand with hers.

'Ye did nae deserve tae ha'e sich a mess fer a wife, wi' the washin' no' done and filth aboot the place, but Ah jist couldnae mak meself dae it... Ah'm gettin' better noo, an' Bessie says she kens ither wimen who gae soft i' the heid efter babbies. Ah'm tha' sorry, Sean... tha' sorry....'

They were both crying and he kissed their joined hands, struggling to speak.

'Naw, Sarah, it wasn't you, it wasn't because of the *washing..*'. He took a deep breath. 'I didn't get the job at Stonebyres, or the other ones I was trying to get. I needed to bring in money and started to gamble, at the cards.' He kept his eyes lowered, not wanting to see her response to his words. 'I learned a few tricks, years ago, and found I could take a good amount off the men in Lanark. Then, I was found out. Or maybe they just got tired o' me winning so much. These are bad men, Sarah. They gave me a battering and, well, that's how I came to be taken to the prison.'

He paused and she gripped his hand tightly. 'Ah ken a' that. Joe and Kyle Macinnes telt me the night ye were taken.'

He sat upright, pushing his hair back off his brow. 'Ye know?'

'Aye, an' Ah still love ye, Sean.'

He gave a long sigh and tilted his head back to gaze unseeingly at the ceiling.

'I'm in trouble, Sarah. The money was not just for you and the children, it was for The Cause. I have been meeting my Irish brothers, colleagues from Ireland who, like me, have had to flee from their homeland because of their beliefs.

'We all pledge money for the Cause, a free Ireland, and I couldn't tell them I had no employment, no means to give support. For years they've counted on my contribution and when I started to win at the cards, it seemed the easiest way to raise it. I never told them where the money came from, some have deeply held views on gambling and, of course, I was also cheating...' Now that he had started to unburden himself, he carried on in a flow of confessions.

It was dark by the time he finished and they suddenly realised that the children had fallen asleep where they played, with Davey curled up on the floorboards beside the beds. While Sarah settled Robbie in the cot beside her own son, Sean re-kindled the fire and lit the lamp, talking as he worked.

'When I left the prison they wanted me to sign on for the army. I cannot be part of the King's army. It is against all I hold true! They were forcing me, saying they could throw me back in prison if I refused, so I told them I would.'

'Och naw!' Sarah cried, rushing towards him.

He took her in his arms and held her tight. 'I only said I would, so I could leave the jail. I said I was coming home to see ma family and they've given me papers to take up to Lanark tomorrow morning.' He held her at arm's length, 'I *cannot* join the army. They will come looking for me when I don't report to the office so... I have to leave here... now.'

'Where will ye gae? Can Ah come wi' ye?' Even as she uttered the words she knew it would be impossible.

'There's Bryson's men out to find me, and the Guard will be after me... I have to be far away from here by morning. I will go to the city, Edinburgh or Glasgow, get lost among the people and find work. Proper work, ma darling. And then I'll send for you and the children.'

'Fer truth?'

'When I have a place to stay and income to keep you all, yes, I will. Until then, you're better off without me....'

'Naw! Oh Sean, Ah cannae bear the thocht o' ye leavin' me agin!'

He kissed her passionately and held her in a long embrace. Then, abruptly, he prised her away from him and went to the door.

'I'll send for you all.'

Then he was gone.

Chapter Eleven

"Is there for honest poverty
That hings his head, an' a' that?
The coward slave, we pass him by
We dare be poor for a' that!
For a' that, an' a' that,
Our toils obscure, an' a' that,
The rank is but the guinea's stamp,
The man's the gowd for a' that."

Robert Burns

In the dying days of 1798, chilling north easterly winds brought snow clouds billowing down across the country.

At first the snow falls were greeted with acceptance by the adults and pleasure by the children. However, as the days went on and the tiny, icy flakes built steadily into a thick blanket, it rekindled memories of the harsh winter of '95.

To take advantage of the sudden cold spell over Hogmanay, an ice rink was prepared by a group of curling enthusiasts from the town and the first day of the New Year found people from all around the area making their way through the white landscape to take part in the game.

Joe was proud to take Donnie with him up to Lanark and walked to Ewing's to collect his stones. Then, placing them on a sledge, set off to show his son the joys of curling.

The sun never managed to break through and even before the close of play the grey ceiling of cloud released another floating curtain of icy flakes. Plans for an after-match ceilidh were abandoned and the women folk gathered up their baskets of food and fought their way home, skirts flapping and heavy capes billowing.

The players carried on, snow swirling around them, sweeping frantically in front of the stones until the cry went up to cease play. A hurried decision was made to award the match to a young Lanark team, who was far out ahead in points anyway and the rinks were abandoned beneath a covering of new snow.

Soon, the playing fields were deserted as everyone sought shelter, hurrying against the gusting, ice-filled wind.

With collars and mufflers pulled up and caps pulled down, Joe and the other men from New Lanark made a hasty retreat back down into the gorge.

Little Donnie, who was revelling in being with his father and among the men, sat on board his father's toboggan, gripping the sides to keep his balance. Eyes screwed up against the snowy onslaught, he was determined not to complain even though the freezing cold bit into his toes and fingers.

On seeing the snow storm whipping past the steamed-up windows and howling in the chimney, Fiona realised that the curling would be cut short. She greeted her husband and son with bowls of hot stew and dry clothes warming on the rack by the fire.

'Yer soaked and ha'e ice a' doon yer backs!' she cried, pulling at Donnie's jacket. ' Get oot o' those cla'es this minute or ye'll both be ill afore the mornin'!'

'Aw Mam, it wer' great!' Donnie's teeth were chattering but there was a huge grin on his shining, red face. 'Can we gae agin t'morra, Da'?'

'Naw, Ah'll be workin'. Mibbee the snow'll stoap an' it'll freeze, like a few years past, an' we can gang up on Sunday?'

When Sunday came, the snow was still falling, on and off, from a leaden sky but the temperatures were higher, making the ice slushy and useless for making a rink.

In Glasgow and on the main trade routes between the towns, travel almost came to a standstill.

The miserable weather and long hours of darkness increased Dale's ill health and he spent most of his time in his study. Even with blazing fires in all the rooms, the Charlotte Street mansion was cold, the air damp, condensation pooling on the window ledges.

Anne Caroline and her sisters absorbed themselves in books, sewing, endless hours of painting by lamp light and writing letters.

The high point of every day was the main meal and Cook struggled to produce pleasing dishes from the decreasing choice of ingredients. Many of the stores were unable to fill her requests and the errand boy would return with the meagre supplies, bracing himself for the tirade of dissatisfaction that would follow.

Nevertheless, three plates of sumptuous savoury recipes were served to her master's colleagues at an important dinner he was giving during the worst of the weather.

All the men lived in Glasgow and given Dale's standing as a banker and merchant, they did not wish to call off. Covering their fine jackets and breeches with thick woollen capes, they made their way through the perilously slippy, snow-piled streets.

Anne Caroline attended the meal which was arranged for mid-day because there were only a few hours of gloomy daylight available for the guests to safely be out in the city. She enjoyed the chance of a break from the monotony of being virtually house-bound. Their only outings had been the short walks to their father's church in Greyfriar's Wynd.

Miss Spears' letters had stopped due to the atrocious weather and she had not heard from Mr Owen for several weeks. Sometimes she became so despondent that she believed he had probably forgotten all about her and was engaged in an intimate relationship with another young lady.

These thoughts threatened to torture her and it became a daily battle to force her attention on to other subjects like reading, embroidery or, more often, to seek solace in prayer.

'My goodness, Dale, your daughter is growing up at a fine pace!' John Clark bellowed, when Anne Caroline left the gentlemen to talk business and pass around the port.

The dining room flickered with candlelight and brilliant flashes of leaping flames in the fireplace. The warmth of the rich meal, good company and fine wine made Dale feel more at ease.

'I thank the Lord for all my daughters every day.' he replied with feeling. 'My dear wife would be as proud as I, had she lived to see them.'

'Make the most of your children,' Clark advised. 'Too soon they will be married and away from under your roof. We only have them for a short time. Borrowed, as it were, until they find their own path in life.'

James MacIntosh lit his pipe and, pushing his chair back from the table, crossed one leg over the other in a relaxed posture. 'My son, Charles, is building a new factory near the city, so I hope to be seeing more of him and his family.'

'They were out at Darnley, weren't they?' Dale asked. 'Isn't that where Tennant has the bleaching fields?'

'Aye, beside his father-in-law's farm. The firm's doing well, very well, and I am proud to say my son has contributed a great deal to its success. They are patenting a new bleaching powder and are hopeful of making their fortune.'

'That's excellent news! I remember when he first said he wished to be a chemist and you were not so confident, eh?'

'He's proved me wrong, and I am pleased for him. More than pleased!'

The other gentlemen at the table added their congratulations, pouring the ruby red port and sampling cheeses from a selection on the table.

'So, where's he moving to?' Dale asked.

'Near the Monkland Canal, in the St Rollox area. It will give them easier ways to ship in the coal they need for the process and, of course, move the product out again.'

'I wish them luck,' said Archibald Paterson, Dale's neighbour, 'in this trade climate it is hard enough to keep afloat, let alone start a new factory.'

'How are the sales of your mills going? New Lanark? Catrine? Any buyers on the horizon yet?'

'It is too early to say,' Dale said, firmly. 'In the spring, perhaps I will hear again from some interested parties.'

'So, you have a possible purchaser? And do they subscribe to your philanthropic measures towards your pauper Boarders?'

Dale recalled Owen's eager young face, his assurances that he was committed to better conditions for the working classes. His words had not been taken on face value. Dale had made it his business to ascertain if Owen was, indeed, on the committees in Manchester he purported to be and was pleasantly surprised to discover that it was the case.

'On first inspection, yes, I would be inclined to believe the standards I have set would be adhered to after a sale.'

'And is this prospective new owner known to us?'

'I would not think so, he is from over the Border.'

323

MacIntosh roared with laughter, 'Sell to a Sassanach? It's no' like ye, Dale!'

Dale just smiled in his good humoured way, 'It's not the land of his birth that concerns me too much, but rather the fact that he is not a practising Christian.'

'Business is business, my friend.' said Paterson. 'Ye cannot lay down how a man believes as a condition for sale.'

Dale cut himself a small slice of hard cheese, mindful of the possible pains of indigestion it might produce.

If Owen was only concerned with doing business with him, that would be one thing. It was Anne Caroline's confessed deeply felt affection for the man that caused Dale to feel uncomfortable. He let the conversation turn away from his impending retirement from the mills and then, when the subject of the war was brought in to play, joined in with the discussion.

'All we seem to read in the newspapers these days is how the French are victorious in their battles.' Paterson said, impatiently. 'This damnable fellow Bonaparte seems to have a gift for rallying his troops!'

'We are losing a lot of men to the war effort,' said Dale. 'Some of my best men have gone from the mills, not all conscripted either! They see it as a chance to broaden their horizons, ignorant of the suffering war brings to everyone. Many have left the Highlands to take up arms, leaving only the weakest to work the land and keep the families. Spinningdale is suffering, I fear.'

'And I hear young Thomas Muir is in France now,' said MacIntosh, 'being praised to the skies and applauded by the Directory for his calls for revolution in our country. They see him as a kindred spirit, wanting to change the parliament.'

Dale looked very grave. 'He may be being celebrated now but the poor man was severely wounded.' They all looked down the table at their host. 'I am in frequent correspondence with his father who tells me that his son was caught in the crossfire of battleships as he sailed to Europe. Half his face was blown apart, shattering his cheek bone and destroying his left eye. He only barely survived.'

'Good God! But he lives?'

'Apparently. He has recovered sufficiently to be treated as the darling of the establishment. Portraits have been commissioned of him... with, his father understands, a patch of folded material draping one side of his head to hide his disfigurement. Oh and they've held processions and fanfares ... the lot! It is of little comfort to his family. There is still a warrant out for his arrest and he is earning himself no leniency from the courts by encouraging the new United Scotsmen movement.

'They may be underground here, but I gather they are aligning themselves with the United Irishmen, a seriously militant group.'

'I have also heard these rumours,' Harrison, a quieter, younger member of the party added. 'A dim view is being taken of Muir's close association with Thomas Paine, no less.'

'Paris is a hot bed of republican refugees. If Pitt tries to smother them here, they just flee across the channel and grow stronger with the help of the French. It is a dangerous time.'

The conversation moved on and Dale began to feel weary. He was tired after·a busy day and, exacerbated by the port, his body ached to relax, his eyes wanted to close. Skilfully, without offending his friends, he drew the gathering to a close.

As he climbed the stairs to take a rest in the study, he thought again of Thomas Muir and prayed that there would be a good outcome for the young man after his harrowing ordeal.

He had stood up for what he believed, been castigated and thrown out of both his profession and his country and now, half-blinded, he was in the thick of a crowd of political revolutionaries. How could he ever return to Scotland? How would his father ever be able to hear his son's voice or look upon his poor, damaged face?

Dale passed his daughters' bedrooms and wondered if he could have borne it if his son had grown up to suffer like Thomas Muir. Even as the thought crossed his mind, he knew the answer: God would have given him the strength.

Later, reading his bible in golden lamplight by the fire, he kept pausing to murmur prayers for Muir, his father and all the other families affected by violence and Man's inhumanity to Man.

He was not to know that on that same evening in France, Thomas Muir was hiding in the little Ile-de-France village of Chantilly.

His role of unofficial representative for political refugees to the Directory in Paris had placed him in a dangerous position, forcing him to leave the city for his personal safety. Making every effort to hide his identity, he awaited the arrival of his Scots compatriots. Two bitterly cold months had passed and with only a small child knowing of his existence and supplying him with food, he was in a desperate situation.

That dark evening on January 26th, as Dale prayed for the souls of his stricken human beings, Muir was overtaken by desolation, cold and the trauma of his injuries.

He died, suddenly and alone.

His efforts to remain incognito were so elaborate and complete that it was several days before his identity was confirmed and the news of his death relayed to Paris.

***

The war with France did not impinge on the lives of the Scotts as they went about their daily lives. So, it came as a shock when a man appeared at their door one evening with news of Joe's old friend from the early days at New Lanark.

'Tam's back.' the man said flatly. 'He wants tae see ye.'

'Whit, Tam Murdoch? Here? In Lanark?' Joe looked at the stranger more closely, he was familiar. 'Are ye merrit tae Beth, Tam's sister?'

'Aye, Ah'm Russell Barr. He's at his Ma's but Ah should warn ye, Tam's no' sae guid.'

'How?' Joe was already reaching for his jacket. The worst of the snow was thawing but it was still a nasty night to walk up to town.

'He's bin woundit... bad, like. They've brung 'im back bu' he's in a gie poorly way.'

On their climb up the hill to Tam's house, Russell explained all he knew of his injuries. He'd been slashed in the arm in a bout of hand to hand fighting and when the wound become infected they had to amputate it right up at the shoulder. For weeks he was nursed in a field hospital and then brought back to England on a small boat, along with other wounded soldiers. A further few weeks were spent at a camp a few miles south of London and he was supposed to have been brought back to Scotland before the new year, but the weather had delayed this still further.

'He's suffering frae his arm, an he's as thin as a skeleton, jist bones, is a'. Ah'm warnin' ye noo, fer tis a hard thing tae see.'

Joe tried to prepare himself but still felt a terrible wave of pity and horror when Mrs Murdoch, bowed with angst, took him to his friend's bedside.

The small back room where he lay was lit by a couple of candles, guttering in a jar. They sent distorted, moving shadows across the walls and showed the cadaverous head and shoulders of a man lying beneath the rumpled covers.

'Tam! Yer hame, at last....' Joe started.

'Whit Ah have nae left in the mud i' France, Aye, Ah'm back.'

His voice was all that was recognisable for Tam looked old, shrivelled, and his eyes were sunk deep into shadowy sockets.

They spoke of Fiona and the new babies, Rosie now being married and Sarah's two children, although Joe omitted any mention of Sean. Tam was listening but his eyes wandered and from time to time he would take a sharp breath with a sudden jerk of pain.

'Its' rough fer ye.' Joe said gently. 'Is the pain bad?'

Tam closed his eyes for a second, swallowing with difficulty and holding his breath. Then, after a long sigh, he looked up at Joe.

'Has Sam been back?'

Joe gave a start. 'Sam? Ma brither, Sam?'

'Aye. Ah wis servin' wi' him some months past. He said he'd be back tae see ye a', noo yer Da's deid.'

'How is he?' Joe's head was reeling.

'Och, he's a'richt. Risen tae a Major. We got chattin' yin nicht an' Ah said Ah wer' frae Lanark. When he telt me his family were frae Douglas an' Ah heard his name, Ah said Ah knew ye... ye wer' ma pal. He wanted tae knaw a' aboot ye an' the ithers.'

'Ye telt him aboot Meg? An' Ma?'

'Aye. He wis fair cut up aboot wee Meg.' Tam closed his eyes again and for a moment Joe thought he was asleep, then he licked his cracked lips and spoke again. 'He felt guilty aboot leavin' ye a'. He telt me tae sae sorry tae ye, Joe.'

Joe reached out and touched Tam's good arm, then squeezed it. 'It wis nae his fault. Faither wis gaun tae kill him, we a' ken whit happened. Ye tell him we're a'richt noo, a' New Lanark? An' aboot Fiona?'

Tam murmured something but the words were lost as he fell into an exhausted sleep.

Joe left shortly afterwards and ran most of the way back down the road to the village, filled with the news of his brother.

It was a huge relief to all the family to hear that Sam was alive and well. Yet, this knowledge brought new anxieties. Now that they knew he was serving as a soldier, every snippet of news of the war became of interest and the more they learned, the more they feared for his life.

Joe took to visiting Tam regularly, whenever he was going to Ewing's workshop or collecting supplies from Lanark. He would ask for more information, anything, about Sam, about the war, the life in the regiment, but Tam wouldn't answer. Having delivered his message, he wanted to shut out all memories of the dreadfulness he had witnessed.

Slowly, with his mother's faithful nursing, he began to gain a little weight and was persuaded to rise from his bed every day, inching his way back to life.

By the time the woodlands were alive with green shoots and bird song, Tam was well enough to take walks to the High Street and even venture to the tavern.

He was given a hero's welcome but made it very clear from the start that he never wished to speak of his time in the army. His empty sleeve and useless stump were reminders enough, but while his body healed, his mind was too damaged and just shut away the whole episode, out of sight.

Except when he was alone, especially at night.

***

The spring also brought Rosemary's wedding.

After a simple ceremony, Rosemary and her new husband held a reception at their home in Kelvinside.

It was a gracious, red sandstone terraced house which, as Rosemary's more mercenary friends teased, would have been reason enough to become Mrs Peckham, without the gentleman in question also being so charming.

After the months of preparation for the grand event, it all went very pleasantly. Rosemary looked beautiful in a pure white, wide-skirted crinoline, insisting on old fashioned hooped petticoats and gathered ruffles of lace edged silk.

'These flimsy, narrow dresses we wear nowadays are not enough for my Special Day,' she told Anne Caroline. 'I wish to have the most glorious gown any bride could ever have!'

The lavish food, spread on tables down either side of their drawing room, and the expensive wine, were gifts from Rosemary's parents who felt quite peeved that she chose to host her reception in Mr Peckham's house, rather than her family home.

Rosemary was adamant, telling them 'It will also be *my* house, and I wish to show it to my friends.'

Anne Caroline and Rosemary's other close friends guessed that Rosemary's desire to show off her very advantageous marriage was too strong to be denied. The Kelvinside residence far outshone her father's house and, without a thought to her parents' feelings, she simply decided on the most prestigious venue.

Anne Caroline enjoyed the wedding enormously, acting as a bridesmaid for the service and dancing the evening away with a string of young men who she barely knew but made pleasant partners for the party.

The day of the wedding was made even more memorable because she received a letter from Mr Owen that very morning.

Since the heavy snow of winter, he had written a couple of times but this letter held important news. He was coming up to Scotland in just a few weeks time and would be accompanied by his business partners, Mr Barton and Mr Atkinson. They were keen to see the New Lanark Mills for themselves and, if all was in order, would then be requesting a meeting with her father.

It was a sunny summer's day when the three partners of the Chorlton Twist Company of Manchester alighted from their coach in New Lanark. William Kelly welcomed them to his office and they formally signed the visitors' book before commencing a guided tour of the mills.

The day was very warm but when they entered Mill One and were taken to the doors of the various work rooms, the heat intensified along with the roaring, reverberating sounds of the spinning jennies.

The active looms stretched the whole length of both side-walls, their iron wheels and gears working two thousand spindles.

Several women tended the machines and forty or fifty small children scurried about in white tunics, their shaggy hair and bare feet layered with cotton dust. Each was intent on their own task, with the Overlooker, a bearded man in a loose white shirt and breeches, pointing out instructions as they ran errands, mended threads, brushed up the dust and crawled beneath the whirling spindles collecting debris.

'So many children,' Owen said, above the noise. 'Some seem no more than babies.'

'All the children are very well cared for here,' Kelly had to raise his voice to be heard. 'Mr Dale pays particular attention to the welfare of his Boarders... the orphan children who are lodged in Mill Four.' He gestured to the group to leave the room and, once out in the comparative calm of the stairwell, he continued.

'Would you care to see the schoolrooms? We have over five hundred regular pupils now and more than a dozen teachers.'

'That would be of great interest, thank you,' Owen allowed the other men to walk in front of him. Judging by their facial expressions and the many questions they were asking of the manager, his colleagues were impressed by what they were seeing.

After being shown examples of the children's work and a brief view of one of the neat dormitories, they strolled back up the hill towards the office. Kelly had instructed his clerks to prepare up to date reports on the mill's production and he invited his visitors to take a seat while they went over the figures.

The two older gentlemen were sweating in their wigs and cumbersome, formal jackets, being obliged to loosen their cravats and unbutton their waistcoats to give some relief from the humidity.

Owen appeared pale and calm beside them, only the wet curls of his neatly cut hair sticking to his forehead, giving an indication of the hot weather.

From all the detailed notes and lists taken on his previous inspection, Owen was thoroughly conversant with the workings of the mill and the expected out-put. He ran a practised eye down Kelly's figures for the last quarter and commented on various areas where production was up or employment figures were down.

All the anomalies were discussed and explained to his satisfaction and, after taking refreshments, the Englishmen called for their coach.

'It has been a pleasure,' Mr Atkinson said warmly, shaking Kelly's hand. 'I hope we meet again in the not too distant future.'

'Likewise, sir. If you are looking to invest in cotton mills, I can assure you that you could do no better than New Lanark.'

Mr Barton joined in with his appreciation of the tour, then, looking over Kelly's shoulder at a magnificent clock, exclaimed, 'My word, you have a splendid timepiece there! I don't think I have ever seen the like before!'

They all turned to admire the beautiful clock.

330

'No, you will never have seen another like that one.' said Kelly, proudly. 'It is unique. I made it myself and it is driven by the water, like the mills, and keeps the time for the village.'

'Good Lord,' mused Mr Atkinson, taking out his spectacles and hooking them carefully around his ears. He leaned closer and inspected it in every detail. 'Miraculous....' he murmured, 'quite miraculous.'

In its rounded wooden case, the clock's face held several dials: one for the hours, minutes and seconds, one for weeks, one for months, one for years and one calculating every ten years.

Owen also thought the clock was very fine and was particularly pleased to be ending their visit on a pleasurable note, with his partners in such high spirits.

It was a cheerful party who climbed aboard the coach and rattled their way up the winding hill to Lanark. They were to stay the night in town, at the Clydesdale Hotel, before continuing to Glasgow the following day.

***

When she heard the familiar muffled clang of the great iron gate at the end of Charlotte Street, Anne Caroline rushed to the window.

A handsome carriage with two grey horses was drawing to a halt outside the front door.

'Mr Owen is here!' she cried, pressing against the pane of glass to catch a glimpse of the figures climbing out into the street.

Mary and Jean joined her, moving between the two large, street facing, bedroom windows.

'I cannot see him,' complained Mary. 'There is one much older gentleman, in a top hat, but the others have already mounted the steps. Perhaps these are different business men to see Papa?'

'No, no... Mr Owen wrote to me with the date and time, it must be the party from Manchester.'

She left the window and went nearer the doorway to the upstairs landing. It would never do to be seen lurking near the staircase, but she could make out voices from the hall. When Robert Owen's

331

distinctive tones could be heard, she felt a nervous shiver run up her spine.

He was actually here, in the house, ready to speak with her father. An attack of nerves forced her to retreat to the dressing-table stool to sit down.

Downstairs, Owen and his partners left their hats with Renwick and were shown into the library. Mr Barton and Mr Atkinson were as amazed by the great collection of books and ornaments as Owen. They wandered about the room noting interesting titles on the spines of the books and admiring the paintings and porcelain.

They were not kept waiting for long before the butler returned to escort them up to Dale's study.

After the initial introductions were made, the meeting moved rapidly to the nub of the matter.

Dale clasped his hands in front of him on the desk and gave the three men an expectant appraisal.

'And so, gentlemen?'

Mr Atkinson told him of their visit to New Lanark the previous day and of the discussions between the partners regarding the purchase of the mills.

Dale, astute businessman that he was, then questioned them closely regarding the financial position of the Chorlton Twist Company. He found them sufficiently affluent to allow a realistic degree of certainty that any transaction with them would be honoured.

No price for the mills had been mentioned. As the meeting progressed and they could assume that Dale was prepared to dispose of his business to their company, Mr Atkinson decided to bring the subject out in to the open.

'Well, sir, given that you wish to sell the mills at New Lanark and we are of a mind to buy them, may we enquire your terms for the sale?'

Dale leaned back in the creaking chair, a glimmer in his eyes. 'I must profess that I am at a loss to put a fair price on them. My brother James and Mr Kelly may know better than me, because for the last year I have not taken such a close role in their management.' His gaze alighted on Owen. 'But, Mr Owen knows better than I do the value of such property at this period, and I wish that he would name what he would consider a fair price between honest buyers and sellers.'

While keeping his composure, Owen was non-plussed to be put in such a position in the company of men with far greater experience in business than his own.

Drawing from his knowledge of the last inspection and the size and production of the mills, together with the finances available among his partners, he quickly assessed a figure.

'Sir,' he said, 'It appears to me that sixty thousand pounds, payable at the rate of three thousand a year for twenty years, would be an equitable price between both parties.'

Dale regarded him for several long, thoughtful seconds, then smiled, saying, 'If you think so, I will accept the proposal as you have stated it, if your friends also approve of it.'

Owen turned to his partners, almost holding his breath in anticipation and to his surprise, smiles spread across their faces.

Nodding and stating their agreement, all the gentlemen shook hands on the deal.

Owen savoured the moment, looking from his friends to David Dale and glancing around the sunlit, book-lined study with its unusual octagonal walls.

A vase of fresh roses sat on a table by the window, an embroidered fire screen covered the fireplace opening, silver topped ink wells and pen holders lay gleaming on the desk, and the deep voices of the merchants, relieved and buoyant to have the sale agreed. It was a scene to be remembered.

As soon as Owen and his colleagues left the house, Anne Caroline knocked at her father's study door and enquired about the outcome of the meeting. She was delighted to hear that New Lanark had been sold to Owen and then asked again as to her father's views on the man himself.

'He is obviously a good businessman, but, I am afraid to say, my dear, that as far as giving my blessing to him as your future husband, I have not changed my mind.'

Tears stung her eyes as she wrestled for self control.

'But Father,' she pleaded, 'I have known him as a friend now for over two years and he has been consistent in every respect as a fine and honourable man. I beg of you to re-consider.'

Dale's serious expression brooked no further discussion but, as she left, Anne Caroline ventured to say;

'I have spoken with him on the subject of his religious beliefs and he assures me that he would never interfere with or prevent me from following my chosen church. He feels deeply for me, Papa, as I do for him. However, I will never marry a man who you will not embrace as part of the family, so I will respect your wishes.'

The next day, when Owen joined the Dale daughters for a walk on Glasgow Green, Anne Caroline met him with dreadful mixed feelings. After their long time apart, she yearned to be with him more than ever, however, her words to her father had not been said lightly.

'Papa is very satisfied with you on all counts in your transactions regarding the mills, but, Oh, my dear Mr Owen, I regret he will not agree for us to be married.'

Owen was extremely disappointed.

The walk took on a poignant air and, as they talked, they sought comfort from the fact that they would at least be able to spend some time together over the following weeks.

'My partners in the newly formed New Lanark Twist Company wish me to stay in Scotland for the next month or so to oversee the changeover of management. I shall be travelling to Lanark as soon as I have attended to my regular customers in Glasgow, probably early next week.'

'Oh, but that is fortuitous! My sisters and I are preparing for our summer holiday at the New Lanark cottage and will be there very soon ourselves!'

The thought of being together for the summer made Dale's resistance to their union only slightly easier to bear.

'Oh Rosemary,' Anne Caroline confided in her friend as they walked beside the Kelvin river. 'I am at my wits' end as to how to cope with my emotions concerning Mr Owen. I love him so much and I know he cares for me as fondly.... It is so difficult to believe that we cannot be together like you and Mr Peckham.'

'Mr Owen is held in high regard by all who have met him. Your father's views are really very trying,' Rosemary sympathised. 'Especially when you have reassured him that Mr Owen would not stop you following your Christian faith or attending church.'

'Perhaps, if I asked some of our mutual friends to extol Mr Owen's virtues to Papa, he might take heed of them? Mr MacIntosh and Mr Paterson are both acquainted with him and have been most flattering in their remarks about him.'

Anne Caroline sighed and watched some ragged children scrambling around on the riverbank, guddling for trout. The tall grasses and pink campion shrouded their little bodies where they lay on their stomachs, reaching down into the water among the stones on the riverbed. Suddenly, amid a splash of silver spraying water, a fish was grabbed and thrown up onto the slope.

The girls watched from the far bank, smiling at the innocent pleasure on the children's faces.

'I wish I was a child again,' Anne Caroline said, despondently. 'Summer days were filled with games in the garden or walks picking wild flowers among the hedgerows. Now, my head is growing so full of worries and my heart so heavy with the fear of losing the man I love, that I cannot seem to find joy in anything anymore.'

'I am sure it will resolve,' Rosemary told her brightly, although she felt it was doubtful that Anne Caroline's father would relent.

***

Dale did not accompany his daughters to New Lanark the following week. Recently, he was finding it too tiring to travel far from Charlotte Street and preferred the comforts of his well appointed mansion to the sparse little house in the country.

Owen was already in Lanark, having taken a room at the Clydesdale Hotel for an unspecified length of stay. Most of the work he was undertaking to ensure the smooth transition of the mills into new owner-ship was dealt with in Kelly's office. As the Dale's cottage was just next door, he noticed Anne Caroline's arrival immediately.

Before returning to the hotel for the night, Owen called on her and they arranged to meet for a walk the next morning.

He reminded Anne Caroline of her offer to show him the wonderful waterfalls further up the valley. Had she not mentioned to him how Lady Ross impressed on her that if she wished to show Corra Linn to any of her guests, they would be more than welcome?

The morning brought a blustery breeze whipping at the trees, so Anne Caroline tied her bonnet firmly in place and slipped her favourite warm shawl around her shoulders. Toshie and her sisters were accompanying them for the stroll but when Jean heard they were going to see the Falls, she decided to stay behind and content herself with the sampler she was sewing.

'The walk is not too long, I have taken it on many occasions,' Anne Caroline told Owen as they left the house and set off towards Caithness Row.

Washing hung from the windows like bunting, flapping and waving in lively animation along the curved stone buildings. The road to Bonnington estate left the village by means of a narrow path behind the Highlanders' tenements and to Anne Caroline's dismay she saw a long black wagon was taking up most of the space between the walls and the sheer hillside.

The dung heaps were being cleared.

This was a regular and excessively smelly operation but could not be avoided. So she held her handkerchief to her nose and they walked briskly past the men shovelling muck from the offending middens.

'At least in the country one is quickly free from the stench of human waste.' Owen said in a sensible tone when they were beyond the worst of it. 'In the cities it pervades the air and there are places in Manchester where the streets are rarely cleaned. The rats grow as large as cats!'

Anne Caroline laughed and then, catching her toe on a raised stone, she stretched a hand towards him to save herself from tripping.

'Are you all right?' He was immediately attentive.

'Yes... silly of me!' she gave an embarrassed laugh.

'I feel you should take my arm for support throughout the walk, for your safety...'

She needed no prompting and saw the flirtatious twinkle in his eye when she slipped her arm through his, 'What a very good idea,' she agreed, smiling impishly back at him.

To allow them a little privacy, yet keep within the bounds of propriety, Toshie walked some distance behind the couple. The younger girls were entertained in a competition to see who could find the most varieties of flowers and grasses.

It took a long time for Owen and Anne Caroline to reach the woods above Corra Linn. They kept stopping to admire the countryside or pause in their step to speak earnestly to one another, one topic running seamlessly into the next.

'There!' Anne Caroline exclaimed, when they entered the stone pavillion high above the gorge. It was aptly named the Hall of Mirrors because the walls were lined with mirrors to reflect the waterfall. 'Did I not tell you it was a spectacular sight?'

Owen was stunned by the view and on turning his back to the Falls, he marvelled at the reflections of the torrent falling all around him.

'I have heard people speak of the Falls of Clyde but never did I imagine them to be so wondrous! They are truly magnificent!'

The previous few days had seen rain falling heavily across Clydesdale and the ensuing water from this downpour was still surging between the cliffs.

'It was this tremendous power which inspired my father to build the mills further down the valley,' Anne Caroline told him, staring out at the cascading water. 'Listen to it! Look at the mist of spray it sends high into the air! It never fails to fill me with awe.'

Owen stood beside her, struggling to make out her words above the never-ending roar of the water. Her face was flushed and beautiful in the daylight, her lips parted in delight at the view. When she glanced sideways to see if he was enjoying the sight, she realised that his attention was not on Corra Linn, it was focused on her.

'I hope we can return here many times,' he said, a strange nervousness to his voice. 'Together.'

'I would like that, very much. If only it could be so.' she smiled up at him and placed her hand on his arm. 'Shall we return to the village now?'

Away from the deafening rumble of the river, the atmosphere between them relaxed again and Anne Caroline spoke of her early memories of visiting the Falls.

'That was many years ago, on one of the first visits to our cottage here.'

'The mills were built about fifteen years ago, am I right?'

'Yes, well, I was only a child when the first mill burnt down, but I remember it well. It was a terrifying sight.'

'You were staying in the village?'

'No, the house was not yet built. Indeed, there was only the one mill then. However, after the fire, father brought in more builders to reinstate it and then the other mills grew up beside it.'

She reached out her free hand to tap a foxglove bell and send a bumble bee buzzing out of its hiding place.

'I will miss it.' She sighed. 'My sisters and I have known the village nearly all our lives and seen it grow before our very eyes. My father showed me the plans, I can recall the detailed drawings, and although the mills are no doubt excellent, I feel it is the village and all the hundreds and hundreds of families who know it as their home which is his greatest achievement.

'Why, Julia was just a baby when we took our first holiday here! It is a magical place and has found a special place in all our hearts.'

She smiled at him, wistfully.

They walked slowly back down the valley with Owen in a quieter, more thoughtful mood than on their exuberant ascent towards Bonnington House.

New Lanark *was* a special place.

The whole gorge, with its tumultuous waterfalls and sheer cliff sides, was set apart from the rest of the world. The village itself, and the community Dale had forged there, was self contained and unique. He could hardly believe that he was now the manager of such a place and yet, despite its profitability its attraction to him would be reduced without Anne Caroline.

Like all the challenges throughout his young life, he could not accept that she would never be his wife. He had to do something to alter her father's opinion of him but he was so engrossed in the administration for the sale that, for the moment, he could not think of how to gain Dale's acceptance.

The New Lanark residents were in a state of shock and upset at the fact that the mills were no longer owned by David Dale.

Some of the older women wept at the news, despairing for their way of life and grieving for the loss of such a kindly master. Among the men and the younger workforce, there was a real fear that jobs would be cut and several started to make enquiries about alternative employment. There were few opportunities for work around Lanark unless they considered going into the mines or working on the land. As the mill work also gave them lodgings at a very reasonable rent and schooling for their children, leaving the village was a depressing option.

'Weel, it'll no' matter twa beans tae me whit this new maister does,' Bessie announced to Fiona and Sarah one evening. They were sitting out in the street along with many other clusters of families and neighbours, making the most of the light evening.

'How no'?' asked Sarah, stitching away at a new coat for Mrs MacTavish next door.

'Ah'm no' bein' hired agin. Ah'm too auld, they tell me, sae Ah'm oot o' a job come September.'

'Yer no' tha' auld! An' ye dae a grand job!' Sarah was taken aback. 'Whit'll ye dae?'

'Ah dinnae ken. Jist sit here an' look oot ma eyes.... Auld an' done, tha's aboot the sum o' it.'

Fiona laughed. 'Away wi' ye, Bessie! There must be summat ye can be daein'? Ye could look efter Lily MacKinnon's three lassies an' let her gae bak tae work, fer a start! She's bin askin' aboot an' nae body will tak them on.'

'Ah'm no' surprised!' said Sarah, 'They're richt wee tinkers, the MacKinnon weans, an' they fight like cats!'

'Och weel,' Bessie sighed and pulled herself to her feet. 'Ah'll haul ma auld bones up the stairs an' see tae the dishes afore ma lads come hame. They'll look efter their auld mither....'

'Ye say 'auld' one mair time, Bessie, an' it'll be the last thing ye say! Ah'll dae awa' wi' ye mesel',' Fiona was smiling but there was sympathy in her eyes as she watched her friend draw her shawl around her and rustle back through the tenement doorway.

'We'll hae tae find her summat tae dae,' Sarah said. 'She's sae used tae bein' busy an' earnin'. We cannae ha'e her gaun like Mrs Pollock, an gie up the ghost frae lack o' work.'

'Tha's whit Joe wis sayin' aboot Tam, jist the ither day. Tam's sae doon in the dumps wi' his arm an' a', sae Joe taks him up tae Ewing's wi' him noo, an' that wee Melanie is teachin' him his letters.'

Fiona yawned and stretched her arms above her head. 'Tam's bin a bit better since. Gi'es him summat tae dae, an' anyhoo, mibbee he can mak some money one day frae bein' able tae write.'

'Its gettin' sae dark Ah' cannae see tae thread ma needle,' Sarah murmured, licking the end of a long piece of cotton and making another attempt to find the eye of the needle.

She was earning enough each week to pay her contribution to the household and also put a little away. This was her personal fund, her secret savings for when Sean sent for them to join him in the city.

It was both a frightening and exciting prospect, but most of all it kept a glimmer of hope alive within her heart that life would not always be as it was today. One day, she would hear from him, she was certain of it. Until then, she worked tirelessly to keep her children healthy and secure more orders for her dress-making.

Following Fiona's example, she was taking a pride in her appearance again and her efforts were appreciated by the men in the village. She was not looking to attract another man, her clean braided hair and pretty dresses were all in preparation of seeing her husband. None the less, their admiring glances and flirtatious comments did much to boost her self-confidence.

The sale of the mills meant little change to Sarah's life, but she was concerned for Fiona, Cal and Rosie.

It was through Rosie that they heard the latest news from the office. The new owners were English, which was bad enough, but it was now known that one of them was the slim young man who could often be seen walking with the Miss Dales.

'Yon lad we saw wi' Miss Anne Caroline,' cried Fiona, 'walkin' doon by the river the ither efternoon? Naw, he's too young tae own a' this! He disnae look much aulder than ma Joe! Are ye sure?'

Rosie's little mouth set in a line. 'That's the very man. Robert Owen they cry 'im, an' Ah'll tell ye summat else!' she paused for effect, 'He's sweet on our Miss Dale, an' frae the look on her face the ither day, she's no' complainin' at his attentions either!'

This was a startling piece of information but the most alarming fact about Mr Owen only came to the surface on the following Monday.

Owen had not attended any of the Sunday church services held in the village. Feeling snubbed by the lack of his presence, some of the older congregation made it their business to find out which church he preferred in Lanark. It did not take long to discover that Mr Owen was not a religious man, indeed, he had been known to speak out against organised religion.

'In the name o' God, why has yer brother sold the place tae a man who's not a Christian?' Kelly asked of James Dale, who could not reply.

Their heated exchange was overheard by Gerard MacAllister, so within hours of the bell tolling the end of work, his wife had informed the entire village.

Calum wandered down the river with his fishing rod; a bottle filled with ale in his tackle bag. It was a cloudy evening with a light breeze disturbing the surface of the water, perfect for fishing. He found a soft patch of grass and sat down to tie on the fly. During the winter months he had patiently plaited long horses' tail hairs into a line, with a wispy tapering end to which he could attach the flies.

As he observed the flies skimming the river, carefully matching their shape and colour to his homemade efforts, he remembered his own encounter with the man who was now the mill owner.

He liked Mr Owen, no matter what the gossiping housewives were saying. From that brief exchange about the mare with the girth galls, Cal formed the impression that he was a good man.

He took a swig from the bottle, pushed the cork back in and then stuck it in the cold water between some rocks. A large plop sounded mid-stream and all thoughts of Owen and the mills left Cal's mind. The fish were on the rise so all his attention was trained to feeling his way with his bare feet on the slippery rocks and wading quietly out into the current to cast his line.

Over the coming days it soon became a familiar sight to see Owen and the elder Miss Dale walking around the village together.

Toshie and Giggs looked on them with compassion, knowing that Mr Dale was against their friendship. In their business affairs with Owen, both James Dale and William Kelly quickly grew to respect the diligent, polite manner in which the young man carried out his duties. He was always willing to discuss matters with them and held firm views on punctuality, manners and fair treatment. These were all attributes that David Dale shared and the more they got to know Owen, the more they felt sympathetic towards him in regard to his hopes to be with Anne Caroline Dale.

Kelly sent regular reports up to Glasgow and would often praise Owen's attitude or plans. He informed Dale that his youthful looks did not do justice to the wealth of experience he so obviously possessed.

However, word also got back to Dale about the regular romantic strolls his daughter was taking with Owen and Dale sent a letter to Anne Caroline.

'Papa wishes us to return immediately to Glasgow!' she declared tearfully to Owen the next time they met.

He took her hand, 'I, too, have received a summons from your father. He wishes to talk to me, although he does not say if it is to do with the mills or our relationship.'

They looked into each other's eyes with so many questions and wishes but only David Dale held the answers.

Owen left for Glasgow the next morning but it was the middle of the day before Toshie and Giggs finished packing up the carriage to take the girls home. Mrs Cooper was miffed by the sudden curtailment to the family's visit. She helped to oversee their departure with annoyance etched on her face, her back stiff, giving curt monosyllabic responses to any queries from the staff.

After all the trouble she took to provide good meals and a high standard of comfort and now the Dales were barely through the door than they were away again.

Anne Caroline boarded the carriage and sat down heavily with a churning stomach. She could see some Highland women pegging out washing and carrying buckets to the lade for water. There was nothing unusual in their actions but as they went about their business, barefoot, chatting and calling to one another in their brightly patterned skirts and blouses, it dawned on Anne Caroline that she might never look on them again.

What if her father forbade her to see Mr Owen? If he decided to call a halt to the country holidays now the mills were sold?

When the horses were sent forward and the coach lurched up the hill towards Lanark, she strained to catch last glimpses of the rooftops she knew so well. When the last view was lost behind tree tops, she realised she might never again see the hundreds of chimney pots and bell tower; features of a place so dear to her that a tear escaped and trickled down her cheek.

The roll of the carriage came to a sudden, rocking halt. The coachman was shouting to men on the road in front of him and Jean and Toshie pulled down the side windows to see what was happening.

Work was just being completed on two gate houses, built on the brow of the hill to mark the entrance to New Lanark. They were of a smart design, matching the appearance of all Dale's buildings in the valley, and were replicas of each other sitting face to face across the road.

Between them, a wagon load of stones lay on its side. Several men and little boys were busily unhitching the horse and clearing the wagon of its load so it could be hauled upright.

Joe was the manager of the team and seeing Dale's carriage approaching, he walked towards it calling apologies.

'We'll ha'e it cleared in a jiffy!' he shouted.

'What a dashing man!' Jean giggled, peering out at Joe.

Toshie was amused but hid it well with a reprimand. 'Miss Jean! That is not appropriate!'

'But he is!' Jean insisted. 'His hair is as golden as corn and even at this distance I can see his eyes are the clear blue of the sky on an icy day...'

Giggs patted her on the hand. 'You are reading too much romantic nonsense, the man is a rough labourer, it is not seemly to talk of him like that.'

Jean took another look at Joe, man-handling massive rocks to the side of the road.

'And if he were a Prince would I be able to say he was handsome?'

'That would be different.'

'How very silly.' Jean declared. 'It should make no difference at all. I will ask Papa, for surely it should make no difference what a man does for his living on Earth. If God has made him with such perfection, it should be appreciated, whether labourer or prince?'

Anne Caroline watched her little sister's forehead crease with thought and said, 'I agree, it is very silly, but unfortunately my dear, that is the way in our society.'

The road was cleared and as the carriage trotted past, Joe bowed his head politely and Anne Caroline raised her hand in greeting. On seeing her wave, Joe returned a wide smile of recognition.

'Tha' were all the Dale lassies,' he said to Tam, who spent most days sitting on the wall near where Joe was working. 'The aulder lass looked upset... her eyes were... Och, Ah dinnae ken whit it wis, but she looked awfy sad.'

'Mibbee noo her Da' disnae own yon mills, she'll no' be doon this way agin?' Tam offered.

That thought had not occurred to Joe.

He turned to look after the carriage with a renewed awareness of its occupants, watching it disappearing off towards the town in a cloud of dust, the horses' rhythmic hoof beats softening into the distance.

All of a sudden, it hit him how strange New Lanark was going to be without the Dales.

Chapter Twelve

*"Withal, he (*Dale*) was a genial, humerous man. He was given to hospitality and he would sing an old Scotch song with such feeling as to bring tears to the eyes."*
W.G. Black

When Anne Caroline arrived at Charlotte Street, she was surprised to see Mr Owen's gig standing by the house. On asking Renwick of his whereabouts, she was informed that Owen had been closeted in the study with her father for the past two hours.

Suffering the effects of their long journey and with her head still filled with the rumble of the bumpy roads, she went up to her room and lay down on the bed. The swaying motion of the carriage caused a disorientating dizziness but it was not just this physical discomfort that caused her to feel unwell.

Jean and Mary comforted their sister, trying to calm her with kindly platitudes, but they were also acutely aware of the meeting that was being conducted only yards away along the landing.

Eventually, the study door opened and the two men came out.

Anne Caroline sat bolt upright. Heart pounding, she swung her legs off the bed and swept her hands down her long cotton skirts, chiding herself for creasing the fine material.

Listening intently for any sounds or words from the two men as they descended the stairs, she quickly ran a comb through her hair and checked her appearance in the mirror.

Breen appeared at the bedroom door.

'Miss Anne Caroline, your father wishes you to join him in the drawing room.'

Jean clasped her sister's hand and wished her good luck, as anxious as Anne Caroline to know the outcome of their father's discussions with Mr Owen.

'My dear,' Dale greeted his daughter in a normal, genial manner. 'I hope the journey was not too tiring?'

Robert Owen stood by the fireplace, his hands behind his back, his face blank of any expression. When she looked directly at him, he bowed his head and spoke quietly.

'Miss Dale.'

Her eyes were flashing between the two men, trying to gauge their mood and desperate for them to speak.

'Mr Owen and I have had a long talk.' Dale said slowly, walking across the room to stand beside the young man. 'I won't beat about the bush, me dear. I understand that you two would wish to be married and although I had my reservations, I have just informed Mr Owen that I will no longer stand in your way. You have my blessing.'

'Oh Papa!' she ran to him, throwing her arms around him and kissing him effusively on the cheeks.

'I take it that meets with your approval!' he chuckled, gently releasing her hold.

'You have made me the happiest person alive!' she cried and turned to Owen.

He caught hold of her hands and kissed them, a joyous smile lighting his face and sparkling in his eyes.

'Oh Miss Dale, Anne Caroline, it is I who am surely the happiest. Your father suggests that we be married in September and he would like the ceremony to take place in this house.'

'My goodness!' she was astonished at the progress of the arrangements. 'So soon! I think that would be wonderful!'

'Well,' Dale looked from one to the other. 'I will see you at dinner, my dear daughter.' Smiling, he held out his hand to Owen who grasped it firmly. 'I will see you anon, Mr Owen.'

'Indeed. Thank you, sir.'

Dale left the drawing room and strode across the hall to his library.

His change of heart regarding Owen was brought about by many factors.

It pained him to refuse his daughters anything and seeing Anne Caroline's desolation had been hard to bear. The reports from Kelly and his brother James told of a hard working affable young man, and those of his colleagues in Glasgow who knew Owen, were of a similar mind.

Even his friend, Professor Garnett, who hailed from Manchester, knew him and spoke of him in warm, affectionate terms. Professor Garnett was travelling through Scotland to research his up-coming report for the Society of Bettering Conditions and Increasing the Comforts of the Poor. While in Glasgow, he called at Charlotte Street and enjoyed an afternoon and a few glasses of claret with Dale.

'I found your venture at New Lanark most rewarding,' he said, while they strolled through the back garden to take a seat under the rose arbour.

Carolina would have been gratified to see it was blooming in profusion.

'I am glad to hear it.' said Dale. 'The production is good and we are continuing to discover new markets to fill the gap caused by our lost customers in Europe.'

'Yes, yes, the yarn is being produced in massive quantities, but it is heart-warming to see such a fine example of how so much work can be undertaken without causing distress to the workforce. I saw many happy faces and heard a great deal of laughter while I was there. The paupers were almost plump with the food you provide for them and the school gave an outstanding exhibition of what can be achieved.'

'I am a strong believer in education.' Dale took his seat, arranging himself so that the afternoon sun did not catch his eyes. 'You and I can read the bible, learn the teachings of the Lord, and it is our duty to ensure everyone has the opportunity for such knowledge. Sunday schools are insufficient, there needs to be regular tuition to make it worthwhile.'

'And I believe you are disposing of the mills? To a Manchester company?'

'The Chorlton Twist Company. They have registered a different trading name for this acquisition, now being called the New Lanark Twist Company.' Dale took a sip from his wine glass. 'The sale is done. One of the partners, a Mr Robert Owen, is there at this moment organising the take over.'

'Ah, Robert Owen. I know him well. Oh, they will be in excellent hands in that case.'

'Ye think so? he assured me that he holds the same views as I on the welfare of the children. Am I right in accepting that as a fact?'

'There are few who hold such strong views on the care of his workers. He has long been a member of the Manchester Literary and Philosophical Society, an elite group and he holds his own on the floor, from what I have heard. Dr Percival knows him very well, of the Manchester Health Board.' Professor Garnett looked thoughtfully at a butterfly sunbathing on the lavender and added, 'precocious but trustworthy sort of chap, Owen.'

Now, surrounded by the scent of bees-wax polish and leather bound volumes, Dale remembered Garnett's words.

He was entrusting the life and happiness of his beloved daughter to this young man. It was a major step and he wished that his wife was beside him to discuss the matter. Anyway, during their long meeting before Anne Caroline returned from New Lanark, Dale had probed and questioned Owen until he was satisfied that he had done his duty as her father.

The matter of religion was left unresolved, but Dale was a true Christian. He did not bear grudges or condemn people and so, in due course, he accepted Robert Owen into the family.

***

The wedding was arranged for 30th September.

Throughout the intervening weeks, the rooms of Dale's mansion were alive with visitors, dressmakers and florists. The household staff excitedly set about scrupulously dusting and polishing in preparation for the great day.

Then, when there were only days to go, the kitchen downstairs became a hive of activity. Ovens were filled and refilled with cakes, pastries and every type of sweet meat that Cook could produce from basket upon basket of provisions hauled in to the bursting larder.

Adding to the hustle and bustle of the house came Anne Caroline's grandparents, the Campbells. Now elderly, they chose to arrive a couple of days before the event so they could rest after the arduous journey from Edinburgh and be refreshed for the memorable occasion of their first grandchild's wedding.

Dale preferred not to preside over his own daughter's marriage and asked the Reverend Mr Balfour, a Church of Scotland minister and friend, to perform the ceremony.

On the morning of the wedding, guests were welcomed at the door and shown into the drawing room which was bedecked with flower arrangements. A space was cleared down the centre to allow for rows of chairs so everyone could sit down to witness the service.

Only their closest friends were invited and Dale greeted them all with his customary cheerful smile. The formality of his customary choice of black jacket and breeches relieved for this auspicious occasion by the addition of a gold satin waistcoat.

Claud Alexander, with his wife Helenora and sister Wilhelmina, were among the first to alight from a procession of carriages, having stayed with friends overnight in the city.

'We would not miss dear Anne Caroline's wedding for the world!' cried Helenora, resplendent in a billowing gown and large feathered bonnet. 'It seems only yesterday that she came to stay at Ballochmyle as a small child! But we were just remarking how that must have been more than ten years ago?'

'The same year as the great fire, eleven years ago' Dale agreed, 'aye, a great deal has happened to us all since then.'

The tall figure of James MacIntosh came through the door with his son Charles, sharing a carriage with his business partner Charles Tennant and accompanied by all their wives. Their excited chattering voices were soon joined by Rosemary Peckham and her husband and further guests. The gentlemen's dark jackets contrasting sharply with the ladies' colourful foaming lace and rustling silk gowns.

Archibald Paterson was the last to arrive, slapping Dale on the back and ushering his wife towards the open drawing room door in mock haste.

'Only live ten yards from ye door and I wager we are the last to our seats!' He winked at Dale, lowering his voice. 'Mrs Paterson is rarely dressed by this hour o' the morning, you are witnessing a miracle!'

When Anne Caroline descended the stairs with her sisters in attendance as bridesmaids, the room was full and she was met by the low murmur of their voices.

'Is Mr Owen here?' she asked her father, who was waiting in the hall to escort her into the drawing room.

'Of course, he is.' he told her, his eyes shining with emotion. 'Ye look beautiful my dear, he should be very proud to have ye as his wife.'

Anne Caroline gave a shy smile. She was extremely pleased with the appearance of her gown and those of her sisters, having agonised over many details.

The results were enchanting and very fashionable, being simple white, narrow dresses, caught in below the bosom by a velvet ribbon and with a floor length panel of the same material draped down the back from their shoulders. Exquisite embroidery, incorporating sequins and soft pastel colours, adorned the hems and neckline.

The dazzling finished effect of the five girls in their shimmering white dresses was worth all the hours of standing for the seamstress and last minute fittings and adjustments.

Holding a bouquet of pale pink and cream roses, Anne Caroline laid her hand on her father's arm and they walked into the room to meet the guests.

The front row of chairs had been left empty, except for one. Owen jumped to his feet as soon as they entered and waited until everyone was seated before resuming his seat beside his bride.

To the amazement of all, the service was over in less than one minute.

Reverend Balfour asked Robert Owen and Anne Caroline to stand up, then asked if they wished to take each other in marriage and when they nodded he proclaimed, 'Then you are married and may sit down.'

They looked at each other in astonishment and then turned to look over their shoulders at the expectant audience.

Was that it? Were those few words sufficient to join them in matrimony?

After a brief, silent pause, a ripple of congratulations trickled through their friends until there was suddenly laughter and clapping. Chairs scraped back and guests headed through the crowded room to be among the first to wish them happiness in their new life together.

The party began to disperse to the dining room to enjoy the splendid array of dishes and Owen could contain himself no longer. He left his wife's side for a few moments to take the opportunity to ask Reverend Balfour why the ceremony had been so short.

'It is usually longer,' he beamed, 'I generally explain to the young persons their duties in the marriage state, and often give them a long exhortation! But,' he glanced over at Dale's portly figure in deep conversation with Archibald Paterson, 'I would not presume to do this with Mr Dale's children while he lived and was present, knowing that he must have previously satisfied himself in giving them such advice that seemed satisfactory and sufficient.'

After a short spell of mingling with their well-wishers and sampling Cook's delicious dishes, Anne Caroline retired upstairs with Rosemary and her sisters and prepared to leave the house.

It was the only part of the whole affair which caused Anne Caroline any sadness. It was arranged that they would immediately depart Glasgow and travel south to take up married life in Manchester.

Leaving her friends and family was a terrible wrench. Despite assurances from Owen that they would return regularly to visit New Lanark and therefore she would have ample opportunity to see her father and sisters, it still hurt to say goodbye.

The time had now arrived and there was a nervous knot in her stomach when she entered the bedroom, shared for so long with Jean. All her clothes and personal belongings were already packed, only her travelling attire lay out on the bed. She gathered up the pale pink day dress and moved behind the screen to change, while the other girls sat around on the bed and chairs, chatting among themselves.

Listening to their familiar voices and laughter, she was nearly overcome with sorrow at their imminent farewells. Then, buttoning her dress and adjusting the lace on her cuffs, she pulled herself together and reminded herself of her dear husband. Wherever he was, she wished to be, so Manchester would not be so hard to bear. One great comfort was that Toshie would be accompanying her to their new home.

All the guests, family and servants came out onto the street to wave the couple away. So it was amid cheers that their carriage trotted out through the gates.

The roads were very bad and the journey tediously long, but Owen was in such high spirits that he kept his bride and her maid entertained by pointing out the sights as they drove down over the border and into England.

After several stops, they neared the end of the journey and Owen suddenly leaned towards Anne Caroline and pointed out a small house lying just beyond the road.

'Well, my dear, you see that dwelling? What do you think of our future home?'

She looked at the low building which was very poor and commonplace and felt misled and disappointed.

'It is... different from the one you had described to me.'

He sat back but could not keep the mirth from showing in his eyes and she realised, as they carried on along the road past the wretched building, that he was joking.

Toshie was also relieved, having feared that her poor young mistress had been lead down the garden path and Owen was going to subject her to very low living standards.

Owen's actual residence, their new home, was a much pleasanter house altogether.

Greenheys was a large building, well placed within an extensive garden and had been built for a wealthy merchant. No expense was spared on Honduras wood doors and plate glass windows and there were fireplaces in most of the main rooms.

Owen had been living there for over two years, having purchased it with a friend. The house was so big that they divided it down the middle to make two self contained homes.

His friend had the side with the front door so Owen took his new bride through a door at the side which he used as an entrance. It lead into the house through an attractive conservatory, abundant with well tended plants and polished furniture.

They were met by an elderly couple, Owen's housekeepers, who bowed and curtsied to Anne Caroline. Then, without further ado, the man disappeared outside to the stables and the old woman hurried off to the kitchen to finish preparing their evening meal.

'Oh this is charming!' Anne Caroline cried, walking from room to room and circling round to see the cornices, alcoves, views and the arrangement of the accommodation.

She was very tired after the journey but felt an enormous relief at finding her new home to be so comfortably appointed.

'I like this house,' she thought, exploring up the stairs, 'I can be happy here and with my darling Robert at my side, it will be a wonderful life.'

***

351

'Manchester?' Sarah screwed up her face in disgust. 'They're gonnae be livin' in Manchester?'

'Aye, that's whit Gerry telt me,' Rosie said firmly. 'Tha's in England. No' tha' far doon, but a guid lang way awa'.'

'D'ye think we'll e'er see Miss Dale agin?'

'Ah dinnae ken. Mibbee aye, mibbe naw.' Rosie had taken her husband's habitual expression as her own.

'Weel, if she's wi' the man she loves, Ah wish her a' the happiness.'

Tam had given them a basket of late peas from his father's allotment and they were sitting together shelling the peas at the table. Only the younger children were playing around them, Davey and Donnie being old enough now to go down to the school with Fiona.

There were voices on the stairs and then Bessie came in with a postman.

'*This* is the Scotts' hoose, no' the yin below.' She was telling him, then turning to Sarah, 'There's a letter fer ye, hen, an' it wis aboot tae be put at the door o' Mrs Gavin. She's that stupit, she'd probably open it an' then throw it on the fire if it wisnae fer her!'

Sarah took the letter and stared at it. The words meant nothing to her but she didn't want to open it in front of Bessie and the postman who were still arguing about something at the doorway.

It was only when they left that she took it out of her apron pocket.

'Rosie, this can only be frae Sean. Ah'm that feart at whit it says... but Ah need tae knaw...will ye read it fer me?'

Rosie wiped her hands on her apron and found a knife to open the envelope.

Her eyes scanned down the page and then she looked up at her sister. 'Aye, its frae Sean. He writes, 'My darling Sarah, I hope someone reads this to you for I know you do not have your letters. I have a place for you and the children, please come to Biggar next week, Thursday or Friday. I shall be at the Cross Keys Hotel and we can travel on together. Your loving husband.'

Sarah seized the paper from Rosie's hands and held it reverently in front of her, smoothing the edges and running her fingers across the lettering. Sean had touched this paper, he had held it as she did now. She kissed it, wet tears running down her cheeks.

Rosie carried on shelling the peas. Every time Sean came into her sister's life, there were tears: happy tears, sad tears, angry tears. How long would this re-union last, she thought, long enough for another baby to be on the way and then he would be off again, or in prison?

Sarah had no such doubts. Sean had sent for her, they were going to be a proper family again. That was all she wanted to know and all she needed to know.

Joe and Fiona were very sceptical and even as she wrapped up the last of the children's clothes on the morning of her departure, he was imploring her to stay.

It was still dark in the room and the family were dressing and eating porridge by the light of the fire and an oil lamp. As Fiona nursed baby Robert and chased after her older boys to eat their breakfast, Calum was trying to fit Cathy's little arms into the new coat Sarah had made for her especially for the journey.

Joe finished shaving and pulled his work smock over his head. 'If ye'll no' see sense an' stay,' he said, seriously, 'at least gi'e me yer word ye'll come hame agin if things get bad?'

'It'll be fine, Joe. Ye'll see!' Sarah said brightly.

She was hitching a lift up to Lanark with one of Bessie's boys who had a loan of a pony and trap for the week. From there she would have to pay for a place on the coach to Biggar, but this could easily be afforded from her carefully hoarded savings.

'Promise me!' he demanded.

Sarah was looking healthy and well again, a far cry from the poor creature she became when she was living with Sean. He remembered the Irishman, drunk and dissolute, the town girls fawning over him, and wished his sister would tear up the letter and stay in New Lanark.

'A' richt, *Ah promise*, but ye needn't be frettin,' Joe. He'll tak care o' us.'

The mill bell began to toll, calling the workers to start the day.

Rosie had said her farewells to Sarah the night before but Fiona wrapped her arms around her and held her tight, before forcing herself to let go and whispering '*Sealbh math dhuit'*.

Sarah knew it meant 'good luck' and smiled boldly back at her friend.

'Thank ye, Ah'll miss ye a', but Ah ha'e tae be wi' ma man. Ye ken?' the last was said with feeling, because Sarah could tell that Fiona was struggling to understand her trust in Sean.

'As Joe says, mind ye ha'e a hame wi' us if it doesnae work oot.'

Calum hugged her and murmured something unintelligible before hurrying out the door. He understood her need to change her life but feared what the future held for his sister beyond New Lanark.

Joe picked up her bundle and, taking Cathy's hand, helped them down the stairs.

Bessie was outside in the cool dawn air, standing beside the little trap waiting to say goodbye. She had tears in her eyes and her chin was crumpled as she kissed the girl on the forehead, hugged the children and turned quickly away.

'Ah wish ye a' the best,' she called, voice breaking. 'Cheerio the noo!' then she took hold of the banister and pulled herself wearily up the stairs.

Joe pulled his sister into his arms, embracing both her and little Stephen. He was choked with tears but Sarah's jaw was set in a determined line: her mind focused on her reunion with Sean, not the reality of saying goodbye to Joe.

Then he lifted Cathy up on to the trap and she wriggled along the bench beside Bessie's son to allow Sarah to climb aboard.

'Bye then,' she said. 'Take care o' yersel', Joe.'

Waves of anxiety flowed through him and, regardless of Bessie's son only feet away, Joe reached up and squeezed her hand.

'Ah love ye dearly, lass. Ye tak care o' yersel an the bairns. Get Sean tae send us word tha' yer safely wi' him. Mind an' ye dae, fer Ah couldnae bear tae lose ye as weel as Sam.'

A sudden spark of panic flashed into Sarah's eyes as the enormity of what she was doing hit her.

'Ah love ye too, Joe. Ah'll get 'im tae tell ye.'

In that instant, he saw the terror, as if she was waking from a nightmare, then she seemed to shut it away and busied herself with tucking her shawl around the baby.

'It's no' too late tae stay....' he cried, but she was already speaking.

'We'd best be awa'.' She attempted a smile. 'Bye, Joe.'

He walked to the end of the Row beside the trap and then watched it trail up Braxfield Row, the sturdy pony between the shafts straining into the harness.

Dawn was brightening the sky, showing pale grey behind the black silhouette of the steep hillside.

It was autumn, October, eleven years to the month from when the Scotts had clattered down that same hillside in the bucketing rain, miserable and homeless. Meg and Ma were both laid to rest in the little graveyard, Rosie married and in her own place and five new little children had come in to their family.

The village lay silently around him, all the rush and crowds of the workers were now contained inside the four great stone mills. His eyes roved over the massive buildings and the glimmering ribbon of water in the mill lade.

These huge mills were the reason they were all here, they were responsible for keeping the family and putting bread on the table and a room to live in. Without them he would never have met his beloved wife.

He was proud of being part of the teams that broke the rocks and built the walls. He felt gratitude towards the whole village for giving his family a home and teaching him a trade, but he too wished to leave its confines.

Fiona deserved more than one room in a factory tenement and he sometimes berated himself for not achieving more in his life. Perhaps Sarah was right to leave the valley and take the plunge into a new life over the horizon.

Joe started to walk back towards Fiona. There was no more he could do for Sarah, she was set on her own path. Although he was not a church going man, he found he was beseeching God to take care of his sister and her children.

**

Anne Caroline's absence was felt keenly by her family and the servants at Charlotte Street. After the excitement of the wedding and the continuous entertaining while hosting the Campbells, they were suddenly left with a strange feeling of emptiness.

Jean, now an assured young lady of fourteen, took over many of her elder sister's duties and would meet with Breen and Cook in the mornings and then take the regular walk with her younger sisters on Glasgow Green. Autumn blustered its way into the bare, short days of winter and the air chilled to frosty nights when the shutters were closed by five o'clock. The aroma of oil lamps and coal smoke replaced fresh air and fragrant flowers.

Their father combated the loss of his elder daughter's presence by a reassertion of his business dealings, seeking to divert his attention by finding buyers for his other mills.

James MacIntosh, his partner in the Dalmarnock Dyeworks, was also keen to take it easier in day to day affairs and they discussed various approaches from other mill owners. So far, few could either raise the required money or fulfil Dale's high standards for their continued management.

Claud Alexander did not wish to buy out Dale's share of Catrine but was of a similar mind as his friend to find a new owner who would continue the benevolent ethos at the little mill village; created so carefully by the two men.

'Find us another Owen!' Alexander had quipped, on leaving the wedding reception.

Alas, it appeared to Dale that these sort of enlightened businessmen were exceedingly thin on the ground.

As he looked over production figures and costs for his mills, especially the most northern village at Spinningdale, Dale became fatigued at the thought of trying to sort them out. More and more, he just wished to follow his calling in the Church and be with his daughters.

One afternoon, with the rain splattering against the drawing room window, he laid down his Bible and gazed into the fire. Margaret and Julia were at the piano playing a soft duet while Jean and Mary took it in turns to practise the lady's steps of a new dance.

It was peaceful beside the crackling fire, several lamps already lit to aid the weak, white light filtering through the windows. A question regarding a long standing venture he had embarked upon many years before was playing on Dale's mind and he found himself wishing he could speak to Owen about the matter.

Around the same time as he formed a partnership with Arkwright and Dempster to create the New Lanark Mills, the other gentlemen built a mill at Stanley, in Perthshire.

Although Dale put no money into the business at the time, his continued association with Dempster, MP for Perth, meant he had been kept aware of the progress of this factory. In fact, two mills were finally built, one cotton and one flax and he was now being asked to invest in the enterprise. The figures were not good, the war and rising cotton prices were hitting Stanley badly.

That afternoon he received the very bad news that the flax mill had burned to the ground. New capital was required to support the re-building and allow production to continue in the cotton mill or the village, now housing and giving work to over three hundred people, would have to be sold.

Should he put his money in that direction? Would an injection of capital really secure the future for the people of Stanley, or would he just be throwing good money after bad? He wanted to mull it over with someone who understood mills, understood the needs of people.

It had become clear to him, just as his colleagues informed him months earlier, that Robert Owen was clever in his profession and had a natural flair in management. Anne Caroline's letters indicated that he was also a kind and caring husband so Dale's regard for him was growing every day and he was sorry that they lived so far apart.

'It would be very pleasant', he thought, 'to converse with him on these issues. I have been too long on my own with these trade affairs, it would be a relief to hear another's point of view'.

'Papa? You look very serious.' Jean dropped down into the chair beside him in a cloud of bouncing brown ringlets and blue petticoats.

'Do I, my dear?' he gave her an affectionate pinch on the cheek. 'I am too old for business nowadays, I prefer to sit by the fire and read.'

'We like it when you are down here with us, not stuck up in your study all the time.'

He gave a throaty chuckle. 'Then I shall have to renew my efforts to sell the other mills, then I can be with you all the time.'

She jumped to her feet again and kissed him on the nose, giggling. There was a strong resemblance between Jean and Anne Caroline, both taking after their mother in colouring and the shape of their faces.

Dale felt a maudlin mood threaten to engulf him.

'Why don't we have a song?' he declared in an effort to keep his low spirits at bay. 'Mary, ye know some of my favourite ballads, the ones we sang last Hogmanay...do we have the word sheets from last year?'

She tripped off to find them, Dale threw more coal on the fire and they all clustered around the flames. It was a pastime they always enjoyed in the winter but this year, although no-one mentioned it, they were acutely conscious that there was one person missing.

***

It seemed to the villagers that little was different in the affairs at New Lanark following the change of ownership. However, behind the scenes, things were not going as smoothly as had been anticipated.

Owen and his partners conceived a strategic plan to achieve the production they required, but it was not being implemented.

William Kelly did not seem to be interpreting their orders correctly, or, more worryingly, he did not appear to be abiding by them at all. The various changes that were to be executed were not happening and on writing for explanations their queries were either rebuffed or left unanswered. It soon became clear that both Kelly and James Dale were just carrying on with the work plan they knew and understood.

Any orders from Manchester were shelved in favour of relying on old working practices which, they believed, were perfectly adequate and had always produced good results.

Mr Atkinson was alarmed by this lack of co-operation and Mr Barton became very irritated that although they owned this mill village north of the border, the Scotsmen running it took little heed of their masters in Manchester.

It came to a head at a meeting near the end of the year.

Anne Caroline was reading by the fire in the gracious front room at Greenheyes when Owen arrived home early. She was not yet used to the long hours on her own and found them difficult to bear and lonely, especially now that the hours of daylight and inclement winter weather allowed for few walks to relieve the monotony.

Owen's friends were mainly batchelors or businessmen but he had gone to considerable trouble to introduce his wife to the few married couples he knew in the area. The wives were kind and hospitable and it was through these ladies that she found a church to attend on Sundays.

Otherwise, she would spend the days on her own or with Toshie.

So it was with surprise and pleasure that she heard a horse's hoof beats from outside the window and saw her husband dismounting.

'My dear!' she called, hurrying towards him as he came through the conservatory door. 'Is everything all right? It is barely one o'clock?'

He kissed her fondly, as they had grown accustomed to do on every meeting, and put his arm around her to walk to the hearthside.

'I have news, which I hope you will find agreeable.'

She raised her eyebrows expectantly.

'My partners have asked me to return to New Lanark to take over its governance.'

'Return? For how long?'

'To live there! I would be in sole charge of the mills and village.' He smiled at her, his eyes lively with the challenge of this new responsibility. 'We will be nearer your family, what do you say to that?'

'I am delighted! Although, that is not to say that I am not content here, with you. Wherever you wish us to live, I will be happy to follow. But... yes, Robert, I can truly say that I am very happy with the news!'

'We will leave in a few weeks time, early in the new year. There is much to be done before I go, and then we will ready ourselves for this adventure.' He kissed her again, 'Oh my dearest, I have long wanted to put in to practise my own theories for organising a small community. This will give me the chance to carry out all the changes I wish to make... it is a most *wonderful* opportunity!'

After informing Toshie, who was as thrilled as her mistress, Anne Caroline sat down to write to her father and tell him of their forthcoming journey back to Scotland.

His response came speedily, insisting that they make use of the cottage in New Lanark as their home and wishing them post haste.

Having been lulled into a false sense of security by the apparent seamless changeover of owners, New Lanark was thrown into a frenzy of gossip on hearing of Owen's return.

Rumours abounded that Kelly and James Dale were to be sacked and then came a wariness of how many other alterations might be coming with such a youthful manager, an Englishman, taking over the reins.

'Och he was a' richt when he wis here afore,' Joe said, reasonably. 'Ma worry is tha' the buildin' work is a' done, an' Ah doubt if he will be like auld Dale an' want tae be makin' mair hooses.'

'There's talk that he's gonnae cut back the workers,' said Rosie, 'put people oota work an' mak' the rest o' us work mair oors.'

'Where did ye hear tha'' Fiona asked.

'Gerry heard that wis one o the things tha' Mr Kelly wis upset aboot an' wouldnae take a part o'. An' they're no' wantin sae many weans. De ye think they'll jist send them bak tae the Poor Hoose?'

'Naw!' Fiona was horrified. 'They cannae dae tha'! can they? No' efter a' Mr Dale's done fer the bairns?'

Rosie sighed. 'Weel, ma Gerry says there's gonnae be a lot of things changing aboot the village, an' we'll ha'e the owner living in the middle o' us a' the time. It's no' gonnae please a lot o' folk aroond here, Ah can tell ye!'

As the end of the year approached and plans were being hatched for the customary Hogmanay celebrations, a letter came for Joe from Sarah.

Written in Sean's hand, but signed by Sarah, Fiona read it to him as soon as she came home from the school. It told him that she and the children were well and living with Sean, closing with, 'I think of you all often and send my love.'

There was no return address.

To mark the start of the year 1800, the bonfire was bigger than ever and, as was now customary, the Highlanders carried out tables and chairs from Caithness Row for everyone in the village to contribute food and drinks to the ceilidh. They were favoured with a crisp clear night, a shining half moon bathing them in light within hours of the last red glow of sunset disappearing behind the surrounding hills.

When the mill bell chimed for the end of the last working day of the century, workers streamed out from the buildings.

This was the end of the Eighteenth Century and they were eager to see in the Nineteenth Century with plenty drinking, dancing and merriment. Kyle led the fiddlers in popular jigs and the gathering crowd whooped and danced around the flames.

Even Mrs Cooper donned her warmest bonnet and cape to step outside the front door and watch the spectacle.

After trying to persuade Bessie to join them, Fiona and Joe left Robert in her care and took Donnie and Davey down to the festivities. Calum carried Davey on his shoulders, an almost happy expression on his face. He was pleased to be free from work for the following day's holiday and with the news of Sarah being safe, he felt more comfortable with his life than he had in years.

The Scotts' room was a much more peaceful and tidy place to live without her, yet he would never have wished her so far away.

His own plans to move out were, once again, put to the back of his mind.

When the countdown began for the stroke of midnight, Fiona and Joe stood with their arms around each other and she pointed out the beautiful moon directly over the village.

'See the moon? Tis sae bonnie. Ah wonder if Sarah is lookin' at it. If she is, Ah wonder if she's thinkin' o' us?'

Joe gazed above him at the gleaming white crescent floating in a sea of inky black space.

Perhaps his sister was seeing it, just as he was, at that very moment in time. All over Scotland, clocks were striking midnight to herald the New Year, the start of a new century, and the ancient church bells in Lanark pealed out across the frosty countryside.

Perhaps Sam was also sharing its light? Wherever they were, he prayed they were safe and happy.

He looked around the cheering crowd. These were his neighbours, his workmates, his friends, and seeing their jubilant faces he hoped this new man, Owen, was worthy of stepping into Dale's shoes.

Maybe this was as good as life could get, maybe the days of feeling secure were coming to an end? He fervently hoped not, but no-one knew what the future held so he must make the most of these good times.

With tears in his eyes, he kissed Fiona, held his tankard high and joined his fellow villagers in a rousing chorus of Auld Lang Syne.

*

NEW LANARK

LIVING WITH A VISIONARY

C A HOPE

The story continues.... Robert Owen is now in charge of the village. As he takes up the reins, implementing sweeping changes, life will never be the same again for the Scotts or indeed any of the inhabitants of New Lanark.

Throughout this period in Britain, William Pitt (The Younger) is Prime Minister and King George 111 is on the throne.

Alexander of Ballochmyle, Claud, mill owner (wife- Helenora)
Alexander, Wilhelmina, sister of Claud
Arkwright, Richard, 1732-1792 mill owner, engineer
Atkinson, Mr, partner of Owen in the Chorlton Twist Co.
Bayley, Thomas
Barton, Mr, partner of Owen in the Chorlton Twist Co.
Black, David, tobacco merchant
Braxfield, Lord, Lord Justice Clerk, Robert MacQueen 1722-1799
Brown, Mary, cotton broker
Burns, Robert, poet 1759 - 1796
Campbell of Jura, John, banker, David Dale's father in law
Currie, Dr, friend of David Dale
Dale, Anne Caroline "Carolina" (wife of David) 1753-1791
Dale, Anne Caroline, (1778- 1831 Mary, Margaret, Jean and Julia- Dale's daughters (died in infancy -Arabella, Christian and Katherine)
Dale, David 1739 - 1806
Dale, Hugh, brother of David 1741- 1794 (wife-Margaret, son – David)
Dale, James, half brother of David 1753 – 1819 (wife – Marion Haddow)
Dale, William, 1784-1790 son of David Dale
Dempster, George, 1732-1811 lawyer and MP for Perth
Drinkwater, Peter
Hamilton, Gilbert 1744 - ? businessman, Lord Provost of Glasgow 1792-94
Hardy, Thomas, reformer 1752 - 1832
Kelly, William, clockmaker, engineer and mill manager
MacIntosh, Charles, chemist 1766-1843 (wife-Mary, née Fisher)
MacIntosh George, businessman 1739 - 1807
McGuffogs, drapery shop owners
Muir, Thomas, reformer 1765-1799
Muir, James, Glasgow hop merchant, father of Thomas

Owen, Robert, 1771-1858, social reformer, mill owner
Paterson, Archibald, businessman
Percival, Dr Thomas, 1740 - 1804
Pitt, William, Prime Minister 1759-1806
Ross, Lady Elizabeth Lochhart
Scott Moncrieff, Robert, banker
Sinclair, Mrs, needlework teacher at Glasow City Hospital 1780s
Spears, Miss
Tennant, Charles, businessman 1768 – 1838 (wife-Mary)

Guide to the Dialect used in this Novel

aye – yes
auld lang syne – old, long days ago: days now in the past
bairns – children
besom – a naughty, cheeky or bad girl/woman
bin – been
brither - brother
cannae – cannot
chap – knock (chap ma door – knock on my door)
cheerio - goodbye
cla'es – clothes
crabbit – bad tempered, snappy
cry him – call him (his name)
dinnae fash yersel' – don't upset yourself
disnae – doesn't
dour – glum
douth – depressed, gloomy
drookit – soaked
dunno – don't know
efter – after
gae – go
gaun – going
gowd – gold
greetin' – crying (tae greet – to cry)
guid - good
ha'e – have
haud – hold
haun – hand (gi'e me a haun – give me a hand, help me)
havering and footering – prevaricating (havering – talking
   rubbish)
heid – head
jennies – engines (spinning jennies – engines for spinning)
jist - just
kens – knows (ye ken – you know)
lummock – clumsy, lumbering
mair – more (onymair – anymore)

mind – remember
mon – man
mony – money or (in context) many
muckle oota a mickle – (making) much out of a little
neeps – turnips
nicht – night
noo - now
nuthin' or nuchin' - nothing
ony – any
oot - out
Overlookers – mill supervisors
richt – right
skelpit erse – smacked bottom
sumf – idiot, stupid
tae – to
tatties - potatoes
telt - told
thocht – thought
t'morra - tomorrow
vennel – narrow lane, close
weans – small children
wee - small
whaur – where
wheesht – shush, be quiet
whit – what
wid – would
yin – one
yon – that or there

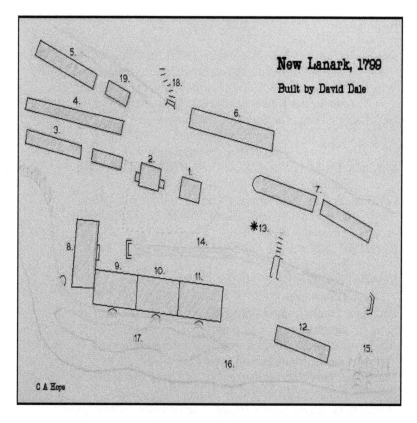

Author's Impression
David Dale's New Lanark in 1799

1. David Dale's House
2. Manager's House
3. Rows (first workers' housing)
4. Double Row
5. Braxfield Row
6. New Buildings
7. Caithness Row
8. Mill One
9. Mill Two
10. Mill Three

11. Mill Four
12. Iron Foundry
13. Site of Bonfire*
14. Mill Lade
15. Dundaff Linn
16. River Clyde
17. Island
18. Steps to Lanark
19. Road to Lanark

*Site of Bonfire – the only fictional place marked on this drawing.

369

Bibliography

Donnachie, Ian and Hewitt, George (*1993*) *Historic New Lanark,* Edinburgh University Press, Edinburgh

Whatley, Christopher A (*2000*), *Scottish Society 1707-1830,* Manchester University Press, Manchester

New Lanark Trust, *The Story of New Lanark*
 Living in New Lanark
 The Story of Robert Owen

McLaren, David J (*1990*) *David Dale of New Lanark,* CWS Scottish CO-OP

Griffiths, Trevor and Morton, Graeme (2010) *A History of Everyday Life in Scotland 1800 to 1900,* Edinburgh University Press

RCAHMS *New Lanark Buildings and History,* Broadsheet 15

RCAHMS *Falls of Clyde, Artists and Monuments* Broadsheet 14

Podmore, Frank, (repro of pre 1923 book) *Robert Owen: A Biography*

Mackay, James A, (1992) *Burns: A Biography of Robert Burns*, Mainstream Publishing

MacIntyre, Ian (2009) *Robert Burns: A Life*, Constable

Sinclair, John, *"Old" Statistical Account of Scotland*

Black, W G, *David Dale's House, Transactions of the Regality Club,* Glasgow

Grateful thanks to:
Lorna Davidson
New Lanark Trust
Scottish Wildlife Trust at the Falls of Clyde
Mitchell Library, Glasgow
Burns Museum, Alloway (National Trust for Scotland)
New Lanark village in general